Also by Douglas Jackson

CALIGULA
CLAUDIUS
HERO OF ROME
DEFENDER OF ROME
AVENGER OF ROME

and published by Corgi Books

SWORD OF ROME

Douglas Jackson

CORGI BOOKS

TRANSWORLD PUBLISHERS
61–63 Uxbridge Road, London W5 5SA
A Random House Group Company
www.transworldbooks.co.uk

SWORD OF ROME
A CORGI BOOK: 9780552167918

First published in Great Britain
in 2013 by Bantam Press
an imprint of Transworld Publishers
Corgi edition published 2014

Addresses for Random House Group Ltd companies outside the UK
can be found at: www.randomhouse.co.uk
The Random House Group Ltd Reg. No. 954009

The Random House Group Limited supports the Forest Stewardship
Council® (FSC®), the leading international forest-certification
organisation. Our books carrying the FSC label are printed on
FSC®-certified paper. FSC is the only forest-certification scheme
supported by the leading environmental organisations, including
Greenpeace. Our paper procurement policy can be found
at www.randomhouse.co.uk/environment

Typeset in 11/13pt Sabon by
Kestrel Data, Exeter, Devon.
Printed and bound by
CPI Group (UK) Ltd, Croydon, CR0 4YY.

2 4 6 8 10 9 7 5 3 1

For my mum, June

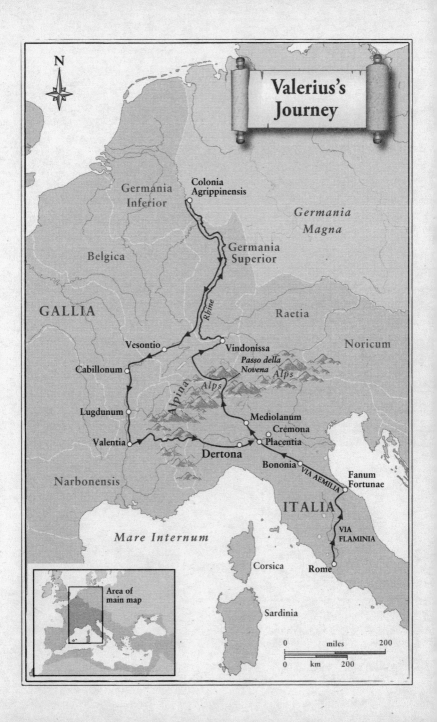

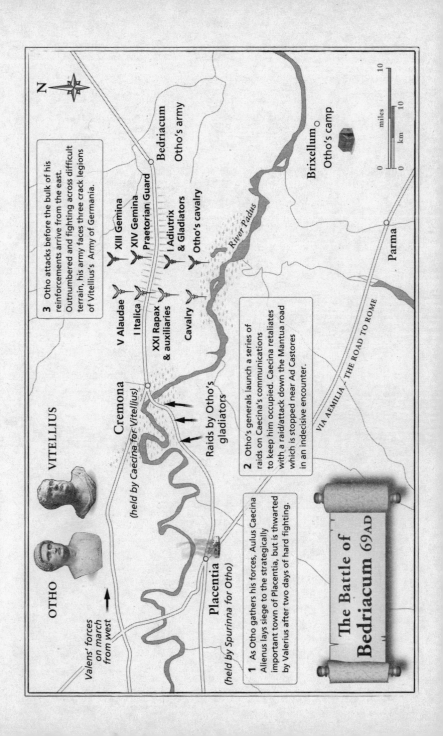

N

OTHO

VITELLIUS

Valens' forces on march from the west

Placentia
(held by Spurinna for Otho)

Cremona
(held by Caecina for Vitellius)

Raids by Otho's gladiators

XXI Rapax & auxiliaries

V Alaudae
I Italica

Cavalry

Bedriacum
Otho's army

XIII Gemina
XIV Gemina
Praetorian Guard

I Adiutrix & Gladiators

Otho's cavalry

River Padus

Brixellum ○
Otho's camp

Parma ○

VIA AEMILIA – THE ROAD TO ROME

1 As Otho gathers his forces, Aulus Caecina Alienus lays siege to the strategically important town of Placentia, but is thwarted by Valerius after two days of hard fighting.

2 Otho's generals launch a series of raids on Caecina's communications to keep him occupied. Caecina retaliates with a raid/attack down the Mantua road which is stopped near Ad Castores in an indecisive encounter.

3 Otho attacks before the bulk of his reinforcements arrive from the east. Outnumbered and fighting across difficult terrain, his army faces three crack legions of Vitellius's Army of Germania.

miles 0 10
km 0 10

The Battle of Bedriacum 69AD

The story I now commence is rich in vicissitudes, grim with warfare, torn by civil strife, a tale of horror even during times of peace.

Cornelius Tacitus, *The Histories*

SWORD OF ROME

I

Southern Gaul, May, AD *68*

She had died protecting her child; that seemed obvious. A tiny hand, the fingers already turning blue in the stifling heat, lay palm upwards just visible beneath the edge of the shabby grey cloak that covered her body. The raven hair fluttering in the soft breeze was still lustrous where it hadn't been clotted by blood and brain matter from the terrible wound in her skull. Gaius Valerius Verrens was thankful he couldn't see the mother's face. He raised his eyes to the crows and buzzards circling in improbably blue skies, their cries of irritation at being disturbed from the feast an unlikely lament to the fallen. With a feeling of weary resignation he remounted the big roan and surveyed the swollen clusters of dead that lay like stranded maggots across the field of half-grown corn between the woods and the olive grove.

'They would have hidden in the trees.' He frowned. 'But whoever killed them must have flushed them out and then ridden them down when they tried to flee.'

'What does it matter?' The speaker's voice managed to combine impatience and arrogance in equal measure.

'They're just a few barbarian peasants. We are wasting time.'

Valerius turned to consider his companion. It exasperated him that Marcus Salvius Otho could be so irritating, and at the same time so difficult not to like. Only a few years older and of the same senatorial rank, the man insisted on treating him as if he were a junior tribune on his first campaign. A rich man on a rich man's horse, Otho had curly dark hair and a face that had never known hunger. Heavy brows arched above liquid, almost feminine eyes; sensitive eyes that softened a nose like a ship's ram and an overweening sense of his own importance. The cavalry escort, a troop of mounted archers from some wild tribe of the Vascones mountains in the northernmost region of Hispania, rested their horses in the shade of the nearby olive trees. They had been in the saddle for eighteen days since leaving Carthago Nova, the last few through the chattel-stripped, fear-ridden landscape of a failed rebellion. Exhaustion and hunger were written stark in the deep lines on their faces. Valerius kept his voice low enough not to be overheard.

'It matters because, judging by the hoofprints, there must have been fifty of them, which means they outnumber us two to one. If they're a marauding band of surviving rebels, they would think twice about attacking regular cavalry . . .'

'Those rebels, as you call them, are our allies,' Otho sniffed. Valerius felt a familiar twinge of conscience at the reminder that he was himself a rebel. True, Nero had earned his enmity by his treatment of Valerius's former commander, Corbulo, General of the East, but a gut-wrenching, very Roman part of him agonized over conspiring against a man born with a divine right to rule. He shook the thought from his mind. Nero had sown the seeds of his own destruction by his ill use of the army, the Senate and the people. The fruits of that sowing had become apparent two months earlier when the Gaulish aristocrat Gaius Julius Vindex had raised the southern tribes against the Emperor. Somehow, Vindex, the rustic senator, had convinced Otho's patrician patron, Servius Sulpicius Galba, governor of Hispania Tarraconensis, to support him. But Galba had been too slow to act, leaving Vindex's ill-disciplined and badly led rebel army to suffer inevitable defeat against the elite Rhenus legions the Emperor sent against him. Now Galba, whose ambitions for the purple remained undiminished, was back in Hispania, and he had dispatched Otho to Rome in a bid to persuade certain powerful men that change was necessary. If Otho succeeded, he was confident the ageing Galba would name him his heir. If he failed, all he could look forward to was a painful end. It was Valerius's job to get him there.

Valerius shrugged. 'Since the defeat at Vesontio they're hunted men with swords in their hands, bellies to fill and nothing to lose. If they sense weakness, they will attack, allies or not. I'd guess we're too strong for them, but' – he pointed to the dead woman – 'if these people were killed by auxiliary cavalry we have a different problem. The legions which destroyed Vindex are loyal to the Emperor and still quartered at Lugdunum, less than fifty miles north. If they take us, the best you can hope for is to be strung up from the nearest tree.'

Otho swatted at the flies plaguing his horse. 'Then we must avoid—'

'Shit.' Valerius reacted instantly to a howling shriek

that split the silence like an executioner's sword as thirty horsemen burst from the cover of the trees on the far side of the field. He spun the roan and dragged Otho's mount by the bridle back into the shadow of the olive grove.

'Form line,' he roared. 'Serpentius? With me in the centre. Two men to guard the governor.' The field was heat-baked, as flat as a legionary parade ground and three hundred paces wide. By now the enemy horsemen – Batavian auxiliaries, judging by their war gear – were a quarter of the way across, but Valerius took the time to issue precise orders. He rapped out the commands, roaming the line as he shouted each word in their faces. 'Swords only.' The long, razor-edged *spathae* hissed from their sheaths. 'Straight to the charge. Stay tight with me. We hit them once and we hit them hard. Leave them screaming and bloody then circle back to cover the governor. Understand?'

The decurion commanding the Vascones grunted his acknowledgement and barked an order to his men, at the same time urging his mount out of cover and into the sunlight. Valerius was already in motion. After the months spent in the saddle with Corbulo's cavalry the roan might have been a living extension of his body. He felt the comforting presence of Serpentius, his Spanish freedman, pull up to his right knee. Their eyes met for an instant, and Serpentius nodded. No need for spoken orders. Valerius reached across his body and slid the long blade of his *spatha* from its scabbard on his right hip. Neither man carried a shield, though each of the cavalry troopers held the light leather roundel the auxiliaries favoured. He checked his horse to allow the Vascones to form on him and looked up just as a slight stutter in the Batavian ranks and the strident cry of urgent orders confirmed what he had suspected. He felt a savage heat well up inside him. The Batavians had seen a small huddle of mounted men amongst the bodies of the villagers they had themselves slaughtered, and marked them as local lords or magistrates, rich pickings compared to the farmers and tanners who lay bled out among the stalks. When they had launched their surprise attack from the woods the last thing they had expected was to be confronted by a full troop of cavalry. Now they must face a fight they hadn't bargained for or break away, leaving their flank exposed to the rampaging Vascones, already screaming their war cries as they pounded over the dry earth.

Valerius saw the enemy come on, confirming that the Batavian commander had made the right choice. But that still wouldn't save them.

Three hundred paces separated the converging forces and they closed at a rate that would have terrified and bewildered a foot soldier. Valerius's mind was that of a veteran cavalryman, effortlessly judging angle, distance and speed. He sensed fear and confusion in the enemy ranks and that awakened the killer inside him. All the long months of frustration and fear as he and Serpentius had stayed one step ahead of Nero's assassins were condensed into a ball of fire at his core. He wanted to slaughter these cocky German bastards.

'Close the ranks,' he roared. 'Hold the line.' The order was echoed by the curved trumpet of the unit's signaller. It was a question of nerve. When cavalry met cavalry the accepted tactic was to charge in open order, to avoid individual collisions that would cripple man and horse, but Valerius was inviting just that. His racing mind took in every detail of the enemy. The thunder of hooves pounded his ears and the Batavians were a sweat-blurred wall of horses and men that surged and rippled, the gaps opening and closing as each rider attempted to keep station on the next. Lance tips glinted in the sun. Had he miscalculated? Would their leader order a volley? He imagined the chaos if the spears arced into the close-packed ranks. No, they were closing too fast. If they waited to get within throwing range they wouldn't have time to draw their swords and no man willingly went into battle defenceless. Instinct told him to pick a target, but it was still too soon. Think. Stay calm. You command. Today he must suppress the battle madness that made war a joy. Gaps opened in the Batavian line as countless hours of training prevailed and they resumed their natural formation. The enemy horse overlapped the Vascones by eight riders. Logic dictated that when the two lines met and the Vascones were checked, the Batavians would wrap around Valerius's flank and the slaughter would begin. But Valerius didn't intend to be checked. His plan was to smash through the Batavian centre. But first something had to break.

Seventy paces.

The faceless mob took shape as a line of glittering spear points and glaring-eyed, bearded faces, lips drawn back and teeth bared. A wolf pack closing for the kill.

Fifty.

It must be soon. But not yet. Patience.

Thirty.

'Boar's head,' Valerius screamed, and his command was instantly repeated by the signaller's insistent call.

At his side, Serpentius effortlessly switched his sword from right hand to left and put the reins in his mouth. The Spaniard reached to his belt and in a single smooth movement drew back his arm and hurled one of the two Scythian throwing axes he always carried.

The spinning disc of razor-edged iron took the centre horse of the Batavian line in the forehead and the beast reared and swerved, setting off a chain reaction as riders hauled their mounts aside to avoid a bone-crushing collision. For the space of two heartbeats the centre of the disciplined Batavian attack splintered into chaos. It was long enough. Valerius nudged his mount right and the Vascones automatically followed. The boar's head was predominantly an infantry tactic, a compact wedge designed to plunge like a dagger into the heart of the enemy, but every Roman cavalry unit practised the manoeuvre. At Valerius's command the auxiliaries had moved seamlessly from line into an arrowhead formation, with Valerius, Serpentius and the signaller at the tip, aimed directly at the point where the stricken horse had swerved aside. Valerius hit the gap as the Batavian to his left tried to close it. He was already inside the rider's spear point and he could smell the fear stink on the man's wool over-tunic as his *spatha* swung in a scything cut that split ribs and breastbone, jarring his wrist and drawing a shriek of mortal agony from the other man. The dying Batavian reeled in the saddle even as Valerius's angle of attack slammed his horse aside, creating more space for the rank behind. A simultaneous scream from his right told him that Serpentius had drawn blood and then they were through and clear. There was barely time to take a breath before he shouted his next orders.

'Wheel left. Form line.'

He had intended to smash the Batavian attack and retire to protect Otho, but the instant he turned he recognized an opportunity too tempting to ignore. The charge had carved the Batavians in two and now the riders to the right of his line milled in confusion a hundred paces away. Six or seven men and two horses writhed in the dust where Valerius had struck the centre. Those on his left were closest and had held their nerve, but they were pitifully few, with perhaps a dozen troopers still in the saddle. Valerius still had more than twenty men and now he launched them against the nearest Batavian survivors.

'Kill the bastards!'

The Vascones charged in open order while their enemies were still re-forming, and the Batavians had barely reached a trot before the Spanish tribesmen were among them, cutting right and left and howling their war whoops. Valerius picked out a mailed figure in the centre of the line and it was only as he closed that he saw how young the man was. Calculating eyes shone from a pale, determined face beneath the rim of a helmet that shone like gold. The Batavian drove his spear point at Valerius's chest and only the speed of fear allowed the Roman to deflect the shaft upwards with the edge of his sword. He felt a bruising crunch as the point clipped his shoulder and ducked to avoid the ash shaft swung like a club at the side of his head. Still, the cavalryman was able to batter his shield into Valerius's body as they collided, almost knocking him from the saddle. They circled like fighting dogs, snarling and seeking out a killing opportunity. Valerius saw the moment his enemy's eyes widened, the mouth opening in a final scream as the auxiliary felt the edge of Serpentius's sword crunch into his neck between helmet and mail. In the same instant, Valerius rammed his *spatha* between the gaping jaws. He felt the jarring impact as the iron point met the back of the skull and hot blood spewed from the boy's mouth to coat his sword hand. His victim was thrown back, already dead in the saddle, and his pony ran for a few strides before the body fell to sprawl among the corn stalks.

'Must be getting slow,' Serpentius muttered. 'I've seen the day you'd have had a chicken like that for breakfast and spat out his bones.'

Valerius gasped his thanks and turned to survey the battlefield. Four or five dismounted Batavians still battled for their lives on foot, but the rest were dead or dying, and the survivors of the enemy left flank were still milling about where they had been when the Vascones had charged their comrades. 'Enough,' he ordered the cavalry leader.

The man looked mystified. Serpentius spat something in his own language and the officer called his men off. The surrounded Batavians formed a wary circle, but when Valerius ordered them to lay down their swords they complied readily enough. He heard the sound of hooves and Otho rode up with his guards. 'Why have you spared these traitors?'

'Because they're not traitors. They were only obeying orders, just as we are. Think about it. If your mission succeeds, in a few weeks' time we'll all be fighting on the same side, so what's the point of killing them?'

'They would have killed us.'

'I accept that, but—'

'Then I'm ordering you to kill them.'

Valerius raised his sword and Otho edged back. 'I gave them my word that they'd live.'

The other man bridled. 'I—'

'Look.' Serpentius pointed to where the remaining Batavians were trotting back towards the edge of the wood, where another, larger force had appeared. Valerius bit back a curse as he saw that the newcomers vastly outnumbered his men.

'Form up,' he roared. 'Senator Otho, retire to the rear.'

He heard a sword being unsheathed. 'I've done enough retiring for today.'

Serpentius laughed and Valerius shook his head wearily. 'Very well, but stay close to this Spanish rogue. And if he says run, by Mars' sacred arse, you run.'

By now the Batavian horsemen had reached the larger force. Valerius squinted in the bright sunshine as some sort of heated discussion took place among the enemy, punctuated by a sharp cry as one of the riders pitched from the saddle.

'Now why would they do that?' Serpentius asked no one in particular.

'If the left flank had attacked us while we were busy with their friends,' Valerius suggested, 'they would be sitting here and we would be lying in the dust trying to push our guts back in. I think whoever commands has just given his opinion on their lack of action.'

'A forceful kind of officer,' Serpentius commented. Valerius nodded, but his eyes never left the cavalrymen on the other side of the field and his fingers tightened edgily on the hilt of his sword. Serpentius could count too and his horse tossed his head as it sensed his concern. 'There are a lot of the bastards.'

'There are, but . . . ah, I wondered when he'd make up his mind.' A single horseman trotted across the bloodied ground towards them. When he reached halfway, he rammed his spear into the turf and advanced another ten paces before raising his hands to show he was unarmed. Valerius nodded to Serpentius. 'Get the men back into the shelter of the trees and take the prisoners with you.'

'Watch him,' the Spaniard warned. 'I don't like the look of this one. If he'd kill his own, he's not going to worry overmuch about turning you into buzzard bait.'

'When did you become my nursemaid?' Valerius didn't wait for an answer, but every sense screamed at him to be wary as he kicked his horse into a canter. Before he reached the lone Batavian he heard the sound of hoofbeats, and slowed to a walk as Otho joined him. 'You're an even bigger fool than I thought.' He didn't look at the other man, but let the anger turn his voice hard. 'You'll get us both killed.'

'Always the hero, Valerius. You never let anyone forget Colonia and the Temple of Claudius. Do you think that my not having fought makes you a better man than I? Or perhaps you disapprove of the fact that I was once Nero's friend?'

Valerius reined in and studied his companion. He could feel the Batavian's eyes on them. 'I counted your wife as a friend. She did not deserve what happened to her.'

Otho's face froze and his hand slipped to his sword. 'Perhaps one day I will kill you for that,' he whispered.

'Perhaps you will, but for the moment we have more important things to do. Like staying alive.' Valerius hauled his horse round and together they approached the enemy.

He was dressed, like his auxiliaries, in plaid tunic and trews with a cloak of wolfskin, but his chain-link armour was close knit and of the highest quality. If that wasn't enough to declare his status, he wore a heavy gold torc round his neck that was worth a year's wages to the legionary who claimed it. The first thing Valerius noticed were his eyes, which were an empty washed-out blue that reminded him of sea ice. He had only seen eyes like that in one kind of man: a man who could kill without feeling and compassion and would keep on killing long after other men would be sickened by it.

As he drew the roan to a stop, the pale, expressionless features forced their way into his consciousness and his heart fell as recognition dawned. They exchanged salutes. It was the Batavian who spoke first.

'You have a decurion among your prisoners? Younger than his comrades—'

'Gaius Valerius Verrens, late of Legio X Fretensis.' The young man's lips pursed in annoyance at the interruption. He glanced at Otho, expecting a similar introduction, but Valerius ignored him and the governor of Lusitania was sensible enough to keep his identity to himself.

'One of Corbulo's officers? You are a long way from home. Claudius Victor, prefect Third Augusta Batavorum, attached to Legio IV Macedonica. I repeat my question.'

'I am sorry. He was very brave.'

The Batavian nodded slowly. 'And now I must kill you.'

Valerius looked across the field to where the enemy dead lay. 'You have already lost twenty men. Why would you wish to lose twenty more?'

Victor shrugged. 'What are soldiers for?'

'True,' Valerius conceded. 'But it makes their officers seem careless if they lose too many.'

The thin lips twitched, but if anything the pale eyes grew colder. 'Then perhaps you would like to surrender? I can have three hundred men here by nightfall. You have nowhere to run. Patrols like ours are sweeping every district between Arausio and the river. Every pass to the east is guarded. I doubt you will want to go north. To the south, the sea. We could talk about your mission, which intrigues me. Late of Corbulo's Tenth, but I would guess more recently with the traitor and coward

Galba.' He waited for a reaction, but when none came he ran his eyes over Otho, taking in the expensive horse, the fine clothes and the well-fed features. 'Why would the pretender send a patrol so far into the territory of his enemies? A patrol with, let me guess, a *praetor* . . . no, not a *praetor*; these clothes belong to man of great means. A senator then, or of senatorial rank . . . ?'

Otho's horse sensed his unease and moved beneath him. Valerius decided the conversation had gone on long enough. 'Surrendering to your tender mercies does not appeal,' he said casually. 'I have a better proposition. Since we both know you are lying about the patrols – we saw no sign of them yesterday – I suggest you allow us to withdraw to the river. If we are unmolested I will leave my prisoners and the wounded on this side of the ford.'

'And if I refuse?'

'I will personally kill them, one by one, and take their heads.' The words were said carelessly, but he kept his eyes as cold as the other man's. 'You must make your decision now. If you agree, you may recover your dead.'

Claudius Victor stared at him for a long time. Valerius had a feeling the Batavian wanted to tear him apart with his bare hands, but even as he watched the eyes lost their menace. 'Very well,' he said. 'I do not wish to appear any more careless than I do already. I accept.' As he spoke, he moved his horse closer and Valerius's hand strayed towards his sword. But the Batavian was only studying every detail of his face, taking in the lines, the scar that disfigured him from brow to lip, and the fathomless dark eyes that gave a hint to the qualities of the inner man: strength, determination and lethal intent. When he was satisfied, Victor looked down at Valerius's carved wooden hand as if he had only just noticed it. 'Not something to be easily forgotten,' he said, almost to himself. 'I will remember you, cripple; killer of my brother. We are a patient people, and when we meet again, as we will, I will take great pleasure in killing you in the old way.' He nodded and turned away, and Valerius and Otho rode back to the Vascones.

'How do you know the slippery bastard won't come after us anyway?' Otho asked. 'He didn't look like the kind who would care too much about a few prisoners, especially if you killed his brother.'

'No,' Valerius didn't look back. 'But he's lost a lot of men and I doubt his troopers would thank him for losing any more, especially if we keep their heads. The head is the repository of a Batavian's soul. That's why they keep skulls as trophies: to deprive their enemy of his. They're a hard people, the Batavians; good soldiers, but quick to anger. If Victor sacrifices his men, the next head they take might be his.'

'What did he mean by killing you in the old way?'

Valerius turned in the saddle and looked back to where his enemy watched implacably from the far side of the field.

'It's not encouraged these days, but the Batavians liked to burn their prisoners alive. Slowly.'

II

'We don't have any choice. We have to go back.'

Otho shook his head. The suggestion was unacceptable. 'Our only option is to carry on. My orders from the governor of Hispania Tarraconensis were clear.'

Valerius noticed the aristocrat didn't refer to Galba by the grandiose title the governor had awarded himself – Lieutenant to the Senate and People of Rome – and wondered what that signified. They had stopped to rest near the burned-out ruins of an estate on the west bank of the Rhodanus, the great river that linked Lugdunum with the port of Massilia. He walked to the pebble shore and looked out across the glittering waters, east, towards home.

'You heard what the Batavian said. Every pass to Italia is guarded. By now he will have reported back to his headquarters and the place will be swarming with patrols, every one of them looking for a party of twenty-five men, led by a well-dressed aristocrat on a fine horse. You cannot change what you are and I cannot hide twenty-five men. We must go back. It is for . . .' Valerius knew it wasn't worth appealing to the man's instinct for self-preservation, which lagged many leagues behind his political aspirations, 'the good of the Empire. If you die, who will Galba be able to rely on? Titus Vinius, whose only loyalty is to himself? Cornelius Laco, a drunkard too lazy even to harbour ambition?'

The other man frowned. It was the same question Otho had been asking himself since Galba had tasked him with this mission. And the closer he came to the sword points of the enemy, the more he doubted his patron's motives. A few years earlier Marcus Salvius Otho had been as close to Nero as anyone in the young Emperor's increasingly debauched court: close enough to offer him the sexual favours of his wife, Poppaea. But Poppaea had captivated the Emperor and Otho had been ordered to divorce her. He had become an embarrassment and a liability. It said much for his powers of persuasion that he had been sent into virtual exile as governor of far-away Lusitania, Rome's most westerly province and a rural backwater, rather than quietly executed. Galba's bid for power had given Marcus Salvius Otho an opportunity to return to Rome with honour and the promise of advancement, but the opportunity came at a price and with a high risk. To claim it Otho would have to march into the very heart of Nero's Rome and just one slip would bring torture and death. But the governor of Lusitania did not lack courage. He shook his head. 'My mission is too important.'

Valerius took a deep breath. 'There is another possibility. Two men might get through where many cannot.'

'Who?'

The one-handed Roman glanced to where the cavalrymen were walking their horses. 'Serpentius has a leopard's instinct for survival. He lived through four years and a hundred fights in the arena and he has saved my life more times than I care to remember. If anyone can reach Rome, he can.'

Otho nodded thoughtfully. 'Then he can guide me.'

Valerius shook his head. 'You are too conspicuous and too important to risk. I don't know the details of your mission, but I understand why you were chosen. Senator Galba believes you have access to men on the Palatine and in the Senate who can persuade Nero to give up the purple and declare Galba his successor. That may be true, but it is also possible that Marcus Salvius Otho is being asked to place his head in the lion's jaws.' He hesitated, waiting for a reaction, but Otho remained silent, barely breathing and tense as a full-drawn bowstring. 'What if there was another man, with similar access? A simple soldier, but one who once wore the Gold Crown of Valour? A bauble, and an undeserved one, but a bauble which impressed the impressionable. Even the Emperor was dazzled by its glitter. And there were others.'

Otho's eyes turned calculating. 'Perhaps my mission would be beyond the wit of a simple soldier?'

'It is true that I am no politician.' Valerius shrugged. 'But Nero chose me to hunt down Petrus and I won Corbulo's trust even when he thought me a spy.' And, he thought, you know I brought secret messages of support to Galba from Vespasian in Alexandria, even if you don't know the price he asked. 'How can I make a decision until I have more details of Galba's plan?'

Otho made him wait, pacing the river bank while he turned the proposition over in his mind before beginning to speak. 'Nero is finished. He has lost the Senate, the people and, more important, most of the army. He clings to power in Rome only with the aid of the Praetorian Guard. His is a fortress made of straw and it

31

only needs the slightest push to topple it. My mission is to persuade the Guard to provide that push.

'Nymphidius Sabinus, who holds the Praetorian prefectship with Tigellinus, is the key. He will convince the Guard to abandon the Emperor and support Servius Sulpicius Galba. However, he is understandably nervous and seeks assurances that Galba will meet his price. You will visit him at his house on the Esquiline Hill, behind the Fountain of Orpheus, and hand over this seal. It is the token which will prove your identity. Tell him that Galba will pay whatever it takes to buy the loyalty of the Guard.'

'Whatever it takes?'

Otho nodded. 'Senator Galba was reluctant; he is not a generous man. But he was persuaded when I pointed out that every Emperor since Augustus has had to pay his dues to the Guard. Claudius handed over fifteen thousand sesterces a man and counted it a bargain for an Empire.'

Valerius stifled the questions that Otho's statement raised in his head. All but one. 'And you are certain Nymphidius has the power to do what he claims? Tigellinus has kept a tight rein on the Guard for five years. It would not be like him to lose control now when he needs them to keep his own head.'

'Forget Tigellinus.' Otho spat the name and Valerius belatedly remembered the part Nero's favourite had played in separating Poppaea from her first husband. 'He is finished. They say he wanders the palace like a spectre, afraid of his own shadow, or, worse, the Emperor's. As for personal terms, you may offer Nymphidius everything short of the succession.' His eyes glittered and for the first time Valerius realized the true extent of his ambition. 'That prize belongs to only one Roman and it is not some rustic nearly man from Etruria.'

Valerius nodded, but his mind was already elsewhere. He'd come to understand that Otho's arrogance was like a tribune's sculpted breastplate: a protection against those who would question his authority rather than those who sought to harm him. The governor of Lusitania was a much more complex personality than he first appeared, a fact confirmed by Otho's next words.

'Be careful, Valerius.' He laid a hand on the younger man's arm. 'Your peril does not only lie on the road. Galba's freedman Icelus has languished in the *carcer* this past month, and two others who set out on our mission have not been heard of since they reached Rome. Nero is weak, but even a cornered pig can be dangerous.'

Valerius nodded his thanks. So, he thought, the game begins again. He remembered the many nights in Gnaeus Domitius Corbulo's tent on campaign in Armenia and the mind-twisting game of strategy and nerve the general had played so skilfully. Caesar's Tower: four levels, a thousand combinations, but only one winner. Nero had feared Corbulo, his greatest general, and had ordered his death. Valerius himself had only just escaped with his life, with the general's daughter Domitia. His hand strayed to his pouch, feeling for the Caesar stone he had taken on the day Corbulo died, before he remembered that he had given it to Domitia in Alexandria. Where would she be now? The likelihood was Rome, and that was one of the reasons why he had volunteered to continue Otho's suicidal mission to the city. The other reason was darker, cast a shadow over his mind, and was one he would share with no man, not even Serpentius.

'When will you leave?' Otho's voice cut through his thoughts.

'At dusk.' He had considered heading downriver to Massilia and taking passage on a merchant ship, but he knew Nero would have agents watching Ostia and every other Roman port for Galba's couriers. 'We'll travel by dark, staying close to the Via Aurelia until we clear Aquae Sextiae. The coast road will be watched and it will be safer to take to the mountains. Better to get there alive than not at all.'

Otho nodded distractedly. 'Arrange for your servant to switch saddle blankets with my mount, but make sure he does it out of view of the escort.'

He saw Valerius's look. 'Five thousand gold *aurei* sewn into the lining. A poor exchange.' He smiled. 'Atlas will be glad to have someone else carry the load, but it grieves me to part with it.'

But Valerius's mind was already reaching out towards the distant mountains that lay between him and his destiny. He was going into the unknown again, but he hadn't bargained on carrying an Emperor's bounty.

III

Rome, 6 June, AD 68

The city glowed like multi-hued gold in the pale early evening sunlight. Beyond the walls and the low rise of the Aventine, the greater mass of the Palatine Hill dominated their view. The marble palaces of the Emperors gleamed as if they were studded with diamonds and, just visible beyond them, the pale bulk of the temples of Jupiter and Juno on the Capitoline were backlit by a sea of fiery red: the terracotta roof tiles that covered plebeian and patrician alike. Valerius hitched his cloak to better disguise the wooden hand that identified him as clearly as any banner. He could visualize the seething mass of humanity that fornicated and farted, plotted and squabbled beneath those roofs. The stink of corruption, physical and political, permeated every inch of the seven hills, but still he smiled. 'It's good to be back.'

'Then why are we standing here in this stinking gutter when we could be inside the walls with a warm bed and a warm woman?' Serpentius growled.

Valerius shook his head in mock dismay. 'Trust a Spaniard to be always thinking of his own comfort, even if it will eventually kill him. In case you hadn't noticed, the gate guards are searching every man for weapons, and experience tells us there'll be a spy on every second street corner. Before I go into the leopard's lair I want to know whether he's eaten or not.'

'And how do we find that out?'

'From an old friend.'

'Does he live far from here?'

'Not far, that's why we came to the south gate.'

The Spaniard sniffed, testing the air until he found what he wanted. 'Well, I'll be in the tavern over there until you come back.'

Early next morning, Valerius was making his way along the Vicus Patricius when six Praetorians appeared from nowhere to surround him. He looked around for Serpentius, but the gladiator had vanished at the first sight of the black cloaks.

'You are under arrest.'

'May I be permitted to ask why?'

'On the orders of the Emperor.' The decurion's words sent a shiver of unease through Valerius.

'Very well.' Valerius raised his arms. As the Praetorian searched him for hidden weapons he noticed that the few passers-by who risked a glance in his direction did so with a mixture of fear and pity, but most didn't even look. Clearly, no one wished to be tainted by association with whatever crime he was accused of. The decurion's eyes turned shrewd when he saw the wooden hand and Valerius knew he had been recognized. Only time would tell whether it was for good or ill.

When the soldiers were satisfied, they marched him up the cobbled Nova Via before turning right on to the Clivus Palatinus, and the palace complex that sprawled across the hill. It had been four years since he last visited this place, for the interview with Nero that had led him on the fateful mission to track down the Rock of Christus and almost cost him his life.

His captors pushed him through a guardroom and from there into the depths of the hill to an evil-smelling, windowless cell. He was not surprised; death had always been a potential outcome of this quest. Gaius Valerius Verrens had faced death many times, not least in the flame-scorched furnace of the Temple of Claudius as Boudicca's champions broke in to slaughter the last of Colonia's defenders. It was there that his right hand had been taken, and now the Emperor's guards removed the walnut fist on the leather stock that had replaced it. He had steeled himself to accept whatever horrors they planned for him, but when the mottled stump was revealed he cried out as if he could again feel the long Celtic sword carving through flesh and blood and bone.

When they were done, his captors left him with his thoughts and the damp already beginning to eat into his bones. He closed his eyes, willing his heart to stop thundering. A face swam into focus. This wasn't how it was meant to be. Had his informant got it wrong? Had he been betrayed? He ran the conversation of the previous day through his mind.

'Whoever sent you has misread the situation entirely. Nymphidius is a country-bred boor who struts like the cock of the dungheap because he believes Nero is finished, but he does not control the Praetorian Guard.'

'Then who does?'

'Offonius Tigellinus.'

'They said he had gone into hiding.'

'Is that so different from staying in the shadows?' His old friend had raised a cultured eyebrow. 'It does not *mean he has lost his power. He understands the position better than anyone in Rome. He fears the outcome, but he can still influence it. If any man can bring Nero down it is Tigellinus.'*

The information should have reassured him, but for a moment his guts churned with panic, as if the entire hill were pressing down on him. Eventually the feeling passed, and he huddled into the corner where, despite his closed eyes, true sleep evaded him. Instead, he found himself in a half-light world where dream and imagination swirled and eddied until he wasn't certain where the one ended and the other began. A female presence hovered on the edge of his consciousness. Some instinct told him it was the shade of the Trinovante girl who had betrayed him almost a decade earlier, or Fabia, the beautiful courtesan who had given her life to save his, but he knew his mind was shielding him from the truth. There it was, a narrow, sculpted face with a wide mouth and flashing chestnut eyes: Domitia Longina Corbulo. Her message was that she released him from his vow, the vow to avenge the death of her father. But how could someone else release a man from a solemn pledge made over his general's still warm body?

Three days, or was it four? There was no way of telling, with a filth-spattered bucket for his waste, and food and water pushed through the hatch whenever someone remembered. At some point he found himself reliving his first meeting with Servius Sulpicius Galba, the man whose ambition had brought him to this place, and quite possibly his death.

Eighteen months earlier, in the chaotic hours after Corbulo's suicide, Valerius had fled Antioch with Serpentius and Domitia, one step ahead of Nero's executioners. When they reached Alexandria the general's old friend and rival, Titus Flavius Vespasian, had taken Domitia into his protection. But Vespasian was less certain what to do with the two men who were now being blamed for Corbulo's death. In the end, they had been exiled to a remote desert outpost, where they spent six months training the general's Nubian cavalry for his assault on the rebel province of Judaea. Their exile only ended when Vespasian summoned them to carry a message to Carthago Nova in Galba's province of Hispania Tarraconensis. Then, no one had any inkling that a geriatric patrician with a reputation as both a snob and a skinflint had ambitions for the purple. But with Corbulo, most loyal of the loyal, forced to fall on his sword, Nero's generals knew that the only way any of them would be safe was if their increasingly erratic master could be deposed. By the time Valerius reached him, Galba had allied himself with Vindex and his rebels.

On first acquaintance, Servius Sulpicius Galba was a dried-out stick of a man with all the attraction of a well-gnawed bone. Tall, thin and stooped, he had a broad forehead and a gnarled skull that gleamed like a legionary's helm, and he wore the permanent expression of someone who had just sucked on an unripe lemon. He seldom smiled, because to do so would reveal the absence of any teeth, and his hooked patrician nose was perfectly shaped for looking down on those he felt were beneath him.

Valerius had pondered how to address the man who aspired to be the next occupant of Nero's throne. 'Caesar,' he bowed.

'I am not your Caesar,' Galba snapped. 'I will govern Rome for the people and the Senate, not for personal aggrandizement. The Empire needs stability and firm management and I will provide it. This has always been my destiny. Only a patrician, a man of maturity and long military experience, is capable of providing the leadership Rome needs. You have Vespasian's letter?'

Valerius reached into his pouch and handed over the scroll. Before opening it, the old man peered at the seal, checking it hadn't been tampered with. His bony hands shook as he read it and Valerius wondered how any man could believe those hands capable of steering the Empire on the steady course it needed. His head had been filled with an image of Gnaeus Domitius Corbulo, a true leader: resolute, firm and battle-tested; loved by the men he pushed to the very limits of their mental and physical endurance. Corbulo would have made a great Emperor, but he would never have taken the purple while Nero lived. By ordering his death, Nero had deprived himself of the one man who had the power to hold the Empire together. This old man would never have dared to stir from his bed while Corbulo lived. Yet here he was, and it seemed he held Nero's fate in his hands, because he produced a sour, tight-lipped smile.

Otho had been hovering in the background waiting to be told the contents of the letter, but Galba ignored him. 'General Vespasian tells me here that you are a man of resource who can be trusted?'

'General Vespasian honours me.' Valerius had felt Otho's eyes on him. What had Vespasian got him into?

'I may have work for a man of resource.'

Valerius shook his head at the memory just as the cell door burst open and two guards armed with naked swords strode in. They stood over him while two others bound his arms tight with rope and dragged him out into the corridor and down a set of steep steps. His throat turned dry at the sight of the horrors that awaited

40

him there. The brazier glowed so bright the walls were painted red and the very air seemed to sizzle. On a table lay instruments of torture that needed no identification. He wanted nothing more than to be returned to his dark, damp cell and left there to rot if need be.

They fixed his bound arms to a hook on the wall, so that his toes could barely reach the ground and his muscles quickly felt as if they were on fire. When they left, he had never felt so alone.

Only he wasn't alone.

From the far side of the room he heard a soft scratching sound, the sound a rat makes when it tries to chew its way into a wooden corn store. Gradually, Valerius pinpointed the source of the noise as two bright ovals of reflected light. As he watched, the ovals rose and in the brazier's glow he became aware of a human shape; naked and skeletal surely to the point of death, but with a hugely engorged manhood. The – thing – approached until it was stopped by the bars of a cage, where it stood gnawing with filed teeth at what looked to Valerius like a human thigh bone held between two claw-like hands. He found he had stopped breathing and drew in a huge gasp of fume-tainted, overheated air.

'You are fortunate that our Egyptian has been recently fed.' Valerius flinched at the unexpected voice from the doorway. The tone was conversational, almost apologetic, but it was belied by the bright blade Offonius Tigellinus held in his right hand. 'The Emperor found him amusing, like a pet crocodile, but I fear he is bored of his tricks. He hasn't come to see the entertainment for more than a year.'

Valerius had no illusions what was meant by *entertainment*, but he buried his fears and focused on his jailer. Tigellinus wore none of the trappings that went with his position as prefect and commander of the Praetorian Guard, but his tunic was of the finest material and a gold chain belted it at the waist. Tall and thin, he had a bald head with a fringe of mousy hair that clung to the back of his skull like a frightened squirrel. If it hadn't been for the sword, you might have thought him harmless, which would have been a mistake. According to Valerius's agent, Tigellinus was still the most dangerous man in Rome.

'I thought we had an agreement.'

'We do.' The Praetorian prefect nodded gravely. 'I spoke to our mutual friend last evening. If you are what you say you are, I will put the arrangements in place and you will go free, just another poor coward who gave up everyone he knew at the first sight of the Egyptian. It is a process which safeguards us both. But our bargain depends entirely on the answers you give in the next few minutes. First, you should know that I am aware of certain facts and that I can surmise certain others. I tell you this so that you understand that I will know if you stray from the truth. Of course, you do not know which facts, which should make you all the more careful what you say.' He frowned, and for a moment he seemed quite lost. 'I have served the Emperor loyally for five years, but now that his focus turns to military affairs I fear that I can no longer be of so much use to him. It is my wish to retire, with honour and suitably recompensed, to my estate beyond Fidenae. The question is whether you are able to fulfil your promise to facilitate this.'

'And that, as you are all too aware, Tigellinus,' Valerius kept his voice as reasonable as the other man's, 'is a question that can only be answered by cutting me down from here.'

'What guarantees have I that you will keep your word?'

'None.'

A sharp intake of breath seemed to indicate that all the hours playing Caesar's Tower with Corbulo hadn't been wasted. 'Then tell me why I should not call the guards and have you stripped and tethered for the Egyptian's pleasure . . . and mine.'

'Because I am your only hope, Offonius Tigellinus. Galba will rise and Nero will fall. It is only a matter of how and when. If the legions are forced to besiege Rome, the mob will tear the Emperor apart and his faithful lieutenant with him. You have heard it, Tigellinus, the baying for blood and the cracking of sinews; indeed you have instigated it.' Tigellinus shook his head and Valerius saw something other than superiority in the dark eyes. Raw fear. 'Your only hope is for a peaceful change of rule and the protection of the victors; your only salvation the fact that you fully cooperated in ensuring it. Would you rather these gifts were in the hands of your fellow prefect Nymphidius?'

Tigellinus spluttered. 'Put your faith in that blustering pig and the Great Fire of Rome will seem like a flickering candle compared to the inferno the gods will wish on this city.'

'Then help me, and Galba will hear of your heroics.' Even chained to the wall with the drooling Egyptian eight paces away, Valerius struggled to disguise the contempt in his voice. A million Romans had lived in fear because of this man's tyranny. Thousands of innocents had died horribly because he had pandered to the whims of a gilded man-boy driven mad by omnipotence. Of all the men in the Emperor's inner circle Lucius Annaeus Seneca alone might have curbed Nero's excesses. By engineering the philosopher's death Offonius Tigellinus had condemned Rome to years of terror and ultimately brought her to the brink of civil war. Now, it seemed, he was the only man who could save her.

'What would you have me do?' The words were accompanied by a shudder of distaste. 'He is insane, you know. He wanted to open the cages of the arena and fill the streets with wild beasts. To poison the entire Senate. Only the voice of reason stayed him.' A faint light shone in the depths of Tigellinus's dark eyes and Valerius wondered how many of these outrageous claims were true. The Praetorian paced the room, each time he approached the cell drawing a soft mew of anticipation from the Egyptian. 'When I urged him to bring the African legions to Rome, he refused, because he mistrusts Mucianus and he fears Vespasian. Now he has sent the Fourteenth to hold the mountains and recruited a scratch legion of marines from Ostia to hold the city against attack. Marines? Does he think Galba is going to sail up the Tiber?'

'Perhaps you should not have killed Corbulo?'

Despite the softness of Valerius's voice, Tigellinus recognized the threat contained in the words. 'That was not my doing. I would have saved him if I could, but the Emperor insisted. Even at the last he could not be swayed.'

'Why?

Tigellinus blinked. 'Why?'

'Why did he have to die?' Valerius saw emotions chase one another across the pale face as the Praetorian sought some avenue that would not condemn him.

'Fear and envy,' he said eventually. 'The Emperor looked at Corbulo and saw the better man. He feared his strength and was envious of his popularity. When Corbulo overstepped his *imperium* by invading Parthia, Nero's anger grew beyond control.' The knowing glint in Valerius's eyes forced a change of direction. 'And the plotting, of course,' Tigellinus hurried on, the words tumbling over each other. 'His son-in-law stood against that very wall and implicated him in conspiracy with Piso and his scum. By then he had condemned half of Rome, but his naming of Corbulo could not be ignored.'

'He was Nero's most loyal general. He would never have betrayed him.'

'Yes.' Tigellinus's voice took on a terminal weariness. 'But when has loyalty ever been enough to save a man?' A long moment passed as they stared at each other, the silence broken only by the animal-like snuffling in the background and the soft sputter of the glowing coals. 'I ask again: what would you have me do?'

Valerius smiled at the incongruity of a man in chains dictating to a man with a sword in his hand. 'Let it be known among the Guard that Nero is planning to escape to Alexandria. There is no dishonour in abandoning an Emperor who himself abandons his people.' He saw the Praetorian's startled glance. 'Yes, it is true, Tigellinus. It seems that more than one rat is preparing to leave the sinking ship. But can you convince them?'

'And if I do?'

'You have your life, your estate and whatever plunder you have managed to lay your bloodstained hands on.'

Tigellinus ignored the insult. 'Your word on it?'

Valerius nodded. 'On my honour, though it makes me sick to the stomach to say it.'

'And Galba? Will he pay what they ask?'

'Senator Galba will know of your part in the peaceful handover of power. You have his freedman here?' Tigellinus darted a guilty glance at the doorway. 'Then I hope he is not too damaged, because we will send him with the glad news, and the message that Offonius

Tigellinus alone is responsible for his salvation.'

Tigellinus came forward and used the edge of his sword to cut Valerius free. As Valerius rubbed the stump of his right wrist, the Praetorian prefect went to the table and retrieved the walnut fist with its leather socket from a cloth sack which had sat among the hooks and the knives. It was only then that Valerius truly believed he might leave the chamber alive.

Valerius used his teeth to tighten the leather ties and Tigellinus made one last suggestion. 'You must still meet Nymphidius. He is much less a danger on the top of his dungheap than if you try to keep him out of the farmyard. Let him think he is in control. Let him offer the tribute and accept the acclaim. His arrogance will take care of the rest.'

'Very well. And Nero?'

'It will be as you suggested.'

Valerius flexed the fingers of his left hand and picked up the sword from where the Praetorian had laid it on the table. Tigellinus's eyes widened and he opened his mouth to shout for aid, but the younger man strode past him towards the cage. 'The Emperor will no longer be in need of a pet.'

IV

Valerius could feel it in the air around him: that sense of foreboding that came with the approach of a summer storm. In many ways Rome was a city already under siege. Serpentius had almost given up hope by the time he'd returned, pale and exhausted after four days and nights in the cells below the Palatine. Now the Spaniard recognized a new sense of purpose in his Roman friend.

In the stifling, airless depths between the four- and five-storey *insula* apartment blocks that filled the capital's poorer areas life took on a frenzied desperation. Men and women fought each other over the dwindling stocks in the shops and streetside stalls, and the whole city seethed with fear and uncertainty. Either Nero had repealed the decree that prohibited civilians from carrying weapons or his supporters had decided they were safe to ignore it. Bands of thugs armed with cudgels and knives stood at every junction, unhindered by the Praetorians or vigiles, questioning or 'arresting' those who caught their eye. Anyone foolish enough to appear rich or even mildly prosperous was likely to come under suspicion. It was well known in the stews of the Subura and the tight-packed hovels on the slopes of the

Collis Viminalis that the Emperor had been betrayed by the upper classes and the Senate. Dressed in the dusty work gear of a pair of itinerant builders Valerius and Serpentius had little to fear, and any keen-eyed bully who questioned their disguise would be quickly dissuaded by the aura of sheer savagery that cloaked the former gladiator. As an extra precaution, Valerius had wrapped his wooden fist in the folds of a rugged cloth sack of the kind workers used to carry their heaviest tools. His companion carried a similar bag, which, from the way he handled it, held equipment of considerable weight.

Tigellinus had arranged temporary accommodation for them out by the city wall near the Porta Salutaris. It was typical of its type, two dusty rooms on the fourth floor of a creaking *insula* block, with water drawn from a pump in the yard and a night soil pot you emptied in the stinking drain that ran down the centre of the street. They discovered why it was so readily available when they woke before dawn to the terrified screams of pigs being led to slaughter in the pork market beyond the wall.

On this day, their route took them down the Vicus Longus and into the teeming filth of the Subura before they turned left up the slope past the Temple of Juno Lucina and the sixth shrine of the Argei.

'Watch out.' Serpentius pulled Valerius to the side of the street at the familiar sound of marching feet in hobnailed sandals. They stood back beneath the awning of a fruit stall as a mismatched unit of soldiers stumbled past and veered off towards the Porta Tiburtina. Each of the men carried some kind of weapon, but they were dressed in a mix of blue tunics and civilian clothing. Some had helmets and armour, but most did not. They walked with a curious rolling gait, and those still dressed as civilians stood out because of the heavily muscled upper bodies and arms that gave them the look of acrobats or wrestlers. Many were clearly foreigners; swarthy and dark-skinned, like the Syrian cavalry Valerius had commanded in Parthia.

'These must be the marines Nero is forming into a new legion. Sailors, too,' he said.

'They don't look like much,' Serpentius spat. 'Sunshade operators.'

Valerius laughed at the reference to the sailors' traditional onshore task of erecting the great sailcloth awnings that protected amphitheatre crowds from the fierce heat of the summer sun. 'I don't know. They all look tough enough, and they're volunteers. Equip them properly and give them the right training and they might surprise you.'

'No time for that,' Serpentius pointed out. 'If it had been anyone but Old Slowcoach the legions would already be marching across the Milvian Bridge. Corbulo would have shoved an eagle up Nero's arse by now.'

It wasn't how Valerius would have put it, but he knew the Spaniard was right. Where speed and determination had been needed, Galba had proved slow and timid. He should have reinforced Vindex at the start of his rebellion. Instead, he had begun his march too late. If he had continued his advance, the likelihood was that the two German legions who had defeated the Gaul would have joined him, or melted away in front of him. In the aftermath of the victory at Vesontio, while their blood was up, they had urged their own commander to proclaim himself Emperor and march on Rome. Lucius Verginius Rufus had refused, but it showed that his legionaries were ready to gamble all for change.

'Nero is a desperate man, and forming the marines and sailors of the Imperial fleet at Misenum into a legion shows the level of his desperation. Since the time of Caesar and before, Roman citizenship has been a condition of joining a legion. Most of those men were *peregrini* – foreigners – and some of them are probably former slaves.' Valerius grinned as he felt the Spaniard's withering glare. 'Not that it makes them any less brave.'

When the marines were out of sight they hefted their workmens' sacks on to their shoulders and continued up the hill to where the road opened out and the *insulae* began to give way to more prosperous townhouses and villas. When they reached a small square Valerius laid his burden aside and drank sweet water from the Fountain of Orpheus, which provided a supply for those locals not rich enough to have one of their own. Nymphidius Sabinus was clearly not among them. His villa sprawled across the top of the slope with a view down towards the tiled roofs and marbled pillars of the Forum. Valerius left Serpentius sitting by the gate and made his way to a servants' entrance in the side wall. His knock was eventually answered by a grizzled bruiser with disconcerting eyes that never looked in the same direction at the same time. Valerius concentrated on the left one and announced that he'd been summoned by the master of the house to discuss a price for replastering the slave quarters.

The doorman sniffed. 'Stay here and I'll get the factor.'

'I was told to speak to the master.'

The man carried an overseer's staff and Valerius could see he was tempted to reward such impudence with a beating. He prepared to block the first blow, but a voice from inside froze the overseer in place.

'What's going on, Clodius?'

'Some dirty labourer demanding to speak to you. I was just going to kick his insolent arse back on the street.'

A tall figure appeared behind the doorman and a meaty hand pushed him aside. 'Idiot. Didn't Julius tell you I was expecting a tradesman? Let him in.'

'I'll just search—'

'Don't waste any more time. I need to be at the Castra Praetoria in an hour. You, come with me.'

Valerius bowed and followed the man towards the villa. Nymphidius Sabinus had the build of a boxer, with a powerful chest, and legs that appeared too short for his body. His head was set square on broad shoulders and he wore his flame-red hair cut military short. He led the way to the end of the garden, far enough away from the house to ensure no servant could overhear their conversation. His features were as florid as his head, as if he were permanently angry or had been drinking heavily, but when he spoke there was no hint of a slur. 'You've come from Galba?'

For answer, Valerius drew the seal Otho had given him from inside the neck of his tunic.

Nymphidius's eyes gleamed, but he pointed at the building as if he were identifying some defect that needed work. 'The old bastard is taking his time.'

'Rome's lieutenant is consolidating his position and making certain nothing will go wrong. I'm sure you can appreciate that.'

The big man turned and brought his face close to Valerius, lips drawn back and teeth bared. 'Give me any more of that horseshit and I'll have Clodius beat you black and blue just to hear you squeal. It's all right for Galba and that fornicating bastard Otho. If anything goes wrong they can jump on a ship and fuck off to exile in Africa. I'm the one with my balls on the butcher's block. That's why the price has just risen.'

Valerius met his stare. 'I was told to offer you a thousand *aurei* now and a thousand when it is done. With twenty thousand sesterces a man to the Guard on the day the Senate proclaims Servius Sulpicius Galba Emperor.'

Nymphidius's right hand shot out and long fingers closed on Valerius's throat. Valerius reflected that he could have broken the arm with a single movement, but he was playing a part and that part required that, for the moment, the Praetorian prefect be allowed his fun.

'The Guard will take what I give them,' the big man growled. 'I've already got them eating out of my hand like tame finches. As soon as Nymphidius Sabinus says the word, Nero is finished. The only question is what happens after. Who's to say I haven't had a better offer? The price is two thousand *aurei* now and another two when it's done.' His eyes turned calculating. 'You're no lowly courier, are you? Galba wouldn't have sent someone without the authority to negotiate.'

Valerius managed a nod and the fingers at his throat relaxed and dropped away.

'Good. As long as we understand each other. Galba is an old man; he must be close to seventy. He can't last much longer. He needs someone reliable to advise him and that someone will be me. He also needs an heir.' Valerius almost smiled at the other man's undisguised ambition, and the unlikelihood of its ever coming to pass. Nymphidius Sabinus saw himself as a potential Emperor, but Galba would recognize him for what he was: an overbearing, country-bred bully with the manners of a rutting boar and the habits to match. He had as much chance of becoming heir as one of Nero's ceremonial elephants of taking flight. But he was also central to the plan. Otho had warned Valerius to offer Nymphidius anything but the succession, but Otho wasn't here. Valerius knew that Nymphidius would never agree unless he got what he asked for. He nodded gravely.

'I think that can be arranged.'

'Don't think.' Nymphidius glared. 'You speak for the old man. I want to hear you say it.'

Valerius took a deep breath. 'Servius Sulpicius Galba will appoint you his heir as soon as he is invested with the purple.'

Nymphidius stared at him. It could be months before Galba reached Rome, and more till his investment. Valerius could tell the Praetorian commander would have liked the announcement to be made earlier, but he had played all his bargaining chips. His ruddy features relaxed and he nodded. 'Very well. I'll start approaching the Praetorian cohorts as soon as I see the colour of your money.'

Valerius shook the sack free from his wooden hand and Nymphidius's eyes widened a little as he saw the walnut fist. The sack was half filled with sand to conceal what was kept within and to deaden the sound of metal upon metal. Inside were hidden twenty smaller bags, each containing one hundred golden *aurei*. Serpentius carried a similar load and the weight of coin had come close to breaking their backs on the long trek up the hill. Valerius retrieved one bag from the sand and opened it to show the buttery glint within. 'Perhaps we can find somewhere more private to complete our discussions.'

Nymphidius laughed and draped an arm like a tree branch over Valerius's shoulder. 'Bugger having two rooms replastered. I think I might have the whole place rebuilt.'

V

'It's done,' Valerius said. 'The Praetorians will abandon Nero and hail Galba as Emperor tomorrow. According to Tigellinus the Senate will follow within hours. He's finished.'

'Does that mean we can get out of Rome?' Serpentius's weathered face showed something like relief. 'This place reminds me of that day in Oplontis before the earthquake. Like a pot ready to boil over.'

Valerius considered the suggestion. Weeks of living with the constant threat of torture and death had left their mark on both men, but Galba's mission was only half complete and he had his own reasons for staying. Reasons he wouldn't reveal even to the Spaniard. 'No,' he said finally. 'We have to see this through. The latest rumour is that Rubrius Gallus and his men have declared for Galba. If it's true, the only military force of any consequence loyal to Nero this side of the Alps is the marine legion. I want to know more about them.'

Their chance came later that day, on the way back from the Castra Praetoria, where Valerius had been attempting to gauge the mood of the Guard. Raucous voices bellowed from the doorway of a bar in the shadow of one of the giant water castles that provided reservoirs for Rome's aqueducts. Valerius recognized the song as a pornographic shanty he'd heard roared by naval oarsmen. He nodded to Serpentius and they slipped inside into the gloom. It was the usual crossroads tavern, a low-ceilinged room with a stone bar inset with large urns filled with *posca*, the cheap, lead-sweetened wine favoured in these places, and others brimming with stew of indeterminate origin. Ten men seated around a rough wooden table took up most of the space and they gave off an air of cheerful menace that was as much a result of the power of their combined voices as of their bulk, which was substantial. They ignored the newcomers and Valerius squeezed through to the bar, where he ordered a jug of wine and two cups. He and Serpentius took their places a little to one side of the group and supped their wine while the singing subsided and the men began to talk in the coarse, easy manner of shipmates. Now that his eyes were accustomed to the dark, Valerius could see that they were a mix of races, including easterners, probably from Syria, Judaea and Egypt, where the navy recruited, and a Nubian, whose size marked him out even among these men chosen for their strength and power when hauling on a fourteen-foot oar of seasoned oak.

'If we're a legion, when the fuck are they going to give us proper uniforms?' The complainer was a bull-necked Syrian with thick curly hair and guttural, almost incomprehensible Latin. His refrain was taken up by the bearded man next to him.

'Aye, and weapons. If they expect us to fight this Galba and his traitors we need shields and spears and training in how to use them.'

Valerius lounged back on his bench, apparently concentrating on his drink, but taking in every word. It seemed one of the few Romans among them, seated at the far end of the table, disagreed with his shipmates' view. 'Nah, we won't have to fight. Soon as the old fart hears that the crew of the *Waverider* is coming to get him, he'll shit himself.'

The crude boast brought roars of '*Waverider*' and a new burst of singing, but one voice, more sober than the rest, cut across the noise. To Valerius's surprise it was the Nubian's, and he was listened to.

'We won't get proper uniforms, nor proper pay, until we're a proper legion and we're not a proper legion till we're trained. I don't know about you, oarmates, but I wouldn't much fancy taking on a legion. We're tough enough . . .' he waited until the roar of agreement had subsided, 'but some of us have seen those boys at work and being tough and brave didn't do the opposition much good. I think they'll use us to garrison Rome while we're hardened up for land fighting. The regular legions can defeat the traitor, the way they beat the Gauls. As long as we're to eventually follow the eagle, I for one will be satisfied with that.'

'Aye.' The man opposite, a bearded brick wall with an accent from somewhere up on the Danuvius, nodded. 'Juva is talking sense as usual. We will fight if we have to, but we must be patient for our eagle.'

A pause in the conversation gave Valerius his opportunity. 'Perhaps I could offer you gentlemen a drink?' he suggested. 'It would be an honour to help slake the thirst of Rome's protectors.'

'Are you laughing at us?' the Danuvian demanded, his red-rimmed eyes threatening. 'I don't like the stink of you, or your dangerous-looking friend.' He turned to his mates. 'I think we should take them out the back and drown them in the piss barrel.'

The proposal was greeted by roars of approval and Serpentius reached for his knife as the bulk of the sailors rose to their feet, but Valerius placed a restraining hand over the Spaniard's and the Nubian Juva growled at his shipmates.

'No. He's right. If we are to be soldiers, we should act like them. With discipline. We are here to protect Romans, not do them harm.' He turned to face the two men. 'But why should you want to buy us a drink?'

Valerius shrugged. 'There have been rumours that a new legion is being formed from the navy. From what we've heard it sounds as if it's true. You men are sailors; I'm interested to know why you should volunteer to fight on land.' He pulled back his sleeve to show the walnut fist. 'I have fought on land and sea and I know there's a big difference.'

Juva studied the artificial hand. 'Perhaps not a good enough fighter on either.' He grinned.

Valerius met his eyes with an unblinking stare. 'Good enough to be still alive, my friend.'

The Nubian froze. For a moment he looked like a great panther ready to spring. Then he laughed. 'Where is this wine we were offered?'

They waited until the owner had served up jugs of wine, and while his comrades took up their filthy refrain once more Juva joined Serpentius and Valerius by the wall. He picked up his cup and drank deeply, slurping in appreciation. Valerius refilled the cup and the Nubian nodded his thanks.

'Why do we fight? You think it is for money?' the big man growled. 'True, a year at the oars pays less than half what a soldier earns for a year behind the eagle, but why would a man die for money? No, it is partly pride. Who would want us as we are, the dregs and scrapings of a dozen ports? *Peregrini*. Orphans and bastards and the abandoned. A sailor is despised, except by his own kind,' he waved an expansive hand that took in his roaring shipmates, 'while a legionary has the world's respect. But even that might not be enough. So there is more. Divine Nero in his wisdom has decreed that all, even the lowest among us, *even a former slave*, will become a Roman citizen on the day his enlistment expires, and that enlistment will be deemed to have begun the day he first took ship. Can you understand what that means, Roman? In just ten years, if I live, the byblow of a Mauretanian pirate and a Nubian house slave will be permitted to wear the toga.' As he spoke, his eyes glistened and his voice rose. 'No man will have the right to raise a hand to me and I will have the right to stand in judgement over other men.'

'Then I congratulate you, Juva of the *Waverider*, and I will pray that you live to see that day. But for now, what do your officers have planned for you?'

'That is a spy's question.' The eyes narrowed further, but Valerius was ready for the accusation.

'Not a spy's.' He lowered his voice. 'A question from one with a family and friends who fear for the future. You spoke of garrisoning Rome while others fight, but I fear that is not to be. The reason the naval legion exists is because the Emperor's generals have deserted him. You are all he has left.'

'There is the Guard,' Juva said defensively. 'They are oath-sworn to their Emperor.'

Yes,' Valerius agreed, wincing internally at having to deceive an honest man. 'There is the Guard.'

Juva stood up, knocking the table back, his great bulk

cutting out the light from the doorway. 'Whatever happens, we will fight and if necessary we will die for the man who has given us our hope and our pride. Perhaps you are a concerned family man, perhaps not, but it is time to go.'

The other men fell silent as the mood in the bar changed. Valerius and Serpentius rose slowly and backed away, Serpentius stumbling with a curse as they reached the doorway. As they emerged into the sunshine, Valerius reflected that he'd got at least part of the information he came for: Juva and his shipmates would back Nero to the last. But he had a feeling it might come at a price.

That feeling was confirmed as the two men set off in the direction of the Vicus Longus. When they'd walked a hundred paces over the baking cobbles Serpentius hissed a warning. Valerius glanced back to see four of the sailors following in their wake. It seemed Juva regretted his impulse in letting them go so easily.

The men were still with them when they reached the Vicus. Valerius's first instinct had been to lose them, but Serpentius purposely held back and he waited to see what the Spaniard had in mind. By the time they reached the narrow streets of the Subura, the sailors were only a dozen paces behind. This was Rome's poorest district, a tight-packed haven for gangsters, thieves and pimps where a life wasn't worth a shaved *sestertius* and no sensible man would come to another's aid.

'Is this wise?' Valerius muttered.

'If we lose them, they'll just keep looking. We need to convince them we're not worth the pain. Where better than this?' He lifted his sleeve to reveal a gnarled wooden cudgel he'd picked up from a pile of weapons at the door of the tavern.

Valerius grinned. 'I think I know just the place.' He

stepped up his pace, increasing the distance between the two men and their tail. When they had gone another fifty paces he turned to his left on to the Via Subura, a road that would eventually take them out towards the Esquiline Gate. As they walked, he explained his plan to Serpentius and the Spaniard nodded agreement. They took another turn, into a warren of alleyways hemmed in by apartment blocks, which eventually brought them to a crowded square with a fountain in the shape of a fish at its centre. Serpentius darted to the left and lost himself in a crowd in front of a tavern called the Silver Mullet, before disappearing up a street which ran parallel to the alley they had just left. Valerius continued onwards. He knew the sailors would be suspicious that they'd lost Serpentius, but that couldn't be helped. He kept his pace steady; there was no hurry now. Eventually he saw the dark shadow of a narrow passage that cut off at right angles ahead and to his right. Now he slowed, allowing his pursuers to catch up. The locals here had an unerring sense for impending trouble and he felt them drifting away like smoke until he was alone in the narrow street with the four sailors. He passed the darkened entrance to the smaller alley without a glance and carried on a few steps before swinging round to face the enemy, a short sword miraculously appearing in his left hand. The first two exchanged glances at the sight of the bright iron, but they didn't break stride. The one to the left was armed with a sword and the other hefted a nailed club. They knew they were facing a fighter, but with odds of four to one in their favour they were confident their opponent was already a dead man.

The second pair of sailors were big and tough and alert, but they had never faced someone with Serpentius's speed and skill. The Spaniard darted from the Alley of the Poxed Tart already swinging the stolen club to take the nearest man on the bridge of the nose, smashing bone and cartilage and leaving him momentarily paralysed. As the sailor's companion turned to face the threat, Serpentius rammed the head of the club into the V formed by his ribs below the breastbone, driving every ounce of air from his lungs. If he wished, either could have been a killer blow, but Serpentius had weighted them to disable. For good measure he swung the club right and left, rattling each of the sailors on the skull just above the ear, buckling their knees and dropping them heavily to the festering rubbish that littered the cobbles.

The two men facing Valerius's sword heard the cries of their oarmates and froze, not even daring to turn and check the new threat.

'We have no quarrel with you,' Valerius said carefully, 'and we mean you no harm.' Given the circumstances it seemed an unlikely claim and he saw suspicion and fear harden their faces. 'You're not dead, are you? And neither are your shipmates. All you have to do is pick them up and take them back the way you came. You first.' He gestured to the man on the left, the big Danuvian from the tavern. The sailor hesitated, but Valerius nodded encouragingly. 'Believe me, this is not worth dying for.' The man exchanged a whispered word with his friend. His eyes never left Valerius's blade, but he nodded agreement and went back to help the two men who lay groaning under Serpentius's watchful eye.

'Tell Juva I wish him well and that he doesn't have to concern himself with us,' Valerius said.

The last man nodded slowly before turning to help his shipmate. They took a man each and shouldered them down the street, edging their way past the Spaniard as he whirled the cudgel like a child's toy.

They watched the sailors go. 'Will they fight, do you think?' Serpentius asked.

'They don't lack courage,' Valerius said. 'And Nero has been clever enough to offer them something to fight for. But they won't stop Galba.'

The Spaniard snorted derisively. 'Maybe they won't have to. We'll all have died of old age before Old Slowcoach gets here.'

VI

9 June

By early summer Rome was a whirling sea of rumour and gossip, each tale twisted and chewed over as a dog gnaws an old bone, and less likely than the one that preceded it. Nero had called on his old friend King Tiridates of Artaxata and an army of Armenians and Parthians was already marching to his aid. He had filled a ship with the contents of Queen Dido's treasury and set off to found a new Empire in Africa. He had laid down the reins of power and pledged to make his career on the stage. He was already dead. Other stories were closer to the truth. Two more legions in Moesia had deserted his cause. Vespasian, who had yet to openly declare for Galba, had guaranteed Nero's safety and offered a place of exile in Alexandria. This last scenario, Valerius knew, the Emperor's opponents wanted to be true, and his new friend Nymphidius Sabinus, joint prefect of the Praetorian Guard, did what he could to make it seem so, sending loyalist elements among his cohorts to Ostia to await Nero's coming. Within hours of their departure their more avaricious comrades accepted an offer from

Nymphidius on behalf of the Lieutenant to the Senate and People of Rome of thirty thousand sesterces a man, ten years' pay by Valerius's calculation. Where Galba would find the money was another matter. The old man might be rich as Croesus, but Valerius doubted that Rome's most notorious skinflint would be pleased to hear he had paid twice as much for his Empire as Claudius two and a half decades earlier.

Still the Senate wavered. Galba had not moved from his base in Hispania and the legions of Verginius Rufus, battle-hardened and angry, lurked around the headwaters of the Rhodanus in Gaul. Galba had the authority, but Rufus had the power. If ever Rufus wanted to be Emperor, now was his chance. But, through fear, or loyalty, he did not take it.

It needed one more push, and only one man could provide it. Valerius packed a thousand *aurei* of Otho's Emperor's bounty in the builder's sack and went to visit Offonius Tigellinus. By late afternoon the deed was done and the Senate declared Emperor Nero Claudius Germanicus Caesar an enemy of the people.

The house Valerius sought lay close to the Temple of Diana on the Aventine Hill overlooking the Circus Maximus. Substantial and well built, it might have been the home of a prosperous merchant. He doubted it would have been the first choice of the woman who now occupied it, but perhaps she had good reason for selecting a modest residence. This visit was a distraction from his mission, and a potentially dangerous one, but Valerius was bound by the vow he had made to her father, and even if it had not been so, his heart would have drawn him here.

The thought of seeing her again turned his legs weak

and he fidgeted at the entrance like a nervous schoolboy until a doorman answered his knock and showed him inside. Domitia Longina Corbulo's face showed surprise when she recognized him, followed by a frown of suspicion as the doorman announced him by the assumed name he had given. But she would not have been her father's daughter if she hadn't instantly recovered her poise. She ushered him through to a light-filled room with an open roof and a small pool at its centre. On a bench in one corner an elderly woman looked up from her sewing and frowned. Domitia took a seat on a second bench and waved Valerius to a cushioned marble ledge a few decorous feet away.

'You should not have come here, Valerius.' She smiled. 'I am a respectable married woman, you know.'

He shot her a warning look at the use of his true name, but Domitia only laughed in that unaffected way he remembered. If anything, she had grown more lovely in the two years since they had parted, the lithe figure fuller than he remembered, but the deep brown eyes still with their mocking glint. Not a girl any longer, but a true Roman lady. A respectable married woman. She would be nineteen.

'Do not concern yourself. Cassia is deaf.' She exchanged smiles with the old woman. 'She sees no evil, because I ensure there is none to see, and she hears nothing at all, which I find useful. When he went to take up his praetorship in Sicilia, my husband left me with a hag whose tongue was as sharp as her ears, but I rid myself of her before she could do any damage.'

Valerius allowed himself a smile. 'Still as formidable as ever.'

'I may be married, Valerius.' Her words were accompanied by a smile, but they held an iron core. 'Some day

I may even be owned, but I will never be ruled.' She held his gaze for what seemed an age. At the very heart of her was the same resolve that had made her father who he was: Gnaeus Domitius Corbulo, general of the armies of the East. 'I thought you must be dead.'

The change of direction caught him off balance. He remembered the desperate escape from Antioch as the Emperor's agents closed in after Corbulo's death. The resolve she'd shown even as her world was being torn apart. 'I should have been. In Alexandria, Vespasian kept Nero's assassins at bay, but when we left for Hispania they followed us through Africa and Mauretania. They came close in Leptis, but Serpentius saved both our lives.'

'He is with you?'

'He has business in the city.'

She nodded, slightly distracted. 'And you have been with Governor Galba?' He could hear the doubt in her voice.

'You disapprove of what he is doing? I would have thought—'

'No.' Domitia shook her head. 'It is just that he seems so . . .' She searched for a word he knew was 'feeble', but came up with 'old'. The next words came in a rush. 'A true soldier would already have been at the gates of Rome. A true soldier would not have waited. You would not have waited, Valerius. You would have destroyed that man . . . that monster.'

He felt the heat of her passion, the same heat that had seared them both on the sun-scorched Egyptian beach where the shattered wreck of the *Golden Cygnet* had lain rocking in the shallows. He darted a glance at Cassia, but the old woman was concentrating on her needlework. *That monster* . . . the man who had ordered her father's death. Nero. 'That is why I came. I wanted you to know that he will fall, probably before morning. Who knows what might happen. The city could be dangerous for days, even weeks. Perhaps it would be safer if you left.'

She shook her head. 'I will be safe enough. I have a protector who will provide me with guards.' She saw his look as the alternative meanings of the word 'protector' registered and gave a bitter laugh. 'No, Valerius, he would not dare. He was part of the escort General Vespasian provided from Alexandria. Now he follows me around like a devoted puppy, but sometimes . . . sometimes I see a look in his eyes that troubles me. When this is over I will send the puppy away with his tail between his legs.'

'And who is this . . . protector?'

This time the laugh was genuine. 'Surely you're not jealous, Valerius? That was in another lifetime. He is seventeen, just a boy.' He could have reminded her she was the same age when she had become his lover, but he doubted she would see the irony. They talked for a while longer, tiptoeing around the subject that linked them like one of the shackles binding the prisoners in Nero's death cells beneath the Palatine. It was not his place to raise it, and when Domitia declined the opportunity he sensed the interview was at an end. They rose together, somehow coming closer than either intended. He could smell the scent of the perfumed oils on her body, and something more subtle below it.

'Was that the only reason you came, Valerius, to warn me?' She said it lightly enough, but the words made his head spin. When he spoke he seemed to have pebbles in his throat.

'No. I wanted to see you again, for one last time.'

There was a moment – a long moment – when he wondered if she wanted him to take her in his arms and kiss her. He wanted it, and he knew she knew he wanted it. But neither moved. Eventually, her face twisted in a grimace that might have been pain or regret and she reached out her right hand to place something in his left. He looked down at the blue Caesar stone polished by the touch of Gnaeus Domitius Corbulo's fingers.

The whispered words were so faint that, afterwards, he wondered if he had heard them at all.

'Restore his honour, my Hero of Rome. Finish it.'

VII

Later, the only thing Valerius would recall clearly of that night was the walk from the Aventine to the Clivus Palatinus where he found Serpentius waiting. The rest was like being at the centre of someone else's dream. An impossible drama played out in an alternative world.

'You know what to do?'

The Spaniard nodded. 'We have all the exits covered, including one or two only Tigellinus knew about.'

'If he comes out, you follow him and send word to me,' Valerius warned him. 'There's to be no trouble in the city. It's unlikely the mob will support him, but we can't afford to take the chance. His marines are still loyal. If they're drawn into a fight with the Praetorians there will be a massacre.'

'So this is what it's like to make history?' Serpentius shivered despite the warmth of the evening. 'It feels as if the gods are blowing on the hot coals of a dying fire. Will it make a difference?'

Valerius thought of all the years of opportunity squandered under Nero's rule. The thousands of dead souls now crying for revenge. Had it been any different under Claudius? Or Caligula? Or Tiberius? 'I hope so.'

The Spaniard straightened. 'Then that has to be enough.'

Valerius took a deep breath and walked swiftly to the gate, where the palace guards stepped aside without acknowledging his presence.

'Nero has abandoned the Golden House,' Tigellinus had said at their most recent meeting. 'He feels safer on the Palatine, surrounded by people he can trust. No one will stand in your way. He has been told an officer will report the latest situation. Phaon, his freedman, and a few of his slaves will not abandon him, but neither will they oppose you.'

The receiving room was as Valerius remembered it, vast and intimidating, with the great marble statue of Laocoön and his sons being tormented by pythons dominating the left of the chamber and bathed in light as he opened the double doors. Only the right side of the room, around the golden throne set atop a dozen stairs, was properly lit, as if the throne's owner wished to remain blinded to the reality that lay beyond the reach of the lamps. The throne was empty.

Valerius stepped inside, closing the door behind him, and stood in the darkness, listening. At first there was nothing apart from the soft swish of a fan attempting to stir life into the thick, heat-heavy air. Then he heard it, a low muttering from the far side of the room, beyond the open windows that led to the balcony. He focused on the sound and walked towards it, placing each step to minimize the noise of his nailed sandals on the marble floor. Gradually the words became clearer.

'I am lonely, Mother.' The voice of a young man, soft and pleading. 'Why did you desert me? All I ever wanted was to please you.'

'Please me?' Another voice, this time high-pitched,

a woman's. 'Why, you murdered me, ungrateful child, stabbed me on the shore; hard stones in my back and my blood mingling with the salty sea.'

Valerius shivered as he listened.

'Not me, Mother. Some fool who overstepped his orders. You deserved so much better than that tawdry end.'

'And Seneca, who was your friend, was that also a mistake?'

'I miss Seneca.'

'And Britannicus?'

'Did I ever make you proud, Mother?'

'What mother would not have been proud of a son like you? Each time you sang, you sang for me. Every triumph, you dedicated to me.'

'Mother?'

'Yes, Caesar?'

'What must I do?'

The shrill voice was replaced by an urgent hiss. 'Run, Lucius. You must run and never stop.'

'There is nowhere to run.' Valerius's voice had all the finality of a marble tomb closing. He stepped from the shadows and the stocky figure on the balcony froze, silhouetted against the dying light, his eyes bulging, pale with fright. All the blazing glory and deadly threat that had made him the object of awe and fear was gone now. Where there had been an Emperor, now there was only a man.

'You?'

'Yes, Caesar.'

'You should be dead.'

'I come with a message from Gnaeus Domitius Corbulo.' Even in the gloom Valerius saw that pallid flesh grow paler. 'He bears you no ill will, despite the calumnies you heaped upon him. He seeks no revenge, though I, for one, would not hesitate to avenge him. All he asks is that you act with the nobility of your line. It is finished. Today the Senate decreed that you should be scourged to death. You have seen men scourged; backs bared to the bone and flesh in tatters. Could you stand the kiss of leather and iron? And even if you escaped that, what fate awaits a man forsaken by his people? Fight and you will lose. They will tear you apart for the horror you brought upon them. Run, and they will find you, wherever you flee.'

'Alexandria . . .'

'Vespasian will send you back.' Valerius kept his voice hard and unflinching; the voice of a judge passing sentence. 'Africa? The governor is loyal, but how long can he protect you? The rest have already deserted you. You are an Emperor without an Empire. There is only one way.' Valerius reached beneath his cloak and drew his sword from its scabbard. It was the cavalry sword Corbulo had given him so long ago. He remembered the long, eagle's face, the comforting certainty; the dying breath.

Nero saw the sword and ran shrieking from the room.

The road was familiar, the old Via Salaria that led out to Valerius's family estate at Fidenae, but he did not need to travel that far. Serpentius was waiting by a gateway with a troop of Praetorian cavalry and he recognized the entrance to the villa owned by Nero's freedman.

'He came here with Phaon and four others. Slaves, we think,' the Spaniard informed him. 'The place is surrounded. There's no way out.'

Valerius nodded. He reached into the pouch at his belt and his fingers settled on the small blue stone

Domitia had placed in his hand. Corbulo's master piece in Caesar's Tower. He picked it out and weighed it for a few moments before disappearing into the darkness of the walled garden. Serpentius heard a short squeal of terror and the horses shuffled nervously at the sound. The screech of an owl made his fingers automatically form the sign against evil before the sound of voices left him oblivious to all else.

'Will you never leave me alone?'

'I will follow you to the ends of the Empire if need be. You have too much blood on your hands.'

'So it must be now?'

'Yes, it must be now.' Was it some night creature or the soft hiss of a sword being drawn?

'Here?'

'No, here would be better.'

'Will it hurt?'

'Only for a moment.'

'I cannot.'

'You must.'

A sharp cry followed by soft, pitiful sobbing. 'See, I cannot. Help me, my Hero of Rome.'

'For Rome.'

The words were followed by a prolonged wistful sigh; the kind of sigh a great actor might make before leaving the stage for the final time. A shadowy figure reappeared, stooping to wipe something on the long grass. The Spaniard went to stand at his friend's side. 'So it is finished?'

Valerius looked to the north, where the wolves of the Rhenus were gathering. He remembered the limitless ambition in Otho's eyes. Galba's bony hands shaking as they unrolled Vespasian's scroll. How long would those hands be able to keep their grip on the Empire's reins? A peal of thunder broke the silence and lightning flashed over the distant hills. All the ingredients for mischief and the gods were already stirring the cauldron. 'What if this is just the beginning?'

VIII

At first it went well. Galba, typically, did not move until official word of his acclamation by the Senate reached him in early July at Clunia, in the north of Hispania. Only when he had the sealed leather scroll in his hand did he don the purple cloak and begin his march. Another man would have hurried to Rome before someone stepped in and tore the prize from him, but the Emperor-elect was a patrician who took the trappings of his new status seriously. With the recently constituted Legio VII Galbiana, a barely trained rabble of Spanish peasants under Roman centurions and officers, in the van, he made his stately way across southern Gaul, while Otho cursed at his side. All this Valerius would discover later, along with more sinister intelligence of which he was about to receive forewarning.

Fortunately for the new Emperor, the man most likely to usurp his position, Verginius Rufus, had been among the first to accept his elevation, before retiring with his Rhenus legions to Moguntiacum. Rufus kept his command, for the moment, but Fonteius Capito, governor of Germania Inferior, had not been so fortunate. Unable to make up his mind whether to support the new Emperor, he had been accused of treason and executed by two of his own officers. It helped that most Romans perceived Galba as a great statesman; also that he was old, and therefore unlikely to be around for long. Since he had no living children there would be no Galbanian dynasty, but a judiciously chosen heir in whose selection they might have some say. Valerius had a feeling they would be disappointed.

Throughout July, the tension eased from the city like air escaping from an overblown goatskin, but by August, with the heat bouncing from Rome's walls like a furnace and the Senate acting like rabbits at the mercy of an imaginary weasel, the populace became increasingly impatient. And none more so than the naval legion.

'They should have sent them back to Misenum,' Serpentius said balefully as he and Valerius passed another tavern brawl involving men in blue tunics. Having spent the two months since Nero's death kicking their heels and waiting for something positive to happen, the two men were as frustrated as anyone else in Rome. Even the Spaniard found the relentless heat and dust of summer oppressive, and the Tiber, never the most sweet-smelling of streams, filled the whole city with the reek of an open sewer.

'The Senate is frightened to make a decision,' Valerius pointed out. Normally the senators would have left the city in August for their holiday homes at Baiae, Neapolis and Oplontis, but with the advent of a new regime none had dared. 'Any decision. An Emperor ordered the marine legion's creation and now only an Emperor can decide their future. They are neither one thing nor the other, and, worse, they are frightened. When Nero called, they volunteered, to stop one man. Galba. That man is now their Emperor and Emperors are not known for tolerance or mercy. Their future is uncertain at best and painful at worst.'

'Then why don't they run?'

'If they run, it will prove their treason and Galba will hunt them down, as Crassus hunted down Spartacus. Their greatest strength is in their unity and a display of their loyalty. If they can convince Galba they are worthy of his trust and he has the sense to accept it, perhaps we will yet see them march behind an eagle.'

'Aye,' Serpentius spat. 'And perhaps one day when I back the Greens they will win.'

It was towards the end of the month, and still with no sign of Galba, that Valerius decided to visit his sister Olivia at the family estate at Fidenae, to the north of the city. Conveniently, it also allowed him to meet another obligation.

They could hear the laughter from the wayside tavern long before they reached it. A single bullock cart stood in the yard, alongside six horses being fed and watered by a stable boy. Valerius reined in beside them and left Serpentius to see to their mounts.

A large man in a formal toga sat at a table heavy with a dozen dishes, telling a story Valerius had heard before about an African tyrant and his performing elephant.

'It got to the end of the tightrope, wobbled for a moment with a look of extreme displeasure on its sad features . . . fell off and landed on his head. You've never seen such a mess. They had to clean the old man off the floor with a bucket and brush. His wife rushed in, screaming, "Is he hurt?" The elephant handler carefully looked his beast over and replied, "No, he seems fine."'

The man's six companions roared with laughter and

the storyteller beamed. His smile grew wider when he noticed Valerius at the door.

'Enter the ghost of Achilles.' Aulus Vitellius raised a silver cup that was certainly not from the inn's stock. 'Gentlemen, I give you a true warrior. May I introduce Gaius Valerius Verrens, Hero of Rome and special envoy to our lord and master, the Caesar of the South. Valerius, my aides, Lucius, Gavo, Octavius and . . . the rest.' Valerius met the frank stares and nodded a greeting. Vitellius's reference to his work for Galba proved he trusted his aides, but he had always been trusting. Perhaps too trusting. Today, though it was barely midday, he was at his loquacious best. 'Landlord! This calls for more food and more wine. A toast, to one Aulus Vitellius, the newly appointed governor of Germania Inferior, may his legions be victorious, may he prosper among the barbarians, and may his creditors wither on the vine, be swallowed by blackbirds and shat out like the manure they are to do some good for a change.' Someone passed Valerius a cup and he joined in the toast, laughing with the rest.

An aide moved to allow Valerius to squeeze in beside his old friend on a bench designed for three, and below the table he slipped a well-stocked purse into the folds of Vitellius's toga. 'Perhaps this will help keep the manure at bay for a little longer,' he said quietly.

The new governor of Germania Inferior studied him like a long-lost son and his eyes turned moist. Valerius knew that his friend was busily weighing the purse in his hand and would by now have calculated its value to the last *as*. He saw the deep-set eyes narrow, then widen, and finally Vitellius gave a roar that made all five of his chins quiver like waves in a storm. Valerius felt himself engulfed in two enormous arms and drawn into a suffocating embrace. Eventually, Vitellius released him and they sat back, each studying the other with a mixture of pleasure and wariness.

They had first met in a riverside fort on the Dacian frontier when Vitellius cheerfully admitted trying to have Valerius killed, then almost certainly saved his life by offering him a position as military adviser when he left to govern his African province. He had changed little since their eighteen months together in Carthage. His thinning hair was mostly gone now, and he was perhaps a little heavier around the middle – hardly surprising in a man who could eat three large meals a day and still be demanding more when everyone else was crouched in the *vomitorium*. Many made the mistake of confusing fat with foolish and lumbering with slow-witted. In fact, Vitellius's bumbling self-mockery disguised a shrewd brain that the Emperor Claudius had recognized by making him consul. He had been a friend and intimate of Nero, but, as the Emperor's power waned, he had hidden away on his estate until Servius Sulpicius Galba had called him back to service. It was Vitellius who had revealed to Valerius that Otho's evaluation of the situation in Rome was flawed, and that there could be no transfer of power without the help of both Praetorian prefects, and Vitellius who had arranged the meeting in the Palatine dungeon with Nero's former favourite, Tigellinus.

Vitellius fumbled the purse into a secure position and murmured his thanks. 'You would think a man of any intelligence could not fail to return rich from his province, but I was struck down with an almost terminal case of honesty.' He shook his head in mock sadness as he repeated the refrain Valerius knew so well. 'After all those years of avoiding it, my conscience finally caught up with me. How could any man let those people starve?'

Valerius knew of many governors who would cheerfully have watched their people starve, and profited from it by raising the price of what little wheat was left. Instead, Vitellius had purchased grain from Rome at exorbitant prices and had it shipped over to Africa at his own expense. It had made him hugely popular among his citizenry, who had petitioned Nero to recompense him, but a laughing stock in the Imperial capital. He was still waiting for his money. 'And now you have an Emperor's confidence again.'

Vitellius gave him a shrewd look. 'Perhaps you know more than I do. I have my appointment and an opportunity, that is true, but who is to say why it has been offered.' He raised the silver cup and drank deeply, wiping his lips with the back of a plump hand. 'My predecessor, Capito, despite his mistimed and fatal hesitation, was a man of action, which I, let us be quite open, am not. He was also a man of means, which I,' his moon face split into a grin, 'notwithstanding some recent good fortune, am patently not. Therefore, by our new Emperor, I am seen as harmless, perhaps ineffectual; a man more likely to shout "Bring us more wine, you lazy bastard"' – the tavern owner laughed and added another three jugs to the table – 'than "Let us march on Gaul". Yet he may have mistaken me. I am not without ambition.' He gestured to one of the aides and the man disappeared outside to return a moment later with a polished rosewood box, three feet in length and five inches across. Serpentius appeared watchfully behind him, a threatening, whip-thin presence with a curled lip who drew uneasy glances from the young aristocrats who served Vitellius. The governor laughed

81

at their discomfiture. 'I see you still have your Spanish wolf, Valerius. A wise decision in these uncertain times.' He stared at the former gladiator, seeking some sign of acknowledgement, before his eyes registered recognition. 'Didn't you win me money when you butchered Caladus the Thracian at the old Taurus arena?'

Serpentius's eyes narrowed and he took his time before replying. 'If I did, you were fortunate indeed, because Caladus fought again twelve times under the name Rodan. Not every gladiator who spills his blood on the sand is a dead gladiator.'

Vitellius's plump features twitched first to understanding, then to outrage, before he spluttered with laughter. 'Fortunate indeed. I will remember that the next time I make a wager.'

He waved away the young aide and flipped the wooden box open. Inside was a sword that took Valerius's breath away. The *gladius* was like no other he'd seen, the hilt wonderfully worked in spun gold, with precious stones decorating the scabbard and a miniature legion's eagle on the pommel. 'Divine Julius himself carried this sword.' Vitellius slipped it free from the scabbard and Valerius saw the blade had been worked so skilfully that a pattern like silver smoke ran its length. 'I have borrowed it from the Temple of Mars Ultor, where my brother is high priest. Rome has need of it, Valerius. Aulus Vitellius has need of it.'

At another time, Valerius might have smiled at this foolishness, but he could see that Vitellius was in earnest. 'You are going to war, my friend?'

The other man shook his head. 'No. But there is a name to be made by the man who defends the Rhenus, and perhaps takes the battle beyond it in the manner of Germanicus. If that man carries the sword of Julius

Caesar, his other deficiencies might be overlooked. Leave us, please,' he ordered the young men, 'and make sure the cart is well provisioned.' The aides shuffled out and Valerius nodded to Serpentius to join them. Vitellius lowered his voice. 'Who knows,' he said carefully. 'If the next Emperor is an old man and it is such an onerous position, he may feel two years, perhaps three, is enough before handing the reins of power to a younger, more energetic candidate.'

Valerius stared at him. Vitellius had commanded a legion on the Danuvius and as governor of his province, but his conceit in thinking that he could follow Galba to the purple was astonishing. Yes, he was of the proper patrician stock, but if Galba dismissed men like Marcus Salvius Otho and Titus Vespasian, how likely was he to appoint as his heir a fat man who thought stealing Caesar's sword made him a great general? But now was not the time to disabuse his friend of his ambitions.

'Then may Fortuna favour you.' He raised his cup. 'What news do you have?'

A lifetime in politics had taught Vitellius the value of having a long list of contacts throughout the Empire, and now they were proving their worth. 'You have just come from Rome, so you know of the unrest among the naval militia?'

'I know they call themselves a legion.'

'Exactly. They will not fight, but Galba should have ordered their disbandment. By delaying he is only storing up trouble. And I fear that is not our new Emperor's only misjudgement.' He reeled off a list of officials, including two of senatorial rank, whom Galba had ordered executed before he left Spain. 'Anyone who did not greet his appointment with sufficient enthusiasm, and their families with them.' Valerius looked up, startled, and

Vitellius nodded sagely, picking at the remaining food. 'Yes, even Nero at his worst only used such barbarity sparingly. It seems my old friend Servius has discovered a taste for blood. He has a delicate path to tread and I fear he treads it with all the care of a wandering buffalo. In Gaul, his conscience tells him to reward the rebels he failed to support, not understanding that this puts him at odds with the legionaries who saw their comrades fight and die defeating them. It is said that he has already called for the head of Mithridates of Petrus because he's heard the old bugger has been ridiculing his looks. In Africa, Clodius is refusing to send grain supplies to Rome, a decision probably taken when Nero was alive, but his days are numbered. Verginius Rufus is deposed in Germania Superior, but he may survive.' He frowned, the movement setting his great jowls wobbling. 'There is one thing that puzzles me. I hear rumours from Rome of chaos and disruption in Syria and Judaea, yet my agents assure me they are not true. The source of these tales appears to be Nymphidius Sabinus. Can you think of any reason for him to do that?'

Valerius laughed. 'Not unless he is using them as a goad to hurry our new Caesar to Rome, where he belongs.'

Vitellius nodded gravely. 'You have not lost your nose for conspiracy, Valerius.' Valerius sensed there was more to come, but the new governor of Germania Inferior was in no hurry. 'I have also heard tales of some remarkable exploits by a young cavalry commander. These tales, along with everything else that happened in Parthia, were supposed to be suppressed, but Aulus Vitellius is not without his friends. Still the soldier, Valerius?'

'It seems the only thing I am good for.'

The fat man smiled. 'My new position comes with

a certain amount of responsibility, but also a certain amount of power. One aspect of that power is a say in the appointment of legionary commanders. Galba believes the Fifteenth Primigenia's legate is of suspect loyalty. He wants to foist some young upstart *quaestor* from Baetica on me, but I believe that if I insisted he would appoint my own candidate, particularly as you have already been of service to him.'

Valerius had been listening, but not quite taking in what Vitellius was saying. Slowly it dawned on him what he was being offered.

'I . . .' His heart swelled until it filled his mouth and the words would not come. Not an African legion or a temporary command, but five thousand of Rome's finest, marching behind the eagle of a legion with a pedigree that went back to Pompey the Great.

'There is no hurry to accept, I assure you. I doubt I will be in Colonia Agrippinensis until November.'

'I am honoured by your faith . . .'

'Of course, I understand you must complete whatever mission Galba has assigned you. But you may write to me at any time, and,' he took Valerius by the wooden hand, 'remember that the offer stands for as long as I have the power to make it, and that as long as Aulus Vitellius lives you may call him your friend.'

Vitellius hauled himself to his feet. He picked up the wooden box from the table and pulled the sword from its cloth covering. The *gladius* looked small and insignificant in his big hands and as he swung it in a clumsy practice cut Valerius had a terrible sense of foreboding. But Vitellius was oblivious of his gloom. As he lumbered towards the door and the appointment that was his destiny he turned with a smile. 'The world will hear more of Aulus Vitellius.'

Valerius watched him go and the words seemed to echo round the room, but his mind held only a single thought.

He had been offered a legion.

IX

An hour after leaving Aulus Vitellius, they turned through the gateway and on to the track leading to the villa. A flash of white among the trees to their right told Valerius they'd been sighted by a watch slave now sprinting to announce the arrival of strangers.

And he was a stranger. It was almost two years since he'd left home to travel to Syria and, for reasons he couldn't explain, he hadn't visited or sent word since he'd arrived from Hispania all those weeks ago. The rough road twisted through low hills cloaked with untidy ranks of grey-green olive trees that stretched away into the distance. It was long enough to allow time for alert defenders to set up an ambush and provided ample cover from which they could hurl their missiles at hostile invaders with impunity, at least until the latter had organized themselves. This was where he had spent the first dozen years of his life and he knew there were barely visible tracks through the trees that led to caves and gullies where his people could retreat and either hide or, if necessary, attempt to fight the attackers off. Regular troops would persist and the end would be inevitable, but the kind of men who would find a run-down place like this an attractive target were bandits and brigands; bands of deserters. They would not relish giving their blood with no guarantee of profit. As the calculations ran through his mind, he realized with a shiver why he was making them.

When they reached the house he was still lost in thought, and the cry of welcome from Olivia came as a shock.

'Valerius! Why did you not warn me you were coming? I wasn't even sure you were alive.'

When he saw his sister looking so well he felt like laughing. There had been days when he had held her in his arms and been certain she wouldn't survive the hour. The last time he had seen her the shadow of the illness still lay upon her features, but now her cheeks showed a country housewife's glow and she had put on weight. Olivia had always scoffed at the pampered life of a Roman lady, even when she had been forced to live it. Since the deaths of her husband and their father she had become her own woman, and that woman looked at home in a simple homespun *stola* with flour dust on her face. She was flanked by her ancient servants, Granta and Cronus, their father's freedmen who looked after the actual running of the estate, though what that amounted to these days he had no idea.

Belatedly he became aware of another presence, hanging back in the shadows. Olivia saw his look, and with an almost imperceptible nod invited the man forward. He was of mid-height, perhaps a hand span shorter than Valerius, but with the angular hardness that comes with life outdoors, and truculent, unyielding eyes that said he was ready to deal with whatever came at him.

'Lupergos.' Olivia's voice cut across Valerius's thoughts and demanded he look at her. When he did, the message he received dared him to challenge what she said next. 'He is my – our – estate manager.'

Valerius left it just long enough to send an equally unmistakable reply before he nodded. Lupergos bowed and backed away. In an instant the tension drained from the faces of the two freedmen and they approached with the traditional traveller's welcome of a bowl and cloth, a loaf and a flagon of pure water from the well behind the house. Olivia invited him to stay the night and he saw the flash of surprise on Serpentius's face when he agreed. The villa was a sprawling place laid out on a single level, and Valerius remembered it fondly. The last time he had been here much of the paint had been peeling and the plaster cracked, but as Olivia led him to his room he was surprised to see fresh, glowing white everywhere, and signs of repairs to floor and ceiling. Their eyes met, and there was that challenge again, but he said nothing. He found a fresh set of clothes that fitted and joined her in the atrium. She'd always been fascinated by his travels and she listened for over an hour as he spoke of the vast, forbidding landscapes of southern Armenia, the heat-seared deserts of Arabia where the wind could strip a man's flesh, and the jewelled seas and emerald cliffs of the Hispanic coast. Somehow, there was no time to discuss the estate's domestic arrangements.

Eventually, he said: 'I think I will inspect the estate. Perhaps Lupergos would like to join me.'

He saw the momentary flare of concern in her eyes, followed by the acknowledgement that this moment could not be avoided. 'Of course. If you wait by the barn, I will fetch him.'

Lupergos appeared a few minutes later and without a word they headed off up the valley to the south slope, past the rows of grape vines to where the oldest olive trees grew. This was Valerius's land; all this fertile red earth in the miles-wide bowl between the hills. He loved it, and it was part of him, just as he was part of it. But he felt no particular desire to work it. In truth, since his father's death it had become Olivia's and he was content with that. He had his own life to live, and it wasn't anchored to the soil, however welcoming. Below the earth lay countless cubits of finest quality marble that made the Emperor's bounty he had carried from Gaul look insignificant, but he was the only man alive who knew it and that was the way it would stay. To get to it, they would have to strip the estate bare, tear the trees and the vines from the ground by their roots and gouge great canyons in this beautiful land. No man would say that was Gaius Valerius Verrens' legacy. No matter what it cost.

As they reached the olives, Lupergos began to talk unhurriedly in a thick north Etrurian brogue that marked his class as much as the rustic clothes he wore. 'I will cut the maturest trees back, but not too much because they produce the finest oil. The oldest of them are only ten years from the end of their useful life. We must plant their replacements now, unless we want a drop in production.'

'You think the slope will take it?' Valerius spoke for the first time.

Lupergos gave a tight-lipped nod. 'The land is rich and we are better supplied with water than any of our neighbours.'

He had more to say as they turned east through the most productive vines and Valerius was impressed by the Etruscan's grasp of land husbandry and viniculture. Eventually, they set off for home, but almost as if they'd planned it that way, they stopped and faced each other before they were within sight of the villa.

'You are a Christus follower, Lupergos?' It was a provocative question. An admission of guilt could be a death sentence. The other man's nostrils flared. Valerius saw his muscles tense and readied himself for the assault that threatened to come, but eventually Lupergos nodded. Valerius relaxed, but his expression didn't change. It had seemed likely, and made sense, because Olivia had worshipped the Judaean mystic since her encounter with his disciple Petrus two years earlier. 'Well, I don't care about that. What I care about is Olivia and my land, and if you take liberties with my sister or my property I'll pull your guts out through your arse and make you watch as I feed them to my pigs. Do we understand each other?'

The colour in Lupergos's cheeks flared and his breath came quick and hard as he considered his response. 'She said you saved her life. Is that true?'

Valerius nodded, remembering the battle in Poppaea's burning mansion above the Bay of Neapolis.

'Then I'll give you that, just this once. Do we understand each other?'

Valerius looked into the hard eyes and grinned. 'You know about the land. What do you know about killing people?'

The answer, it turned out, was not much.

Valerius took him towards the estate's entrance and explained what he wanted. 'Not one watcher, but two, one either side of the gate, with some kind of signalling system back to the villa. Keep it simple. And defenders. How many? How well armed?' As they walked along the track towards the house he pointed to the low hills and told Lupergos about fields of fire. 'It will be up to you whether to fight or run, but you must create the conditions to fight and win. Three concealed enclosures – forts – with enough room for ten men in each. Archers.'

'But where will I find archers?'

'The slaves. They are young enough and strong enough. They must learn to fight for what is theirs as well as ours. I will send a man to teach them how to use a bow and wield a sword.'

There was much more and Lupergos accepted it without question. The stocks of food and water in the caves and gullies. The valuables that must be left unconcealed to encourage the invaders to take just enough and go. The escape routes and rallying points in case everything went wrong.

But as they reached the house, Lupergos could no longer conceal his curiosity. 'But why now? I know you are a soldier, but . . .'

'I don't know why, Lupergos, just as I don't know why I know it will rain tonight, but it will. All I know is that somewhere out there the wolf is waiting and if I'm not here to protect what is mine, then you must.'

The Etruscan nodded thoughtfully and walked off to his quarters. Olivia was waiting for Valerius by the villa's front door. She took his arm as they entered. 'He is a good man, Valerius.'

He smiled without looking at her. 'Then that is enough for me.'

Before they parted, she took his left hand in both of hers and placed something in his palm.

When he looked down he saw it was the tiny gold amulet in the shape of a boar, the symbol of the Twentieth legion, that he'd placed round her neck when he had believed she was dying three years earlier. He had brought the necklace back from Britannia, where it had been crafted for Maeve, the Trinovante girl he had loved, and lost to Boudicca. Fortuna had favoured Olivia since she'd worn it, but it brought to mind the Caesar token Domitia had handed him that now shared an Emperor's grave. He tried to return it, but she only smiled.

'I think your need is greater than mine.'

Valerius and Serpentius took the road to Rome as the worst heat of the afternoon sun faded the following day. When they reached the first of the roadside tombs that lined the Via Salaria outside the city walls they were met by a galloping messenger. The man reined in and Serpentius was about to thrust his horse between the threat and Valerius when he produced a seal that identified him as one of Tigellinus's servants.

'How did you find us?' Valerius demanded.

'My lord has eyes in many places.' The young rider grinned. 'But it helped that when I asked at the house they said you had set off to visit your estate. There is only one road.'

'Well?' Valerius raised an eyebrow.

The messenger bowed in the saddle. 'My master did not commit this news to paper because he felt it was important enough for you to wish to hear it at the first opportunity.' He took in a breath and recited the words he had learned by rote. 'Last night, Nymphidius Sabinus, who holds the joint prefectship of the Praetorian Guard, denounced Servius Sulpicius Galba before his men as a traitor and a false Caesar and declared that with their support he intended to don the purple himself. In their outrage at this betrayal, the loyal soldiers of the Guard turned upon Sabinus and struck him down. Nymphidius Sabinus is dead.'

Valerius breathed a sigh of relief at the final, fatal sentence. He saw again the red face and bulging eyes and felt the threatening fingers at his throat. What was it Tigellinus had said? *'Let him offer the tribute and accept the acclaim. His arrogance will take care of the rest.'* 'What else did your master say?'

'He said that it seemed someone informed Nymphidius that the Emperor had decided to make another man his heir and the knowledge pushed him over the edge. The judgement of the gods, he said.'

Valerius exchanged a wry look with Serpentius. 'It seems our new Emperor rides with the gods at his shoulder after all.'

The Spaniard grinned. 'But sometimes even the gods need a little help.'

X

October, AD *68*

It was the thunder season and a storm was coming. Still, half of Rome had turned out to line the Via Flaminia and welcome their new Emperor. Valerius rode with Serpentius as far as the Milvian Bridge, which spanned the Tiber a mile beyond the great tomb Augustus had built to house his family. Since he wasn't part of any formal celebrations he'd decided against the toga that might have been expected of him, instead wearing a simple belted tunic with the stripe of his rank, and a finespun woollen cloak. He was surprised to see hundreds, perhaps thousands, of men milling about beyond the bridge and being kept from the road by a wary line of Praetorians. Among the figures hemmed in on the loop of dry ground between the road and the river, he noted the distinctive blue tunics of the marines of the Misenum fleet. The area was pockmarked with makeshift tents of cloth and leather that indicated they'd been waiting overnight, or longer. Curious, he talked the soldiers on guard into allowing him over the narrow bridge. He recognized the commander of the Praetorians as Helius, one of the escort Tigellinus had provided on the night Nero died.

'When is the Emperor expected?'

Helius gave a shrug of irritation. 'No one knows. He should have reached the bridge two hours ago. They're getting restless.' He nodded towards the group of seamen.

'Why are they here?'

'To force the Emperor to confirm them as a legion. They've a long list of demands.'

'Demands?' Valerius didn't hide his disbelief. 'You don't demand anything from an Emperor. You get down on your knees and plead.'

A wry smile touched the other man's lips. 'I know that, but I'm not sure they do.'

Valerius searched the road ahead for the glint of sun on the gleaming armour of the Imperial escort that would signal Galba was close, but he could see nothing. There was still time. He made his decision. 'May I talk to them?'

Helius hesitated before giving his consent. 'At your own risk, but I doubt they'll listen. A lot of them have been drinking since dawn.'

'I'll take the chance. Stay here,' he told Serpentius. 'Just this once I think it would be riskier with you than without.' He unbuckled his sword and handed it to the Spaniard, who gave a snort of disgust. Valerius shook his head. 'I'm going to talk, not fight. I don't see any weapons, so I should be safe enough.'

He rode along the line of Praetorians until he saw a familiar bulky figure towering over the men who surrounded him.

'Juva!' The big Nubian turned at the shout. He was with the group of oarsmen from the tavern and they eyed Valerius with suspicion. The Roman dismounted and handed the reins to one of the guards before forcing his way through the hard-eyed sailors until he reached the crew of the *Waverider*.

Juva's nostrils flared and anger seemed to make him grow even larger. His eyes took in the expensive cloak, and the striped tunic and gold-linked belt beneath it. 'So the simple workman is an eater of larks' tongues and buggerer of little boys? Our friend in the tavern was a rich man in a poor man's clothes. I was right, Roman, you are a spy. We have no piss barrel to drown you in here, but the river is handy. Perhaps we should tie you in a sack and throw you in. I am sure we can find a cock and a dog. We already have the rat.'

Valerius ignored the threat and allowed his gaze to range over the mass of waiting sailors and marines. His instinct told him they would make good soldiers and he felt an affection for their kind he could scarcely explain. They were the type of men he'd served beside and commanded in Britannia, Africa and Armenia: hard, sometimes cruel, and always cynical, who'd cut a throat without blinking an eye, but would share their last crust or sip of wine with the man next to them the night before a battle. 'Why would you want to drown me when I am here to help you?' he said reasonably. 'Look at you. Do you think the Emperor will speak to a rabble? At least try to look like soldiers and have your officers form you into your centuries and show him some of that pride you boasted of.'

'We have no officers.' The speaker was the man whose nose Serpentius had broken. 'The cowards would not come. They do not deserve to lead men like us. We'll elect our own officers when we have our eagle.'

This laughable concept made Valerius blink. 'What

makes you think the Emperor will even speak to you? Why should he do anything for men who volunteered to fight against him?' He turned to Juva. 'You would be doing them a service if you took these men back to the city. Better to wait until the Emperor has been acclaimed and had a chance to address the Senate.'

Juva shook his head. 'Lucca is right. There are better men here than the officers they assigned us. Florus there,' he indicated a grinning, buffalo-shouldered youth in the blue tunic of the marines, 'has killed five men in single combat and is not yet nineteen. Glico,' a stern-faced older man with lank grey hair and dead eyes nodded, 'took command when we burned out a pirates' nest on the Carthaginian coast, after the marine centurion was killed.' Juva's words confirmed Valerius's initial evaluation. These men were born fighters who had survived and prospered in a hard service. Yet they all deferred to the Nubian, who continued: 'We did not volunteer to fight *against* Galba. We volunteered to fight *for* Rome. In any case, it is too late to turn back now. It would look as if we were running away and this legion does not retreat.'

'Then you are a fool and no soldier,' Valerius told him. 'Or you would know that a tactical retreat can sometimes be the making of a victory.' The big man's eyes smouldered, but he seemed to see sense in the advice. Valerius continued: 'If you have no officers, who does lead you?'

'Come with me,' the Nubian said.

'Gaius Valerius Verrens.'

'Is that supposed to mean something to me?' The man sitting on a stool in front of one of the tents wore a blue tunic and the insignia that identified him as a centurion of marines. He waited for an answer, but Valerius was happy to let his obvious status and natural authority answer for him. Eventually, the disease-pocked face creased in a thin smile. 'Tiberius Milo, third century first naval detachment.'

'Juva tells me you lead these men?'

The marine shot the big Nubian a wary glance. 'Someone has to. We've been waiting for months for this, scavenging what rations we could, more vagabonds than soldiers.' He drew himself up and pride swelled his voice, which was that of an educated man and came as a surprise, emerging as it did from a mouth with a single blackened tooth. 'We were promised we would be constituted a legion not just by Nero, the man, but by the Emperor of Rome. All we want is for the new Emperor to honour that promise and give us the rights and privileges any legion can expect. We want a legion's pay and a legion's weapons and when we're not on campaign we want to sleep in a legion's barracks, not on the streets.'

'Then I suggest you start acting like a legion.'

The brutal certainty in Valerius's voice made Milo flinch as if he had been struck a blow. 'Do you speak for the Emperor?'

Valerius stepped closer, keeping his voice low and ignoring the threatening presence of the men who had appointed themselves the marine's bodyguard. 'No, but I speak as a soldier who knows this Emperor.' He repeated the argument he'd already used to sway Juva. 'If he negotiates at all, he will not negotiate with a rabble. Line your men up in their centuries and their cohorts, get rid of the drunks and the camp followers. If you have the opportunity, tell him what you were promised and ask him to consider it. If you issue ultimatums, he will not even look at you. Treat him with courtesy, because he is an old-fashioned man who demands it. If you do, he will treat you in the same way. He may ask for time to consider his decision, but that is his right and you would do well not to question it.'

Milo's eyes drifted from the scarred face to the artificial hand. Eventually, he nodded. 'Very well—' His eyes widened as a distant roar cut him off in mid-sentence. Without another word, he charged into the nearest clumps of men, dragging them into some kind of formation and shouting garbled orders. 'Form up. Get the men into their sections. Come on, you bastards. If you want to be a legion, start looking like one.'

Valerius shook his head at the chaos around him. He found Juva staring at him.

'Will he accept us?'

The answer was no. Servius Sulpicius Galba would look at these men and see them as what they were, an untrained mob, a hindrance in his procession towards the Empire's greatest honour. And that was how he would treat them. If they were fortunate, he would consider their case – at his convenience, not theirs. It could take months. But that wasn't what Juva wanted to hear. 'If the gods are with you.'

The big man nodded. It was enough. As the Nubian ran back to his men, Valerius pushed his way back towards the Praetorian line. He was halfway there when he discovered the gods were laughing at them all.

The first sign of trouble was men in civilian clothing wandering among the newly formed sections whispering to one man and then another. At first he thought they must be encouraging the marines to straighten up or stay in line, but something on their faces bothered him: a combination of slyness and barely suppressed excitement. The feeling was reinforced when he saw a figure he recognized moving among a nearby cohort. It was Clodius, Nymphidius Sabinus's doorman.

'You! What are you doing?'

Clodius turned with a dangerous light in his eyes. 'What the fuck is it to you?' At first there was no recognition of the workman who had visited Nymphidius in the commanding figure wearing a rich man's clothes, but there came a moment when the eyes changed and Clodius's hand slipped to his waist. Valerius felt a thrill of alarm when he realized the other man wore a short sword beneath his cloak. What was going on?

The only way to find out was to ask and he started forward. Clodius saw his approach and drew his blade, but his expression faded from belligerence to confusion when he realized his opponent wasn't going to be checked by the sight of gleaming iron.

A peal of thunder cracked somewhere to the south and for a fleeting moment Valerius was reminded of the night Nero had died. Then a new noise began to shake the air. The sound of raucous cheering.

Galba was coming.

XI

Pride swelled the chest of Servius Sulpicius Galba as the acclamation of the crowd filled his ears. The Emperor-elect struggled to maintain his habitual grim expression. The fleshy lips jutted, his rheumy eyes narrowed like those of a warrior squinting into a blizzard, and his long, hooked nose was set at an angle that allowed him to see a hundred paces ahead, but not the flower petals strewn beneath his horse's hooves. He wore a purple cloak and a general's armour, the breastplate and the helmet with its horsehair crest gleaming with golden ornament. At his side hung a long soldier's sword, because, even at seventy, that was how he saw himself. If he was stern it was because he had learned that sternness kept those he commanded at a proper distance. If he was unyielding it was because he believed being unyielding was the only way to ensure his soldiers' obedience. He was not interested in their liking or their respect. All that mattered was that they obey.

It had been a long ride from Clunia, in the north of what had been his province, an almost impossible journey for a man of his years. For most of the thousand miles he had travelled in a sprung carriage, but he had been in the saddle often enough to impress his escort of auxiliary cavalry, now reinforced by the seven hundred Batavian troopers of the Imperial Guard. The Batavians had ridden from Rome to meet him three days earlier, while he rested at Falerii and accepted the fawning homage of the ambitious senators who had stirred themselves to greet him there. Yes, a long journey. One full of lessons for those who thought to oppose him. Painful, but satisfactory and salutary lessons. He had not been cruel. He was not a cruel man. He had not acted out of fear. No, he had acted decisively, as an Emperor should.

Other lessons were on his mind now. Nymphidius Sabinus had betrayed and attempted to usurp him, and had paid the price. But what of those who had supported and encouraged him? He had their names, from the same senators who thought to grovel their way into high and profitable office. Those senators would be disappointed. Servius Sulpicius Galba did not buy loyalty. Loyalty must be freely given or it was not loyalty at all. That was another lesson to be learned.

As he rode this final stretch of road, with the cheers of his subjects ringing in his ears, he felt an unlikely and unusual lightening of the spirit. Since crossing the border into Italia he had been beset by a persistent and irrational horror that it would all be taken away from him before he could reach Rome. And now Rome was in sight. A blur of smoke on the horizon. He was here. After all the long years and long miles he had at last reached the pinnacle of his career. It was a pinnacle he had not sought, but when it had come within his reach he had stretched out for it with all the vigour of a much younger man. Rome was his. And not just Rome. The Empire. Nero had brought the world's greatest power to the brink of ruin. The Empire's coffers were empty. Somehow they must be refilled, and Servius Sulpicius Galba was the man to fill them. Had he not made a fortune that was the envy of other men, and that after being cheated of his rightful inheritance by Tiberius, of pestilential memory? He would begin by discovering the whereabouts of the money Nero had squandered. And then he would recover it. Naturally, those who had received it would complain, but by the very fact that they had received it they were Nero's men, and guilty by association.

Until now the cheering had been set at a certain pitch, dictated by the preponderance of women and children among the crowd, but now it altered to a deep bass rumble. He had been aware of a shadow ahead and to his left, between the road and the Tiber, and now the shadow resolved itself into ranks of men. His first thought was that someone had disobeyed his order and paraded the Guard. They should not be here; they were needed to ensure the city was safe for his arrival. But where were the gaily coloured standards and the bright flashes from armour polished to a mirror shine? No legion ever paraded in so unsoldierly a fashion. None was so poorly equipped. The men he could see were bareheaded and ragged. At last, he recognized the blue tunics among them and with a grunt of irritation realized they must be the naval militia he had been informed about in Falerii. An annoyance and an irrelevance, to be disbanded and sent back to their rowing benches in his own time. He felt his heart stutter. Were they a threat? No, by Jupiter they were not, because if they thought to threaten their Caesar he would decorate the roads with them from here to Neapolis in a display that would make Crassus proud.

The road narrowed as it reached the bridge and he would have passed them by without a glance, but a small group of men pushed their way past the guards into the space ahead of him. His first instinct was to have his bodyguard sweep them aside, but the sense of anticipation in the hundreds – thousands? – who waited in their ranks to his right somehow pierced the thick carapace of his patrician dignity, and he waved his guards back and drew to a halt.

Milo's legs threatened to give way as he looked up at the magnificent figure on the white horse. He had not wanted to be the seamen's leader, but his natural authority had set him apart and he had been driven on by other men's flattery and zeal. Those men were now standing safe among their shipmates and he wished that Poseidon would whisk him back to them. But Milo had led boarding parties and battled pirates and he had a responsibility and he had a just cause. He produced his smartest salute.

'Hail, mighty Caesar. Tiberius Milo and the first naval detachment salute and greet you.'

He didn't notice Galba's twitch at the name Tiberius. The Emperor continued to look down on him as if he were some strange animal encountered on a mountain path; a rodent with two tails, or a bizarrely patterned snake. Milo took his silence as leave to continue.

'We, the men of the first naval detachment, are here to seek confirmation of the rights and privileges granted to us by your predecessor, Nero Claudius Germanicus Caesar.' Another twitch, almost a flinch, and this time Milo did notice. His speech slowed and became hesitant. The words that had sounded so fine when he had memorized them seemed hollow and weak out here on the road. 'Nero Claudius Germanicus Caesar,' he repeated nervously, 'who called us from our barracks and our galleys at Misenum and bade us take arms and fight – for Rome.'

His comrades sensed his nervousness and shouts of encouragement came from beyond the line of Praetorians protecting the road. 'You tell him, Milo!' 'We want what we were promised!' 'Let us fight!'

For the first time, Galba acknowledged the presence of the men by the road with a long look of aristocratic disdain. When his gaze returned to Milo and the five men accompanying him his expression had changed to one of curiosity. First and foremost, Servius Sulpicius Galba was a lawyer; his zeal for fairness and justice, if it had ever existed, was long gone, but he still had a zeal for the facts that would determine the outcome of any case.

'And what are these rights and privileges you speak of?'

Milo swallowed, but when he spoke his voice was strong and it carried to the men he had brought here. 'The right to march behind an eagle as a properly constituted legion of the Empire. The right to bear arms as legionaries of the Roman state. The right to Roman citizenship at the end of enlistment; that enlistment to be twenty-five years and its start date determined by the date of signing up to the recruit's first ship. The right to the full pay, privileges and conditions of a legionary soldier at current rank held.' Each sentence was greeted by roars of approval that swelled in volume. 'The right to a pension and a grant of land at completion of service.'

Galba seemed unaware of the silence that followed and it stretched out until it became almost unbearable. Slowly, the shouting began again, but as it built in power the Emperor raised his hand for quiet.

'These rights you speak of are indeed the universal rights of a legionary, and it is correct that any man who fights behind an eagle standard is entitled to them . . .'

'Aye.' A huge shout went up and Milo grinned as he tasted the first fruits of victory. But beneath the rim of his gilded helmet Galba's eyes contained a lawyer's sly glint.

'Yet,' he affected puzzlement, 'did I not hear you say "granted"?'

'The Emperor Nero Claudius Germanicus Caesar . . .'

'Nero Claudius Germanicus Caesar is no longer Emperor, but I will forgive you that.'

'. . . paraded us before him and pledged that we would be a legion.'

'But he did not *make* you a legion,' Galba pointed out, his tone that of a father gently lecturing a five-year-old child. 'I see no eagle, no cohort standards, none of the trappings of a legion. Perhaps it was *intended* that they should be granted, and if they had been granted I would confirm them, but it is clear to me that they have not. Am I to be bound by the whims of my predecessor?' He turned his mount so he was facing the men behind the Praetorian line and raised his voice. 'I must have more time to consider your position. The Empire awaits my decision on many matters of great import. Would you place yourselves before the feeding of our people, the restoration of our finances, the enormous backlog of decisions that require so much consideration? Of course not.' The Emperor shook his head at the unlikelihood of such a thing. 'When my predecessor called upon you he was not of sound mind. In his delusion he believed we were an Empire at war, when the truth was that his acts might have caused one. Does the Empire need another legion when my ambition is for peace and stability? Can it afford another legion when it has so many other priorities for its resources? All these things your Emperor will consider in time. You must form up and march back to your barracks at Misenum.' Satisfied he had dealt with the situation, he turned his mount and walked it past the perplexed Milo and his fellow negotiators.

But he had underestimated the determination of the sailors and marines. At first there was a shocked silence, but soon the shouting started again. 'No!' 'Give us our standards!' 'Let us fight for Rome!' 'Give us our eagle!' Galba didn't even look in their direction. He had denied them their wish to be a legion, yet in his mind they were just that, with a legion's discipline that would keep them in place as he passed. But they were not a legion. The marines would have stood, but the oarsmen surged forward past their leaders and through the thin line of Praetorians who were too greatly outnumbered to stop them. They surrounded the first troop of cavalry, calling out and jostling, the shouts soon distilling down to a single chant: 'Give us our eagle!'

Trapped in the crowd, Valerius found himself swept along with them. He looked desperately for Serpentius and the horses, but the Spaniard was nowhere to be seen above the sea of heads. His eye was drawn north, to where the Emperor sat, unable to move in the midst of his escort, his stony face as purple as his cloak. He knew that behind Galba the backed-up units would be wondering what was happening; he could almost feel the hands of the cavalry troopers tightening on their spears and their sword hilts.

Still, the situation could have been resolved. He could see Milo moving among the men, trying to push them back away from the road, and there were others, Juva among them, urgently talking and reasoning. Valerius did the same, trying to herd away men who could never have told you why they had surged on to that road, except that they had followed everyone else. Even so, Valerius knew they were one wrong word away from a riot.

'Betrayed!'

The cry from Clodius froze Valerius's blood and there was a moment's silence before it was taken up by first one voice, then another, until that single word drowned out all others. Clodius brandished his sword above the crowd and it was joined by several others.

'No!' Valerius tried to fight his way towards the blade, but even as he tore at the sailors between, he saw more bright flashes above the crowd and heard shouts of alarm from the nearest Imperial cavalrymen. Panic rippled through the protesting sailors the way a summer breeze touches every bent head of a ripened field of wheat.

Clodius was almost within reach. It was as if Nymphidius had reached out from the grave to put a torch to the tinder-dry foundations of the Empire and Valerius tried to puzzle why. Well, he would know soon enough. He reached out for the doorman's raised arm.

Like the stoop of a swooping eagle, something dark clouded the very corner of his vision. Before his mind could even evaluate it as a threat, his head seemed to explode and his vision starred into a thousand vibrant colours before his world went dark.

XII

Servius Sulpicius Galba's certainty that he had won over the sailors and marines made the change in mood all the more shocking and his mind fought to comprehend what was happening as the mass of men pressed his escort more tightly around him. He felt the first rise of panic in his ancient patrician breast.

'This is an outrage,' he spluttered. 'Clear them away.'

The commander of the escort leaned forward to advise him against such a drastic move. He had dealt with crowds like this before and he judged that the men were motivated more by enthusiasm than by anger. Give them time and they would disperse. But before he could say anything the swords appeared. 'Charge them!' The Emperor would never be certain he gave the command, but in three swift movements the advance escort disengaged from the crowd, re-formed and charged.

There were a hundred and fifty men in two ranks. If they had been the Batavians of the Imperial Guard, whose duties as part of the Emperor's personal guard included crowd control and dealing with bread riots, the casualties might have been limited to a few cracked heads and broken bones. But these men were the wild

110

Spaniards of the Vascones who had escorted Valerius into war-ravaged Gaul and they knew only one way to treat an enemy.

Spears first; men spitted like pigs as they cowered away from the charging horses and the screaming bodies flipped clear of the long iron-tipped lances with a trained lift of a powerful arm. Galba's personal escort hustled the Emperor away to the rear of the column, leaving a gap for the following cavalry wing to form up. The prefect commanding the Batavians might have hesitated, but Galba howled at him to ride the agitators down. He formed his men into four ranks and gave the order. 'Draw swords. Advance.'

This time there was no charge. Instead the cavalry pushed forward in a steady, relentless line, the heavy cavalry *spathae* chopping down on head and shoulder, splitting skulls in two and carving great chasms in flesh and bone. Blood spurted shoulder high, screams split the air and soon every sword dripped red. The cavalry horses were trained for this work and as they shouldered their way into the mass of terrified, unarmed sailors they snapped with yellowing teeth at faces and the hands raised to protect them. A man could take a sword cut and laugh about it five years later. A man whose face has been torn off by a horse must live in darkness for ever. The Batavians soon realized that their opponents were unarmed and the rhythm of the blows slackened, the strength going out of the cuts. But it is the nature of war that if one side weakens the other will take advantage. In the respite, powerful arms hauled one of the leading cavalrymen from his saddle. In seconds he was stripped of his weapons and uniform and his naked body battered by fists and feet until he was broken bone and bruised and bloody meat. His comrades saw, and

111

resumed their carnage with renewed effort. There would be no more mercy. Not far away, the three centuries of the Praetorian Guard securing the bridge were caught in the midst of a thousand men fighting for their very survival. A few guards dropped their weapons and were ignored, but others were overwhelmed by the sheer numbers of men. Somehow their commander managed to form the majority into a defensive circle round which the sailors surged and swirled as the cavalry compressed them from two sides. Those trapped on the road closest to the bridge made to escape the relentless carnage in a panic-stricken mob, but the span was only wide enough to take a single cart and dozens were crushed when one man fell, bringing down those behind.

Valerius felt as if he was drowning amid a sea of legs and his dazed mind told him that if he didn't get up he would never rise again. He forced himself on to his stomach, but his arms seemed to have lost their strength and when a heavy foot crashed into his back he knew he was finished. A wave of bodies flowed over him as the defenceless seamen fell back to escape the swords and spears of the cavalry. From nowhere, heavy, dark-skinned legs appeared to plant themselves on either side of his body like a bulwark against the tide. He felt himself being lifted to his feet.

'To the river. It is our only hope.' Juva had to shout to make himself heard above the tumult. His voice was steady enough, but the wide eyes told their own story and Valerius could see the Nubian was on the verge of panic.

'Wait.' Valerius took a moment to allow his senses to clear. He knew what could happen when an infantry formation broke in front of cavalry and it was clear the sailors must break soon or be massacred to a man. To his front he could see the mounted Spanish spearmen. They had been slowed by the mass of bodies in front of them, but the long lances continued to do their work. To his right a pink haze marked the harvest of the Batavian swords. Milo, the marine who had negotiated with the Emperor, rushed up to join them, his face pale with shock.

Hoarse shouts of command alerted Valerius to the position of the Praetorians, still in their defensive circle on the edge of the road. The trapped sailors had identified them as the next threat, but they had come here to talk, not fight, and there was no concerted attempt to attack the guardsmen. In the midst of the formation, Valerius recognized the stocky figure of Helius. He saw a chance, just the slimmest chance, of avoiding a total massacre, and turned to Milo. 'Can you still control these people?'

Milo looked at the chaos of desperate men around him. 'I can try.'

'Trying isn't good enough,' Valerius snarled. 'You must succeed or you are all dead. We only have minutes, maybe less.'

The marine centurion glared at him. 'I will succeed.'

In short, urgent sentences, Valerius explained what he needed. The marine swallowed and looked frantically from the line of cavalry towards the Praetorians. 'I will do my part, but can you do yours?'

'Juva?'

The big Nubian nodded and used his huge bulk to carve a path through to where the circle of Praetorian shields protected their bearers from the fury of the sailors. Determined eyes glared out from below helmet rims and short swords were held ready to dart out at the nearest threat. Valerius positioned himself in front of Helius and walked forward with his arms raised and the distinctive wooden fist clearly visible. He knew the terror of the shield line and the way the eye and hand worked outwith the brain's control. As he came within *gladius* range his heart beat against his ribs. All it would take was a single jab from the snarling, wild-eyed figure behind the curved *scutum* and his guts would be spilled on the earth.

'I greet you, Helius of Mutina.' He kept his voice calm, but pitched loud enough to be heard above the chaos all around. 'I am Gaius Valerius Verrens, Hero of Rome, honorary tribune of the Guard.' The appointment had been made by Nero and was purely temporary, but as far as Valerius knew it had never been rescinded. What mattered was that Helius believed him. 'This is a terrible mistake, Helius, but it is within our power to avoid an even greater disaster. We must talk, but it cannot be with a sword at my throat. Put aside your shield and allow me through.'

He saw the Praetorian blink, the moment recognition dawned, and the disbelief at what he was being asked to do. Helius's eyes flicked to Valerius's shoulder, where Juva's commanding presence protected his back.

'He will make sure I and I alone enter, Helius. You must trust me.'

Helius shook his head at his own foolishness, but he stepped back and allowed Valerius to pass. The sword point followed him all the way. 'One sign of a trick and I'll personally deliver your head to the Emperor.'

The centre of the Praetorian circle was an oasis of calm at the eye of the tempest. For the first time Valerius was able to lower his voice to less than a shout. 'It is the Emperor who has caused this, Helius, and if we do not do something it will blacken his name throughout history. You heard these men. They are not traitors, or mutineers. They came here to show him their loyalty and this is how they are repaid.'

The Praetorian scanned the uproar around him, his eyes flickering between the immediate threat of the marines surrounding him and the area where the Batavian swords still rose and fell and stained the very air scarlet. 'Why should I do anything? I have a responsibility to my men and we are safe enough here.'

'You are safe enough as long as they don't attack you, but unless you act soon they know the only way they can stay alive is by taking your shields and weapons. I have already told my Nubian friend here that.' Helius's gaze flicked to Juva, who waited outside the circle, and his hand tightened on his sword. Valerius shrugged. 'Yes, you can kill me, but that won't change anything. Do as I say and you can save thousands of lives.'

The certainty in Helius's eyes faded. 'What can I do that will change this?'

Valerius told him his plan.

'You're mad. Either you'll get us all killed or I'll end up in the *carcer*.'

'I will take full responsibility, Helius, but we need to do it now.'

Helius closed his eyes and for a moment Valerius thought he had failed. Then: 'Oh, shit. Disengage!' he roared. 'Form column on me. First century to the front.'

The near-suicidal command was greeted with confusion in the Praetorian ranks before the ingrained discipline of decades brought obedience. Juva's shipmates from the *Waverider* had created enough space for the manoeuvre and in four quick movements the Guard were advancing unhindered through the sailors towards the narrowing gap between the Vascones and the

Batavian cavalry. Valerius marched beside Helius and he thought he could see confusion in the cavalry ranks and a hint that perhaps their attack was being pressed less forcefully. Instinct told him that someone on the Emperor's staff would be trying just as hard as he to stop this turning into a massacre. Still, he couldn't take that chance. Helius roared out his orders. 'Single rank. Form line. Third century oblique left.' The Praetorians spread out in a thin defensive line across the Spanish front, with the third century angled to face the Germans.

Now puzzlement and consternation was clear on the faces of the cavalry. Killing a crowd of mutinous sailors on the Emperor's orders was one thing. A full-scale battle against the Praetorian Guard was another. Milo took advantage of the hesitation to order his men back behind the Praetorian line and the cry went up to retreat to the river. The bloodied sailors and marines faded away, leaving their dead and dying behind, and their tormentors to face the wall of Praetorian shields. A few of the Vascones attempted to force their way through, and the order went up from Helius to act defensively. On the right flank, the Germans stood their ground, apart from a section beyond the end of the line who galloped among the fleeing seamen hitting out with the flat of their swords.

Juva had appeared at Valerius's side, but now he turned to go.

'You saved my life,' Valerius reminded him. 'Stay with me and I will guarantee your safety.'

The big man shook his head. 'My place is with my shipmates.' With a last dejected glance at the carnage around him, he walked away.

Valerius looked towards the river. Hundreds of sailors crowded the bank, but a thousand and more waited uncertainly in the space between. The killing had stopped. The shrill cry of a trumpet sounded amid the ranks of the Imperial column and the Vascones wheeled away to disappear up the Via Flaminia. A group of officers from Galba's staff appeared and began talking animatedly with the prefect commanding the German cavalry wing. Helius stood in front of his men looking bewildered, and as Valerius watched one of the staff men trotted over to the Praetorian's side and began barking questions at him.

The sound of hooves close behind announced the arrival of Serpentius leading Valerius's horse. 'I saw you were in trouble, but I couldn't get to you,' the Spaniard said apologetically. He looked at the dog-legged line of crumpled bodies and the sword-slashed wounded now walking or crawling to join their comrades in the space between the road and the river. He shook his head. 'Idiots.' It wasn't clear whether he meant the victims or their killers. 'What happens now?'

A reinforced cohort of legionaries – perhaps fifteen hundred men – approached. For a moment, Valerius feared they would draw swords and the killing would begin again. Instead they began to use their shields to herd the seamen into a smaller area. The bemused sailors showed no resistance.

'What happens now?' Serpentius repeated.

Valerius touched the side of his head where he'd been hit – he still wasn't sure with what – and his fingers came away sticky with blood. 'If the Emperor has any sense he'll understand that this was nothing but a mistake and send the sailors back to their barracks in Misenum. Bad enough killing so many of his own people without stirring up any more bad feeling.'

But he knew that for Servius Sulpicius Galba it would

not be a question of sense or otherwise. The Emperor had issued a direct order to the seamen to disperse and that order had not been obeyed. Deep in his gut, Valerius sensed there was more trouble on the way.

And it came sooner than he'd expected.

'Gaius Valerius Verrens, I arrest you in the name of the Emperor.'

XIII

Two weeks after Galba's bloody entry into Rome Valerius stood in the atrium of the luxurious villa Marcus Salvius Otho had allocated himself. Only his host's intervention had saved him from facing the same charges as the marine legion. Now he listened in growing disbelief as Otho outlined the punishment Galba had devised for the survivors of the massacre at the Milvian Bridge.

'Decimation.'

For a moment the word shocked Valerius into silence. Surely it wasn't possible? 'But no legion has suffered decimation since the time of Crassus, and none for two hundred years before that. In the name of Mars, even Caligula didn't order decimation when the Rhenus legions threatened to rebel. The head of Gaetulicus was enough for him. The Emperor should know that, since he was the man Caligula sent to take it.'

'Yet there is a certain logic.' Silhouetted against the window with his back to his guest, Marcus Salvius Otho shrugged. 'Our Emperor is an old-fashioned man and he has resolved upon an old-fashioned punishment for an old-fashioned crime. He wished to include you among the ringleaders of the mutiny. It took all my charm and diplomacy to persuade him otherwise.'

Valerius waited to discover the price for this unlikely munificence, but Otho continued to stare from the villa window out towards the marbled bulk of the Palatine. The injustice of it – no, it was more than injustice, it was madness – drove Valerius to impotent rage. Decimation meant that one man in every ten, regardless of service or worth, would be drawn by lot, taken out and slaughtered. 'There was no mutiny. There were misunderstandings, there were mistakes, someone,' the fury in his voice made the other man turn, 'panicked. Those men went to the Milvian Bridge to give Servius Sulpicius Galba their oath of allegiance. To prove their loyalty. Now a hundred of them are dead, two hundred more are wounded and our Emperor wants to slaughter another five hundred. To make a point? It is beyond stupidity. It is insane.'

'I suggest you guard your tongue, Valerius,' Otho said lightly. 'It is fortunate you are among friends.' Valerius shot him the look this vacuity deserved and the other man acknowledged it with a wry smile. Having Otho for a friend would be like having a cobra for a house guest; always interesting, but ultimately fatal. 'In any case, why should you care for a few thousand of Poseidon's playmates who could just as easily be killed in a freak storm the next time they sail? They were foolish to volunteer to fight for a madman like Nero and more foolish still to risk the wrath of a man well known to have a *spatha* for a spine.'

Indeed, why did he care? Juva had saved his life, but it was more than that. 'Because they are men who volunteered to fight for Rome.' He stared at the patterned marble floor, which with its depiction of gods and monsters and frolicking centaurs reminded him of the absurdity of what had happened by the Tiber. 'They may not look much, but they have spirit and they have courage. Haven't they suffered enough, seeing their comrades butchered and maimed? More to the point, Rome has suffered enough. Ever since Seneca's fall the Empire has lived in shadow. It needs a chance to draw breath; peace and stability, not more blood spilled on the streets.'

'Spoken like a politician rather than a soldier. Perhaps it is time you took your place in the Senate?' A dangerous edge to Otho's voice made Valerius look up. No softness in the eyes now. They bored into him like glittering arrowheads. 'Sometimes wise words are enough, but . . . You are still a soldier, Valerius? Well, soldier or politician, let me set you a puzzle. Tomorrow the Emperor will slaughter five hundred of your faithful mariners to prove his strength of will. To execute them, he will use the loyal soldiers of the Praetorian Guard, in order to test that loyalty. In one week's time he will go before the Senate and repudiate the thirty thousand sesterces per man offered to the Guard by Nymphidius Sabinus, whom he will condemn as a traitor acting entirely in his own interests.' He paused to allow the significance of his words to register and in the intense silence Valerius imagined the reaction of hard-eyed soldiers like Helius to being cheated. Eventually, Otho continued. 'Not content with this, he intends to replenish the Empire's coffers by a series of punitive taxes on anyone enriched by Nero, which will impoverish half the men he is addressing in the Curia. As a simple soldier, or a politician, what is your opinion of the combined results of these policies?'

For the second time in a few moments Valerius

fought for the right word to describe the indescribable. 'Anarchy.' Otho nodded for him to continue. 'By killing the sailors who volunteered to protect Rome, he risks losing the support of the people. By disowning Nymphidius's bounty he guarantees losing the support of the Guard who placed him in power. By taxing those who have thrived under Nero – not just his favourites – he places himself in grave danger of losing the Senate. Why?'

Otho turned back to the window, staring hard as if he could somehow reach into the mind of the man who inhabited the palace that filled his view. Galba had taken up residence on the Palatine in preference to the Domus Aurea because Nero's great Golden House was a symbol of everything he despised about his predecessor. 'Because he is Servius Sulpicius Galba. He believes – knows – that his bloodline makes him the noblest Roman alive. That his fortune makes him infallible. That the gods had always intended he should be Emperor. And that an Emperor's duty is to rule, not to be advised or directed. Every one of these decisions is patently wrong, yet he sees them as a symbol of his strength.' Otho's voice turned weary. 'We chose him because he was old and because of his lineage. Now it seems that the very age which made him an ideal candidate befuddles him and the glory of his ancestors blinds him to reality. We were wrong, Valerius.'

A chill like a damp fog settled over Valerius as he understood why Otho had saved him. He shook his head. 'I conspired in the end of one Emperor, Marcus; do not expect me to help bring down another. For the gods' sake, if not mine.' Even as the words were spoken, he realized that somewhere in the house men were hidden waiting for this moment. All it would take was one word. In Rome's eyes he was already condemned. Otho would not even need to justify it. But deep in the labyrinthine maze of Marcus Salvius Otho's mind a contest had been taking place and a slight upturn in the thin lips signalled an unlikely victor.

'Very well,' the former governor of Lusitania said lightly. 'Who am I to deny a man his conscience? But it will only happen once, Valerius. Tomorrow we will witness the gory fruits of Galba's wisdom and as those men die you can tell me how it balances on the scales beside your scruples.' He hesitated and his voice became serious again. 'Very soon this Emperor will have another decision to make, and that decision will affect all our futures. If, as I fear, he chooses wrongly, Gaius Valerius Verrens will also have a choice to make. Be sure it is the right one.'

Valerius didn't hear him leave the room, but when he turned he was alone with his thoughts. And fears. Not fears for the future of Gaius Valerius Verrens. But for Rome.

They had been held in pens like cattle, and like cattle they were led to the slaughter. Five hundred men, drawn by lot from their centuries, stumbling in chains up the Via Tiburtina, followed by the comrades who would watch them die. The men of the naval militia were unarmed and guarded by three cohorts of Praetorians, with a full cavalry wing of archers standing by to fill the air with death at the first sign of trouble. Valerius surveyed the scene of humiliation and despair with a sickness in his stomach and a feeling of terrible dread at what was to come. He rode with Serpentius along the marching ranks of the living and the soon-to-be dead, looking in vain for Juva and the crew of the *Waverider*.

He could see that the seamen had been roughly handled and barely fed in the two weeks since Galba's bloody march into Rome, but they marched with their heads high, showing at least some still had their pride.

'Poor bastards,' Serpentius said, as a throaty growl went up from a thousand throats when they recognized the place of execution.

In Divine Caesar's day, the lost, the friendless, the destitute and the nameless dead – anonymous victims of the assassin's dagger, unwanted girl children or exposed babies – had been thrown into pits on the Esquiline beyond the city wall, to rot where they lay among the rubbish and the filth. But the pits had proved too noisome for Augustus's sensitive nose and they had been covered with earth to four times the height of a man and turned into a park under the direction of the Emperor's favourite, the poet Maecenas. The new disposal ground lay well away from the city, out towards the River Teverone. Here, among the smaller pits stinking of death and corruption, a greater excavation had been dug, enough to hold five hundred corpses and more. No burial rights for the men who had defied Galba, and no memorial, just an unmarked grave among Rome's nameless, faceless pariahs.

A large crowd had already gathered to witness their fate and a fourth cohort of Praetorians was waiting to hustle the prisoners to a cleared area beyond the great pit, where they lined them up in ranks of fifty. The remainder of the sailors and marines were kicked and pushed into three sides of a square that faced the condemned men across the gaping trench. Valerius watched from a nearby grove, his eyes still searching for Juva's bulk and waiting for some reaction. But for several minutes nothing happened. It was as if they were all waiting.

For what, became clear when the rattle of chains and horse brass announced the arrival of a new column, headed by the Emperor himself. Galba rode a white stallion, resplendent in his cloak of Imperial purple and the gilded armour of a Roman general and flanked by his closest aides, Vinius and Laco. Otho lagged to the rear among a cluster of senators Valerius guessed was smaller than Galba would like. Behind them came a separate group of twenty prisoners and these Valerius did recognize. Milo, their reluctant leader, marched at the front, his chest out and disdain for the proceedings written on his peasant's face. Among the men behind him stumbled two of the *Waverider*'s crew, Glico the veteran sailor and Lucca, the big oarsman, but no Juva.

A substantial platform had been raised beyond what was now the left-hand face of the square and Galba and his retinue took their place on it as the last of the chained men were lined up in front of him facing the pit. Valerius held his breath in the unnatural silence. Not even the rustle of leaves disturbed the heartbeat before Galba rose to his feet.

'If he had any sense,' Serpentius grunted, 'he'd spare them and we'd all go home happy, but then he didn't come all this way to do that, did he?'

'No, I don't think he did.'

Galba allowed his bleak gaze to roam over the condemned men and their comrades, eyes bright with an emotion only he could identify. He made them wait what seemed like an eternity and as the tension built Valerius suppressed an urge to cry out.

'Get on with it, you bastard.' The savage plea came from the back of the ranks, but there was no reaction from the man it was aimed at.

Finally, the Emperor's harsh voice rang out across

125

the reeking landscape of death. All here had been condemned by their actions, he told them, but it was an Emperor's prerogative to temper justice with mercy. Therefore he had decided that only one in ten must die and the others would be allowed to return to their ships under guard, while their centurions would be reduced in rank. None of the orator's tricks for Servius Sulpicius Galba on this day. He knew them well enough, the extravagant gestures, the *tricola*, the repetitions, but they were for the Senate and those who could appreciate their subtleties. His only affectation was a raised arm, the finger pointing across the great open death pit almost directly at Valerius, in a pose that aped the armour-clad marble effigy of Augustus Caesar that stood on its pillar in the Forum.

'The heirs of Augustus have brought Rome to the brink of ruin; nay, beyond the brink,' Galba continued. 'To restore her to her past glory we must return to the old ways. Not the ways of the Republic, which was an excuse for corruption and nepotism where weak men could rise because they had the patronage of the strong. The ways of my grandfather's grandfather. When new men understood their place and patricians acted like patricians. That means the old ways of hard work, prudence and respect. And the old ways of justice, which is why we are here. These men,' he waved an arm towards the chained ranks, 'fought and killed the soldiers of the Empire.' Valerius bridled at this mindless exaggeration, only for Galba to immediately surpass it. 'Not only did they defy their Emperor, they threatened his person. There is only one sentence appropriate to such a crime. Death. A harder man might have insisted that the guilty should be crucified beside the Via Flaminia in the manner in which Marcus Linius Crassus of blessed memory dealt with the rebels of Spartacus.' He paused, turning to glance at the men who stood behind him. 'Some among my advisers would urge me to show even greater mercy, by executing those who led, but not those who followed. But what kind of man would that make your Emperor? A man who will sell his principles for popularity. A man who bends with every wind. A man who accepted this position, but does not have the strength to adhere to its principles.' He glared at the massed ranks, challenging any to dispute him. 'That man is not Servius Sulpicius Galba. An example must be made that sends a message to every man, woman and child in the Empire, and in your dying you may console yourselves that you are your Emperor's instrument and his messengers. Men will look upon your passing and say: This is Galba's Rome. A Rome which will not take a backward step. A Rome where strength and justice prevail.'

He was about to order the sentence to be carried out, but a flutter of applause from the senators interrupted him and he turned to acknowledge it. The interval gave Milo the opportunity he had waited for. With a rattle of chains, he turned to face the Emperor.

'You talk of strength and justice? Then have the strength to exchange our lives for the rest. The fact that we twenty have been singled out makes us guilty in your eyes. So be it. But let our comrades, who even after all this would pledge you their loyalty, live.' The tough little marine seemed to grow in stature then, even in his rags and his fetters, and the demand brought a rumble of approval from his comrades. A centurion of the Guard stepped forward with his vine stick raised, but Galba, with an amused half-smile, waved him back, and Milo continued. 'If that is too much for you, then at least temper justice with fairness. We who stand before you were selected without a ballot. That means twenty men are about to die who, under the terms of your sentence, should not.' Valerius's respect for the condemned man grew. Milo had nothing to lose, but he was clever too. He knew he could not save them all, but by pointing out that twenty of the men had been condemned unlawfully, he was telling every witness that if the sentence was carried out it made the man who pronounced it as guilty as the men who now stood before him. In effect, Galba could not order their deaths without becoming a murderer himself.

For a moment, Valerius believed the tactic might succeed. But Otho had claimed the Emperor was as inflexible as a cavalry *spatha*, and now he proved it.

'A pretty speech by what we officers would call a barrack lawyer, but not one that changes my decision.'

Milo had expected no less. At least he had tried. But he had one final truth for his Emperor. His face twisted into a bitter smile and he looked out over the festering pits and the mass grave. 'Then truly men will look upon this and say: *This* is Galba's Rome.'

The Emperor went rigid and his mouth worked, but no words emerged. It was left to Vinius, sitting next to him, to rise and give the order to carry out the sentence. A centurion marched forward and took Milo by the arm, but the marine was not finished. He began to rattle his chains as he was dragged towards the pit and the refrain was immediately taken up by the hundreds of condemned men, a rhythmic clanking that seemed to make the very air shake. At the same time an inhuman drone began to issue from the throats of the four thousand men ranked in legionary formation. Valerius saw Milo smile before he was forced to his knees and the first sword slashed down, the first blood spouted from the severed neck and the first head fell into the pit. Centurions ran among the ranks, lashing out at the sailors and marines, but the bass hum grew in volume with every man who died; a sound that managed to combine contempt for the perpetrators, hatred of the man who ordered it, and pride in their comrades. Now the drone was punctuated by the cries of the men brought forward. Lucca began it in a voice as big as his stature, and the same words were repeated, again and again, only cut off by the fall of a sword.

'I die for Rome.'

'I die for Rome.'

'I die—'

Valerius forced himself to watch every blow, and by the time the last condemned man was brought to the pit edge he could feel tears streaming down his face. The crowd, in that way of the mob, had begun by cheering every blow, but had quickly been won over by the courage and bearing of the victims. Their cries for mercy were ignored. Serpentius looked across the field of death to where his Emperor sat stone-faced, watching the last of the spectacle. 'Bastard,' he spat.

By then, Valerius only had eyes for Marcus Salvius Otho.

XIV

Rhenus Frontier, November, AD *68*

The wine tasted sweet on his lips, but there was a hint of fruit, too. A Nomentan, he guessed, but how could one be sure? Still, much better than the tanner's piss they had served on the galley that brought him down the Rhenus. The journey from Italia had been pleasant enough, though long. He had found the air of the high Alpine passes oddly invigorating, but the food of the locals execrable. Who could live on cheese, no matter how many hundred ways it was presented? Things improved markedly when he joined the Classis Germanica ship at Basilia, where the Rhenus wound its way from the Alps into Germania Superior, and the rising waters had carried him swiftly and in no little comfort. The week-long delay at Moguntiacum, a hundred miles upstream from the palace at Colonia Agrippinensis, had been inevitable but worthwhile. Hordeoinius Flaccus, the legate who had just taken over from Verginius as governor of Germania Superior, had been keen to show off his troops and keener still to hear the latest news from Rome.

Aulus Vitellius selected another roast duck – his third – ripped off a leg and sighed with pleasure as he bit into the firm meat. And now he was here at last, with the tiresome ceremonies confirming his appointment behind him. When he had picked the bird clean a slave appeared with a bowl and he washed his grease-slick fingers before drying them on a fresh cloth. 'Now remind me of our dispositions,' he said to the man in the place of honour on the couch to his right.

Gaius Fabius Valens had barely touched the food, content to watch the unequal epicurean battle unfold as the new governor of Germania Inferior ate his way through enough rations for three or four men. Dark and intense, Valens was as thin as his host was fat, with an air of suppressed anger that made other men wary. It was said that he had personally removed the head of Vitellius's predecessor, and, if he was being honest, the new governor admitted he found Valens a little frightening. When the general spoke, it was sparingly and through clenched teeth, as if he were unwilling to part with the words.

'My own legion, First Germanica, is stationed at Castra Bonnensis, which you passed on the left bank of the river.' Vitellius nodded. He remembered the large fort dominating the river bend five miles upstream. 'Numisius Rufus commands Fourteenth Gallica at Castra Novaesium, the same distance to the south, and Fifteenth Primigenia and Fifth Alaudae, legates Lupercus and Fabullus, hold the swamp country further downstream at Vetera opposite the Frisii, who like our old foes the Chatii and the Cherusci have been suspiciously quiet this year.'

Vitellius called for more wine, using the delay to run the names and positions of his legions and the Germanic tribes they kept honest through his mind. 'You believe I should be concerned?'

Valens shook his head. 'The campaigning season is past and the tribes have withdrawn to their winter encampments. Our only concern would be if the river ice reaches a thickness that would allow them to cross, but it is more than twenty years since it last froze over completely.'

The governor shivered, not with fear, but at the thought of its becoming any colder than it already was. Colonia Agrippinensis was a surprisingly civilized place and not at all what he had expected. Most Roman settlements on the Rhenus frontier were like Castra Bonnensis, large forts built to hold a legion and its associated auxiliaries. Over the years a small town would grow up around the gateway to supply the wider needs of the seven or eight thousand men within: bars, brothels and bakers, tanners and tunic makers. Colonia was different. The city had originally been a settlement for the Ubii, a Germanic tribe forced from the eastern bank of the river by their more powerful neighbours. But nineteen years earlier the unfortunate Ubii had been displaced again, when Claudius had ordered the establishment of a *colonia*, a planned town, settled by retired legionaries. Which was why Colonia Agrippinensis was like a little piece of Italia dropped on to the damp, gloomy flatlands of Germania: a tidy grid of streets enclosed by a defensive wall, with plastered houses, a forum and, most important, the governor's palace, a comfortable two-storey villa built round an open square. But there the similarity ended. The land around Colonia was a veritable swamp, the air damp enough to swim in and, in November, cold enough to shrivel a man's extremities, even when he was wrapped in a voluminous woollen toga. The heated floor made it bearable, but even so the wind whistled through every gap. As the whole world knew, Aulus Vitellius was a man who liked his comforts. A full belly was all very well, but cold feet? Belatedly, he realized Valens was still speaking.

'. . . Julius Civilis.'

Vitellius smiled. 'Ah, and how is our Batavian Pompey?'

'If you chain a wolf, I suppose you should not be surprised if he howls. Better that Nero should have executed him along with his brother. Better still if he had left them to rot in Britannia, and their savages with them. Fine soldiers the Batavians may be, but an auxiliary in his own land is a recipe for trouble. There's bad feeling between the tribesmen and the legionaries who man our signal stations on the island. Bar brawls and the occasional stabbing.'

Vitellius frowned. A decision would have to be taken about Civilis, a prince of the Batavians, but also a Roman citizen. A year earlier he and his brother had been accused of treason. The brother had been executed, but for some reason Nero had spared Julius, and Galba had now sent him home in chains. It was a complication he didn't need. 'I am told to expect a delegation from Noviomagus in the next few days.'

Valens nodded. 'They will ask you to release him as a signal of your trust and to make an auspicious start to your reign as governor.'

'And you would advise what?'

'A year ago . . .' The other man hesitated and a shadow crossed his face that sent an even deeper chill through Vitellius. He had been a politician for more than thirty years and he recognized the signs that confirmed the hints that had been dropped in Moguntiacum.

'Please continue,' he said carefully.

'A year ago I would have flayed his barbarian carcass and fed what was left to my catfish. The Batavians wouldn't have liked it, but they would have accepted it because our strength and our resolve was not in doubt.'

'And now?'

Valens, never a man to advertise his feelings, went as still as one of the statues of Vitellius's predecessors that lined the walls. A leopard ready to make the final leap. 'May I be frank, governor?'

Vitellius kept his face as impassive as his interlocutor's, and the First Germanica's general took it for assent to continue.

'The situation has changed. This morning, you took the salute of the elite first cohorts of the four legions of Germania Inferior, as fine a body of men as ever carried a sword for the Empire. Most of them have soldiered on the Rhenus frontier for their entire service. It is a largely thankless duty; dull garrison work, extreme watchfulness, permanent readiness for war, and the occasional patrol beyond the river that is as likely to be ambushed as not. The opportunities for glory are slim. Likewise the opportunity for profit.' Vitellius noted the change in tone that identified the importance of profit and nodded wisely. 'Six months ago those same men marched into Gaul to put down the revolt of the traitor Gaius Julius Vindex. Many of them shed blood and lost friends, but they won a great victory; the traitor was dead and his army scattered. They were promised glory and plunder, and they believed they had won both. Yet soon they discovered that the traitor was no longer a traitor, but an ally of the new Emperor, Servius Sulpicius Galba. Their victory was for nothing.' There was another subtle change in the voice as Valens continued, a hardening like ice forming on a pond. 'Far from being glorious it brought them only ignominy and scorn. What booty they took had to be returned. Now they hear that the Emperor has lavished rewards on the Aedui, the Arverni and the Sequani, the very tribes they vanquished, while they have nothing to show but their wounds. As I am sure you have been told, the Rhenus legions are seldom happy with their lot, but I must tell you they have never been unhappier than they are now.'

As Valens continued, Vitellius carefully laid the cup he held on the table at his side and crossed his jewelled fingers to prevent the other man from seeing them shaking. The news of his troops' unhappiness didn't come as a surprise. Flaccus had suggested as much of his own legions, who resented the dismissal of their former commander, Verginius Rufus. Personally, Vitellius thought Verginius was fortunate to still have his head. The fact that he had turned his legions down when they tried to proclaim him Emperor only delayed the inevitable. Yet there was opportunity here as well as danger.

'I will, of course, make suitable representations to the Emperor to ensure they receive the rewards they deserve,' he said very deliberately. 'My personal means do not allow me to make the gifts I would like to make, but I will do what I can. Arrange for me to visit each unit in turn, beginning with First Germanica, and make the occasion an awards ceremony. I'm sure some of your men were honoured for their actions at Vesontio, but it is the way of these things that exceptions are made and the deserving are missed. We will ensure that all who are worthy receive the promotions and *phalerae* they deserve.' He smiled, thinking of his old friend Valerius Verrens. 'Perhaps we might include at least one Gold Crown of Valour?'

'An excellent suggestion. I will see that it is done.'

Vitellius nodded his dismissal and Valens rose to his feet. He bowed and was making his way to the door when he appeared to have an afterthought.

'We agreed that I could be candid. You have a lineage as distinguished as any man in Rome. As governor of Germania Inferior, four legions are at your disposal; probably the most powerful unified command in the Empire. Those legions have no taste for our new Emperor and that is unlikely to change. The three legions of Germania Superior are of a similar mind. None of these legions have yet sworn an oath to Servius Sulpicius Galba. They are the keys to Rome for any man with the courage to grasp them.'

With a curt nod the legate marched from the room. Despite the chill air, Vitellius felt the sweat running from his hairline and down his cheeks. Candid, indeed, and no afterthought. Valens had thought through each and every word. He had sought no response, thank the gods. This was just a planting of a seed. What to do? Have one of his legates arrested within a week of arriving in Colonia? It was unthinkable that Valens would not have foreseen the possibility, and the man who had hacked the head from Fonteius Capito would have no hesitation in doing the same to Aulus Vitellius. On the other hand, Valens would not have made the approach unless he had the support, or at least the approval, of the other legates in Germania Inferior, and perhaps those at Moguntiacum.

Was it possible?

Galba was old and weak. Would his soldiers even fight for him? In any case, the legions of the Rhenus frontier outnumbered those in Italia by at least two to one. It *was* possible. But only if a man had the courage to take what was offered. He reached for the polished rosewood box that held Julius Caesar's sword, but it was as if his hands refused to obey his mind. His fingers came within an inch of wood, but they would go no further.

A sign?

He took a step back and drew in a huge breath to calm his racing heart.

To accept was to risk everything. To refuse was unthinkable.

Very well. He would do what Aulus Vitellius did best.

He would do nothing.

XV

Rome

Valerius watched the predictions Otho had made about Galba in the aftermath of the Milvian massacre come true one by one. Not content with repudiating the thirty thousand sesterces a man Nymphidius had promised to the Praetorian Guard if they delivered Rome, the Emperor decided he no longer had need of the German cavalry of the Imperial Guard. The Batavians and Tungrians were paid off and sent home humiliated, where their tales of Galba's perfidy would further inflame the Rhenus legions against him. The Guard accepted the loss of a fortune with a lack of protest that made Valerius uneasy, but Galba decided was a vindication of his unyielding rule. In the Senate, Nero's former favourites had no choice but to accept their impoverishment in the knowledge that the alternative was the loss of their lives and those of their families.

'In his own way he is as mad as Nero.' Otho's lips twisted into a bitter half-smile. 'He will listen to no one but Titus Vinius and Cornelius Laco. He has handed the consulship to Vinius, and Laco is to command the

Praetorians. The two most worthless creatures in the Empire are made the most powerful.'

Valerius had never seen him so disheartened. Since he had arrived in Rome, the former governor of Lusitania had worked tirelessly to extend his influence and rebuild relationships with the senators he had offended during his time as Nero's companion in dissipation and debauchery. Serpentius, who had ways of finding out things he had no right to know, said there were rumours of tens of thousands of sesterces changing hands.

'They say he has pushed himself to the financial limit to reward his new friends,' the Spaniard said. 'And that he has many friends. When he dined with the Emperor last week, they were attended by a double century of Praetorians and it was Otho who gave them a gift of a hundred sesterces each.'

'The Emperor still keeps you close,' Valerius pointed out to Otho. 'He has given Vinius and Laco the power they have because he knows they will do nothing to stand in his way. He will not make a degenerate and a known thief his heir, or a man who cannot make up his mind whether or not to rise in the morning. If not you, who?'

'A hundred others.' Otho's voice betrayed his frustration. 'Power and position for all . . . all except Marcus Salvius Otho. He keeps me close because he does not trust me and so he can lecture me on morals. Apparently, the stories he has heard about my time with Nero *offend* him. He invites me to deny them, but what is the point when his spies can confirm them, along with a dozen others? Was the man never young?'

Valerius smiled. 'You are wrong, Marcus. All of Rome talks of you as the next Emperor. He will name his heir soon and that heir will be you.'

Otho turned to him and Valerius almost flinched when he saw the look in the other man's eyes. 'Let us hope so, Gaius Valerius Verrens. I have been weak and I have been foolish, but I have given this man my loyalty. I will not allow him to betray it. I will not stand by and watch everything we have worked for destroyed.'

Brumalia, the winter festival honouring Cronos and Demeter, came and went with no announcement, as did the procession of the consuls to the Temple of Jupiter Maximus at the turn of the year, when Galba led his fellow consul Titus Vinius to the Capitoline and received the adulation of his people. On this day, by custom, every legion in the Empire would renew its oath to the man who ruled it. Otho passed the time in a fever of anticipation, awaiting the summons from the Palatine.

But when a summons came eight days later, it was for Valerius.

The Imperial messenger who arrived at the house he had rented on the Esquiline Hill gave no indication of why Galba had sent for him, so Valerius made his preparations with care. Previous experience of visits to an Emperor made him well aware of the deadly risks involved. He found a stylus and scratched out a letter for Olivia and a second to his old acquaintance Gaius Plinius Secundus instructing him to transfer sole control of the estate at Fidenae to his sister, and left them with Serpentius.

'You know what to do with them,' he told the Spaniard. 'And I meant to give you this when we were in Carthago Nova, but there never seemed a right time.' He threw Serpentius a leather bag that clinked when it landed in his hands. 'If anything happens to me, go back to your people in Asturia. Go with my thanks and become a bandit or a king. Whether as slave or friend, you have never failed me. You have saved my life more times than I care to remember, but you have your own to live.'

The Spaniard weighed the bag in his hand, before tossing it back. 'If he was going to kill you he would have done it before now.' His dark eyes glittered in the lamplight. 'I threw the bones last night. There is a storm coming, a storm that will threaten everything we know, but I did not see your death.' Valerius waited for more, but Serpentius turned his back and resumed sharpening his long sword.

Valerius had fought in more skirmishes and battles than he could remember, but he could feel the fear toads squirming in his stomach when the guard escorted him into the Imperial palace. He had been here often enough to understand how uncertain such a moment could be.

The Emperor had set up court in the enormous receiving room where Valerius had surprised Nero six months earlier. Titus Vinius – accusing eyes staring from puffy, tight-lipped features – and Cornelius Laco, the indolent patrician who had taken Offonius Tigellinus's place as Praetorian prefect, huddled together at the bottom of the stair leading to the golden throne. Another man, his features so bland he could be lost in any crowd, stood to one side. Valerius realized he must be Icelus, Galba's influential freedman, and the third member of the triumvirate who controlled access to the Emperor.

The heady odour of incense or some strongly perfumed oil made his head spin as he stood between two Praetorians of the palace guard until the whispered conversation ended. Eventually, the Emperor waved him forward to the foot of the steps. This was the first time Valerius had seen him properly since the day of the naval legion's decimation and he realized that the strains of office had already laid a permanent mark on the old man. Galba had always been spare, but now the bones on his face stood out like knives from flesh the texture of parchment, and the nose was less majestic eagle's beak than meat hook. But the harsh, imperious voice remained unchanged, and when he spoke Galba sounded as if he were a judge passing sentence.

'Gaius Valerius Verrens, your actions during the treasonous insurrection on the Via Flaminia perplexed and pained me. Only your previous sacrifices in the service of the Empire swayed your Emperor towards leniency.' Valerius kept his face emotionless, but he could feel the eyes of the other three men boring into him as the tone changed almost imperceptibly. 'You are familiar with our governor of Germania Inferior, Aulus Vitellius?'

Now he understood how a mongoose felt when confronted by the cobra. But he was angry too. Galba already knew the answer to his question, so what was the point of all this play-acting? 'I was fortunate to be military aide to the honourable Vitellius when he had his province of Africa during the consulship of Licinius Silianus and Vestinus Atticus,' he said stiffly.

'So, familiar rather than merely acquainted?' Vinius this time, a patrician questioning an inferior.

'I would count Aulus Vitellius as a friend.'

Laco picked at his manicured nails and Icelus drew a wax tablet and a stylus from his sleeve. Vinius exchanged glances with Galba before speaking again. 'You have pledged your oath to Servius Galba Caesar Augustus?'

Valerius looked up at Galba in confusion. 'I gave the Emperor my oath in Carthago Nova.'

'He requires you to give it again.'

'Is my loyalty in question, Caesar?'

Galba waved a weary hand. A pained expression crossed his lined face – and something else. Valerius was astonished to realize that the Emperor of Rome was a frightened man.

'We require certainty,' Vinius insisted.

Valerius restrained the urge to snarl in defence of his impugned honour. Once? Twice? What difference did it make? He straightened to his full height and said the words in the powerful voice he had once used on the parade ground. 'In fulfilment of my vow, I gladly pledge my loyalty to Servius Galba Caesar Augustus, Emperor of Rome.'

Galba slumped forward and his voice was barely audible. 'Gaius Valerius Verrens, your service for the Empire is well documented. Now your Emperor requires your service once more. This information must go no further than this room – on pain of death. On the kalends of Januarius the legions of Germania Superior refused to take the oath of loyalty to their Emperor. They have mutinied.' Valerius closed his eyes. Mutiny. But in Germania Superior, not in Vitellius's province. 'There has been no insurrection yet and there must not be. You will carry dispatches to Aulus Vitellius at Colonia Agrippinensis, with the Emperor's greetings, and certain other instructions the wording of which has yet to be decided. You will also carry an oral message from his Emperor, who requires his faithful servant to crush this mutiny with all speed and any means necessary. That is why it is vital the message is carried by someone he knows and trusts. You will be followed in time by a delegation from the Senate, but it is crucial that in the meantime Vitellius ensures the legions of Germania

Superior stay in their barracks and make no threatening moves towards Rome or Gaul.' Anger turned the pale features a bright pink. 'This has been coming since they tried to put Verginius in this chair, but they have no leader now. Flaccus is a weakling to have allowed it to come to this, but if Vitellius holds his nerve they will realize they have no alternative but to submit to their Emperor's will.'

This time the spinning in Valerius's head had nothing to do with the perfumed smoke. Why him? There were other men in Rome who knew Vitellius better, men of higher rank whose word would carry more force. But he knew why. Galba would certainly have been informed about his part in Nero's downfall. Furthermore, the details of Valerius's mission to track down the man Petrus would be in the Imperial vaults, and his escape from Alexandria a step ahead of Nero's assassins had marked him as a man of resource. He had no choice; that had always been clear. And what about the practicalities? Colonia was almost a month's travel from Rome by the most direct route, which was over the western Alps to the head of the Rhenus. He would have to travel through country controlled by the mutinous legions. There would undoubtedly be checkpoints and patrols. The one thing in his favour was that the weather had been unusually mild. Traders had been turning up in Rome for weeks marvelling at their ability to get through the mountain passes at this time of year.

He made his decision. 'I cannot travel officially. I will take one good man and letters confirming me as a merchant with authority to travel through Italia and Germania. We will also need a warrant to use Imperial remounts, and papers allowing us to pass through Helvetia.' This last to Laco, who sighed as if being asked to perform some enormous labour. Valerius turned back to the Emperor. 'I should begin immediately, Caesar. Even managing thirty miles a day, it will take us more than three weeks if all goes well.'

The Emperor frowned. 'The wording of my dispatch to Aulus Vitellius requires delicate drafting. It cannot be hurried. Three weeks, you say? Then a day or two is of no matter when balanced against the importance of the message. Report to Prefect Laco tomorrow morning and we will see what we can do.'

Valerius bowed and backed away towards the door. As he left the room he was surprised to find Vinius at his shoulder.

'You are right to urge speed, Verrens, but he will not be moved on this. I will be surprised if it is complete even in two days. He has other priorities.' He glanced at the younger man's wooden fist. 'I was with the Eighth when we invaded Britannia. Late to the games and little more than an escort to Divine Claudius, true, but I know how tough the Celts can be. You are your Emperor's hope, young man, but I know he can count on you.'

He turned away, leaving Valerius with the odd feeling that he might have misjudged Galba's new consul. But Vinius's warning counted for nothing. It would take five full days for Galba to draft his message to the governor of Germania Inferior, and by then it was already too late.

XVI

The nature of the other priority taking up Galba's time became clear the next day, with disastrous consequences for the new Emperor and for Rome. Titus Vinius – who to Valerius's astonishment turned out to be one of Otho's new friends, thanks to the young senator's timely offer to marry his daughter – sent word. The scribes were to write later that the omens were bad, that thunder crashed and rolled and lightning split the sky, but the day Valerius remembered was one of those still winter miracles, with pale blue skies and barely a hint of breeze to stir the standards of the Praetorian Guard as Servius Galba Caesar Augustus announced his choice of heir.

He and Serpentius joined Otho as he rushed to the Castra Praetoria just in time to be present when the man in whom he had placed his trust, his loyalty and his life shattered his dreams and destroyed him politically and financially. By rights, the Senate should have been told first, before an announcement to the people from the rostra in the Forum, but Galba hoped the honour he paid the Praetorians might make up for the thirty thousand sesterces a man he had robbed them of. As

Serpentius said later, it was a 'true measure of the idiot's judgement'.

They watched from close to the gateway as the Emperor took his place on a reviewing platform on the Praetorian parade ground, part shadowed by the great red-brick barracks that lined the walls. Five thousand men of the Guard stood silent and motionless in their ranks. At Galba's side waited a dark-haired, unsmiling young man of medium height with the soft, careless features and empty eyes of those born to rule. He was of an age with Valerius and his face stirred a memory. A memory of a family graced with power and riches for generation after generation, but one in which the aptitude for survival appeared to have become extinct. A father and a brother executed by Claudius. Another brother murdered by Nero, and this one until recently exiled for his part in his family's intrigues. Valerius shook his head. Why him? And why now? The Praetorians listened in mute puzzlement as the Emperor began the speech that would become the suicide note for his rule. Of all the men at the Castra Praetoria that day, Servius Galba Caesar Augustus and the young man at his side were among the few unaware of that fact.

Galba began with a long preamble extolling the virtues of the Praetorians before he came to the point. 'A man reaching the twilight of his lifetime needs an heir, and never more so than when that man is Emperor. Rome requires firm leadership. History tells us that to ensure such leadership requires a man of special character and impeccable ancestry. A man young enough to provide a prolonged period of stability, yet old enough to make the kind of mature decisions that face any great ruler.' Valerius glanced at the man beside him, thinking that Otho might have been listening to a eulogy about himself. The handsome face remained emotionless, but his eyes glinted like sword points as he stared at the two figures on the distant platform. Galba's voice grew in strength as he continued. 'I present to you Lucius Calpurnius Piso Licinianus as a young man of great stature. A young man who was born to rule. The blood of the triumvirs runs in his veins. The blood of Pompey the Great and Marcus Linius Crassus, the men who saved Rome from the scourge of Spartacus. Perhaps not the blood of Caesar, but with the strength of a Caesar, and the wisdom of a Caesar.' He paused and won a few cheers from the tribunes and the centurions in the front rank, but from the mass of troops behind there was only sullen silence.

'One last chance, old man. Now is the time to offer them their money.' Valerius wondered if he had imagined the hissed words that emerged from Otho's lips.

But there was no offer of reward from Galba, just a long list of the Piso family's accomplishments, their consulships, the temples they had endowed and the great games they had sponsored. Throughout it all, the expression on Piso's face never altered from self-satisfied complacency. He had held no public office, not even a lowly quaestorship, yet now he was being offered control of the greatest Empire the world had ever known, and he accepted it as his by right.

'Patrician, politician, soldier and citizen,' Galba continued. 'We all want the same for Rome. Strength and stability, prosperity and peace . . .'

'What about glory?' The voice came from somewhere at the back of the Praetorian ranks and was quickly followed by a second. 'Aye, and what about loot?'

'There will be glory enough for all in the new Rome,' the Emperor promised, ignoring the second shout. 'But first we must draw breath and take time to recover from the last ten years of the tyrant's rule. It has left us bleeding and bankrupt. Great men have lost their lives and their families, while others have lost the will to rule. And a new Rome needs a new morality. All of you know the tales of debauchery, excess and the worst kinds of corruption sponsored by *that man*, perhaps some of you were even forced to witness it.' Otho went very still, but otherwise gave no reaction to what was the nearest he would get to an explanation for why he had been overlooked. 'Marriage and family will be the watchwords of the new Rome. Thrift and enterprise will see the Empire's finances restored . . .'

'I have heard enough. Poor soldiers, he will bore them all to death.' Otho stalked out of the gate towards the Porta Viminalis. Valerius followed, puzzled by the patrician's response to his personal disaster. Where he had expected fury there was only a cold resolve that was much more frightening.

'So all Rome speaks of me as the new Emperor, Valerius? Well, we will see.' They took the left fork on to the Vicus Patricius past the twin temples dedicated to Mephitis and Isis. 'Vinius tells me you have renewed your oath.' Valerius's steps faltered at the unexpected and unsettling statement. A comment that hid a question he was reluctant to answer. Surprisingly, Otho didn't press him, but carried on through the crowds, looking neither right nor left. Valerius hurried to catch up. 'He also said that Galba has given you an important mission. For once, he has made the right choice. An honest man, who is sometimes too honest for his own good. A proven soldier he can trust to carry out his orders whatever the obstacles or the cost. A man whose loyalty to his Emperor is not in question. Something of a unique combination, I would suggest, in these days when the loyalties of so many are being tested. Yes, our Emperor has chosen well.' He stopped in the centre of the street and turned to face his companion. People looked on in surprise to see the well-known figure without the lictors that were his due, but Otho ignored them. His eyes were bleak and his voice turned cold as stone. 'I pray that you leave on your mission for the Emperor soon, Valerius. Loyalty is a fine thing, but loyalty to the wrong man can be dangerous, and, in the wrong circumstances, a combination of loyalty and honesty can be fatal. The climate in Rome can be unhealthy at this time of year.'

He turned to leave, but Valerius caught his arm. 'What have you done, Marcus?'

Otho shook his head and pushed the hand roughly away. 'It is not a question of what Marcus Salvius Otho has *done*. It is what the Emperor has done and cannot be undone.'

Why was he here, when the last parting had been so final?

He asked himself the question as he trudged up the slope of the Aventine to the house Domitia had rented. She had made it plain there was no place for him in her life. Yet here he was. He knew he might not return from Galba's mission and this could be his last chance to see her face. He wanted her to know he was leaving the city, but not leaving her. He also wanted to warn her.

Otho's words still haunted him. He couldn't bring himself to believe anything would come of them, but the implication was clear enough. If one Emperor could be overthrown, why not another? But to take the purple Otho would need strength and support, and from what Valerius, who was as close to him as any man, knew of him, he didn't have enough of either. If he did anything rash the most likely outcome was that he would go the way of all the others who had stood in Galba's path. Old he might be, but the Emperor had shown he wasn't frightened to swing the executioner's axe. No, if he tried, Otho would fail, and where did that leave Valerius and his oath of loyalty? Should he warn the Emperor? Yet what did he have, other than a vague threat? And what he knew, Vinius would certainly also know.

Here it was. But the house looked different. Even in winter the shutters should not have been closed this early in the day. No one answered the door, and when he stepped back to study the upper storeys he was certain he saw a twitch of movement between the wooden slats, as if someone had just drawn away in a hurry.

'What do you think you're doing?'

It was less a question than an accusation. He turned to find a young man glaring at him. The youth was as tall as he was, but slim and pale; about seventeen years old, with sandy, tight-curled hair and acne-dotted skin. His clothes were expensive in cut and quality and matched what appeared to be a high opinion of himself, judging by the dismissive expression he wore. He stood with his fists bunched in a pose he obviously believed was designed to frighten. Valerius had faced blood-crazed Celtic champions who wanted to tear out his throat with their teeth, and the thought that he should be scared of this babe in arms made him laugh aloud.

'I'm minding my own business, boy,' he said. 'Perhaps you'd like to do the same.'

The insult only made the young man angrier. His pallid features turned a belligerent brick red as Valerius turned his back and continued to study the house. 'This is private property.'

'It is property which belongs to a friend, and—' The only hint of danger was the sound of rushing feet, but Valerius was already turning to meet the threat and he used his right arm to block the cudgel scything at his head. He grunted as the blow landed, but the thick cowhide socket which attached the walnut fist to his forearm took most of an impact that would have smashed another man's bones. At the same time he brought his right foot round in a sweeping arc that knocked his assailant's legs out from under him. Not the boy, but some hired thug who'd appeared from the gods knew where and whose head now smashed sickeningly off the cobbles. A second attacker, short, running to fat and much too slow, had been at his partner's shoulder, but Valerius's violent reaction made him hesitate for a fraction too long. While he was still trying to work out what to do with the curved knife he carried, Valerius brought the walnut fist up in a backhand smash into the angle of his jaw. Teeth flew like hailstones as the man's head snapped back and he collapsed groaning beside his friend. By now the first attacker was trying to push himself up with his elbows. Valerius crouched beside him and took the greasy hair in his left hand. A short-arm jab with the right connected with the thug's temple and the man's eyes rolled back in his head.

Valerius kicked the knife and the cudgel away and turned to where the young man stood, frozen to the spot, dark eyes wide and mouth gaping. He put the walnut fist under the boy's chin and closed his mouth with a click of teeth. 'You should choose your hired help more carefully,' he advised. 'Too slow and too stupid, and they both stink so much that I smelled them before I heard them coming. Why did you order them to attack me? I told you I was only minding my own business.'

'I am guarding—'

'He and these bully boys have been hanging around for days, ever since the mistress left, your worship.' The expression of righteous outrage came from Domitia's doorkeeper, the man who had ushered him in on his previous visit. 'I told them we didn't want them here, but he insisted they wouldn't leave until he knew where she'd gone.'

'What business is it of yours where the lady of this house is?' Valerius turned on the young man.

The youth bristled. 'That is my affair.'

Valerius glanced casually at the two men groaning on the cobbles. 'What if I choose to make it mine?'

'You will pay for this.' The young man spat his defiance. 'My uncle will have you thrown in the *carcer*. These are two of his personal bodyguards.'

'And who is your uncle?' Valerius asked, somehow knowing he wasn't going to like the answer.

'Titus Flavius Sabinus, Prefect of Rome.'

Merda.

XVII

To my friend G. Valerius Verrens, greetings from your brother in arms. How I miss our desert banquets of sand and dung flies, savoured to the musical accompaniment of the Nubian auxiliaries whose howls so entertained us that I fell to dining with cloth stuffed in my ears. This innovation had the added attraction, of course, of rendering your rustic chatter interesting and your Spanish friend's witticisms quite comic. I trust he is well and this letter finds you still basking in the glow of our new Emperor's gratitude, and that the fruits of victory taste sweet upon the tongue, for it seems clear to us here that your mission on behalf of my father was an unqualified success. General Vespasian sends his regards and good wishes. For my part, I have spent the past three months with a stylus in my hand instead of a sword, and my backside, more used to a saddle, has grown soft as an Egyptian dancer's. The reason for this enforced lack of hostilities is my father's insistence that the armies of the East must remain on the defensive until the intentions of our commander are made clear. The invasion of Judaea was a complete success and we made great progress in the months after you left Alexandria. The Jews are worthy opponents and fanatical defenders of their ground, but, as you know, our legionaries are a match for any enemy. We took Tiberias and Tarichaea in the late summer before marching on Gamala, one of their hilltop strongholds. I had the honour of leading the assault and you will be pleased to know, my Hero of Rome, that your friend has equalled you in the matter of honour. I accepted the Crown of Valour from my father's hands, though I modestly ascribe my success to the men of the Third Gallica who did most of the actual fighting.

Valerius smiled at his friend's understatement as he read the letter in the house on the Esquiline. Since the day they'd met, Titus Flavius Vespasian had never tried to hide his envy of the Corona Aurea – the Gold Crown of Valour – Valerius had won defending the Temple of Claudius against Boudicca and her rebels. To win the Corona Aurea, a man had to be first over the walls in the assault on an enemy city or carry out some other act of almost suicidal courage. Vespasian would never have given the award lightly, and Valerius knew Titus must have performed an astonishing feat in front of the whole army for the general to present his own son with one of Rome's highest military honours. Titus continued his report:

We made further progress after the turn of the year, but, with so much uncertainty in Rome, my father took the decision in June to pause. Everything remains in place for the final suppression of the

*revolt, but, thus far, there has been a singular lack
of direction. I am sure the Emperor has his reasons
for this, but it has been difficult to sit back in the
knowledge that the war could have been won by
now. Even as I write, the Jews will be reinforcing
their fortresses and strengthening their defences,
but the reason I do so at this time is that I will soon
be visiting you in Rome. I leave in one week and
my father has entrusted me with dispatches and a
letter commending me to the Emperor, for reasons
of which I know you are aware . . .*

How could he not have seen it? Titus's letter had
arrived the day he had been summoned before the
Emperor and, in the chaos since, he had missed the
significance of the short passage he had just read. *A
letter commending me to the Emperor.* A letter with the
same message Valerius had carried orally to Galba in
Carthago Nova. Take away the diplomatic language and
the meaning was clear: here is my son. Announce him
as your heir and you will have my support in everything
you do. But Galba had made Piso his heir. Where would
Titus be now? And how long would it take for the news
to reach him? He wouldn't continue his journey only to
be humiliated, Valerius was certain of that. He would
turn about and go back to his father. Which raised yet
another question: what would his father do? Vespasian
controlled the best part of six legions in the East. He
was a man of enormous principle, but also a man of
enormous pride. Galba's refusal to consider Titus was
as good as a slap in the face.

But that wasn't what had made him reread the letter.
He scanned the pages until he found the passage he was
searching for.

I hope very much to see you when I reach Rome,
but there are many others I must visit. Among them
a young gentleman who accompanied a friend of
yours, and of mine, on the day she took ship back
to Italia. I shall not name the lady, for reasons
we both understand. From the tone of his letters
it seems he was quite taken with his shipmate,
and she with him. He has been sent to my uncle,
Sabinus, in the hope he will learn the craft of
diplomacy and the intricacies of politics, but he is
young and easily bored, and I fear he will be more
often found at the games. You may see him there.
He is my brother, Titus Flavius Domitianus.

Titus Flavius Domitianus.

The young man he had threatened and whose bodyguards he had left bleeding was Titus's brother. Vespasian's son was Domitia Longina's protector?

But no longer. His breath caught in his throat as he turned his attention for the third time to the letter from Domitia the doorman had passed to him. It was in a code her father had perfected and they had agreed to use in the dangerous weeks that followed Corbulo's death. In it, she explained how what had begun as a flirtatious game to pass the time on the ship bringing her back from Alexandria had become something much more serious in the mind of Domitianus. When he had begun to appear at the house at all hours of the day and night, she had decided the only way to cool his ardour was to put some distance between them. There was more. She apologized for the abrupt nature of their last parting and he read into her words something that created a liquid feeling inside him and made his heart soar, despite the voice in his head that cried caution. Hidden in the dry groups of anonymous letters was a hint of genuine affection, and perhaps more than affection.

She had left a few days earlier for the country house of an aunt outside the northern city of Dertona. According to the doorman she planned to spend three months there, before returning to Rome in the spring.

It was an odd choice of destination in winter, but Dertona was known for its benign climate. He consoled himself that at least she would be safe from Domitianus there.

And if Otho's doom-laden prediction came true, the further away from Rome, the better.

The following day Valerius took Serpentius to check whether Laco had the Emperor's letter. He still hadn't told the Spaniard the detail of their mission, only that they were going on a journey and he should arrange food, horses and warm clothing. But the former gladiator's nose for trouble was already twitching.

'There's a rumour in the market that they've got some kind of problem up north. That wouldn't have anything to do with our trip, would it?'

'Would it make a difference if it did?'

Serpentius grinned. 'I suppose not. Even with Fabiana's company, life has been a little dull lately. It's time we were out of the stink of the city and back on the road.'

Valerius returned his companion's grin. Fabiana was the pretty slave girl who looked after the house and he'd never even suspected. It seemed the Spaniard had added discretion to his already wide range of talents. How many years had it been? Seven? Eight? He tried to remember the day Serpentius had tried to kill him on the packed sand of the gladiator training ground, but, except for a snarling face filled with murderous intent, it was a blur of sweat and pain. The lines on the face still looked as if they had been hacked out with a knife, though they were deeper now. Grey stubble on the cheeks, but still the same fire in the dark eyes. Still the same old Serpentius; thin as a stockman's whip and just as tough, quicker than the striking snake he was named for and twice as dangerous. Old? He realized he had no idea what age the Spaniard might be. He had saved Serpentius from certain death in the arena by recruiting him for a mission that, ironically, had almost killed them both. In turn, the former gladiator had pledged to serve him and a bond existed between them as strong as any blood oath.

'What else have you heard?'

'It sounds as if our friend Otho is finished.'

Valerius was startled enough to stop in the middle of the street. 'What makes you say that?'

The Spaniard shrugged. 'Seems he'd been telling everyone who'll listen that the Emperor would make him his heir and used the fact to borrow money. Lots of money. Now that Galba has named Piso they're all calling in their loans. You've seen what he's like. Never leaving his room. That panicky look in his eyes? And what about all the coming and going? They're not all debt collectors.'

'He still has friends.'

'Not friends with that kind of money.' Serpentius laughed. 'No, he's either planning to run or . . .'

'Or?'

Serpentius turned to meet his gaze. 'Either you run or you fight.'

'Then let's hope he runs. You're right, it is time we were out of the stink of the city.'

When they reached the Palatine, Valerius was surprised

to be escorted once more to the receiving room, where he found Galba and his three advisers huddled in discussion. As he waited for his presence to be acknowledged the voices became increasingly heated. He heard the name Onomastus and it froze him to the core. Onomastus was Otho's freedman and the kind of slimy, double-dealing Greek who gave his compatriots a bad name.

'You must act, before his influence is any more powerful.' The speaker was Cornelius Laco and he was more agitated than Valerius had ever seen him.

'I disagree,' Vinius interrupted. 'We do not have enough evidence. Give them more rope and they will strangle themselves with it.'

'Evidence?' the Praetorian commander demanded. 'He is the Emperor, he does not need evidence, all he needs is suspicion. Just give the word and I will clear out that rat's nest in—'

'No.' Galba's grating voice stopped him in mid-sentence. 'Titus is right. Justice and strength. We will wait, gather evidence, and when the time is right we will strike.'

Laco turned away with a sigh that might have contained the sentiment 'old fool', but Valerius didn't have time to dwell on the implications of what he'd heard, because finally Galba noticed him.

The Emperor called him forward, but before he could speak Laco burst out: 'Why don't you ask him? He's probably one of the bastards.' In the frozen silence that followed, Valerius waited for the question that would either make him a liar or condemn Otho to the axe.

Eventually, the Emperor shook his head, and when he spoke his voice was almost kindly. 'This young man has enough burdens without adding another. I am afraid your mission must be delayed again, Verrens.

There are suggestions of new developments on the Germania frontier. It has become more complex than I first envisaged. I must think on it for a while longer. See Laco after the sacrifice tomorrow and we will discuss it.'

As Valerius turned his back the bickering resumed. Again, he heard the name Onomastus. What did they know that Gaius Valerius Verrens did not? And what kind of deadly game was Marcus Salvius Otho playing?

XVIII

Of all the glories of Rome, Valerius had long ago decided the Temple of Apollo was the most perfect. When Augustus dreamed of having a shrine on the Palatine to rival the Temple of Jupiter on the Capitoline he insisted on a construction on a similar scale. The result was a multi-columned masterpiece of creamy Etrurian marble flanked by an avenue of pillars and surrounded by a hundred statues depicting the fifty daughters of Danaus and their unfortunate husbands. In front of the temple stood an enormous statue of the god, the only one in Rome which rivalled the great colossus in Nero's Golden House. On the roof a pair of gilded chariots of the sun were drawn by eight golden steeds. A magnificent arch, dedicated by the temple's founder to his father, formed the gateway, and martial scenes carved from ivory and plated with precious metals decorated the double doors.

Through this gate Servius Galba Caesar Augustus made his way eighteen days before the kalends of Februarius to preside over the traditional sacrifice and hear the auguries for the coming year. He took his place at the top of the steps overlooking the altar, where he was welcomed by Umbricius Scaurus, the high priest and haruspex. On his right stood Piso, his recently appointed heir, who Valerius had discovered was a pleasant, if not particularly bright young man with little interest in life beyond increasing his fortune and restoring his family's reputation. To the left Galba's fellow consul, Titus Vinius, and Cornelius Laco, prefect of the Praetorian Guard, looked uncomfortable alongside the Emperor's most devoted and loyal servant Marcus Salvius Otho. Valerius, by special invitation of the Emperor, was part of the entourage waiting among the columns for the sacrifice to begin. Otho had greeted him with a dry smile and now he chatted amiably with Laco, who patently struggled to match his pleasantries.

The blast of horns announced the arrival of the sacrifice, a fine white bull led into the shrine by the *victimarius*, a bare-chested young man who had probably brought up the animal from birth. This familiarity hopefully ensured the bull would stay calm throughout the ritual, for any sign of nervousness from man or beast would be taken by Umbricius as a poor omen. In honour of the day, the animal's coat had been brushed to an ivory sheen, its horns gilded and its back draped with embroidered cloth of gold and scarlet. Galba's eyes never left the bull. Valerius noticed that Otho's gaze never left the Emperor. As it was coaxed towards the altar, the sacrifice let out an enormous sputtering fart that made Umbricius frown and the handler's eyes widen. The young man recovered enough to speak quietly in the bull's ear and by some hidden pressure on the neck persuaded it to kneel. Aided by the haruspex, Galba made his way down the steps to sprinkle the ritual dust on the animal's head and back. As he completed his task a second muscular youth appeared, armed with a large axe which he swiftly brought down on the bull's forehead. The blow landed with the sound of a thunder clap. For a heartbeat the animal appeared more surprised than stunned, then its eyes rolled back in its head and it collapsed on its side. Before it could recover a knife was drawn quickly across its throat. The Emperor stepped back, careful not to allow his toga to be stained as blood spurted from the pink-lipped wound to be collected in a bronze bowl by the *victimarius*. Then the sacrifice's body was opened from breastbone to tail and Umbricius stooped low as the steaming entrails flooded out on to the tiles. He flicked at the yards of blue-veined intestine with the *lituus*, his curved wand of office, until he found the gall bladder and the heart. As the seconds passed, Valerius realized he was holding his breath. The priest began muttering to himself. Galba stepped closer to hear what Umbricius was saying, and the blood drained from his face.

'The omens are bad.' The high priest's voice echoed round the temple precinct, drawing a shudder from all who heard him – all except one. 'The gall bladder is black and the heart is swollen. The sacrifice is declared null.' He drew breath and every man there expected him to order forward the next bull. Instead, his eyes fixed on Marcus Salvius Otho. 'There is an enemy at the heart of the Empire.' Galba flinched at the words and a murmur of disbelief punctuated by shouts of 'No' ran through the assembly, but the sardonic smile Otho had worn throughout the ceremony remained in place. 'Foul plots pollute the very air that surrounds us.'

For a moment Valerius believed Galba would use the priest's words as an excuse to have Otho arrested and dragged off to the *carcer*. Icelus and Laco had spent the last two days urging him to do just that. Now the gods had confirmed their suspicions. Someone – it must have been Icelus, because Laco had neither the energy nor the wit – had set this up. If ever there was a moment to act, it was now. But the aged Emperor just looked from Umbricius to the bloody mess at his feet and back again as if he wasn't aware what was happening. Without the support of the governor of Lusitania he would never have had the nerve to make the great gamble that had brought him the Empire. Otho had been with him every step of the way and for all his faults he was a patrician of the noblest Roman stock. Galba trusted Vinius and Laco to do his bidding, but Otho's backing had given him added legitimacy. He was so blinded by the need to be perceived as strong and just that it probably didn't occur to him that Otho might believe *he* had been betrayed. All that mattered was that Servius Sulpicius Galba had done what was right. Eventually, he found his voice.

'Continue with the sacrifice.'

A second bull was brought forward and the ceremony resumed. From his place by the pillars Valerius saw a small olive-skinned man approach Otho and recognized the patrician's freedman, Onomastus. The former slave did most of the talking and Otho nodded gravely. When they'd finished their discussion Otho approached Laco in a way that was almost submissive, bowing to the Praetorian prefect and shaking hands before drifting to the side of the temple and making his way to the gate.

Valerius pushed his way towards Laco. 'I see Marcus Salvius Otho has left. Is something troubling him?'

Laco glared at him. 'If there was, I'm sure you would know better than I. Some foolishness about a new house and meeting the builders. A new slight to the Emperor that I will be sure to report. The man never did have any manners.'

Valerius thanked him equally tersely and considered what he'd been told. If Otho had bought a new house it was the first he'd heard of it, and given his precarious financial position it seemed an unlikely tale. On the other hand, it could be something perfectly innocent that Otho didn't want to air in public. Yet every instinct told him something wasn't right. Careful not to be noticed, he slipped away from the temple to the guardhouse at the top of the Clivus Palatinus where he had arranged to meet Serpentius. He found the Spaniard sitting in the shade of a cypress tree talking to Juva, the big Nubian from the naval militia. His quarry was about to be swallowed by the crowd on the Via Sacra; there was no time for pleasantries. 'I want you to follow Otho. I need to know who he meets and where he goes.'

Serpentius was on his way before Valerius had finished speaking. Juva started after him, then called out as Valerius turned to go back up the hill. 'There is something you should know. The militia has been summoned to the Praetorian barracks. Someone came this morning with an order releasing us from arrest.'

Juva disappeared after the Spaniard, leaving Valerius with another puzzle. Galba had rescinded his order to send the sailors and marines directly back to their base at Misenum and agreed to reconsider their case. But why would he order them to the Praetorian barracks, where a single word could reignite the violence of the Milvian Bridge? The only way he would find out was by asking Vinius or Laco, and that would have to wait until after the ceremony.

He started back towards the Temple of Jupiter with a growing feeling that his world was about to fall apart.

XIX

Serpentius slipped so easily through the crowds awaiting the outcome of the divination that Juva had trouble staying with him. Only the Nubian's great height allowed him to keep the Spaniard in sight till he caught up. Otho remained fifty paces ahead with Onomastus and two of his lictors as they passed the House of the Vestals and the Regia.

'If we end up in the open, drop back,' the gladiator muttered from the side of his mouth. 'You're a bit too conspicuous for this kind of work. Following people is an art.'

Juva shrugged. 'I thought I might be some help if you got into trouble, old man.'

'If I wasn't on business, I'd cut your balls off and make you eat them for saying that. Maybe later.'

'You could try,' Juva growled. The big man continued to watch Otho's progress. 'He's turned left. Do you think he's going to the rostrum?'

Serpentius glanced up at the black man. 'Maybe you are good for something after all.'

He increased his pace. They were in the very heart of the Forum, in the shadow of the Capitoline Hill, with the great bulk of the *tabularium* off to their right and the Rostrum Julium with its captured ships' beaks to their left. Serpentius expected Otho to carry on towards the law courts in the Basilica Julia, which would be crowded with lawyers, prosecutors, jurors, the guilty and the not quite guilty, but the former governor of Lusitania stopped by the 'golden milestone' in front of the Temple of Saturn. Serpentius noticed immediately what another man would not. A group of around twenty men dressed in cloaks stood by the temple steps and their wary, tense faces and the way they carried themselves marked them immediately as soldiers. As he drew closer he recognized Mevius Pudens, a tribune of the Guard, at their forefront.

'Trouble,' he whispered to Juva. 'You watch our backs.'

He edged nearer as Pudens and another of the waiting men approached Otho and began a short, animated conversation. He heard the words 'late' and 'hurry'. But Otho seemed paralysed. He waved an incredulous hand at the group by the steps as if he couldn't believe how few they were.

'There is no turning back now,' Pudens declared, and to prove it he swept back his cloak and drew his sword. 'Hail Caesar.' The shout was clearly a signal, because more swords appeared and the cry was taken up in twenty throats. Someone brought forward a *sella* and Otho was bundled into the chair before it was picked up by four stout Praetorians and carried off past the astonished faces of senators who had emerged from the Curia to discover what the commotion was.

For a moment, Serpentius couldn't believe what he was seeing, but in a crisis the Spaniard's mind was as swift as his actions. He turned to Juva. 'Find master

Valerius and tell him exactly what has happened. They're heading for the Castra Praetoria and he should meet me there when he can.'

Without looking back, he hurried off after the cheering Praetorians and their burden. Otho had recovered sufficient poise to wave and smile fixedly at the mystified bystanders as the little procession passed. Within minutes Serpentius noticed a curious phenomenon. The incident had begun with fewer than thirty men – barely enough to start a riot, never mind a rebellion – but by the time they crossed the Vicus Longus that number had doubled, and more were joining all the time. A few brandished swords, but more followed with quiet determination, out of curiosity and self-preservation; what was happening here could affect them and their families and the more they knew the safer they would be. They emerged from the Subura to be joined by a new influx, among whom Serpentius recognized a few with the broad shoulders and blue tunics that marked the sailors and marines of the disgraced naval militia.

As they stumbled through the streets after the raised chair, rumours danced through the crowd like mini-wildfires; stories and half-truths bouncing from man to man, adding to the confusion and changing shape and meaning as they went. Serpentius could hear the voices around him.

'What's happening?' someone demanded.

A big man in a smith's leather apron replied. 'They say there's a new Emperor.'

'What happened to the last one, the old man?'

The smith shrugged. 'He must be dead.'

'The Emperor's dead?' The lawyer marching to Serpentius's right sounded sceptical, but the cry was taken up by the man next to him and the reverberations

169

rippled out like rings from a stone thrown into a pool.

'The Emperor's dead.'

'Hail Caesar!'

'Who is it?'

'The new Emperor.'

'But who?'

'Must be the boy he adopted,' the smith said. 'The rich one. Maybe he's going to hand out some of his cash.'

The man next to him grinned. 'In that case I don't care who he is. Hail Caesar.'

As they approached the Castra Praetoria, Serpentius pushed and snarled his way forward until he was marching to the left of the chair. When he looked up he saw a curious mixture of terror and elation on Otho's face. The patrician's skin was the colour of a long-dead fish's belly and sweat ran down his cheeks, but his eyes glowed with an almost mystical light, as if the creature inside was experiencing a different event from the vessel that held it.

'Hail Caesar!' The refrain was taken up by a crowd now several hundred strong and they swept through the gates into the barracks as the tribune on duty watched helplessly. Serpentius could only look on in admiration. Otho had taken Rome's most powerful citadel without the loss of a man or a drop of blood. The question was: could he keep it?

The sacrifice of the second bull had just been completed. This time Umbricius declared the omens favourable, as well he might. One attempt to shape Imperial policy was permissible; a second could be fatal. In any case, the Emperor was paying for the bulls. The unfortunate animal had been cut up into small portions, for the gods, and larger parts which would be cooked and eaten later at the sacrificial feast, with the best cuts naturally going to Galba and his favourites. Valerius experienced his usual reaction to the scent of roasting meat: an unlikely mix of hunger and nausea occasioned by the memory of Messor, the young legionary who had been nailed to the door of the Temple of Claudius and burned to death within feet of those trapped inside. He was thinking about how to take his leave when he noticed the tall figure arguing with the guards at the temple gate.

'Juva,' he called. The two guards recognized the one-handed man in the formal toga and moved aside. Valerius stepped close to the Nubian, so their conversation couldn't be overheard. 'What's going on?'

Juva explained what he had seen, making no attempt to interpret it, but stressing Serpentius's plea for urgency. Valerius felt the blood drain from his face. It was starting. He glanced across to where Galba was completing the final rituals of the sacrifice. Was he aware of what was happening? No, of course not. He could see from the complacent faces of Vinius and Laco that nothing was amiss. A moment's hesitation, almost of pain, but there could be only one decision. Otho was a friend, but Corbulo had taught Valerius that honour and duty were obligations that must always rise above friendship. He nodded to Juva to stay where he was and made his way towards the consul and the Praetorian prefect, forcing himself not to hurry and trying to work out what to say without starting a panic. The fate of Rome might depend on the next few moments.

Laco's expression transformed into a snarl as he approached, but Vinius read the seriousness in his face. 'What is it?'

Valerius took them aside. 'A section of the Guard have proclaimed Marcus Salvius Otho Emperor. They are

171

carrying him to the Castra Praetoria and may already be there.'

'Impossible,' spluttered the Praetorian commander. 'I would have known.'

'You idiot,' Vinius sneered. 'You wouldn't notice a rebellion if it started under your fat belly. The Emperor must be told.' He rushed off towards the altar, but was forced to wait while Umbricius made the final prayer to Apollo for an auspicious start to the new year. When he was able to whisper the news, Valerius saw Galba's face go grey and he seemed to shrink inside his toga.

The Emperor hurried across to join Valerius and Laco, with Vinius in his wake. He called Icelus and Piso across to join them and asked Valerius to repeat exactly what he had been told.

'So.' A relieved sigh escaped his lips. 'There are only a few of them?'

'I was told twenty or thirty, but they are on their way to the Castra Praetoria.'

'The Guard will not allow the usurper entry,' Laco said confidently.

'How can you be sure?' Vinius demanded. 'It is the Guard who are taking him there.'

'A few rotten apples.'

'It was a few rotten apples who brought down Nero,' the consul reminded him.

'What must we do?' Galba sounded exactly what he was, a confused old man.

Valerius listened in frustration to the dithering. By now the crowd of senators, priests and visiting provincial dignitaries had noticed what was happening and a rumble of unease ran through them. Eventually he could take no more. 'Act,' he urged the three men. 'Act now. Gather the palace cohort and march on the Praetorian

172

barracks. If there are only a few of them, they won't fight. Guarantee them their lives and you can still negotiate a settlement. Offer Otho the option of exile.'

'And if there are many?'

'If there are many you have enough men to lay siege to the barracks. Bottle them up inside and give their blood a chance to cool. You buy time and an opportunity to negotiate. If Otho had the support of the whole Guard they would be here now, not at the camp. He can't have gathered all ten thousand of them or Laco would know about it. They'll still be about their normal duties outside the city. I doubt if there can be more than four thousand men at the Castra Praetoria.'

'But how can we be certain of the palace cohort's loyalty?' Laco demanded.

'Because they are here and not there.'

'I will talk to them.'

Valerius blinked at Piso's unexpected intervention. 'This is a time to act, not talk,' he said forcefully. But Galba had already leapt at the opportunity to delay a decision that might force him to declare war on his own Praetorian Guard. Valerius used the interval to send a message to Juva to go back to Serpentius for the latest news. While he fumed, Laco paraded the officers and men of the palace guard outside the temple gates and Galba and Vinius discussed the possibility of drafting in the other troops in the city.

'What about the urban cohorts and the *vigiles*?'

'Policemen and firemen,' the Emperor said dismissively. 'Their loyalty lies with whoever pays them, which is currently Titus Flavius Sabinus. They have never rebelled in Rome's history, but neither will they face the Praetorians.'

Vinius thought for a few moments. 'The naval militia

are in their barracks. If we guarantee them their eagle, they will follow you.'

Galba brightened, but Valerius stepped forward before he could speak. 'Someone has called the naval militia to the Praetorian barracks. Otho is no fool. If they've obeyed the summons, he may already have taken their oath.'

The Emperor froze. For the first time it seemed he realized the true peril he faced. Now was the time to take action. Any action. To delay could be fatal. But suddenly Piso rushed to the temple steps and started addressing the assembled soldiers and the opportunity was gone.

Valerius's frustration grew with every word the young man spoke. Around him, the cream of Rome's aristocracy stood waiting for some sign of leadership. Beyond the temple walls he could hear the rumble of growing discontent and demands for information from the mob who had gathered to hear the now forgotten result of the divination. Piso's lanky figure towered over the massed ranks of Praetorians as he harangued them in a powerful voice about the choice between honour and shame. They stood at the crossroads of history, he said. They could save the Empire's reputation and that of their corps by supporting Galba, and expunge the deeds of a few deserters. Otho had condemned himself by his own words and actions. The guardsmen listened with blank faces. Only when he hinted at finally paying the gift they had been offered seven months earlier did he get a reaction. The Praetorians pointed out that if they'd got the money in the first place the Emperor would not be in this position today. At the end, there was no cheering, only a sullen, leaden silence and Galba dismissed them to their barracks because he couldn't trust them to march on their brethren.

Meanwhile, the Emperor's advisers bickered. It had always been clear they had little respect for each other, but now the animosity was in plain sight. Vinius's strident voice rose above the others. If Galba wouldn't go on the attack he should barricade himself into the palace, arm his slaves and wait the plotters out. It was so clearly an invitation to the rebels to take the initiative that for a moment Valerius wondered if Vinius was part of the conspiracy. Laco raged that he would have Vinius executed by his bodyguard and the consul called for his lictors.

'Verrens is right, we must do something,' the Praetorian prefect shouted. 'To do nothing is to invite disaster. What if our enemy is marching on the Senate at this very moment? Every minute we waste allows Otho to seem more of an Emperor to the men who are with him and those he needs to convince. He too will be panicking – we should take advantage of that.'

Galba glared. 'No one here is panicking. We are debating the best course of action.'

Laco bowed an apology, but his face told a different story. His eyes met Valerius's and he shook his head in exasperation at the ineptitude of the man he'd supported. But, from somewhere, Galba suddenly gained a new confidence.

'Yet we can take hope.' The ageing Emperor's voice rose as he grasped at potential salvation the way a drowning sailor grabs for a passing spar. 'We still have the support of the people and the Senate. The army, the legions of Germania Superior apart, is still with us . . .' As he spoke a new roar interrupted him from beyond the walls. 'What is it? What is happening?'

A messenger ran up to Laco, and as he listened the Praetorian commander's face split in a savage grin.

'They're saying Otho is dead. Someone saw him killed. I hope the bastard suffered.'

'This is our moment,' the Emperor said breathlessly. 'Lucius Calpurnius Piso Licinianus, you are to march to the Praetorian barracks and regain control. Take a strong escort, arrest the ringleaders and bring them to your Emperor.'

Valerius saw Piso go pale. This patently wasn't what the young aristocrat had expected when Galba had adopted him as his heir. Still, his chin came up and he raised his fist to his chest in salute.

'There is no guarantee the rumour is true,' Valerius pointed out. 'You may be sending him into a trap.'

But Galba was already celebrating his victory. 'Escort me to the rostrum. I will address my people. Open the gates.'

XX

Serpentius felt himself buffeted by the heaving crowd that followed in the wake of Marcus Salvius Otho. They were five hundred as they passed through the gates of the Castra Praetoria. By the time they reached the parade ground in the middle of the three-storey red-brick barrack blocks their numbers had been swelled to three times that by Praetorians primed for this moment by Onomastus's agents. The Spaniard, a man of the sharpest instincts, could feel the suppressed violence all around him. He had experienced the power of an earthquake and every instinct told him this was the human equivalent.

Another four thousand men waited at attention on the hard-packed earth of the Praetorian parade ground. Otho's bearers carried him to a reviewing stand, and Serpentius found a raised doorstep that allowed him a view of the proceedings while he took stock of what was happening. He was not an educated man, but it did not take a Seneca or a Cicero to understand that he was at the centre of great events. In a matter of minutes Otho had transformed himself from a penniless aristocrat discarded by his Emperor into the man with the power

177

to supplant him. A force that had begun with twenty men now numbered the equivalent of a full legion. Not only that, but they controlled probably the greatest military power base in Rome. Not a hundred paces from where he stood was the Praetorian armoury, with enough swords and spears, shields and mail to equip twelve thousand men, and the treasury, packed with the gold to buy the services of twelve thousand more.

All Otho had to do was convince them he was the man to lead them.

From his marginally elevated position Serpentius realized the guiding hand behind the plot had put all the elements in place to make it happen. The centuries arrayed in their lines on the parade ground were made up of rank and file legionaries; there was little sign of the officers or centurions who might have swayed their allegiance. And in a block at the heart of the black and silver ranks another unit had been given the place of honour: the naval militia who had more reason to despise Galba than anyone else in Rome. Someone had issued the men from the rowing benches with tunics of marine blue so that for the first time they had the appearance of a unified military force. They were still unarmed, but somehow the way they held themselves made them more dangerous than the pampered Praetorian peacocks who surrounded them. Whoever had brought them here and placed them in Otho's hands had made a risky roll of the dice. With his first words the rebel Emperor turned it into a stroke of genius.

He waved an elegant hand that took in the blue-clad ranks. 'Servius Sulpicius Galba denied you the eagle your sacrifices deserved. My first act as Emperor is to grant it to you anew.' A long moment of silence followed and the air crackled with anticipation and something close to wonder as the crowd to Otho's left parted to reveal a section of Praetorians carrying the gilded standard that had inspired the legions as they conquered half the world, from the wintry hills of Brigantea to the deserts of Africa, and the shores of Lusitania to the rocky wilds of Parthia. This was what a legionary fought and died for, and in doing so counted himself fortunate. One of the men handed Otho the eagle. He held it for a moment, the weight of brass and gold evidently a surprise and as if he couldn't quite believe what he had in his hands, before raising it in salute to the men in front of him. It was all pre-planned, a piece of theatre as contrived as any that ever took place on a stage, but Serpentius felt the hair on the back of his neck rise and he saw the emotion in his own face reflected in the expression of the man who now stood next to him. Juva's mouth gaped in a cheer that was lost in the crescendo of sound torn from the throats of the men in blue and taken up by everyone around them. Whether they had come here to support Otho or merely out of curiosity, they were all in his thrall now. 'I name you First Adiutrix, the helpers, because when I needed you you came to my aid. Who will carry this eagle?' With a shout, the front ranks of the new legion surged forward as one, but their leaders pushed them back, and from the chaos a single man stepped clear.

'Florus,' Juva whispered as the young marine from the *Waverider* marched forward with his curious sailor's gait. Serpentius could feel the confusion in the big Nubian. 'What should I do?'

'Go to them,' the Spaniard said. 'It is what Valerius would want you to do. Go to your comrades and serve with honour, whoever you follow.'

When Juva turned to him he had tears in his eyes. He

held out his great meaty hand and the gladiator took it. 'May Fortuna favour you.'

'And you.'

Serpentius watched the broad back force its way through the crowd like a galley through a heaving sea. Juva's century opened to welcome him just as Florus, newly appointed *aquilifer* of the Legio I Adiutrix, accepted the eagle standard, and a new roar split the heavens above the Castra Praetoria. He saw veteran soldiers openly weep as the new legion took the oath from a man who would be either dead or Emperor by the time the sun set.

There were more speeches, but he barely heard them as he pondered whether to return to Valerius. What would happen to the one-armed tribune if Otho became Emperor? He dismissed the thought as quickly as it had formed. Valerius was old enough and wise enough to look after himself. Each of them had stared death in the face often enough not to be too concerned if it came calling again. But since they had returned to Rome Serpentius had watched the shadow that stained Valerius's scarred features fade, and the melancholy that had enveloped him lift. It would be a pity to die now, just when life appeared to have been given some meaning. He knew the reason for the change was the general's daughter and he feared that pursuing her would only bring his friend more pain, but a man, especially one like Valerius or Serpentius, could only live for the moment. And, for the moment, he reckoned he could serve Valerius best by sticking to Otho.

He had them now, that was certain. Serpentius had heard enough military speeches to know. The growls of assent. The pent-up energy of hounds straining at the leash. It could only be a matter of time.

At last. 'You have listened to me. You have heard me. You have not arrested me. That alone condemns you before a man who does not know the meaning of mercy. Servius Sulpicius Galba's hands are stained with the blood of the marines who trusted him, the innocents of high rank and low who refused to acclaim him. He will not forgive.' Otho's final words – 'Are you with me?' – coincided with the opening of the armoury and drew the biggest roar of the day. The swords and shields were snatched up as quickly as they could be handed out, but if Otho believed he had created an army, he was wrong. They were a mob, and they wanted blood.

Apart from a small knife Serpentius had no weapon, but that was no handicap to a man like the Spaniard. A sailor ran past him with a sword held high. With a flick of his wrist Serpentius disarmed the man and with a snarl dared him to try to recover the blade. The sailor backed away; there were other weapons and easier victims. Serpentius trotted after the leaders as they disappeared towards the west gate and the road to the Forum.

Despite the urgency, Galba had taken the time to don his general's gilt breastplate and strap on the long sword he had carried from Hispania. He looked like a leader; all he needed now was someone to lead. But he hadn't bargained for the enthusiasm of the mob. Urged on by senators who had come to show their support, they manhandled him into a chair and hoisted him on their shoulders. Valerius had armed himself with a *gladius* borrowed from a member of the palace guard and along with Vinius stayed close to the Emperor, his progress and movements hampered by the folds of his toga. Whether by accident or design, Laco and Icelus were

181

forced further back. Galba's personal guard struggled to stay within reach of the man in the chair, but Valerius could see from the way they kept glancing at each other that they were in a high state of nerves. A huge crowd had gathered in the Forum and the Emperor and his retinue swirled in its grip like flotsam in an ebbing tide, overlooked by thousands more Romans watching the entertainment from the shelter of the basilicas and temples.

The first warning of trouble came when Piso and the commander of his escort appeared at the far side of the Forum from the direction of the Argiletum. Galba's heir shouted something that was lost in the clamour of the mob, but Valerius did hear the screams that followed a moment later. He looked up as two cavalrymen forced their way into the crowd, slapping at heads with the flats of their long swords and clearing a path for the Praetorian infantry who followed.

He shouted a desperate warning to Galba's escort. Their job was to form a barrier between the Emperor and the threat, using their shields to give him a chance to escape. Instead, they took one look at the advancing horsemen and slipped away into the crowd. Cursing, Valerius drew his sword and forced his way towards the chair. He could see Vinius, his eyes wild with growing panic, attempting to do the same. Galba had seen the approaching threat and screamed orders at the people carrying his chair. At last, they noticed the cavalrymen, but instead of carrying their burden to safety they tipped him from his seat and fled. Valerius saw the Emperor go sprawling and shouted a warning to Vinius. He battered his way towards the stricken man, snarling and threatening anyone who got in his way. Somehow he managed to force himself between Galba and the two horsemen. He risked a glance at his feet where the Emperor lay with his wig askew and his toga around his knees, his eyes dazed and confused. Valerius was tempted to reach down and help the old man to his feet, but the screams grew closer and he turned to find the first cavalryman only feet away. The trooper's eyes glared from beneath his helmet and he roared at Valerius to make way or die. When the one-handed man stood his ground, the trooper urged his horse forward, scattering the crowd as the beast snapped its jaws and flailed with its hooves. Valerius danced out of range of a mouthful of stained teeth and then stepped forward so he was close enough to feel the heat from the animal's body. Then he rammed his sword into its chest. The horse screamed and reared, pitching its rider out of the saddle and almost pulling the *gladius* from Valerius's hand. Somehow, he hauled the gore-stained iron free and turned to seek Galba among the nearby throng. A shout alerted him and he spun to find the dazed cavalryman stumbling towards him with a long cavalry *spatha* held ready to strike. The two men circled each other, looking for the first opening. Valerius had no wish to kill the trooper. Somewhere in the numbed centre of his mind he realized he'd just taken sides in a civil war, but he had no intention of spilling another Roman's blood unless he had to. Not far away men were helping Galba to his feet and Valerius screamed at them to get him out of the Forum. Before the old man could move he was overwhelmed by an avalanche of armed soldiers, their sword arms hacking at the group. Galba's aides recoiled, spurting blood from severed limbs and broken heads. In the same instant Valerius sensed the rhythm of the swords around the Emperor change and a scream of mortal agony told him the two hundred and twenty-one day reign of Servius Galba Caesar Augustus was over. The momentary distraction almost killed him as the cavalryman lunged to pierce the thick cloth of his toga and run the edge of the blade across the flesh above his hip. Galvanized by the sting of the iron he forced his assailant back, making him parry desperately with the now clumsy cavalry sword. Valerius was gladiator taught and gladiator trained to a speed and a skill few other men could match. He was also left-handed, and a left-handed swordsman causes problems for an opponent no right-handed one ever will. He kept the trooper on the move until the man could barely defend himself. A feint and a lunge, and with a sudden shriek the other man fell back, holding his shoulder. Valerius's mind reeled, still filled with the confusion and horror of the Emperor's death. Before he could move he found himself under attack from another three or four men and it was all he could do to defend himself. The only thing that kept him alive in those first few seconds was speed, but when a fifth man joined the Praetorians he knew his life was measured in seconds. For the first time he found the swiftness of his blade matched – outdone – by another man. He concentrated on keeping that dazzling blur of iron at bay, but panic began in his stomach and grew to fill his chest and his mind. It was only slowly that it dawned on him that his adversary, while keeping him on the defensive, was, by some martial wonder, at the same time ensuring his enemies' swords couldn't reach him. He risked a glance at his new opponent, and in the same instant felt the sword flicked from his hand. Serpentius stepped effortlessly between Valerius and the men still bent on killing him.

'Hold,' he shouted. 'Can you not see his right hand? It is the disfigurement we were told to look for. The

Emperor Marcus Salvius Otho Caesar wants to deal with this one personally. There will be no easy death for Gaius Valerius Verrens.'

Still, they would have killed him but for the Spaniard's snarling presence. In his own land, Serpentius would have been a prince, but the Romans had made him a slave, then a gladiator, which had left him all the more fearsome. As the Praetorians stepped back, Valerius had a momentary, almost detached vision of a spearman plunging his javelin again and again into the writhing body of Titus Vinius.

'I'm sorry,' the Spaniard whispered. 'But it was the best I could do at short notice.'

Valerius smiled bleakly. 'So be it. Let the gods decide.'

But he knew the decision whether he would live or die would not be made by the gods, but by Marcus Salvius Otho.

They kept him in a cell for an hour in the disciplinary block of the Praetorian barracks until they brought him before the new Emperor of Rome. As he limped towards the *praetorium* of the great camp, two patricians were just leaving. Valerius was so weary he would barely have acknowledged them, but he noticed one of the men falter and he looked up into the eyes of Suetonius Paulinus, Boudicca's conqueror, the general who had awarded him the Corona Aurea, and more recently sent him on the mission that had led to Gnaeus Domitius Corbulo's death. The general shot him a look of confusion, which quickly turned to scorn. It was plain he knew what he was seeing: a dead man. With an audible sniff he stalked away, saying something that made the other man laugh.

Otho had set up his headquarters in the utilitarian villa which until recently had been the home of Cornelius

Laco and his family. Now he sat behind Laco's desk, sampling Laco's wine, and studied the man in front of him with a look of puzzled irritation. Valerius met his gaze and kept his own face expressionless. He tried not to notice the severed head that sat to one side of the desk. Even in death Servius Sulpicius Galba's glassy-eyed stare personified his outraged dignity.

'How is your wound?' Otho asked.

'I'll live.' Valerius regretted the terseness of his reply even as he uttered the words, but it didn't really matter because it was a prediction he knew was unlikely to come true.

Otho produced a weary smile. 'It really would have been much tidier if you'd got yourself killed like poor old Servius here. Did the silly old goat really think I was going to sit back and let him hand Rome to some upstart who couldn't put on his shoes without the help of six servants? I told them I didn't want Galba's head, but now that he's here I find it quite comforting: a reminder that I did what was right. I didn't do it for myself, Valerius, I did it for Rome.' The words hung between them for a moment before Otho's face twisted into a grin that Valerius couldn't help matching. 'No, that's not actually true. We both know why I did it. I did it because Nero stole my wife and my position and packed me off to a stinking hellhole where the people's only ambition was to add another acre of dust to their worthless farms. I did it because Galba as good as promised that I would sit where Nero sat, and then, just when I had it in my hands, he took it all away again.' He sighed, and for the first time Valerius recognized a desperate sadness in him. 'And now it's done. I'm sorry about all the people who are being killed out there, but I'm afraid I didn't quite understand the force I was letting loose. That's something I've learned today, Valerius, but at least I know I have a lot to learn. Not like Servius. Servius thought his breeding and his upbringing and his wealth made him infallible and that taking advice was weakness. I, on the other hand, am happy to take advice. You see, I am being candid with you.' He picked up a second cup and poured Laco's carefully selected wine. Valerius accepted, knowing it could be the last he ever drank. Otho seemed to confirm as much with his next words. 'Now it's possible that's because you are already a dead man – you'll admit I gave you every chance to join me? – but I prefer to think that it's because you're an honest man. A man I can trust, even though you would not repay me with yours. For instance, what advice would you give me now?'

Valerius frowned at the unexpected question. He had expected scorn, and, at best, a quick death. Instead, he stood here drinking fine wine with his wound throbbing and his head full of puzzles.

'Get your men off the streets, that would be the first step. Be magnanimous in victory. Announce an amnesty for Galba's supporters. Pay the Praetorians what Galba owed them – I assume you've already confiscated his fortune?' Otho nodded. 'Rome is like a boiling pot with the lid jammed tight. It could still explode in your face. Take the heat off and allow it to cool.'

Otho smiled. 'Good advice, and I'll take most of it. Laco, Vinius . . .' He read something in Valerius's eyes and a pained expression crossed his face as he realized his prospective father-in-law was dead. 'No, not Vinius then, but Laco is sitting in the *carcer* waiting for the strangling rope. He can be packed off to some dusty little island where he can be fat and idle for the rest of his days. Piso, though? That would be a sign of weakness.

As Galba's heir he probably thinks it's his turn to be the Emperor, and we can't have two Emperors, can we? He's hiding out somewhere, but they will hunt him down soon enough and by nightfall he will be reacquainted with his adoptive father here.' An aide entered with a document. Otho read it quickly and signed with an assured hand. When he looked up his eyes had turned serious. 'I may have work for you, Gaius Valerius Verrens, Hero of Rome, but first I require something from you.'

'You hold my life in your hands. What more can you want?'

'This is something that must be given freely. Your oath.'

For a moment the air seemed to be sucked from the room. In his mind, Valerius counted the days since he had made his sacred pledge to another man. But that man was dead and his head lay between them on the table, the pale features already dulled to a soft grey by the first signs of corruption. He brought his right hand with the wooden fist across his chest in salute and tried to ignore Galba's accusing stare as the words emerged from between cracked lips.

'In fulfilment of my vow I gladly pledge my loyalty to Marcus Salvius Otho Caesar Augustus, Emperor of Rome.'

Otho nodded gravely. 'What should I do about Germania?'

Again, the question caught Valerius off balance. 'The legions of Germania Superior mutinied against Galba, not the Empire. They have no grievance against you. When they find out he's dead they will take the oath.'

The Emperor shook his head. 'No, you misunderstand the situation. Galba was not entirely honest with you. While he has been showing off his new son, things

188

have changed for the worse. That is why you are here and why you still have your head.' In the silence the manicured nail of Otho's forefinger nervously flicked the rim of the glass cup he held in his right hand. 'You see, Valerius, the Rhenus legions have declared Aulus Vitellius Emperor and they are preparing to march on Rome.'

XXI

Colonia

In the comfort of his personal quarters in the governor's palace in Colonia Agrippinensis, Aulus Vitellius reflected on the dilemma he faced and the opportunities his position offered. How could it have happened? In all honesty, he had no idea. One moment he had been enjoying the unlikely pleasures of this city, the next he had been confronted with their grim faces and their ultimatums. Perhaps he had been too gentle with Flaccus. Perhaps he should have done more to placate the legions of Germania Superior. But Valens had been so certain. And now? Now he understood that Valens was not quite the simple soldier he had believed. Valens had been clever, and he had not. Valens had tricked him.

When word came that the Twenty-second Primigenia and the Fourth Macedonica had refused to take the oath to the new Emperor and taken the governor into custody, Valens had persuaded him that the only course of action was to march on Moguntiacum with as much strength as he could muster. When they saw the forces against them and the situation was explained at spear point, the legionaries would see sense. They had made their grievances known. If Galba was clever, he would accede to a few of their demands and quietly see that the ringleaders eventually ate the wrong kind of mushroom.

Vitellius had pondered the question overnight and concluded his general was probably right. He had ordered the four legions under his command to provide six cohorts each and such auxiliaries as they could spare – in all, the equivalent of three full legions – and given Valens command. But Valens insisted that the expedition would only have the Emperor's authority if the Emperor's representative led it.

That was how he had ended up shivering on the flat plain west of Moguntiacum as he reviewed a parade of twenty-five thousand legionaries, with the eagle standards of the former mutineers from Twenty-second Primigenia and Fourth Macedonica arrayed to his right, and the men of First Germanica, Fifth Alaudae, Fifteenth Primigenia and Sixteenth Gallica to his left. *Twenty-five thousand*. The equivalent of five full legions, the finest fighting troops in the Empire, and that took no account of the cohorts of auxiliaries who would march with them. His heart had swelled at the sight of that vast swath of scarlet and silver, the polished iron of their armour glittering bright in the low winter sun. It was odd that Flaccus had not joined him, but perhaps not *so* odd. The governor of Germania Superior was not the man he had been a few months earlier. The creature freed from the guardroom had been broken in spirit and mind. Valens was proved right, the mutinous legions came to heel, and Caecina Alienus, the personable young man Galba had appointed as legate of Fourth Macedonica, had been most cooperative, given the cloud hanging over his career.

When the time came to administer the oath a hush fell over the whole assembly, a breathless moment that he imagined must be like the pause before a battle charge. As he rode out in front of the two formerly mutinous legions with Caecina and Valens the chanting had begun and he knew how it felt to have a cold iron sword pierce his heart.

One word.

It began with the ten thousand men facing him, but he heard it taken up by those behind. Over and over, until it made the very air throb.

One word.

Twenty-five thousand voices.

'CAESAR!'

'No,' he whispered.

'They will not follow Galba.' This from Valens.

'You have a bloodline as ancient as his,' Caecina pointed out.

'He took the purple by stealth.'

'He is not worthy of the throne.'

'They will follow you . . .'

'Or . . .'

What choice did he have? If he refused they would kill him. He looked from Valens to Caecina.

'There is no turning back.' Valens again.

He lifted his arms to accept their acclaim.

'CAESAR! CAESAR! CAESAR!'

He almost groaned as he remembered the moment, wrapping his cloak closer against the morning chill and calling for another cup of warmed wine. The room seemed to spin about him. Soon he would exchange this . . . yes, this *rustic* mansion, for all its fine carved furniture and glowing mosaics, and the busts of his ancestors lining the walls, for a true palace – Nero's

Golden House swam into his mind – or . . . He took a long drink from the cup the slave proffered.

It was only later he understood it had been Valens who had engineered the failed attempt to make Verginius Rufus Emperor, and whose head would be on a spike when Galba discovered the fact, as he inevitably would. And that the personable Aulus Caecina Alienus had been about to be dismissed by the Emperor following an audit which had discovered a large hole in the accounts covering the years of his quaestorship in Baetica.

Their only hope was to get rid of Galba, and they were using him to do it.

He picked up the case containing Julius Caesar's sword, opened it and withdrew the gleaming blade from its cloth bag. He knew he was no soldier, but truly, there was no turning back.

'And now?' He directed the question at the two legates. It was disturbing that the two men who held his life in their hands patently found it difficult to sit in the same room with each other. Valens continuously darted glances of varying degrees of loathing at his fellow general, while Caecina contrived to convey the impression that only he and Vitellius were present.

'Now we march on Rome,' the commander of the First Germanica said gruffly. Caecina gave a reluctant nod of confirmation.

Vitellius felt a thrill of fear as the reality of what he was now part of was put into words. *We march on Rome.* Do, or die. 'Very well. I will lead my legions south in the spring. We—'

'With the greatest respect, Imperator,' Valens interrupted, reluctantly looking to Caecina for support, 'delay would be fatal. We must act now while we are at our strongest and our enemy at his weakest. If we

193

wait, Galba will be able to call the eastern legions to his aid. Show your leadership now and every man of the Rhenus legions will support you. If you wait for three months . . .'

'Soldiers are creatures of the moment, Caesar,' Caecina agreed. 'You must take the initiative.'

Vitellius smiled. Did they take him for a fool? 'It was my understanding that we do not campaign in winter. Surely we must not act precipitously. There are supplies to gather, funds to put in place, plans to agree and alliances to make. We cannot leave the frontier unguarded. It will take a month to make our preparations, perhaps two.'

Valens produced a wide roll of parchment and unrolled it on the table. It was a map of Germania, Gaul, Belgica, Raetia and Italia, detailed and recently drawn. 'That will be Galba's thinking, but we intend to surprise him. Two columns. Myself to the west, following the river route,' he trailed his finger along the blue lines of the Rhenus, the Mosella, the Sauconna and the Rhodanus, 'and then turning east towards Augusta Taurinorum. One full legion, the Fifth, and six thousand men from the other three legions of this province, plus twelve thousand auxiliaries. In all a force of twenty-three thousand men . . .'

'While I,' Caecina chimed in, taking up a position on the opposite side of the map, 'will lead a force of equal strength from Germania Superior by the more direct route through the Alps.' Vitellius opened his mouth to interrupt, but just then a gust of wind from the opening in the roof blew smoke from the open fire back into the room and Caecina brushed a few spots of black soot from the map before continuing smoothly, 'We will march immediately and push as far as we can, acclimatize the men to the mountains while we wait for the passes to open. There has been less snow than normal. We may not have to wait for long. Each column will be large enough to deal with any opposition it is likely to meet and small enough to move quickly. If all goes to plan, we will combine somewhere around Placentia for the final march on Rome with around fifty thousand men. An unstoppable force.'

'But provisions . . . ?'

'Each unit has supplies for a three-month campaign. The order of march has been agreed. The men are ready. All it requires is your order.' Valens produced a new sheet of parchment. 'And your seal.'

Vitellius toyed with the newly crafted gold ring inscribed with the words *Aulus Vitellius Germanicus Imperator* that the two generals had presented to him. Caecina had claimed it was the work of a famous Celtic craftsman and had come from Gaul, but he was such a dissembler, who knew? Like all the rest of this, the ring spoke of premeditation, much more so than he had realized. Only now did he understand the full extent of his manipulation. Every element of their plan was another bar to the cage that held him. Could there be a way out? He felt the hard eyes on him. The answer was no. Still he did not accept the parchment. 'You say two columns? What part will your Emperor play in this?'

'Naturally, Imperator, yours is the most vital role of all,' Caecina bowed. 'We will fight the battles, but it will be here at Colonia Agrippinensis that the war is won. The Lingones and the Treveri have already declared for you and promised materiel and funds, but there is more to do in Gaul. You must draft letters to the tribal leaders and seek their support. We have had word from Lugdunum that Manlius and the First Italica will not oppose us. From Belgica, Asiaticus sends his best wishes and regard, but warns of opposition from his procurator which will require delicate handling. The legions of Britannia will send men to fight for your cause. All they lack is your call. For the moment, your place is here, but when the time comes it is you who will lead us through the gates of Rome.'

Vitellius studied the two faces, the one hard and unyielding, the other with all the adaptability of an actor's. Could he trust them? It didn't matter. Their three lives – and possibly deaths – were as entwined as any love knot.

He took the parchment from Valens' hand, held a finger of scarlet wax to the candle and dripped the molten sealant in the bottom corner and waited a moment for it to harden slightly. With only the slightest hesitation, he applied the signet that would launch his legions against Rome.

XXII

Serpentius looked back as the soft glow of sunrise painted the red-tiled roofs of Rome scarlet and the air above the city was split by smoke from the first cooking fires. 'Do you think you can convince him?'

Valerius stifled a yawn. They'd been riding in the pre-dawn gloom since the last hour of the fourth watch. The Spaniard's question was the one he'd been asking himself since his meeting with Otho. 'I have to try. Perhaps I could convince the Vitellius I knew in Africa. But the Vitellius I knew in Africa would never have risked a civil war to lay his hands on the purple.'

But he remembered the way Vitellius had looked at Julius Caesar's sword in the tavern beside the Via Salaria. He had wondered even then whether his old friend had his eye on the great prize. But he had thought Vitellius hoped to be named as Galba's heir; for him to have allowed himself to be hailed as Emperor some other factor must have come into play, something that had either tempted Vitellius beyond common sense or forced his hand.

'Tell him it is not too late,' Otho had insisted. 'Tell him I will give him anything short of the crown. He can name his price. He may govern any province that takes his fancy. I will share the consulship with him. I will pay off his soldiers and his generals. I will do anything to save the Empire from the terror and the bloodshed that rides hand in hand with civil war.'

And Otho had meant what he said, Valerius was certain. The Otho who had given him the details of their mission was a new Otho, earnest and thoughtful, determined to hold what he had won, but desperate to do what was right. In the immediate aftermath of Galba's death he had allowed the Praetorians to elect their own commanders, but had tightened his grip on the Guard by ensuring those chosen were his supporters. He had called a special meeting of the Senate while the corpses of the coup's victims still lay festering in the Forum, with the result that no man spoke against him. Galba as Emperor had alienated all but those closest to him. Otho did everything to ensure that none had reason to fear his accession. In Rome, he was in a position of strength, with the support of the people, the Senate and the Praetorian Guard. But the man now reclining in Colonia Agrippinensis had seven full legions, perhaps eight, under his command. For the moment Marcus Salvius Otho had a single one. Until the Balkan legions he had summoned from Moesia, Pannonia and Dalmatia reached Italia, the only forces at his disposal, apart from the Guard and the almost worthless urban cohorts, were the sailors and marines of the new First Adiutrix. Valerius had watched them exercise on the flat ground beyond the city walls and had been impressed by their enthusiasm, but he knew that lack of proper training and the long-ingrained discipline that made a legion a legion would cost them dear in battle.

'I am Emperor by the consent of the Senate and people

of Rome,' Otho had said. 'Vitellius must recognize that.'

And there lay the greatest obstacle to a peaceful solution. For Aulus Vitellius to recognize Otho as his Emperor was to betray the officers and men who had proclaimed him to the purple, and to place their lives in Otho's hands. Even if Vitellius himself agreed to trust Otho, it was possible his legionaries would get rid of him and elect one of their own legates in his place. Valerius's old friend was many things, but he was no fool. Who knew what his reaction would be to the man who put the choice to him?

Valerius turned back to the road and Serpentius took up station beside him. They were dressed as a none-too-prosperous merchant and his servant. The Spaniard trailed a pack horse and the goods it carried had more to do with the journey they faced than the trade that was ostensibly the reason for it. 'We may be travelling on a fool's errand, and one that might end up with us dead, but still I think it is a journey worth making.' Valerius told his companion. 'What are two lives when balanced against the thousands we might save?'

'I don't know about yours, but when it comes to mine the answer is quite a lot.' Serpentius grinned. Otho's secretary had provided them with a travel warrant that would take them anywhere in the Empire and allow them to change their horses at military remount stations. It was the choice of route that worried the Spaniard. 'Safer and more certain to take the river road through Gaul. That's the way they'll come and there's no point in us riding all the way to Germania if Vitellius is already on the way here.'

Valerius shook his head. 'His legions will stay in their winter quarters for another month at least. The one thing I'm certain of is that Aulus Vitellius won't put on his campaign boots until he needs to. He is a man who enjoys his comforts, and being in the saddle for too long isn't one of them. Anyway, you're the hardy mountain man. I'd have thought you'd be glad to get back into the hills.'

'In the middle of winter? I've seen the Alps in summer and I didn't like it then. Only fit for goats and ghosts. You'd have to be mad to want to freeze your *colei* off in the mountains. Why do you think the gods made valleys, warm huts and women?'

They took the Via Flaminia north and east through the mountains towards the town of Fanum Fortunae on the Mare Adriaticum, changing their horses every day at Imperial staging posts. Valerius decided to avoid the official *mansiones*, preferring to stay anonymously at civilian inns and hostels where they didn't have to produce their papers. The warrant was sound enough, but some sixth sense warned him against leaving a trail for someone to follow. There was no need to consult a map; the road ran straight and true, with only the slightest deviation for troublesome river crossings and impassable summits. Near the end of the third day, when they were deep in the heart of the mountains, Serpentius suggested they stop and make camp rather than pushing on to find the next *taberna*. He nodded back the way they'd come. 'I'll double back for a mile or so and take a look. I've had an itch in my ear for the past couple of hours.'

'Do you want me to prepare anything?' Serpentius's instinct for trouble was as finely honed as any animal's and Valerius had long since learned to trust his friend.

The Spaniard shook his head. 'It could be nothing. Just light a fire and prepare the bedding and we'll see what happens.'

He returned less than an hour later and dropped from the saddle to join Valerius in a gully just off the track. 'Two of them dogging our footsteps,' he said quietly. 'They stopped when they smelled the smoke and one scouted to within two hundred paces of the camp. We still have two hours of daylight. An honest man would have ridden past.'

'Perhaps they think we're bandits,' Valerius suggested.

'Not them. I recognize their kind and no bandit would frighten them. Handy men, wary and alert.' Valerius smiled. Serpentius could have been describing himself. 'They're nothing to laugh about,' the Spaniard said seriously. 'If they'd come on us unawares, they might have given us a hard time of it.'

'And now?'

'Now, I think we should give *them* a hard time of it.'

They kept watch on watch through the night, but Valerius sensed the two followers weren't an immediate threat. A nuisance and a potential danger, though. And working for whom? It had the scent of Offonius Tigellinus's work, but Tigellinus was in hiding. His cunning had allowed him to survive Nero's passing, but Otho owed him nothing and the Senate had demanded his head as the blood price of their support. If not Tigellinus, surely it pointed to the Emperor himself, or at least his court, but why would Otho have them followed when he had entrusted them with the mission in the first place?

Next morning they rose before dawn and ate a swift breakfast of rough bread dipped in wine and a handful of olives. Serpentius ensured he made plenty of noise as he loaded the pack horse.

'The likelihood is they've been watching us.' He kept his voice low. 'If they are what I think they are, they won't want to take a chance on losing us. They'll give us a few minutes and then they'll follow. I scouted the road ahead a little way yesterday. There's a place where the trees close in and that's where we'll hit them.'

Valerius listened as he outlined his plan. In battle, it was he who would have led, but in an ambush no one was better than the Spaniard.

The two strangers rode side by side in the pre-dawn gloom, slumped in their saddles and more asleep than awake after a night sharing watches. They were a mismatched pair. A heavy-set older man with lank grey hair, narrow eyes and a harelip, and a handsome, pink-cheeked youth in a hooded cloak of fine cloth, with eyes that despite his fatigue never left the road ahead. Felix, the older man, muttered a stream of curses beneath his breath. At their last camp he'd lost the copper phallus charm that never left his neck and he suspected his partner had stolen it. Young Julius, who wouldn't have touched the cheap trinket with someone else's hands, silently screamed at him to be quiet and wondered how he was going to last another week of this. Outwardly, Felix appeared the more dangerous of the pair, but looks were deceptive. Julius had a predator's cunning and an infinite capacity for patience, matched by the cold, impersonal professionalism with which he disposed of his victims. Only one thing marked them as a team. Both right hands lay close to the blades hidden beneath their cloaks.

Serpentius waited until his targets were past before he angled his run at the nearer horse. Since he was as silent as he was quick, it was doubtful Julius could have saved himself even if he'd been looking directly at him. The young spy reacted at the sound of the final footfall, hauling at the sword on his left hip. Unfortunately for him, the long cloak hindered his stroke, and even if it had not Serpentius was already too close. His hands grabbed Julius's boot and heaved upwards and forwards, throwing the boy from the saddle with a desperate cry. Felix snatched a startled look that confirmed his partner's plight before putting heels to his mount. A spy and a backstabber, he didn't intend risking his skin to help a snot-nosed, thieving pup without the sense to watch his right flank. Cursing the ill fortune that had lost him the charm, he galloped towards safety, unaware that his bad luck was only beginning. When he judged he was clear he threw a last glance over his shoulder, exulting at his escape, and in the same instant Valerius kicked his horse into the road ahead and caught him with a full swing of his still scabbarded *spatha*. The heavy sword took Felix in the mouth and the power of the blow and his momentum combined to flip him backwards over his mount's rear to lie moaning and only half-conscious in the road.

Valerius dismounted and searched the fallen man for weapons. The blow had smeared Felix's lips across his lower face and jagged fragments of enamel showed white amongst the red mess. When he was satisfied, he dragged Felix by the hood of his cloak to where Serpentius was hauling his partner to his feet. The Spaniard took one look at the older spy's face and shook his head. 'We won't get much out of him. This one will have to do.' He rammed his captive against a tree with enough force to make Julius cry out.

Valerius picked up the youth's fallen sword and inspected it. 'Why were you following us?'

Julius's eyes darted between his two captors like those of a whipped dog anticipating the next blow. 'Don't know

203

what you mean, master. We are just simple travellers, as you are.' For the moment he was happy to play the fearful innocent. Experience told him his chance would come, and when it did . . . He kept his voice as plaintive as a child's, and wrung his hands as if washing them clean. What he failed to understand was the mettle of the two men he faced. Valerius read something behind the scared eyes: an unlikely confidence, as if the inner man was mocking him.

'Ask him again,' he said.

Serpentius was facing the boy, a pace away and slightly to his right. Like a striking snake, his right hand came round in a short, vicious hook. Julius gasped wordlessly as the Spaniard's fist hit him harder than he'd ever been hit before. The blow took the spy under the ribs and sank deep into his vitals, knocking the air from his lungs and leaving him bug-eyed with pain. He doubled up and would have collapsed if the Spaniard's left hand hadn't casually reached forward and seized his throat with fingers that felt like an eagle's talons. Julius's face turned a strange shade of pinkish blue and an odd cawing, like the cry of a hungry crow, squeezed from his throat. Valerius nodded and Serpentius relaxed his grip. The Roman waited until the choking subsided.

'My friend here is a veteran of the arena,' he said patiently. 'I need only say one word and he will wring your neck like a sacrificial chicken. He knows a thousand ways to hurt you. We can continue this conversation all day, to your pain and discomfort, but I would rather be on my way.'

Julius licked his lips and flicked a glance at Valerius's wooden fist. 'We—'

'Shay muffing.'

The words were as mangled as the mouth from which

204

they emerged, but their message was clear enough. Julius's lips clamped shut. Valerius placed a casual boot across Felix's throat to silence him. Julius stared at his partner's purpling features, and shook his head. Serpentius smiled and Valerius winced at what was coming next.

'You're a handsome boy. I'd wager you have lots of girls chasing after you. That right?' Suspicion flickered on the spy's face, but there was something in his eyes Serpentius instantly recognized. Pride. And in pride, he sensed weakness. 'Yes.' He turned to Valerius. 'A pretty boy like him would be good with the ladies.' Julius produced something between a squawk and a groan as Serpentius slipped his right hand beneath the expensive tunic and his cold fingers closed on the boy's testicles, squeezing just enough to cause discomfort. Julius's complexion went from red to white in a single moment. 'Of course,' the Spaniard continued conversationally, 'to be good with the ladies, you have to have the right equipment.' The clawlike fingers closed and this time his victim gave a little squeak of anguish. The dark eyes sought Valerius.

'Please . . .'

But this was no time for mercy. They needed answers. Felix squirmed beneath Valerius's boot, though whether that was because of what was happening to his partner or because he was in danger of suffocating seemed uncertain. Valerius nodded to Serpentius and the Spaniard tightened his grip with a vicious twist of the wrist that had Julius shrieking in disbelieving agony. The words came out in a gabble. 'WeweresentbytheEmperor . . .'

'Let him speak.'

Serpentius relaxed his grip and Julius let out a long groan of relief.

'Slowly,' Valerius said. 'And do not miss out any detail.'

The young man swallowed. His body seemed to have gone into spasm and he stood with his knees bent in a defensive crouch. 'We were sent by the Emperor's freedman, Onomastus. Our orders were to follow you as far as the border and ensure you kept to the route. If you deviated we . . . were to report back.'

Valerius noted the hesitation, and it seemed Serpentius had too. Like a conjuror's trick, a curved knife appeared with the point pricking Julius's throat. The young man froze.

'Don't take us for fools, my little spy. Men like you and me don't *report back*. That's not what we're paid for. Now, tell me again, and this time get it right, or I'll cut those delicate balls off, fry them in lard and make you eat them for dinner.'

If it was possible for Julius to go any paler, he did. 'If you stopped for any length of time, or left the road, we had orders to kill you.' Serpentius removed the dagger and the boy dropped his head.

'Now that wasn't so difficult, was it?' The Spaniard brought the haft of the knife round in a vicious backhand swipe that hammered into the young man's temple. Julius dropped like a stone and Serpentius turned to Valerius. 'What now?'

'You should have cut their throats,' the Spaniard complained.

'I gave my oath to the Emperor. I don't think I'd be honouring it if I went around killing people who were following his orders.'

Serpentius grunted and urged his mount up the steep gradient. They were crossing the rocky spine of Italia by now, with frost in the air and chills all around, but tomorrow they would begin the downhill journey to the sea. 'They could come after us. Someone will release them sooner or later.'

'After what you did to the boy?'

'I have a feeling he's tougher than he looks.'

Valerius nodded absently. 'But his friend will know he talked. They sense these things. If we're lucky, they will cut each other's throats.'

The Spaniard acknowledged the possibility. 'You still haven't explained why the Emperor should send men to spy on us.'

'Because Otho thinks it's a suicide mission, and normal people would be reluctant to offer their necks to the sword. Every Emperor is suspicious of his own mother, and with reason, if you remember Agrippina. Otho has been in power for less than a month. He trusts no one.'

'So much for your oath.' Serpentius went quiet for a while. 'Are you saying we're not normal?'

The rock-strewn hillsides echoed with their laughter.

XXIII

They rested for a day at Fanum because Valerius's wound was acting up but next morning he felt fit enough to take the Via Aemilia towards Ariminum, with the hills a constant presence to their left, the misty grey of their peaks combining with leaden cloud to make land and sky a single claustrophobic entity. As they rode further north, Valerius felt the atmosphere around them change very gradually. It wasn't something in the air, but in the people they passed. Faces that had been indifferent became first wary, then openly fearful. Beyond Bononia the road reached out into a flat plain of rich, dark-earthed farmland. Yet despite the evident prosperity they met few fellow travellers, apart from local farmers who scurried away when they saw them, and they found every door and window shuttered and closed against them. Valerius said it was as if they were approaching the heart of a plague-hit province. At the outer reaches the fear was little more than a shadow, but the closer you got to the centre the more it took form, until it materialized as a traveller dying by inches at the roadside or the disturbed earth of a new-filled grave. They found one Imperial way station closed and seemingly abandoned, and by the time they reached Regium Lepidum their animals were close to breaking down.

'If we can't change the horses here, we'll end up carrying them,' Serpentius complained.

The staging post at Regium formed part of an auxiliary cavalry base on the outskirts of the town. By now they were well used to the nitpicking pedants in charge of these places: petty officials who studied every word of the warrant, seeking a mistake that would allow them to refuse two mere civilians. This one was no different. The gate guard led them to a sour-breathed ex-legionary seated at a wooden table beneath a rough shelter overlooking the post's exercise ground and horse lines. The man had a suspicious cast to his eyes Valerius didn't like, and a wariness beyond the usual bureaucratic temporizing.

'From Rome, eh?' The clerk sniffed and threw the warrant back across the tabletop. 'Not worth the paper it's written on. First Nero, then Galba, now this Otho, and who's to say he's still the Emperor, eh? Or that whoever signed this is still in a position to enforce it? We hear there's a new man, the governor of Germania, and he has the legions to back up his claim. It would be more than my job's worth to hand out horses on the strength of this. Why should I risk that?'

'Because if you don't I'll personally ram it down your throat,' Serpentius pointed out cheerfully.

The man glanced towards the exercise ground, where two stable boys were collecting manure.

Valerius shook his head. 'My friend here would eat them alive.' He looked around the outpost and the depleted horse lines. 'The post seems very quiet. Just a few guards and no one on the parade ground. That's unusual in a cavalry fort. Who garrisons this place?'

Normally, the official wouldn't have submitted, but the times weren't normal. The thin one with the scarred head looked well capable of carrying out his threat, even if Didius and Philo intervened, which they wouldn't. Traders, the warrant said . . . 'Perhaps I can spare you a couple of remounts,' he said carefully, pointing to the rail where his spare horses were tethered. 'Take the two closest to us.'

Valerius nodded to Serpentius, and the Spaniard went to check the animals, which turned out to be a pair of bow-backed, short-legged specimens fit only for pack duty and as worn out as the mounts they had arrived on. 'I think I'll take a look at these.' He pointed to the far end of the lines where a dozen or so fitter-looking cavalry horses stood with their noses in bags of hay.

The man rose from his chair in protest. 'They—'

'You didn't answer my question.' Valerius pushed him back into his seat.

'Two troops of the Ala Siliana . . .'

So that was why the man was so nervous. The Ala Siliana had served under Vitellius when he was proconsul in Africa. Valerius, as his military adviser, had led them on punitive expeditions against the tribes in the hills south of Thevesitis, and ridden with them again in Egypt when they had been sent there as part of Titus Vespasian's cavalry forces. Vitellius and the Siliana's commander Tiberius Rubrio had been friends, and if the governor of Germania Inferior was looking for a powerful ally in Italia, Rubrio was the man he would turn to.

'And where are they now?'

The administrator shrugged hopelessly. How had he become trapped up to his stupid neck in politics? He was only an insignificant bureaucrat whose sole joy was to make life difficult for people even less significant than himself. 'They rode north the day after they heard Vitellius's army was marching. They said Rome only has one Emperor, Aulus Vitellius, and I should remember that if I knew what was good for me. I didn't know what else to do.'

Valerius ignored the self-pitying whine. 'You say Vitellius's army is on the move? Where and when?' he demanded.

'I don't know for certain, but one of the troopers let slip that they were heading in the direction of Augusta Taurinorum.'

Valerius left him at the table, a small man overwhelmed by events he did not understand, but who could see trouble on the horizon as clearly as if it were a storm cloud. The two stable boys were preparing the horses Serpentius had chosen and loading the replacement pack animal.

He explained the situation to the Spaniard. 'If what he says is true, Rubrio will have ordered his cavalry to prepare the ground for his old comrade from Africa. They'll scout the length of the Padus valley and the mountain passes west of Segusio that control the road to Gaul, and try to work out which units will stay loyal to Otho and who will support Vitellius. Augusta Taurinorum means his main force is advancing down the Rhodanus.' He frowned. 'I would have thought he'd have waited another month, but I suppose it makes a kind of sense to act before Otho can gather his strength, even if conditions aren't perfect.'

'Does that mean we go back to Rome?'

Valerius thought it over. They could return and present the information to Otho, but some instinct told him that, even though his army was on the move, Vitellius himself would remain at Colonia for the moment. Winter campaigning might be fine for his legions, but the man who would be Emperor would wait in comfort a few more weeks. He shook his head.

'If this fool,' he nodded towards the administrator, 'knows Vitellius's legions are marching, Otho will already have heard from the governors of Belgica or Gallia Narbonensis. I think we can do more good by carrying on. We'll push north and try to get past Placentia the night after next. If we stay clear of any troops we see, it will avoid any awkward questions.'

Before they left Regium, Valerius wrote out a dispatch for the Emperor, telling him what they had heard and that they would continue north. 'Whether it will get through, or if he'll act on it even if it does, is another matter, but maybe it will confirm someone else's information. Who knows, he might even call off his hunting dogs?'

He calculated that it would take two days to reach Placentia and a further two to reach Mediolanum, where he would have a decision to make. The two main routes through the Alps depended on the high passes being open, and that was his greatest concern. He hoped to discover which, if either, was the more feasible. If he had a preference, it would be for the northern route, which he'd studied before he left Rome. It would take them by a safe road to Bilitio and then Curia, through the tribal lands of the Suanetes and the Caluci, and far enough from events in Germania for those tribes to be untouched by the conflict. But Valerius recognized that he might have no option but to take the westerly path. That would lead them to the eastern shore of Lacus Lemanus; too close to the advance of Vitellius's legions for comfort. Either way, they would need a trustworthy guide who could be relied on to keep his mouth shut. The mountains were already visible as a hazy blue line on the far horizon, and he knew that despite the unseasonably mild weather on the plain the conditions would be very different in the high valleys. They would need winter clothing and to replenish their supplies, with little prospect of doing so until they reached the land of the Helvetii.

They rode in silence for another mile; then, without a word, Serpentius handed the leading rein of the pack horse to Valerius and turned his own mount round. Valerius watched him go and felt the hair rise on the back of his neck. By now he knew trouble when he saw it. The Spaniard was gone for an hour before he caught up.

'We should camp by the road tonight. I do not think we have time to make the next town by dark.'

They exchanged glances and Valerius nodded. A few miles further ahead they found an open clearing in an olive grove close to the road. Valerius used flint and iron to light a fire and they cooked a legionary's supper of porridge and bacon over the meagre flames, washed down with wine, of which Serpentius swallowed more than his fair share. The Spaniard began to talk loudly of their time in Africa and then roared out a legionary marching song of more obscenity than originality, urging Valerius to join in with the chorus. Valerius caught his mood and they sang and talked until the fire burned low. They set their blankets in the shadow of an ancient olive, leaving saddles and pack close to the glowing ashes. It was their second day of pushing hard and Valerius's rough bed had never been more welcome. He closed his eyes.

When he opened them he took a moment to realize where he was. The ashes were dead, but the cloud-veiled moon provided what might be called light and created a tangle of contorted shape and shade below the olive branches. On the far side of the clearing something moved, something as swift and silent as a hunting leopard. Serpentius? But the Spaniard's bed was where he had set it, with the shape of a man clearly defined by his blanket. The shadow moved again and now Valerius lost sight of it. His hand went to his sword, but he knew that whoever was hunting him had the advantage. The last thing he would know was the flash of dull iron in the moonlight and the sting of a blade at his throat. His eyes tried to drill into the night, and in a fleeting patch of lighter gloom there it was, slipping menacingly through the darkness towards him. Even as he watched, a second shadow seemed to sprout from the ground at the feet of the silent attacker. A flurry of movement followed and the two figures merged into one, wrestling and falling to the ground. Valerius rushed towards the struggling mass even as one of the shadows raised an arm ready to plunge his knife into the other. His arm snapped out by pure instinct and the man gave an awful cry as the point of the sword speared into his spine. As he slumped forward Valerius pulled the sword free and stepped back, shaking.

A wiry figure hauled himself free from beneath the shuddering body.

'How did you know it wasn't me?' Serpentius's voice held no hint of how close to death he'd just come.

Valerius could find no answer. The truth was that he'd reacted without conscious thought. Only the gods would ever know why he had struck. He stood on shaking legs above the man he had killed. Serpentius tossed him a wicked-looking curved dagger that glinted in the dull light.

'The boy?' the Roman choked.

'I must be getting slow,' Serpentius sighed. 'At least he was alone. Better this way. He would never have given up: it was in his eyes. He was that kind of man.'

'We humiliated him. Maybe that was a mistake.'

The veteran gladiator snorted. 'His mistake. It wasn't the humiliation or the pain that made him come. It was because he talked. His pride couldn't bear that.'

Valerius stared down at the handsome young face that was already losing its definition against the bones of the skull. 'We should bury him.'

Serpentius ignored the remark and wrapped himself in his blanket. 'He can wait until morning. He isn't going anywhere.' When Valerius didn't move, the Spaniard sat up. 'Go to sleep, Valerius. It's going to be a long day tomorrow and the day after and the day after that. And don't waste your time mourning the boy. I have a feeling he won't be the last corpse we see before we're done.'

XXIV

It was still early when they reached the next town. In the middle distance they could see a queue of animals, carts and people at the gates. Valerius drew up his horse and pulled the map of Imperial staging posts from the knapsack tied to his saddle.

'This must be Parma.' He frowned. 'What do you think?'

'Looks like some sort of checkpoint. They'll be questioning everybody who enters. Could be a patrol from the Ala Siliana, or maybe the town has declared for Otho and they're keeping the rebels out. Friend or enemy doesn't really matter. We don't want to get involved.'

They turned off to the right, through anonymous nut-brown fields criss-crossed by trackways and drainage ditches, avoiding the rough huts, farmsteads and occasional small villas that dotted the fertile countryside. Valerius studied the landscape around them. Away from the Via Aemilia the country was free of the threat posed by the bigger garrison towns. Politics and war held no sway here, only the all-encompassing, unbreakable cycle of the seasons and the weather. He felt the gait of his mount alter as its hooves pushed into the soft earth and the bitter-sweet scent of the soil filled his nostrils. The very land exuded a kind of eternal peace that he prayed would never be broken by the armies gathering beyond the western and southern horizons. East, too, because by now Otho's messengers would have reached the legions in Noricum, Pannonia, Dalmatia and Moesia and it could only be days before they marched to meet the threat from Vitellius's army.

Serpentius caught his mood. 'It's good to be away from the road for a while.'

Valerius smiled. 'Yes, but don't be fooled. This tranquillity is deceptive. Somewhere not far from here land just like this was fertilized by the blood and bones of thousands of legionaries who marched north to stop Hannibal's advance on Rome. They failed, but their sacrifice was not wasted, because the delay and the freezing weather killed off all but one of the Carthaginian war elephants.'

Serpentius made the sign to ward off evil; the nearest he would ever come to showing fear.

Without warning, a hole appeared in the previously unbroken layer of cloud blanketing the sky above them and for a few seconds a shaft of sunlight burst through to turn some hamlet on the far horizon into a glittering jewel. For no reason, an image of two towns they would pass on the way north appeared in Valerius's head as they had on the map he had studied less than an hour before. Cremona and Placentia had been founded as military camps to protect Italy from the Celtic tribes of what was now Gallia Transpadana, the lands between the Padus and the Alps. It struck him that, along with the river that divided them, they formed a kind of intricate brooch that held the four corners of the Empire together; a Celtic knot that had to be unravelled before any invader could enter the Roman heartland from north, west or east. Vitellius would have to untie that knot if he wanted to secure the purple. Unless Valerius could persuade him to accept Otho's offer the Rhenus legions would be marching this way, and it was possible that here on this rich plain the future of Rome would be decided. He felt a physical pain at the thought. Was it not enough that they had risked everything to rid the world of Nero? Now Romans must suffer for the greed and ambition of his successors. A kind of hardness developed inside him, as if a stone grew to fill his belly and chest. Gaius Valerius Verrens had never shirked a challenge, but this was his greatest test. He had to succeed, because if he did not war was coming. A war that would divide friends. A war between brother and brother. The worst kind of war. Civil war.

By the time they sighted Placentia Valerius's legs chafed against his mount's flanks and man and beast were weary beyond measure. Even Serpentius rode slumped in the saddle. They had little option but to enter the city, if only to replenish their supplies and seek fresh horses. But the lure of a bed after days of having the cold earth clawing through their blankets and into their bones provided an added incentive. Dusk was falling when they reached the town, which guarded the only crossing point on the Padus for twenty miles and was surrounded by stout walls that showed recent signs of repair. As they made their way to the entrance, Valerius noticed Serpentius cast a sour glance at the city's amphitheatre, a massive wooden structure that dominated the cluster of streets beyond the original city boundary. The former gladiator had fought for his life in a dozen stadiums like it and his friend reflected that it was no surprise he had little love for such places or the people who frequented them. The heavy wooden gates had already been barred and a decurion stepped sharply from a rough hut in the shadow of the twin towers that flanked them. Four spearmen appeared at his back and raw, suspicious eyes looked the two strangers over. Valerius saw the grip on each spear tighten when the men noticed the Imperial brand on their horses.

'Your names and your business?'

'Gaius Valerius Verrens, on the road to Mediolanum, and this is my freedman, Serpentius of Avala. We seek a room for the night.'

The decurion had the lined face of a man who'd been forced to make too many tough decisions lately. He studied the Spaniard, taking in whipcord muscles and the menace in the dark eyes. 'Freedman, eh?'

Valerius shrugged. 'These are dangerous times. Even a humble trader in wheat and barley needs protection. We are on our way to negotiate a price for the next harvest with the farming commune of Claudius Cornelius, though I fear our timing could be better.'

'I'll grant you that,' the soldier agreed. 'But still I cannot allow you entry until I know where your loyalty lies.'

'A trader doesn't concern himself with politics, only with profit,' Valerius said airily. 'But Marcus Salvius Otho was still Emperor when I left Rome, and it is in his name this travel warrant is signed.' He handed over the paper and the decurion studied it. 'Will that suffice?'

'It will suffice here.' He waved at one of the spearmen to open the gate. 'But it would have got you in trouble had you used it at Cremona, where we hear loyalties are confused; or in Mediolanum where they have already declared for the false Emperor, Vitellius; aye, and at Novaria, Vercelae and Eporedia, too, may the gods curse them.'

219

'Is that how it stands throughout Gallia Transpadana?'

'A little more or a little less,' the decurion said thoughtfully. 'We had a squadron of auxiliary cavalry pass through less than a week ago. Their officer demanded Placentia swear its allegiance to Vitellius and damn the killer of old men, Otho. But the men of Placentia know their duty. The Senate and people of Rome made us; sent six thousand veterans to carve out a home here on the Padus, gave them land and the means to work it.' His eyes met Valerius's and challenged him to deny it. 'They were our forefathers. They, and they who came after, paid the price often enough in blood and fire, but we acknowledge their debt. The Senate and people of Rome proclaimed Marcus Salvius Otho Augustus Emperor and it is Marcus Salvius Otho Augustus who has our oath.' He stepped back to allow a young family to pass through the gate carrying what looked like their entire possessions on their back. The grizzled features lost a little of their certainty. 'That officer will have made the same demand of any number of places and more forcefully to the weak than to the strong. Some will have obliged him and meant it, others not – there has been smoke on the horizon where smoke should not be – but most will be like those fornicating bastards in Cremona and pledge their oath to whoever wants it at any given time.'

Valerius thanked him for the information, and enquired his name so he could show his thanks at a happier time. The decurion only grinned. 'As you say, master merchant, these are dangerous times, and in dangerous times things can come back to cause a man pain, even his name. If it pleases you to suggest an extra wine ration for the first century of the town watch, then that is your business. For your kindness I will venture another. A word of advice. The way north was safe enough when it was patrolled by loyal auxiliary cavalry, but that is no longer the case. Beyond the river most of the land is still untamed swamp and forest. Out of sight of the road it is the realm of bandits, thieves and escaped gladiators; outcasts who answer to no man and would cut your throat for the price of that patched cloak you wear. Join a larger group if you can, but, if not, be wary.' He nodded, his advice given. 'If you want lodgings for the night you could do worse than seek out the Fat Sturgeon. It's on the far side of the city – the river side – past the street of the silversmiths, but worth the walk if a man likes his wine sweet and bread that won't break his teeth.'

They led their horses through the gate and into the narrow streets, with their close-ranked tenement blocks and reeking gutters. Thanks to the guard officer's directions they found the inn and discovered the way station nearby, just outside the walls of the fort that dominated the centre of the town. As they passed the fort's gate a century of Gaulish auxiliaries marched out, presumably to relieve the guard manning Placentia's walls. The fort, of a size that would be garrisoned by two cohorts, was sturdily constructed in red brick and confirmed what the man had said: this was a military town, built to withstand invasion and siege. The Gauls were garrison troops and garrison duty had a habit of dulling the senses, but Valerius noticed that these soldiers were hard-eyed and alert and they kept their weapons keen. There were other signs for a man who could read them. Even this late in the day, the streets of the city rang with the clatter of hammer on anvil and the familiar whispering song of a whetstoned sword being given a proper edge. As the two men stabled their horses a cart rumbled past filled with massive boulders. They exchanged glances. Someone had tried to disguise catapult ammunition as building stones, but had not quite succeeded.

'Looks as if they're expecting proper trouble,' Serpentius said.

'It was like this in Colonia before the rebel queen came calling, but I think they are better prepared.'

'Let's hope so.' The Spaniard spat in the direction of a mangy tan mongrel that had strayed too close, but his hard eyes softened as a young woman hurried by with two small children. 'I recall that things didn't end too well for the people in your Colonia. Maybe we should just change horses and move on. It would be foolish to wake up surrounded by our enemies.'

Valerius shook his head. 'I think we're safe enough for now. The houses outside the walls have been prepared for demolition, but the people are still in them. If Vitellius's legions come this way there'll be plenty of warning.'

XXV

Water had shaped the land north of the river, the decurion had said, and as they rode through a damp, clinging fog it sometimes seemed their world was entirely liquid. The road was solid enough, raised like a narrow causeway above the surrounding countryside, but to right and left lay nothing but bog and stunted briar; glittering, slime-laden pools pitting mud as black as Hades' hellhound and circled by noisome plants of silver-slicked green. The air stank of decay and unwholesomeness as if somewhere in the ooze a great fish had become stranded and was slowly rotting away, its putrefying flesh tainting all around it. The only sound, apart from the unearthly shriek of an occasional water fowl, was the low thud of their horses' hooves on the hard-packed gravel.

Serpentius shivered and wrapped his cloak tighter around him. 'Two days of this?'

'It won't improve much before Mediolanum,' Valerius admitted. 'But it will look better when the fog lifts.'

'I should have been born a frog.'

'Our biggest problem will be finding somewhere to bed down. The landlord of the inn said there is a *mansio*, but I'd rather not use it unless we have to.'

'The alternative might be a lily pad.'

Valerius laughed. 'A man who was born in a snow-drift should have no problem with sleeping in a puddle.'

But the humour soon faded. Valerius's prediction that the fog would clear was unlikely to be realized, and so it proved. Riding through the relentless murk placed a strain on man and beast alike. True, the fog hid them from potential enemies, but the opposite was also true, and the sense of threat was ever present. Valerius and Serpentius were not nervous men, but every shadow and every sound posed a potential danger and living on the edge for hour after hour takes its toll on any man's nerves. At one point, Serpentius waved Valerius to a halt because he was convinced he could hear the sound of horses somewhere behind them. After a short but tense wait nothing materialized and they moved on, but their ears continued to play tricks. Was the splash away to their left a leaping fish or a duck taking flight, or someone moving parallel to them through the swamp? Was that the murmur of voices or the burbling of a stream flowing into one of the innumerable lakes they passed? It was impossible to tell. Yet each threat had to be taken seriously and each cost them time. It quickly became clear that, even if they had chosen to, they wouldn't reach the *mansio* before nightfall. Valerius turned to his companion. 'We need to find somewhere to camp.'

'It'll have to be close by the road, then.' Serpentius threw a look of disgust at the swamp. 'One wrong step and we might never get back to it.'

A mile further and the landscape remained nothing but bog and pond and it was beginning to look as if the only place they'd be able to make a bed was in the road-side ditch with their feet in the water.

'Maybe we should—'

'Listen!' Serpentius drew his sword and Valerius strained his ears for the sound that had alerted the Spaniard. Faint, just a whisper on the wind, but when the mind made sense of it, unmistakable.

'A woman crying,' he whispered. 'Here?'

Serpentius shrugged, wary as a hunted deer hearing the distant bay of the hounds. 'It came from up ahead.' His expression said they could either stand around like idiots waiting for whoever it was to go away or do something about it.

'I'll lead; you hang back.' Valerius ignored Serpentius's angry shake of the head and kicked his mare slowly into motion, drawing his sword and carrying it low by the horse's side. With each nervous step he scoured the impenetrable, puffball curtain of swirling fog. In vain. All he could make out was drifting shadows and ethereal, indistinct shapes, any one of which could hide an enemy. His mount hesitated, but the sound of harsh female sobbing raked Valerius's brain like a steel spike and he urged her forward.

After an eternity, a vague form emerged from the misty curtain ahead and he drew the mare to a halt. Tall and slim and wearing a dress of brown drab beneath her cloak, she clutched a swathed bundle to her breast and her shoulders shook with the power of her anguish. When she looked up he was surprised to see how young she was – and how beautiful. She raised a hand to her mouth in alarm when she saw the mounted figure approaching.

'I mean you no harm,' he said hastily. 'Where is your husband – your protector?'

She swayed and he thought she might collapse, but she collected herself and after two attempts found the composure to speak, her voice shaking with emotion.

'May Venus preserve you, master. My husband left two hours since, after our pony foundered. He said he would return soon with a new beast to carry little Gaius and me, but I fear something has happened to him.' The sobbing began again and he hushed her, preparing to dismount, but before he could move she staggered forward to the mare's left flank and clutched at his leg.

He saw the moment her eyes widened when she noticed the sword in his left hand, the feral snarl that changed her face from beautiful to ugly as she dropped the cloth-wrapped bundle to stab the long knife it had hidden towards his groin. He had a momentary thrill of pure horror as the blade plunged towards his body. In battle he had seen men bleed out in seconds from such a wound and he knew there was no surviving it. He twisted desperately in the saddle, but it was the horse that saved him, rearing up in fright so the point missed its mark and slammed into the leather-covered wooden saddle. As the girl struggled to haul the knife free, he lashed out with his foot, raking her with the iron studs of his *caliga* sandal, until she staggered away screaming with blood on her face. But even as she'd struck the mist had filled with shadowy figures who now converged on him, howling. Ragged men, thieves and outcasts had set the girl as bait, and like a fool he had snapped at it. Before he could react he found himself surrounded by rusty blades of every shape and size, each as potentially lethal as a well-sharpened sword. He knew that against these numbers his most effective weapon was speed and he kicked his mount forward to batter another knife-wielding figure aside, slashing widely to his left and feeling the fleshy crunch as edged metal bit home. The satisfaction was short lived, because it was clear this fight could only have one ending. Then, as Valerius

226

prepared to welcome death, Serpentius galloped out of the mist screaming his war cry and smashing his enemies aside, the heavy cavalry *spatha* cutting right and left in disciplined sweeping arcs that struck terror into the men who faced him.

'Ride, Valerius!'

The Spaniard's unexpected appearance froze Valerius's attackers and he used the breathing space to carve an avenue through them. Just when it looked as if he was clear he felt hands grabbing at his cloak and a lithe figure leapt up behind him on to the horse's back, long, dirt-caked nails clawing at his eyes and teeth snapping at his neck. The reaction was automatic. He reversed the *spatha* with a gladiator-taught flick and plunged it into his nemesis's body. A terrible high-pitched shriek pierced him as his assailant fell away and he had a momentary vision of dark eyes wide with horror as the girl bounced on the gravel roadway. With a surge of relief he found himself alone in the mist. Serpentius should have been a heartbeat behind, but when he looked back the Spaniard was nowhere to be seen. Even as the knowledge scarred his brain he heard the unearthly scream of a horse in its death throes. He roared a cry of fear and frustration and turned his mount, hurling her back the way they'd come.

As Valerius burst from the mist a single glance took in the scene. Serpentius's horse was down with a spear in its ribs and the Spaniard's leg trapped beneath its heaving body. Around the dying beast at least half a dozen of their ambushers slashed at the former gladiator with spears and knives. The only reason he still lived was that the others had been diverted by the pack horse he'd led, more interested in booty than in blood. From the corner of his eye Valerius saw the spear shaft that flicked out to trip his mount and that split second's warning allowed him to kick himself free as she went down. The fall took him into a tumbling roll that carried him towards the stricken Spaniard, though every revolution was a torment of crushed and torn flesh. Half stunned, he stumbled to his feet, sword in left hand, and chopped down a bearded figure who stood between him and Serpentius.

'Fool.' The gladiator lunged at a spearman who tried to take advantage of the distraction, drawing a howl as his sword hacked away a careless finger. 'You were free. You should have ridden on.'

'If we're going to die, we die together.' Valerius slashed wildly at two snarling figures who were manoeuvring to take him in the flank.

'I don't intend to die.'

But both knew the decision was not theirs to take.

More bandits appeared from the mist, until the two men were surrounded by twenty or thirty feral figures: an entire tribe of mud-streaked men and women with wild hair, hungry eyes and screaming, gap-toothed mouths. Male or female, they were all armed, and they blocked the road to north and south. With Serpentius at his side Valerius could have cut his way out and spilled enough guts to discourage pursuit. But the Spaniard remained trapped, and unless he could find some way to free him they were both dead. Already, a hulk of a man, previously occupied with plunder, was beating his compatriots forward with his spear butt, urging them to slaughter the two interlopers. Serpentius kicked desperately at his fallen mount, at the same time hacking at enemies who were becoming ever more confident. For every bandit they killed, two took their place. Valerius found himself fighting on three sides and only lived because of the speed of a sword arm that was tiring fast.

He cried out and fell back as a spear ripped the top of his shoulder and he found himself lying beside Serpentius as the eager blades sought out their throats.

The Spaniard's hand clutched at his wooden fist and he knew it was over.

Then the trumpet blew.

XXVI

'You were foolish to travel this road alone.'

Valerius stayed silent, still uncertain whether he could trust the grave young man who had saved their lives. Foolish or desperate, the end would have been the same if the auxiliary cavalry squadron hadn't arrived to scatter the bandit tribe screaming into the mist.

'There was no point in following them,' the soldier went on. 'The swamps are their rats' nest. A fool to tempt them, but a bigger fool to fight them on their own ground.'

Massaging the leather stock where his wooden hand met the stump of his wrist, Valerius nodded to acknowledge the truth of the second statement and the admonition in the first. He could still feel the sting of the spear point slicing the flesh of his shoulder, but the wound had turned out to be superficial. The auxiliary unit's *medicus* had cleaned it thoroughly and thought it unlikely to mortify, which was little short of miraculous given the festering source of the weapon that caused it. They sat by the open fire while the young man's troopers bedded down eight to a room in the cramped accommodation offered by the *mansio*. A few paces away Serpentius lay back on a couch covered in a blanket with his injured foot raised. His eyes were closed, but Valerius knew the Spaniard would be listening to every word. The officer's eyes said he knew it also.

'You are a man of few words for a merchant. I usually find them somewhat garrulous. And then,' his gaze drifted to Valerius's sleeve, 'there is your wooden hand; the mark I was told would identify the man I sought.'

The words were casual enough, but both men understood the threat they contained. Valerius kept his expression blank, but inside his heart hammered at his ribs like a wild beast trapped in a pen. He saw Serpentius tense beneath the blanket. Fight or flight. The appraising glint in the cavalryman's eyes told him bluff wasn't an option. In fact, the officer appeared remarkably relaxed for someone who had just passed what could be a death sentence on two very dangerous men. The troopers' insignia identified them as a *turma* of the Ala Siliana, the Thracian auxiliary unit Valerius had been told had already rejected Otho's claim to the purple. These men were paving the way for Aulus Vitellius's army to march on Rome. Why save the lives of two dangerous enemies? The answer was simple and likely to be very painful. Valerius had counted the Siliana's commander Tiberius Rubrio a friend, but with an Empire at stake friendship meant little, and if Rubrio wanted information he would go to any lengths to get it. Fight then, Valerius thought wearily. Better to go down like a lion than a lamb.

The young cavalry commander recognized the moment of decision. His hand fumbled beneath the cloak at his side and Valerius prepared to throw himself at the sword. What appeared was an innocuous leather document case of a type Valerius had seen many times. He forced himself to relax as the other man continued.

'Not all of us believe Vitellius is our rightful Emperor. Aurelius Dasius, decurion of the third *turma* of Ala Siliana,' the soldier introduced himself, 'and as of last night commander of the Emperor Otho's cavalry in the north,' he waved at the sleeping men beyond the flickering shadows of firelight, 'which currently amounts to thirty-two auxiliaries. When Rubrio declared for Vitellius two weeks ago, I persuaded my troop that there was a more certain way to gain a reward than the promises of plunder he gave: to abide by the oath we swore to the Senate and people of Rome. Word came yesterday that a one-armed man would be travelling north and should be offered what protection we could give. It was fortunate that we heard news of your departure from Placentia. Even so, we were almost too late.'

'But you were in time. Gaius Valerius Verrens.' Valerius rose and offered his wooden right hand. Dasius hesitated just for a second before taking it. 'And for that we are grateful.'

The Thracian brought his face closer, so the Roman could see the premature lines brought on by fatigue and strain. His voice lowered to a whisper, which indicated to Valerius that either Dasius was rightly cautious or, more worryingly, he didn't trust his men as much as he would like.

'Our orders are to escort you as far north as possible without compromising your mission, though that decision is at your discretion. I should add that under Rubrio I took responsibility for the security of these parts, out to the hill country beyond Mediolanum, and have knowledge of the area that might be useful to you.'

Valerius nodded to indicate he understood – understood, but had not agreed. Not yet. He shifted his seat and winced as a pain shot through his injured shoulder. There was a balance to be struck here. On one side of the scales lay the weighty certainty that the tactic of posing as merchants, which had served them well enough in Italia proper, would not protect them in this wild place. In fact, it made them a target. Neither was there any guarantee that two men could fight their way through against the kind of odds they had faced earlier. Death held no fears for Gaius Valerius Verrens, but he had begun to believe that Serpentius was indestructible. The fight with the swamp bandits had proved the lie in that. The truth was that without Dasius's fully armed veteran cavalry they would have been dead. Yet there would still come a time when invisibility was more important than security; in the wrong place, the Thracians would stand out like a Vestal virgin at a Bacchanalia celebration.

He kept his voice neutral as he gave his decision. 'I will accept your offer to take us past Mediolanum. After that we will see.'

Dasius sniffed, uncertain whether he was being insulted, but Thracian enough to be offended anyway.

'When we reach the city you will have a decision to make. East or north. Brixia or Novum Comun. Brixia is the better road and the passes were certainly open a week ago, but it is Vitellius's country and will bring you closer to my old comrades. The way to Novum Comun is more treacherous, but if we follow the river we will be safe enough. After that . . .' He shrugged. 'I know a reliable guide.'

'Novum Comun then,' Valerius decided, more difficult or not. 'What is the country like there?'

Dasius smiled for the first time. 'That you must see for yourself.'

*

233

Even on a winter's day as washed out as a legionary's ten-year-old tunic it was the most beautiful place Valerius had ever seen. From the southern shore he felt as if he was standing on the edge of a precipice. The sheer walls of the valley that held the lake in its dragon's jaws plunged down to be reflected on the slate-blue mirror of the surface, creating the effect of a giant chasm. All around was metal: tree-lined hillsides the colour of lead sling pellets, clouds shot with pewter, and a sky of burnished iron that changed tone even as he watched, like a sword blade turned in the dawn light, to a hundred shades of grey he had no names for. And, all around, silver. Vast, towering mountains of silver, and beyond them, higher still, another range, and another, that made him feel like an ant at the steps of the Temple of Jupiter Capitolinus. The sheer scale of them sucked all the faith from him.

Dasius saw his look and smiled. 'Do not worry. It is not as daunting as it appears.'

Time and circumstance had made Valerius's decision for him. They were seven now, and the better for it. Enough to give the opportunist bandits who inhabited these mountains pause before attacking, but not so many as to draw unwanted attention. And the remnant was the best of Dasius's dwindling band of cavalry. The rest had dribbled away, like water through a thirsty man's fingers. 'They are *getae* at heart,' the Thracian spat. 'The spawn of thieves and robbers. I thought to keep them from raid, plunder and rapine, but all they sought was a better opportunity. They looked on the plump farms and pretty villas we passed at Mediolanum and saw riches for the taking. And in time of war none to come after them when the deed is done. We are better without them.'

The guide Dasius knew proved to be a wiry hillman, made bulky by the thick furs he wore. He had dark skin the texture of leather and slanting eyes accustomed to peering through blizzards. A Celt, his demeanour was surly, even for that taciturn race, and he had the facial expression of a particularly ugly dog otter. He spoke a dialect that was neither Latin nor any other language Valerius had heard, but Dasius understood enough to exchange simple sentences with him.

'His name is Valtir and he calls himself a prince of the Orobii, who were here before the Romans came and will be here when the Romans are gone. This is his land, but he says he welcomes you as his guest.'

Valerius bowed, smiling at the poetic Celtic combination of insult and courtesy. Valtir's claim to be a prince seemed unlikely, but it gave Valerius an idea. With grave ceremony he handed over the curved knife he had carried from Rome. It was only a kitchen blade for cutting up food, but it would be an improvement on the rusting spike at Valtir's belt. The little Celt tested the point against his thumb and his dour face broke into a grin when it drew blood.

'He says he honours you for his gift. If he'd had a knife like this when he was a young man he would have slit many Roman throats with it.' Dasius darted a worried glance at Valerius, but the one-handed Roman only laughed.

'Tell him I am happy for him, but glad I did not meet him when he was young. Tell him there will be another like it if he takes us where we wish to go.'

With Valtir leading on his sturdy, long-haired pony and each second man trailing a pack horse, they made their way north-west to the lake in the next valley, which if anything was even greater in scale than that on which Novum Comun stood. 'Luanus.' The Celt pointed to a small settlement a mile away on the far side of the mirrored surface, and led them down a precarious path cut into the hillside which eventually reached a small pier with a flat-bottomed boat tied to it. Valtir held a conversation with the boat's owner that sounded for all the world like two terriers snarling at each other over a bone, but eventually it appeared he had agreed a price for ferrying men and horses across. It took them four hours and five trips to transport all eight men and eleven animals, and by the time it was done they had no option but to spend the night in Luanus, a mean little place, but at least it boasted a tavern. Next day they rose and broke their fast with bread, oil and olives, washed down with watered wine, before crossing the ridge behind the town and following a broad river valley north. Here at least there was a road, even if it was in poor repair, with bridges that had been badly mended and potholes deep enough to break an ankle. For the first time in a week the sun shone, the skies cleared and Valerius was left to wonder at the dangerous, majestic glory all around. The mountains did not rise; they soared to unreachable summits where only the gods would ever set foot. Elysium would be like this, he thought, with air so clear that it invigorated even a soul as dark as his and chased away the demons that had haunted him for eight years.

Serpentius saw him grinning. 'You won't be smiling so much when you have to climb them,' he pointed out. Still, the appearance of the sun seemed to reinvigorate them all. The Spaniard broke into an incomprehensible song in his own language that seemed to have nothing approaching a tune and Valerius thought he could *feel* the wound in his shoulder healing.

It was obvious to the others that Valtir was as at home

among these peaks as he was on his lake. His mood changed and he chattered endlessly as he rode, and it seemed even Dasius only understood one word in ten. 'I think he says he has never seen the hills so free of snow at this time of year. But the weather means a greater danger of the thunder god calling the mountains down.' He shrugged. 'More chance of an avalanche.'

Valerius found himself warming to the personable young Thracian. It became clear that Dasius had taken an enormous risk by backing Otho's cause. If the wrong man won this fight, he could lose everything, including his family's hereditary lands on the plains beside the Hebrus river. But that was not why he had made his decision.

'I have visited Rome and seen its glory, and I have seen what war does. It is beyond imagination that those great temples could burn, the statues be torn down or the Forum run with men's blood, yet that is what will happen if we cannot prevent it. Rome is the Empire and Otho was chosen by the people and the Senate of Rome.' He shrugged. 'That is enough for me. I do not know the detail of your mission, but I know that your aims and mine are one, and I will do anything I can to help you succeed.'

With those words he kicked his mount and rode ahead. Serpentius drew up beside Valerius. 'He reminds me of another young pup with a head full of principles.'

Valerius smiled and shook his head sadly. 'There is very little of Tiberius Crescens in Aurelius Dasius,' he said.

'I wasn't thinking of Tiberius. The young man he reminds me of is Publius Sulla.'

As dusk fell they reached the head of a third lake, which Valtir told them was called the Verbanus. Valerius decided not to risk the trading post at Bilitio, where there was the possibility of a military presence of unknown loyalty. Instead, they camped by the lake shore. As the campfire waned, the Thracians chattered sleepily in their own language, their faces visible as pale blurs in the darkness. Serpentius stood guard by the tethered horses and Valerius could hear him singing quietly to them. Valtir sat with his hands round his knees, his dark eyes glittering, wearing a frown of intense concentration. As Valerius watched, he rose and called Dasius. Together they approached the patch of brush where the Roman had laid out his bed.

'Valtir is agitated about something,' the Thracian explained. 'From what I can work out, the high passes to Curia will be open, but he talked to a trader making for Bilitio and there is word of trouble between the Caluci and the Suanetes, the tribes who control the area. The tribune in command of the post is advising anyone travelling that way to wait until he sends a patrol to investigate. It could be a week.'

Valerius suppressed a curse. 'We didn't come all this way to sit on our backsides for a week or turn back. We'll have to risk it.'

Valtir frowned and spat something at the Thracian. Dasius shook his head, but the little Celt waved a finger and pointed east where the skyline stood out as a shark-toothed line of unbroken shadows.

'What does he say?'

'He became very excited. He said he did not understand that you needed to hurry. Curia is the safest route, but there is another path, known only to a few. There is a road, for what it is worth, as far as Airolus, but after that we must leave the valley and take the mountains. It would cut your journey by a week.'

238

Valerius felt a surge of hope. 'Is he sure we can get the horses through?'

Dasius snapped a question and the little man frowned. 'He believes so. He would not have tried it any other year, but he thinks the conditions are right. It will not be easy, but we could reach Augusta Raurica on the Rhenus by the time your friends in Rome have finished celebrating the festival of Lupercalia.'

Valerius met Serpentius's eyes. Mid-Februarius, then another week at most to sail downriver to Colonia. Where Vitellius waited.

XXVII

Colonia

'There are many calls on our manpower, Caesar, but ask what you will.'

Aulus Vitellius Germanicus Imperator studied the ring that was the only solid evidence he was who everyone said he was and tried to think like an Emperor. The *gladius* from the Temple of Mars Ultor remained in its rosewood box on a marble table, unopened. He had not dared look at it since Valens and Caecina had sat in this very room and launched their rebellion in his name.

He raised his head and looked into the expectant eyes of the senior tribune who had travelled from Britannia to formally declare the support of the legions stationed there. What would Divine Julius do? Strip the island and order all available men to his side? But that would mean beginning his reign by relinquishing a province won at a terrible price in Roman blood. No, he would not taint his office and sully his person with such a decision. It would have been less complicated if Nero had not withdrawn the Fourteenth Gemina from Britannia and ordered it to Dalmatia before his demise. That would have made it simple. The Ninth Hispania, never a fortunate unit, could have been left with the Fourteenth to deal with the barbarians and he would have summoned the Second Augusta and the Twentieth, victors over the rebel Queen Boudicca, to his side. Think.

'It will be onerous for you, I know,' he saw the tribune flinch, but kept his voice imperious, 'but I wish you – order you – to move half the strength of the Second, Ninth and Twentieth legions to Londinium, along with an equivalent force of auxiliaries, there to prepare for shipment to Germania at the first possible opportunity.' He waved Asiaticus, his freedman and secretary, forward. 'He will prepare your detailed orders, but in general you may expect the army of Britannia to march to Moguntiacum and from there on Rome, with their Emperor at their head.'

The tribune bowed, but not before Vitellius had recognized his disdain at being made to accept orders, even written ones, from a former slave. A slight curl of the lip also spoke of a lack of respect for an Emperor whose girth exceeded his military experience by a factor of two.

When he was alone he felt an enormous weight of expectation and helplessness descend upon his shoulders. He closed his eyes. Sitting in the self-imposed darkness he realized how blind he was to events elsewhere, especially in Rome. By now Galba would be aware of his intentions and gathering his legions from the Danuvius and the East to meet the threat. Thanks to the rivalry between his two commanders, Vitellius's army was split. Unless they could combine they would be crushed. Belatedly, his intuition told him he should have ordered a single unstoppable thrust, but there was nothing he could do about it now. There was only one answer.

'Food,' he shouted. 'Bring me food.'

Every dispatch he received from Valens and Caecina contained less information than the one before, and the intelligence from his spies had dried up. If only he knew what was happening.

Gaius Fabius Valens, commander of the western arm of Vitellius's forces, spat to try to rid himself of the taste of roasting flesh that seemed to coat his tongue and infuse the very air he breathed. The stink of freshly shed blood would stay with him much longer. Damn those Batavian savages. The mounds of burning wood and thatch around him had two hours earlier been the city of Divodurum, capital of the Mediomatrici, a Celtic tribe who had cheerfully prospered under Roman rule for more than a hundred years, but had been momentarily confused as to where their loyalty should lie. Valens had no doubt it could have been negotiated in Vitellius's favour. What he had not known, and what he should have been informed of, was that a long-standing quarrel between the Mediomatrici and their Batavian neighbours had never been properly resolved. When the chief of the tribe hesitated on being faced with a choice between Otho and Vitellius, the eight Batavian cohorts attached to Valens' column had swarmed through Divodurum like a pack of hungry wolves. Now the chief's head was on a spear planted in the city's main square and his people, men, women and children – four thousand at least – were either roasting in the glowing embers of their homes or lying in bloody pieces on its streets. He felt a clenching in his guts and gave a little grunt of pain. This atrocity could have one of two outcomes. Either the rest of the tribe would take their revenge on the Vitellian column – ambushes and delaying tactics, which would cost him casualties he could not afford and time he could afford even less – or word would spread of the terrible consequences of defying Vitellius, with the effect of hastening his passage.

He decided he would sacrifice to Mars for the second outcome. Until now, the gods had been kind. He had marched from Castra Bonnensis on the Rhenus to Divodurum at the headwaters of the Mosella in five days with the Fifth Alaudae at his back. They'd been followed by almost three thousand men apiece from his own faithful First Germanica, the Fifteenth Primigenia and the Sixteenth legion. For three of those days a large bird had been seen shadowing the column and the cry had gone up that it was an eagle, an omen of the greatest consequence because every man here followed the eagle standard of his legion. Valens thought it more likely to be a carrion bird of some sort searching out the inevitable detritus left by twenty-odd thousand men, but he kept his opinion to himself. He considered the journey that still faced him. From the Mosella they would go south to Cabillonum and from there take ship down the Rhodanus to Lugdunum; a veritable highway of rivers. If Fortuna smiled there would be no need for another bloodbath like this, but one way or another he had resolved that an example must be made. He looked towards the south gateway of the city, which had somehow survived the incendiary ravages of the Batavians.

'Septimus!' His chief of staff saluted and Valens gave his order in a low voice. 'Choose three ringleaders from each of the Batavian cohorts. I want them tried and condemned and hanged from the gate by noon. We have no more time to waste on this.'

When the tribune had marched off shouting his orders,

Valens reflected that he would give the Batavians the honour of leading the column from the city. When they marched through the gateway they would have plenty of time to contemplate the dangling consequences of their victory. Speed, he thought; I must make more speed. I must cross into Italia before that untrustworthy whoreson Caecina emerges from the Alps. And what is Galba doing to oppose us? I would have expected confrontation, or at least to have seen scouting patrols.

He had his answer the next day. An exhausted courier rode up to the headquarters tent on a blown, foam-flecked horse. It took him three attempts before he could deliver his message in a voice made breathless by the enormity of it.

'The usurper Servius Sulpicius Galba is dead. Marcus Salvius Otho has been declared Emperor.'

The news hit Valens like a hammer blow. Had it all been for nothing? Just for a moment his mind was overwhelmed by dread, before the fear subsided and he could see clearly again. No, there was hope yet. The tortoise had been replaced not by the hare, but by the rabbit.

Speed. He needed more speed.

Aulus Caecina Alienus stared out over the battlefield. It was not meant to be like this. He had ridden ahead to brief the commander of the elite Legio XXI Rapax, which would form the core of his army, on his duties. Instead, he had discovered that the legionaries of the Rapax had already started a war. At first he had experienced near panic at this loss of control before the campaign had even started, but gradually he rediscovered calm. Caecina was a reluctant rebel, driven to insurrection by his fear of the deranged Valens, and the unfortunate discovery by Servius Sulpicius Galba of his borrowings from the treasury of Baetica. He had been brought up to believe that it was a Roman patrician's duty to use the blood and sweat of his province to become a rich man. How was he to know that this only applied to governors and proconsuls, not a lowly *quaestor* made drunk by the fumes of his own power and led astray by hands as venal as his own? Galba it was who had raised him to the heady heights of legionary legate at the unheard-of age of twenty-nine. Galba it was who had been about to strip him of his command, bring him before the courts and destroy him. Now he had gambled his career and his life on a fat man who thought a hero's sword made him a great general and whose only merit in Caecina's eyes was the gullibility that made him so pliable. A curse on Emperors and may Jupiter's arse rain down bolts of lightning on the head of Servius Sulpicius Galba.

'Send in the First and Second cohorts.' The trumpeter winced at the savagery in his commander's voice and put the curved brass horn to his lips. Caecina allowed himself a grim smile. Let the bastards fear him. The stupidity of the First and Second cohorts had begun this; they could finish it. Rather than wait for the supplies from Moguntiacum, they had demanded provisions and gold from the peaceable Helvetii. With their shamans telling them the worst of the winter was still to come, the tribe who had defied Caesar a century earlier refused, and kidnapped a supply column as hostages. A village burned in retaliation. A patrol was butchered. And now the might of the Helvetii stood on the far side of the river, cornered after a fortnight of bloody hide and seek along the Aarus valley. In truth they were a sorry sight in their furs and their rags, defeated before the battle had even begun. But he could not leave a potential enemy in his rear to ambush or delay the men of the Fourth Macedonica and the Twenty-second Primigenia who followed.

'No prisoners,' he ordered. 'And no old men. Take the women and children as slaves.'

A pity. He was not a cruel man, not like Valens, but a lesson must be taught.

He could have led them, proving to himself as much as his men that he was capable of being a soldier. But he told himself a commander's job was to direct, not to place his person at risk. He watched as the unbroken lines of the First cohort waded through the shallows to the far bank, heard the growl as the tribesmen tried to mask their fear with sound and fury. The first spears flew and fell short, thrown too soon by panicking youngsters. They had chosen their position well, so he could not use his cavalry to outflank them, but also badly, because they had left themselves nowhere to retreat. A faint command and a ripple along the Roman line. A momentary shadow in the sky, followed by the first screams as the heavy, weighted *pila* plunged into the packed ranks of the Helvetii warriors. He saw the glitter as more than a thousand swords were unsheathed and imagined fists tightening on the grips of the big curved shields with the boar insignia, bull-muscled shoulders hunching behind them; the muttered curses and whispered prayers. He urged his mount into the middle of the stream, feeling the instant chill as the freezing waters reached his feet and lower legs, staying just out of arrow range. He was close enough to hear the grunts now, as the legionaries punched the triangular-pointed *gladii* into the men in front of them. The slaughter had begun.

An hour later it was over and he stood outside his

command tent listening to the sound of wailing widows and orphans waiting to be placed in chains and the splashes as the dead and the dying were stripped of clothing and weapons and thrown into the river. They would drift downstream to the great lake where their bloated, rotting presence would be a warning to anyone who stood in the way of Aulus Caecina Alienus and his legions.

'A courier, lord Alienus.' An aide drew his attention to a dust-caked cavalryman in a wolfskin cloak. 'From the south.' The man blurted out his story, and the aide led him away for refreshment.

Galba was dead. Caecina felt a molten surge of exultation. Galba was dead. Without the old fool there would be no prosecution and no shame. He was free. But a moment's reflection allowed the burning to cool. What did it really change? His flattery had bounced off Otho like water off a goose. Otho despised him. He was still trapped. More important, would Vitellius stay firm? There was only one answer to that. The bars that held the fat man in his gilded cage were stronger than those imprisoning Aulus Caecina Alienus. So it would continue. Only the name of the enemy was different.

The courier had brought other important news. It appeared the cavalry of the Ala Siliana were holding the Padus valley for Vitellius and harrying any of Otho's forces they could find. It meant the road to Italia was clear and opposition weak.

He saw it in a flash as blinding as a sword blade in the sunlight. If he could reach Italia before Valens the glory would be his. He would wipe Otho's loyalists away and open the road to Rome. The fat man needed an heir. Caecina had planned to use charm to ensure that he was chosen. With a solo victory, the succession was guaranteed. He saw himself in the purple with a crown of golden laurel leaves twisted in his hair.

Was there anything he could do to ensure success? He tried to think like a commander, like a great general. Corbulo perhaps. What would Corbulo do? He would create a diversion to make victory all the more certain. Yes, he would draw the opposition away from his line of march.

He called his cavalry commander. 'Send the Ala Gallorum Indiana into the eastern passes. They are to carry out diversionary attacks on any forts and harry any patrols. Do not risk casualties, but ensure their presence is known.'

The tribune repeated his orders and rode back to send five hundred Celtic cavalrymen towards Curia, Bilitio and Novum Comun – and an unwitting Gaius Valerius Verrens.

XXVIII

'He says we cross here.'

The road turned east after Bilitio and continued on through the high passes to Curia, from where a man could find his way to the Danuvius and distant Noricum and Pannonia. Valtir had reined in beside a ford where the river tumbled melt-green and foaming, knee deep, over the rocks. Beyond the ford a valley with a faint track at its centre cut through the otherwise unbroken wall of mountains to the north-west. Valerius studied the narrow opening in the iron half-light of the pre-dawn. They had discussed this during the night. The traditional route was the safer and more reliable option. With half the normal levels of winter snow even the highest passes would be crossable. It was a well-travelled path and if they lost their way they would be able to find some outpost or village to set them back on the road. If it had not been for the unrest among the mountain tribes, Valerius would not even have considered the second option. The other road meant they would be entirely dependent on Valtir and entirely lost without him. With a nod and a prayer to Jupiter, controller of wind, snow and storm, Valerius urged his mount into the river.

At first the valley was relatively broad, making the going easy, but soon it narrowed and divided into two at a place where they passed a small settlement. Valtir didn't even acknowledge the right-hand path, which appeared the more inviting, but carried on unerringly. Now the valley walls closed in and the mountains seemed to grow higher with every step. Snow capped the peaks and it began to fall in silken nuggets from leaden clouds that seemed to touch the mountain tops. Valtir led, followed by Valerius, Dasius and the four Thracian troopers, with Serpentius, ever alert, in the rear. One of the Thracians, Laslav, who couldn't be more than seventeen, whooped and reached out to catch as many of the gently falling flakes as he could and cram them into his mouth before they melted. Soon, though, what had been a pretty diversion was transformed into a threat as a white curtain dropped between the riders and the world around them. Valerius darted a glance at Valtir, but the Celt barely seemed to notice the change. If a track existed, only he could see it, and they followed carefully in the hoofprints of his little pony. Eventually, he turned off the road and led them through a clump of scrub to a low shelter carved from the hillside by some long-dead optimist hoping to find gold, tin or lead. They tethered the horses close to the cave mouth, made a small fire and spread their bedding on the cold, hard rock. After a long day in the saddle Valerius slept the sleep of the dead.

He woke shivering, to be confronted by a world of black and white. Valtir stood at the entrance of the cave, silhouetted against the ankle-deep snow that blanketed everything outside. Valerius knew the mountain man would be evaluating the conditions, and everything depended on his decision. Dasius had spoken to the little Celt before they bedded down and he had warned of hard climbing ahead. The Roman suppressed a shiver at the thought of the jagged peaks that had formed an honour guard for their progress and imagined what the words 'hard climbing' would entail. 'Dasius? Ask him if this changes anything.'

The Thracian dragged himself away from the tiny fire and joined the slight figure at the cave mouth for a whispered conversation. When he returned Valtir remained in the entrance as if his presence alone was keeping an enemy at bay.

'He says it will make it more difficult, but not impossible.' Dasius's stolid face twisted in a grimace of concern. 'That is his assessment and I have been with him often enough to believe it will be correct, but . . . My knowledge of his language is slight. Sometimes when he says one thing I think he means another. When he talks of what lies ahead, he sees it only through his own eyes and his own experiences. If I ask him about the horses, he shrugs and says he has made the journey in these conditions before. But I believe he considers only his mount, which is mountain bred, not our own, which are not. When he talks of climbs and obstacles, it is his own capabilities that are foremost in his mind. If there is more snow . . .' He hesitated. 'Sometimes when I look into his eyes I think I see fear there.'

They set off after dawn, with Valtir, as always, in the van, the horses' flanks steaming gently in the frosty air and their hooves crunching the undisturbed white carpet underfoot. The mountain peaks towering over them were hidden behind a curtain of low, grey cloud that held the threat of more snow, and now the trail rose steadily to meet it. Unusually, it became even colder as the day progressed and they wrapped their cloaks tighter and breathed on their freezing hands to provide some semblance of warmth. After a steady climb, the valley curved west and the hills formed an unbroken barrier between Valerius and his goal. Studying the barren, scree-covered slopes he felt a chill that had nothing to do with the cold. It did not seem possible that any man could scale those heights, never mind with horses. He heard awed murmuring of the cavalrymen behind him and knew they were thinking the same. Yet Valtir rode on unconcerned, his pony plodding steadily through the snow. After another hour he allowed the beast to amble to a halt and frowned through narrowed eyes at the snow-covered scarp to his right.

'Here,' he said.

The word was greeted by a gasp from one of the Thracians and a mutter that might have been a curse or a prayer. Dasius rode to Valerius's side and together they studied the soaring slope, which looked exactly like every other hillside they'd passed. Perhaps a little less sheer, but still unscalable.

'Can it be possible?' Valerius whispered. The cavalry-man shook his head and hissed a question at Valtir. The little man's reply was accompanied by a shrug.

'He says it is an old cattle raiders' trail. If they could get cows over it, we can take horses. They will have to be led, but this is the steepest part, and once we are over the rise he claims it becomes easier.'

Valerius locked eyes with Serpentius, who had been born and raised in mountains just like these. After a moment's consideration the Spaniard nodded. 'If he says it can be done, I believe it can be done.'

Valerius turned to the Thracian commander. 'Dasius,

you have escorted us further than I had a right to ask. I release you and your men from your duty with my thanks.'

The young auxiliary's chin came up and he pointed to where his men stood in a huddle by their horses. 'We have spoken about this. Without me, who would translate for the guide? So I stay. And these brigands will not leave me, even when given a direct order and faced with a climb that would daunt an ibex.' The nut-brown faces broke into a collective grin. 'So they stay, too.'

Valerius nodded slowly, embarrassed. He wanted to tell them how he valued their loyalty and their courage and that the hardship they were enduring was worthwhile. But he hesitated because he wasn't certain if that was true. It had all seemed so simple when they had set off from Rome. Find Vitellius and persuade him to bring his legions to heel. Succeed and they would save countless lives. Fail and . . . well, they would cross that ford when they came to it. But here in these gods-cursed mountains he was beginning to think they might never reach Colonia Agrippinensis. Yet what choice did they have but to continue? Dasius answered his doubts with a fierce grin and turned away to help his troopers share the supplies equally between all the horses. Before he went, Valerius reached out with his good hand and touched the Thracian's arm. It wasn't much as a gesture of thanks, but Dasius treated it as if he had been awarded another *phalera* to add to the medals on his armoured chest. His eyes turned grave and he saluted as if he were on the parade ground.

When he was out of earshot, Serpentius said quietly: 'We are fortunate in our friends.'

Valerius couldn't meet his eye. 'Yes, we are.'

Dismounted, Valtir led them in single file, not directly

up the mountain as Valerius had feared, but diagonally across the slope. The guide's little pony skipped across the rocks, but the other mounts had to be coaxed, placing a hoof at a time on a path that was barely discernible to the naked eye. At first it was relatively easy, but soon the track took a sharp turn and they were climbing rapidly, the valley floor suddenly dizzyingly far below. Valtir set such a brisk pace that the breath turned to fire in Valerius's chest. They worked their way up the slope in a series of diagonals, always gaining height and every step increasing the agony in muscles unused to the mountains. The higher they went, the deeper the snow and the more treacherous the going. A pack horse would baulk at the incline and they would halt while it was manhandled from before and behind until it kicked and bucked its way to the next level. Eventually they reached a point where Valtir disappeared over a rise and Valerius found himself looking down into a narrow, snowbound valley that had been hidden by the ridge. His heart raced as he realized that it offered a comparatively safer route through the mountains. Each man who followed stopped to take in the panorama and rest weary legs. If anything, the descent was worse than the climb.

By the time they reached the valley floor, it was too late to continue and men and horses were exhausted. Valtir marked out a circle on the ground and began to clear it, piling the waist-deep snow in a wall along the curve he had drawn. Valerius ordered the others to follow the Celt's lead and eventually they had an enclosure that protected man and beast from the worst of the cold wind. After a mouthful of bread and a swig of wine they collapsed exhausted into their blankets, leaving Serpentius to take the first watch.

Next morning Valerius nudged them shivering and cursing from their beds. Ahead of them the ground rose steadily, but nothing like as steeply as the first climb, and Valtir said they would be able to ride again. They mounted and urged their beasts through the snow, the pack horses trailing alongside. In the thin strip between the snow-capped peaks, the sky cleared to a pristine azure blue, but no sunlight reached them in the valley bottom and the raw cold gnawed at their bones. As they climbed, the gorge narrowed still further and Valerius could see Valtir studying the peaks to the left and right, his head darting like a fearful sparrow searching for a hawk. A boulder-strewn stream surged its way down the centre of the pass in foaming cascades and gradually it forced them deeper into the shadow of the mountains to their right.

Not everyone felt oppressed by the conditions. The irrepressible Laslav and another of Dasius's hardy Thracians, Yoni, began a playful snow fight to warm themselves up, cackling noisily. Valtir hissed a warning.

'He says we should not disturb the gods of this place.' Dasius frowned and made the sign against evil. 'We are close to their home and he is fearful of their anger.'

'Then let us hope we are welcome.' Valerius kept his voice light, but his hand instinctively reached for the golden amulet at his neck.

They were nearing the head of the pass when a sharp crack split the cocooned silence, as if someone had snapped a rotten tree branch. Valerius exchanged a puzzled glance with Dasius, but Valtir was already on the move, kicking his pony violently into motion. A desperate cry echoed from Serpentius at the rear of the column.

'Ride! Leave the pack horses and ride for your life!'

Valerius hesitated and Dasius looked to where his troopers milled in confusion. Serpentius urged his horse past them, grabbing Valerius's reins as he went by.

'Ride, you idiot! Avalanche!'

Valerius dropped the rope to his pack horse and dug his heels into his mount's ribs. His eyes searched the hills above for some hint of the danger that had sparked such fear in Serpentius, but he could see nothing. Was it possible that the Spaniard and Valtir were starting at shadows? Even as the thought formed, his mind was struggling to evaluate the impossible change happening before his eyes. The entire mountain top seemed to slip towards him in a single graceful movement, transforming in moments to a twenty-foot wall of snow the size of a legionary parade ground. It began slowly, so slowly that it didn't seem to pose any threat. Surely they could outride the danger? But, as he watched, the great snow bank began to break up and increase in speed, pushing a blizzard of particles before it. Its advance was accompanied by the surging roar of an approaching thunderstorm, but Valerius's eyes and ears seemed out of time, as if the sound was trying to catch up with what he was seeing. Now he needed no urging and he screamed at his horse for more speed, lashing its flanks in a desperate effort to gain ground. He braved a glance back to see Dasius and his cavalrymen on the move at last, although Yoni stubbornly refused to abandon his pack horse and was already ten or fifteen paces behind. Another crack froze the blood in his veins and he realized that a second piece of the snow shelf had broken free. A despairing look told him it was twice as large as the first, which already powered towards him like a grasping hand, fingers of thundering white powder extending from the main break as if a river had broken its banks and created separate streams. With each passing second the streams grew in power and speed, demolishing everything before them and snapping mature trees as if they were reeds. He heard a sharp cry and looked back to see the man with the pack horse go down in a flurry of white. Now the thunder was so deafening he thought his ears must explode and he dared not look up for fear of what he would see. It was only when his world turned to white shards of ice and something enormous kicked him out of the saddle that he knew they were all dead men anyway.

A moment when time stood still. Darkness. The thunder of his heart and the sound of harsh breathing. Something moved against his chest and he opened his eyes to a world of glacial blue and glaring white. He tried to move his right arm to push the snow from his face, but it was frozen in position. The left too. Gradually it came to him. He twisted and struggled with every ounce of energy he possessed. Kicked out with his legs. He could not move a single inch. He was buried alive. Somewhere close by, another poor soul was mewing pathetically like a newborn child and it took a moment to realize it was the sound of his own terror. The movement on his chest again. Something large smashed into his jaw and pushed his head back. Pain blinded him, but the disturbance had created a small air pocket that allowed him to breathe more easily. He realized that his horse had fallen beside him when the avalanche struck, and was equally trapped, with its head across his body. He willed himself to stay calm. How long would the air last? He wondered idly if he would suffocate or freeze to death, and which was the easier. The horse wriggled again, creating more space, and he realized that their combined heat was melting the snow. That thought gave him the strength to attempt another movement, but the result was the same as before. He was not only entombed, but encased. This time there was no escape.

XXIX

Muffled voices. Fingers hauling at his left hand, which he realized belatedly must be stretched out towards the surface of the snow. Was he hallucinating? No, he could hear the sound of frantically scrambling hands clawing through the snow. The mare shifted against him with a 'harrumph' from her nostrils. He whispered to calm her, but the closer the sounds came the more agitated she grew. She shook her head desperately and the heavy skull smashed against him. He cried out as a flare of agony stabbed through his chest, and slipped into a dead faint. When he woke again the trapped air was stale and thick, hardly air at all. The snow holding him in its grip was hard packed, set solid and thick with earth and stones. How much was above him? He felt himself fading and it was a few seconds before he remembered the earlier digging sounds. The scrabbling had stopped. His rescuers must be resting. But time passed and through the fog that threatened to envelop him he was aware of disappointment. They had given up. He tried to move his right arm again, but with as little success as before. His mind conjured up an image of a fly trapped in amber and he laughed aloud, the sound shrill and almost hysterical in his ears. So this was what it felt like. Death. His mind drifted. He had done what he could; no point in wasting his strength fighting it. Life and death would for ever be at the whim of the gods. No regrets. But was that true? He remembered Domitia and the day they had watched the dolphins from the deck of the bireme carrying her to her father in Antioch. *What if Poseidon were to grant you the ability to choose, this very moment, to turn into a dolphin and swim away with me, to spend our lives roaming the oceans together? Would you accept or would you stand here and watch me swim away alone?* Even as the thought formed, the wall of ice blue in front of his eyes turned into an explosion of blinding white and he gasped as a rush of cold air reached him. A face appeared in the opening.

'You're alive?'

It seemed an unlikely question, but Valerius could see the relief written clear in Serpentius's dark eyes. He produced an approximation of a grin. 'I'm not sure.'

'We'd almost given up on you.' Serpentius continued to work at releasing Valerius's left arm. 'There was no heat in your fingers and you weren't moving. The others wanted to leave you. Then we heard you laugh. Dead men don't laugh.' He recoiled as his hand touched something unexpected. 'Mars' arse, what's that?'

'My horse.'

Valerius sat shivering in a fur after being dug free, Serpentius silent at his side. They had lost Yoni and two pack horses, along with most of the supplies. But Dasius kept the worst news to last. Valtir had disappeared.

'When we turned back to try to find you I assumed he would follow.' The Thracian shrugged. 'We were so intent on digging that no one noticed he'd gone until it was too late.' He pointed to where a set of tracks disappeared up the valley. 'At least we know which direction he's taken, but . . .' He didn't need to say more. It was clear to everyone that without Valtir they could be left wandering for ever in this wilderness.

Valerius winced at the pain in his ribs as he threw off the cloak and got to his feet. 'Then there is no time to lose. We have to get through the pass before darkness comes or a new storm covers his tracks.' Dasius ran off to organize his men, and Valerius turned to Serpentius. 'We'll never catch up with him trailing the pack horse. I want you to take the best mount and follow his trail. If you find him, bring him back undamaged.'

Serpentius spat. 'These are his mountains. If he doesn't want me to find him, he won't be found.'

'I know, but we have to try. Unless we find Valtir we'll never get to Vitellius.'

The Spaniard turned away without another word. Dasius came back just as the former gladiator rode out on Valerius's horse, following the line of Valtir's pony. 'Will he find him?'

'If anyone can do it, Serpentius can. He'll make better time than the Celt because he'll push the horse as hard as he dares. That will give him a chance. For the rest, it depends whether Valtir always intended to abandon us.'

'Sometimes I think we are just the playthings of the gods,' Dasius said morosely.

Valerius laughed and clapped him on the shoulder. 'Then let us provide them with a little more entertainment.'

They reached the head of the pass in the late afternoon. Normally Valerius would have called a halt for the day, but he knew it was vital to make as much progress as possible before the weather closed in. Only when the light was fading and they reached a point where the terrain began to fall away did he relent and allow the Thracians to drop from their saddles and build another snow circle. He hid his disappointment that they had seen no sign of Serpentius, but he was not surprised. The Spaniard had the persistence of a hunting dog; once on a trail he would follow until his horse gave up on him, and then he'd continue on foot.

Daylight saw them perched at the top of a precipitous gully leading down to a broad, flat-bottomed valley that ran from north to south. Overnight snow had made any tracks invisible, but they picked their way down the banks of a stream that cut the gully until they reached the valley floor. The horses skittered nervously as their hooves broke through the snow crust into the bog below, but eventually they found their way to firm ground. Here there was a visible track that, judging by the hoofprints, had been recently used. Dasius eyed the trail uneasily.

'Auxiliary cavalry.' He frowned. 'We were fortunate. They must have passed by while we were in the gully or they would have seen us. A small patrol moving south. I don't understand it. This is Helvetii country and military traffic is strictly regulated. Could they be looking for us?'

'I don't know,' Valerius admitted. 'It's possible Valtir ran into them and betrayed us.' He studied the far end of the valley, which was hidden by scrub and trees. If that was the case, where was Serpentius? And what did Valtir know anyway? He made his decision. 'It makes no difference. Friend or enemy, I want to avoid contact with any local forces. We go north, which I would have done in any case.' He kept the confidence in his voice, but without Valtir he knew there must be a possibility that the north road only led deeper into impassable mountains. They rode off, but they'd only travelled a few hundred paces when they heard a shout, and a troop of a dozen or more cavalrymen burst from the cover of the trees.

'Can we talk our way out?' Dasius shouted.

'Auxiliary cavalry a hundred miles from their unit and a man with a wooden hand and a scroll case with the wrong Emperor's seal?'

'Then we must fight.' Dasius barked an order and Laslav dropped the leading reins of the surviving pack animal. Valerius drew his sword, but the Thracian laid a hand on his arm. Dasius's eyes were bright, but his voice held no fear. 'Your mission is too important. If we cannot stop them, at least we can delay them. Ride!' He slapped the rump of Valerius's horse and in the same instant hauled his own mount to face the enemy. 'Ride!' he repeated. Valerius knew he had no option. To hesitate would be an insult to their sacrifice. With his heart feeling as if it were torn in two, he urged his beast up the snowy track. Behind him he heard the distinctive whoop of the Thracian auxiliaries followed by a cry of mortal agony. He dared a glance over his shoulder and was greeted by a whirling free-for-all of mounted men. In that instant he saw that Dasius had failed. Four of the enemy cavalry broke free from the skirmish and galloped in his wake, the iron points of their spears glinting in the low winter sun. With a muttered curse he dug his heels into the mare's ribs in a vain bid to gain another few yards. His mind whirled as he calculated speed and distance. Could he outrun them? That depended on how fresh their mounts were and how exhausted his own after six days in the mountains. Fight? If it came to it, better sooner, before his horse was blown. But against four? He risked another look, trying to gauge the fighting potential of his pursuers. Germans, or Gauls, judging by the long hair streaming from beneath their pot helmets and the rough plaid of their trappings. Well mounted and riding in close formation, two by two, to make better speed through the snow. When they closed on him they'd spread out to make the most effective use of their long spears. He cringed at the thought of one of those iron blades chopping into his spine. But what choice did he have? If he turned and fought, they'd come at him from four different angles. He might take one, possibly two if he was quick, but by the time the second was dying one of the others would have taken his throat out or pinned him like a rabbit on a spit.

The ground raced past in a blur of white and he almost missed it. A patch of disturbed snow at the entrance to a gully fifty paces ahead. He felt his heart quicken, the heat rising up from his belly. So be it. If he was going to die at least he would die trying to live, not like a frightened deer fleeing from the hounds. The gully flashed past to his left and he let the mare carry on another forty paces before he pulled her up and turned to face his pursuers, throwing away his cloak to give him more freedom of movement. The cavalrymen whooped their encouragement at his defiance. This was better sport than chasing some helpless civilian. Timing. Timing was everything. Every instinct told him to kick the mare into motion. In a cavalry fight a stationary man was a dead man. Speed and mobility were as much his weapons as the sword he held low in his left hand. But for his plan to work he needed them to stay bunched until the last moment. So he gritted his teeth and willed the horse to stay still. It was his good fortune that after Serpentius's departure Dasius had insisted he take one of the cavalry-trained spares, which would respond to knee and heel in a fight. Now! When the auxiliaries were a hundred paces away he urged her into motion. She came swiftly to the canter, but by the time she reached a gallop the enemy had already covered fifty paces. He saw daylight between two of the horses. Don't break yet. Not yet. He had deliberately angled his attack to come at them from their right and their attention was concentrated entirely on the fool who wanted to commit suicide on their spear points. None of them noticed the roan blur that erupted from their other flank.

Serpentius's throwing axe took the rearmost rider precisely on the earpiece of his helmet an instant before the Spaniard's horse crashed into the shoulder of the man in front's mount, cannoning him against his comrade. Valerius saw the flash of a sword, a spray of scarlet and a flurry of snow as one of the horses went down. He didn't have time to enjoy the moment because the rear man on the right flank swerved past the chaos and came directly at him, crouched low in the saddle, spear held loose in his right hand. He would be calculating where his point would strike and rejoicing that his opponent had no shield or armour. Valerius could almost feel the auxiliary's elation and he knew that in the other man's mind he was already dead. But Gaius Valerius Verrens had fought Boudicca's snarling champions without a backward step. More important, he had ridden against Parthian horse soldiers born in the saddle and weaned on mare's milk. Three months on campaign as Corbulo's cavalry commander had taught him more about horsemanship and cavalry tactics than another man would learn in a lifetime. When the time came the grip on the spear shaft would tighten, the arm would tense and the iron tip of the spear would whip up to rip his throat or tear through his heart.

The world slowed, every heartbeat an eternity. His rush had taken him on a collision course with the trooper, but now he swerved violently to his right. In his head he saw the eyes narrow in puzzlement beneath the rim of the helmet. Valerius had deliberately kept his sword low. The German would be expecting a right-handed fighter and that meant an attack down the left flank where the pathetically short blade might have a chance of fending away the spear. Too late for the auxiliary to change course, but the lance point followed Valerius and he knew his opponent's only concern was that he would somehow escape. The cavalryman was aiming for the throat: a sign of his overconfidence. Better and more certain to go for the bigger target. Still, a right-handed swordsman would have been all but defenceless against the blow. But Valerius held his sword in his left hand and now the weapon came up with a gladiator's speed and a veteran's timing. The high strike made it easier for the blade to divert the spear past his left shoulder and position him perfectly for a scything counter that would take the cavalryman's head off his shoulders. He recognized a fleeting moment of terror on the other man's face and at the last moment remembered Otho's final words before he had left Rome. *I will do anything to save the Empire from the terror and the bloodshed that rides hand in hand with civil war.* The heavy blade of the *spatha* dropped to take the trooper across his mailed chest, smashing the rings into his flesh and cracking his ribs as he was catapulted backwards out of the saddle. In a blur Valerius found himself reining in beside Serpentius. The Spaniard was retrieving his axes and rifling the bodies of the three men he had treated with less mercy than Valerius's groaning opponent had just received. The downed man tried to speak, but all that came out was a thin stream of bile that hung in strings from his raw lips.

'Here.' The Spaniard threw a leather bag and Valerius trapped it between his wooden fist and the saddle.

'You might have given me more warning.'

'You're still alive, aren't you? More than you can say for these offal.'

'Dasius . . .'

'I saw.' Serpentius looked towards where the remaining auxiliary cavalry were forming up over the bodies of the Thracian and his men. 'We should go.'

Valerius nodded wearily. 'Where?'

Serpentius vaulted into the saddle and rode back towards where he'd emerged from the gully. 'Why don't you ask *him*? Turns out the little bastard speaks better Latin than I do.'

Valerius peered into the shadows where a hunched figure sat like a whipped dog on his rough-haired pony.

Valtir.

Later, when they'd lost their pursuers, they found shelter in a cave Valtir led them to. 'I feared the thunder of the gods and I ran. Once I had run I was too ashamed to come back.'

'Why did you not tell us you could speak our tongue?' Valerius asked. 'It might have made a difference.'

Valtir continued to quarter the carcass of a small mountain goat he'd trapped before the Spaniard caught up with him. 'Sometimes it is better not to know.'

He darted a fearful glance at the gladiator as Serpentius growled: 'He's been listening to every word we say. We should cut his throat now and take our chances.'

267

The words were said in the matter-of-fact voice of a man discussing the price of eggs and Valtir shrank back against the wall of the cave.

Valerius shook his head. 'No. I don't think he has. Remember how he always slept farthest from the fire? I think he truly didn't want to know, because the minute you thought he did you'd have got rid of him. We all ran from the avalanche, even you. The only difference is that Valtir was quicker and he didn't stop.'

The Spaniard produced a bitter smile. 'First the auxiliary and now a stinking Celt who somehow crawled out after his mother birthed him into a sewer. You're going soft.'

'We're soldiers, Serpentius, even without a uniform or a rank or an eagle to follow. Soldiers. Not murderers. Just because Mars is stirring his cauldron and we're teetering on the edge, we can't just jump in.'

'The auxiliary was trying to kill you.'

'He was doing his duty. Following orders.'

'Aye, and look where following orders got us in Syria. Six months on the run with Nero's assassins breathing down our neck.'

Valerius was reflecting on the truth of the Spaniard's words when Valtir's soft voice interrupted from the far side of the cave. 'I can take you to the soldiers' road.'

XXX

The terrain became progressively easier and Valtir more wary with every mile they travelled west through the mountains. On the second day after losing Dasius and his men they bypassed a fortified settlement at the head of the second great lake they had flanked. 'Dunum,' the Celt said. 'More auxiliaries.' From Dunum a broad valley surrounded by rolling hills led where they wanted to go, but Valtir insisted that they keep to the heights and it was along mountain tracks that they rode, camping where they could with the wind whistling through their fur cloaks, and waking up beneath a blanket of snow. Valtir ignored Serpentius's accusing stare. 'Colder, but safer,' he assured Valerius.

The next day broke bright as a summer morning and brought them eventually to a distinctive hill shaped like a sleeping bear. It was bounded by a river to the north and a well-found road that ran parallel with its western flank. The soldiers' road. And it was well named.

From a clump of trees on the summit they watched an endless column of legionaries pass. Century after century. Cohort after cohort. Ten eight-man sections to each century, six centuries to each cohort, apart from the First cohort, the elite of the legion, which would have eight hundred men: the shock troops who would go where the danger was greatest and the fighting hottest. Thousands of men, perhaps even tens of thousands. They marched south, filling the road as far as Valerius could see. Their breath steamed in the cold air and their armour shone in the sunlight so that it was like watching a glittering river of soldiers; an utterly disciplined, implacable river. Each unit was followed by its baggage, the food and heavy weapons without which no legion could operate.

'I saw two eagles,' Serpentius said. 'But only about fifteen cohort standards.'

'Yes,' Valerius agreed. 'So a full legion and half of a second.'

'And their auxiliaries.'

Yes, their auxiliaries, infantry and cavalry. There had been hordes of them, their identity clear in the oval shields they carried and the less disciplined ranks they kept. A small army, but still an army. And that meant Vitellius had been cleverer than anyone had expected. He'd split his forces in two and now they were closing on Italia like a scorpion's pincers. If one army was blocked by Otho's legions, the other would crush them like a piece of soft iron between a hammer and an anvil. Should he try to get back and warn the Emperor? The chances of bypassing the troops they had just watched march past were almost hopeless. No. Their only chance was to reach Vitellius and somehow persuade him to call off his dogs.

'I have brought you here.' Valtir stood by uncertainly, his eyes flicking to Serpentius.

'And we thank you for it,' Valerius assured him, ignoring the Spaniard's snort of disgust. 'We had a bargain.' He reached inside his tunic and took out a small purse. The Celt frowned, but Valerius pressed it on him. 'What happened happened, but it is in the past. You brought us where you said you would and by the quickest way.' Still the little man hesitated. 'If there is a debt to pay, then pay it by your silence.'

Valtir bristled. 'Valtir is a prince of the Orobii, a man of honour.' He reached to his belt and Serpentius's hand went for his sword, but the Celt pulled out the small dagger Valerius had given him. 'I cannot take this.' He held out the knife in the palm of his hand.

Valerius kept his own hand by his side. 'It is a pity to waste a good knife, but if you cannot take it, then give it as a sacrifice to the mountain gods and pray for our safe passage and our safe return. Only one more thing will I ask of you. When you reach home, send word to the Emperor of what you have seen here.'

Valtir stared at him for a long moment, the narrowed eyes unreadable. Eventually he gave the slightest of nods and went to his pony. He rode off without a backward glance.

Valerius felt Serpentius's eyes on him. 'I know.' He sighed. 'But this is the way it will be.'

The Spaniard made to spit, then thought better of it. 'North then?'

'Yes, north.' Valtir had assured them that all they had to do was follow the river north and they would eventually come to a trading settlement and another, much greater river, which must be the upper waters of the Rhenus. 'We'll keep to the riverbank, and stay clear of the road for the moment.'

'Slow going.'

Valerius nodded. 'That might change. We haven't seen any carts or mule trains, in fact no civilians at all, so it looks as if the road has been closed to anything but military traffic. If it seems clear, we might risk travelling it by dark, but I want to be sure. No point in coming all this way and ending up on a nervous auxiliary's spear point.'

'Like thieves in the night.'

The Roman smiled. 'Is there any other way?'

They waited until the road emptied, soothing the horses, which had become restless in such close proximity to others of their kind, and trying to stop their teeth chattering in the cold that seemed to eat into their bones. The road cut straight as a spear shaft across the flatlands, following the general course of the river. The river, as rivers do, wound its way without any apparent purpose, and its banks alternated between hoof-sucking bog and almost impenetrable brush, dotted by the occasional welcome water meadow. Eventually, their progress was so painfully slow that Valerius decided he had no alternative but to return to the muddy fields that flanked the road or they would never reach their destination.

Serpentius grunted approval. 'We can bed down by the river at dark.'

They made what distance they could while daylight lasted, and the sun was well down before Valerius pointed the mare towards the river. By the time they approached it, the brush was a solid barrier and they wandered upstream until they found what seemed to be a reasonably dry spot to bed down. The only drawback was a cloying, sickly-sweet scent that hung in the air around them and filled their throats and nostrils.

'Mars' sacred arse,' Serpentius spat. When he turned to Valerius his eyes were bleak. 'Nothing we can do to-night.'

The Roman nodded. They both knew well enough what they were smelling.

Valerius woke before dawn, grateful he couldn't remember his dreams. He stretched, wincing at the sharp pain in his half-healed shoulder and bruised ribs, before wandering towards the river to piss among the bushes. Now the smell seemed worse than in the darkness and they practically had to force down the meagre breakfast Serpentius prepared. Daylight showed them camped south of a great bend in the river. Fighting off a disabling lethargy, the Spaniard found the strength to check the road for signs of activity. When he was certain it was safe they saddled up and made their way towards the source of the stench, cloaked in a terrible sense of foreboding at what they would find.

It was a familiar enough sight in its way. Still, Valerius felt the bile rise in his throat. The bodies carpeted the surface of a great eddy the river had dug from the bank, fish-belly white and bobbing obscenely in a froth of greenish foam. They could only have been dead for a few days, but already the expanding internal gases had bloated their corpses and those floating face up had lost eyes and tongues to the buzzards and crows hungry enough to brave the unstable platform.

Serpentius worked his way down the bank and hauled the nearest body half out of the water; a broad-shouldered giant with long moustaches and foul pink craters for eyes.

'Tribesmen. Warriors, and they were killed in a fight.' He pointed to the familiar jagged rip in the man's stomach where a length of blue-grey intestine hung clear, twisting sinuously in the current like a plump eel. He frowned. 'They didn't die in the river. They've been stripped of anything of value; weapons, jewellery, everything. That means they were butchered and then thrown in. Why would anyone do that when they knew they'd be depending on the river for water?'

'Because they're sending a message.' Valerius nodded at the empty fields. 'That's why we haven't seen a farmer or a slave in two days. They're terrified to come near the river or the road, because that's the way the man who's commanding this part of Vitellius's army wants it.'

The next day and the day after they found more of the army commander's messages: bodies in the river or littered like dead fish along the banks. But there was worse to come.

A dark stain hung over what little was left of the Helvetii township; not smoke exactly, rather the shimmering aura of disaster. They rode through what had once been a substantial gateway, hoping to find a few buried stores to supplement their dwindling supplies. The moment he smelled the familiar roasted-meat scent Valerius regretted the decision.

'Bastards.' There was murder in Serpentius's voice as he led his horse through what had once been the main square. To one side, in the angle between two houses, congealing blood caked the earth inches thick and the Spaniard picked up a stained wooden doll that had once been a child's toy. Closer inspection showed that the blood lake was dotted with gobbets of flesh and hanks of blond hair. A sandal formed a small island at the centre and a tiny hand, severed at the wrist, seemed to be attempting to find sanctuary on it. 'Bastards,' the gladiator repeated, remembering another torched village and another dead child. He turned to Valerius with murder in his eyes. 'So this is your Roman peace?'

Every building had been burned, but, at first glance, the job had been poorly executed. It was only when you looked closely that you realized the gently smouldering mounds were not half-burned timbers, but the charred remnants of the former occupants, twisted and blackened, red sinew still showing through cracks in the incinerated flesh, grinning teeth brilliant white in blackened skulls that were the gods' way of showing the true nature of the human form. Old men, women and children, almost certainly, but it was impossible to be sure.

'I don't understand. What we saw was an army marching on Rome. These people would never have dared to oppose them.'

'No, but their menfolk did.' Valerius swallowed hard as he surveyed the destruction and wanton carnage. The combination of rotting bodies and roasting meat filled his throat and made his stomach heave. 'This is another of his messages. "Anyone who opposes me will be wiped from the map. Man, woman and child."' He shook his head as the undeniable truth came to him. 'Strategically, his reasoning is sound. He could not afford to leave an enemy in his rear when he marched south. He doesn't have the troops to secure his supply lines, so he uses terror in their place. Paulinus did the same in Britain.'

'A proper bastard.'

'Have you ever met a general who wasn't?' Serpentius met his eyes with a look of puzzlement and Valerius realized why. He shook his head. 'There's something wrong here. Vitellius would never sanction this.'

'He tried to kill us once. And the boy,' Serpentius pointed out.

'That was politics.'

'If he wants to be Emperor there will be worse than this before they open the gates of Rome to him.'

'I don't know . . . it just doesn't seem right.'

'I suppose there is only one way to find out.'

They urged their horses north towards the distant mountains of Germania, the Rhenus and Aulus Vitellius Germanicus Imperator.

XXXI

Colonia Agrippinensis

'We seek an audience with the Emperor.'

The guard commander ran a jaundiced eye over the ragged figures who staggered wearily up from the wharf on legs that hadn't touched dry land for a week. A younger man, dark hair slicked across his forehead by the incessant rain that had soaked the cloak and Celtic trews he wore, though he was no Celt. A face that had known life, as the old saying went, tanned and determined, the lines of its owner's trials carved deep, and the pale shadow of an old scar running across one cheek. Merchants, he claimed, but merchants with nothing to trade who kept their hands hidden beneath their cloaks. And his companion less savoury still. Features more at home with a snarl than a smile, unless he missed his guess, and the hungry, calculating eyes he'd once seen in a caged leopard. Come a yard too close and you'd find your guts in your lap and your head between its jaws.

'The Emperor is a busy man, as I'm sure you've heard.' The words were meant to dismiss, but Valerius's heart quickened when he heard them. Ever since they'd boarded the river galley at Augusta Raurica he'd been plagued by a terrible fear that Vitellius had already left Germania to join his army. The guard prefect had confirmed for the first time that, at the very least, he was still here. Now all they had to do was reach him. 'It could be a week. It could be a month,' the man continued. 'There's a tavern down by the river, if it hasn't already been washed away. In the meantime, let's see your hands and your papers.'

They complied with the order and Valerius heard the familiar hissed intake of breath as he revealed the walnut fist. 'At least make sure he is given my name.'

The guard stiffened at what wasn't quite an order, but came close. Normally he'd reward such insolence by kicking the petitioners out on their sorry arses into the mud, but these weren't normal times. In any case, what harm could it do?

All right. Name?'

'Publius Sulla.'

'Publius Sulla?'

A hand shook Valerius's shoulder and he realized he'd been drowsing after two hours in a room that was little more than a cell and, judging by the heat, must have stood not far from the furnaces supplying the hypocaust system. He opened his eyes to be confronted by a tall, swarthy man with short-cropped hair and a slightly effeminate manner. A half-stifled yawn escaped his lips and the other man frowned and repeated his question, not bothering to hide his irritation.

'You are Publius Sulla?'

'Publius Sulla died three years ago in a dirt fort on the Dacian frontier. If the name was carried to Aulus Vitellius Germanicus Imperator, he would know that.'

The slight chink of metal on metal drew his eyes to the doorway. Valerius heard Serpentius move and put out a hand to stay him, his eyes never leaving the armed guard accompanying the courtier who'd woken him. He allowed his voice to harden. 'If you had given him the additional information that the Publius Sulla who sought an audience had only one hand, he would also have told you that your guards could keep their swords sheathed.'

He recognized the moment the veiled instruction registered. The man's eyes glittered with suppressed malice, but he turned on his heel and walked out. A few minutes later two guards appeared to escort Valerius through a warren of corridors to an enormous receiving room gorgeously decorated in purple and gold. Colourful hunting scenes decorated the ceiling, with toga-clad gods watching approvingly from behind puffy white clouds while barely clothed nymphs supplied the hunters with arrows. Painted marble busts of Vitellius's ancestors stood on fluted pillars at intervals around the walls, each of them matched by a grim-faced and fully armed legionary with his hand on the hilt of his short sword. All this Valerius took in before his attention focused on the heavily cloaked figure lounging on a couch at the far side of the central fire. A puzzled smile flitted across the corpulent features of Aulus Vitellius Germanicus Imperator, would-be Emperor of Rome, ruler of the two Germanias and commander of seven crack legions, the cream of which were currently converging on northern Italia.

Valerius had deliberated long and hard on how to greet his old friend. Vitellius, even as governor of Africa, had never been a man to stand on ceremony. Yet he called himself Emperor now, and in Valerius's experience Emperors and their courts tended to be obsessively sensitive about protocol. Vitellius would expect the respect his new rank was due, and the titles that went with it. But Valerius had given his oath to another man wearing the purple and he had come here to ask Vitellius to lay aside his claim. At last, he put his wooden fist to his chest in salute. 'Gaius Valerius Verrens at the service of my lord Vitellius.'

The smile didn't falter, but Valerius wasn't deceived. It would be as dangerous to mistake the garrulous, irrepressible Vitellius he had left in the tavern on the Via Salaria for the man before him as it would be to confuse a household tabby with an escaped tiger.

'Lord Vitellius? Not Caesar or Augustus?' Valerius searched for a reply that couldn't be interpreted as an insult, but Vitellius waved a chubby hand. 'No matter; old friends should not be bound by such formality. Has he been searched?' The silent answer must have been affirmative. 'Good. Have him bathed and find him some clothing suitable for a Roman knight. And order the kitchen to prepare fitting dishes for such a pleasant reunion between old friends.' He reeled off a list of exotic fish, fowl and meats that made Valerius blink. 'And the best that execrable cellar has to offer. None of your tavern vinegar.' Again Valerius attempted to pass on Otho's message, only to be baulked by that imperious hand. 'I have much to consider. We will continue our discussion when you return.'

An hour later he was back watching Vitellius eat his way through enough food to sustain a legionary *contubernium* for a week. Eventually, the other man laid down the leg of roasting pig he had been labouring over, sighed, gave a soft belch and washed down a pound or more of pork with a pint of wine. He dipped his grease-encrusted fingers in a bowl brought by one slave and wiped them clean on a soft cloth carried by a second. Satisfied, for the moment, he turned at last to his guest. 'Not hungry, Valerius?'

'Uncertainty tends to take the edge off a man's appetite.' Valerius allowed his eyes to slide over the guards who had replaced the earlier legionaries around the walls. Young men, with hard unyielding eyes. Lucius, Gavo and . . . what was the other man's name, Octavius? . . . yes, Octavius, and three more, all in civilian clothing, but fully armed. Vitellius's closest aides. Men he could trust to do his bidding and keep quiet about it. Men who would happily rid their master of an unwelcome guest, slit his belly, fill it with rocks and sink him in the deepest part of the Rhenus. Vitellius saw the look and laughed.

'If I wanted you dead, would I feed you first?' Valerius had a feeling the answer might be yes. Vitellius would find it amusing. A frown creased the German Emperor's pink features. 'Your presence here poses me a dilemma. The fact that you introduced yourself as Publius Sulla, of fond memory, tells me this is not a private visit to take up my previous generous offer. On the one hand, I am pleased to see my old friend. On the other, I fear that his arrival might be somewhat inconvenient, perhaps even dangerous.' Valerius allowed himself a smile, but Vitellius didn't match it. The governor of Germania picked up the grilled carcass of a small bird, discarded it and chose a larger one, cramming it into his mouth and chewing vigorously to the accompaniment of crunching bones. He swallowed, belched and took a draught of wine before continuing. 'The oak-headed arrow fodder of my personal guard are very capable, but I know that whatever is said in front of them will sooner or later

281

reach ears which, in this case, I would rather it did not. Better to be able to carry out our discussions in an atmosphere of mutual trust and part friends.' The deep-set, pale eyes turned icy and were matched by his voice. 'I am aware that Otho has been trying to get messages to me which have been intercepted by generals who do not wish to trouble me with their contents. I take it you are here on behalf of the man who sits upon the throne that is rightfully mine?'

Valerius didn't reply immediately. Vitellius's words had ignited an unexpected flare of hope. He might have airily dismissed the couriers who weren't reaching him, but it left the question of just who was in control: the Emperor, or the men who led his armies. There was also the question of trust. If Vitellius didn't trust his guards, it meant he didn't fully trust their officers, and by extension those same generals who were keeping information from him. Equally, the fact that the guards were prepared to spy on the man they were meant to be protecting indicated a lack of trust in Vitellius on the part of the soldiers he supposedly commanded. And there lay the dilemma for Valerius. Even if he could convince his old friend, did the man have the power to halt the avalanche he'd set in motion? He felt Vitellius's eyes on him, growing ever more impatient, but he ignored them. This was too important to rush. The legions of Germania had elected Aulus Vitellius Emperor, but had it been by popular consent, or at the instigation of their officers? He had an image of a chained bear he had once seen in the street, its owner encouraging it to dance with lashes of a whip. Was Vitellius the bear or the man holding the chain?

At last, he spoke. 'Marcus Salvius Otho greets you. He chose me to carry his message because he knows of our friendship and is certain you would never believe I would advise you to act against your best interests.'

'Hah,' Vitellius growled. 'Then that is his first mistake. He does not know Gaius Valerius Verrens as I do. If you have a failing, Valerius, it is that you're too honest and too loyal. You will act in the best interests of Aulus Vitellius? No, Gaius Valerius Verrens will act in the best interests of *Rome*, because Gaius Valerius Verrens is wedded to a sugar-dusted image of Rome that has nothing to do with the sewer-breathed reality, and Aulus Vitellius may burn in the deepest pit of Hades if it suits Rome's purposes. So do not feed me an onion and tell me it is a peach. I have tasted enough things in my life to know the flavour of ox manure.'

The words struck like a slap in the face from Vitellius's jewelled fingers. Valerius felt the blood surge to his cheeks as he experienced a rush of anger that wouldn't be constrained by the armed men lining the walls. 'And what is Aulus Vitellius Germanicus Imperator's vision of Rome?' He tried to keep his voice level, but the words emerged with the speed and venom of sling pellets. 'Is it the women and children, every one a client of the Empire, lying in a burned-out town on the Aarus river? It was only the first of many we encountered in the lands of the Helvetii. You asked me if I was hungry. I was hungry when I came here, but not when I saw what we were to eat, because your roasting pig reminded me of a babe I saw not a week ago lying in the ruins of its home, with its mother's blackened bones beside it.' He struggled for words as his head filled with the images he'd seen. 'I hope you enjoyed your pork, Aulus. I would have choked on it.'

'That was none of my doing.' The fat man didn't respond to the anger in Valerius's voice. 'We needed

283

supplies. The Helvetii would not give us them. Caecina said they must be taught a lesson.'

'It was done in your name,' Valerius countered, each word fighting its way through clenched teeth. 'This is Marcus Salvius Otho's message to you. "Tell him I will give him anything short of the crown. He can name his price. He may govern any province that takes his fancy. I will share the consulship with him. I will pay off his soldiers and his generals." You have unleashed the wolves of the North, Aulus. Unless you find a way to call them back, what happened to the Helvetii will happen to Romans from Augusta Taurinorum to the very gates of Rome. Whatever you have heard about Otho, he is an honest man. He means what he says. I would stake my life on it.' He saw the look in Vitellius's eyes as he spoke the last sentence and knew, as if there had ever been any doubt, that he had done just that.

'I must think on this. There are other factors here of which you know nothing. Other lives are at stake. Even if I was minded to give up my claim to rule Rome, which I am not, do you think I could snap my fingers and call back my legions? Those men hailed Aulus Vitellius Emperor and Aulus Vitellius in turn pledged himself to them. What sort of weak fool would I look if I dithered at the first bank? Britannia and Gaul have declared for me. Caecina and Valens are halfway to Rome with close to fifty thousand men, and very soon I will join them. There is nothing to stop us but a handful of auxiliaries. Where are Otho's legions? He has only his palace guard, the Praetorians whose loyalty he has bought, and the mob—'

For all the decisiveness of his words, Vitellius sounded like a man attempting to persuade not the person opposite but himself, and from somewhere Valerius found the courage to interrupt. 'He was hailed Emperor by the Senate and people of Rome,' he said.

'He murdered an old man and stole the purple for himself.' Vitellius's voice hardened again. 'That alone should condemn him. The Senate supported him because it was support him or die. The people? What do the people know? All they care about is their bellies. Otho is not worthy of the throne of Rome.'

The last words were almost a snarl and Valerius caught the other man's mood. 'Yet he sits on the throne of Rome and you do not. If Aulus Vitellius Germanicus Imperator wants the purple he will have to walk over the bodies of a hundred thousand innocents to take it. Could you bear that, Aulus? Could the man who gave up his fortune to feed the starving of his African province use dead children as his stepping stones to the Palatium? If he could, he is no longer the man I called friend.'

Valerius found himself on his feet, chest heaving as if he'd just survived a battle. Vitellius's bodyguards moved to surround him with their swords drawn and a wild look in their eyes. The German Emperor slumped forward in his chair like a man awaiting the executioner's axe. For a moment, Valerius's fate lay balanced on the razor edge of a *gladius*, but before a blow could be struck Vitellius raised himself and waved his aides away.

'Enough, for now.' His voice emerged as a tired croak and he shook his head as if something had torn inside him. 'We will talk again tomorrow.'

Valerius hesitated, on the verge of . . . no, he would not apologize. Two legionaries appeared and he didn't resist as they led him away. They were almost at the door when Vitellius stopped them.

'You have tested my friendship, my patience and my hospitality, Gaius Valerius Verrens. Tonight, as you ponder a foolish old glutton's ridiculous dreams, I ask only that you remember this. His only ambition is the same as your ambition: to make a better Rome. And if he had your certainty he would already be garbed in purple, no matter how many innocents it took to make it so.'

As he was escorted back to the room he shared with Serpentius, Valerius felt as if an arrow had pierced his heart.

XXXII

'Will he do it?' Serpentius lay back on his bed in the governor's guest quarters with his hands clasped behind his shaved head.

'If he were his own man, his instinct would be to come to some sort of accommodation with Otho, but . . .' Valerius sighed, exhausted by the confrontation of the previous evening. 'He is like the driver of a runaway chariot. He has his fists on the reins, but he has long since lost control of his destiny. His lead horses are making the decisions and all he can do is hang on and pray the outcome isn't fatal.'

The Spaniard grunted acknowledgement. 'In the kitchens they whisper of him as the Emperor of the dinner table, because the only important decision he ever makes is what he's going to have to eat on a given day. The real power is Valens. Two months ago, during the Vindex business, he tried to bully Verginius Rufus into making a claim for the throne, but Rufus knew it could be his death warrant. When Galba made Vitellius governor of Germania Inferior, Valens must have felt he was being presented with a bull with a ring through its nose.'

'You've been busy.'

Serpentius grinned. 'So far, I'm an honoured guest. I've been fed and entertained and a plump, pretty slave girl from over the river pumped me for information in a way I didn't object to at all. She seemed pleased with what I gave her, though it wasn't information, and in return she told me the lie of the land here.' He smiled at the memory. 'Valens persuaded the legions upriver to hail Vitellius as Emperor and the governor had no way out. The way she told it, it was like one of those tarts who wave a perfumed veil in your face. Next thing you know, you're flat on your back and your purse isn't where you thought it should be.'

Valerius rose and splashed his face with water from the basin by the window overlooking a courtyard patrolled by Vitellius's personal guard. 'Then the answer to your question is no. He will not accept Otho's offer, because he cannot. Valens and Caecina are the men making the running and Valens won't stop until he's handed the seal of the Praetorian prefect, which will as good as put his hands round Vitellius's throat.'

'So where does that leave us?' The Spaniard pulled back the curtain to check no one was listening outside the doorway. 'If we're doing no good here, we should get out while there's still time. My little plump partridge showed me a passage to the slave quarters and I hear that not every soldier on the Rhenus likes the way things are going.'

A weary smile flickered across Valerius's scarred features. 'You may go with my blessing, but this is a game of power; the kind of game I used to play on campaign with Corbulo. Otho already has very few pieces on the board and it would be against my oath to deprive him of even one. I think there may still some good to be achieved here. What was that you said about soldiers?'

Serpentius scowled, disgusted that Valerius would even suggest he might desert him. 'About two dozen men and four centurions of the Twenty-second up at Moguntiacum objected when the young pup Caecina ordered them to pull down Galba's statues. They're being held in chains and the word is that their tent mates aren't too happy about it.'

Valerius nodded thoughtfully. 'That might be useful to know . . .'

A servant's face appeared in the doorway. 'Gaius Valerius Verrens, the Emperor wishes you to join him to break your fast.'

Vitellius was in the room they had occupied the previous night, already feasting on an array of fruits and meats and spooning honeyed porridge from a wide bowl. His eyes were puffy, but whether that was from the wine he'd consumed or lack of sleep wasn't apparent. He looked up when Valerius entered.

'Forgive me, Valerius, but I find that thinking gives a man an appetite.' He waved ringed fingers in an invitation to begin and returned to his plate. Valerius picked at the food, knowing he should eat more – who knew how this day would end? – but his stomach was churning as in the moments before an attack. When Vitellius was done, the household slaves cleared the bowls from the table.

In the long silence that followed, the German Emperor played with a great jewelled ring on the middle finger of his right hand while he contemplated Valerius with baleful grey eyes that contained no hint of his thoughts. Eventually, he sighed and shook his head.

'You have caused me a deal of trouble, Gaius Valerius Verrens.'

'Only because I wished to save you from more, and worse.'

Vitellius nodded slowly, the great jowls wobbling in rhythm with his movements. 'I apologize for my harsh words of yesterday. It says much for our friendship that you and your Spanish wolf were prepared to come here, even if your mission was a misdirected one.' Valerius started to protest, but the other man raised a hand. 'Hear me out, before you say what you must. Last night I mentioned that other lives were at stake, and that is true. I have set events in motion . . . no, let us be entirely truthful . . . the gods have set events in motion, of which they have placed me at the heart, and over which I have no power and little control. You were right to bring me word of what has taken place in my name. It is an un-worthy Emperor who begins his reign with massacre and rapine, and I will do what I can to make amends for what has happened and to ensure such things do not occur again.' Vitellius paused and Valerius saw what might have been a hint of regret in the deep-set eyes. He remembered a time in Africa when this man had wept over the bodies of starving children and wondered how it had come to this. Vitellius nodded as if he too was remembering those times, but both men knew there was no going back now.

'Marcus Salvius Otho's terms are generous, and you may thank him for me. I have a message for him in return, but first I must explain to an old friend why I cannot accept them. Yesterday we spoke of honesty and loyalty. Most men look at Aulus Vitellius and see a fat man whose only ambition is to get fatter. When they look at Aulus Vitellius Germanicus Imperator,

Emperor of Rome, they will see a fat man whose only ambition is to get rich. But you know better, Valerius. When I said our ambitions for Rome were the same, I spoke the truth. A strong Rome, a prosperous Rome, a Rome untainted by the stain of corruption.' A shadow crossed his eyes and Valerius knew he was thinking of his two lieutenants, but it quickly passed. 'I hope and pray that you see your own honour and loyalty mirrored in the fat man who stands before you.' His lips twitched in a sad half-smile. 'You see, I become poetic in my emotion. Seneca would never have approved. Still,' he levered his enormous frame to its feet, 'I will stand. I owe my loyalty to the men who hailed me Imperator on the field outside Moguntiacum. The men who now march on Rome in my name. In all honour, I could never desert them. There was never any possibility that I would turn back, even if I could. I hope you see that now.'

Valerius nodded, unable to speak for the duck egg that seemed to have lodged in his throat. Vitellius waddled to a cabinet set by the wall and stooped awkwardly to open it, and Valerius's heart sank at the sight of the polished rosewood box. Vitellius smiled when he saw his guest's reaction. 'Yes, Divine Caesar's sword. A sword unsullied and untarnished. A symbol, if you like, of the Rome we both wish to see. In a month five cohorts of the Twentieth Valeria Victrix will arrive from Britannia to join me. One of Rome's most feared legions, I hope you will agree?' Of course Valerius agreed; how could he not? He had served in the Twentieth as a beardless tribune. It had been the men of the Twentieth who formed the fearsome wedges which smashed into the great mass of Boudicca's army, and the men of the Twentieth who led the slaughter that followed. Their reputation was well earned, and Valerius had watched them earn it from Suetonius Paulinus's side. He didn't realize that Vitellius was still speaking until he heard his own name mentioned. He looked up to find the other man's eyes on him and his hand on the hilt of Julius Caesar's sword.

'I said that, unfortunately, the Twentieth's commander's loyalties are less certain than his men's. He has decided to stay in Deva to await events. Since those events are likely to be fatal to his career, the Twentieth will soon be in need of a new legate. I can think of no better man to lead them than Gaius Valerius Verrens, Hero of Rome.' For a moment Valerius's head seemed to be filled with thunder. He saw an eagle glittering proudly above an avenue of polished helmets. His eagle. Glory and fame awaited the man who led the Twentieth. It was already a formidable instrument of war; how much greater an instrument could it be in his hands. A *gladius* at the heart of Rome's enemies. Her shield against those who would harm her. The spear point of her military power.

'I cannot.' The words almost stuck in his throat, but they had to be said.

Vitellius continued as if they hadn't been spoken. 'All you need to do to make it so is to place your hand over mine and make the oath to Aulus Vitellius Germanicus Imperator.'

Valerius looked down at the plump fingers on the jewelled hilt and remembered another man's hand on another sword. That man had died because he refused to visit all this on Rome, and had he still lived Aulus Vitellius would never have dared lift a sword against his Emperor. *A Corbulo does not have the luxury of choice . . . only duty.*

'I cannot,' he repeated. It was said with regret, even sorrow, but there was also a savage conviction in the younger man's voice that made Vitellius blink. 'I have already given my oath to one Emperor. As long as he lives, I will abide by it.'

Vitellius's eyes half closed and in that second Valerius thought he detected a hint of unsheathed iron in the hidden depths, but it was gone before he could be certain. An expression of pained regret twisted the German Emperor's features and he withdrew his hand from Caesar's sword.

'A pity.' He sighed. 'With you at my side it would all have been different.'

The hurt was painful to witness and for the first time Valerius realized how much Vitellius had invested in his offer. With a true soldier like Valerius at his side, he could have cast off the chains forged by Valens and Caecina. With an ally he could trust and a legion in capable hands, he would have had the power to rule Rome as it should be ruled. Valerius felt like a man tied between two horses being whipped in opposite directions. Had he placed pride and honour above his duty to Rome? He had given his oath to a man who had taken Rome by force; a man so degraded he had allowed his wife to be used by Nero to ensure his political advancement. Did that man deserve to be Emperor? He felt Vitellius's eyes on him. All he had to do was place his hand on the sword and repeat the words and he would have his legion. Their time in Africa had proved that Vitellius was a good administrator and a good man. Given the right support, he could be a good Emperor. His hand edged towards the spun gold of the sword hilt. But he could not free himself of Corbulo's reproving stare and now it was Otho's words that rang in his head. *An honest man,*

293

*who is sometimes too honest for his own good. A man
whose loyalty to his Emperor is not in question.*

No.

He stood up. 'I am sorry.'

Vitellius cast off his disappointment with a shrug
and replaced it with a mask of geniality. 'Very well.'
He nodded. 'It is your right. I will provide you and
your servant with horses and a pass that will allow you
transit through my armies without hindrance. I said I
had a message for Otho, and you can do me a service by
delivering it. Tell him I must regretfully decline his offer,
but I will make him one of my own. There is only one
rightful Emperor of Rome. If he relinquishes his claim to
the purple, gives up command of the Praetorian Guard
and hands over the keys of state to the representatives
of Aulus Vitellius Germanicus Imperator, he may retire
to Sardinia and live the rest of his life without fear.'
He reached across the table and in a show of genuine
affection took Valerius's left hand in both of his. 'I must
ask you to leave without delay, Valerius, for once it
becomes known that you have been here it could place
us both in danger. We must say goodbye now, but know
this. Whatever has happened, and whatever will happen,
does not affect our relationship. You will always be able
to call Aulus Vitellius friend.'

The words, so unexpected and so welcome, made
something grow in Valerius's chest. He drew himself up
to his full height and rapped his walnut fist to his left
breast in a salute fit for an Emperor of Rome. As he
walked from the room he felt a wellspring of pity for his
old friend and wondered if he would ever see him alive
again.

If he had stayed, he would have seen Vitellius ring a
small bell to summon Asiaticus. While he waited, he

picked up the ornate *gladius*. Divine Caesar had never shirked difficult decisions. A shuffle of feet announced the former slave's arrival, but Vitellius didn't turn to acknowledge him.

'Send me Claudius Victor.'

XXXIII

Rome

Marcus Salvius Otho paced the long balcony of the great Golden House Nero had created to ensure his name would for ever be linked with the greatest of his divine forefathers. Unlike the late Emperor Galba, Otho had no reservations about living amid the luxurious trappings that the man who sent him into exile had gathered from the four corners of the Empire. The balcony overlooked a beautiful park where deer and antelope roamed by a shimmering lake and he watched the animals for a while, until he could delay the decision no longer. Returning to his desk, he picked up the letter and read it for the fourth time. Otho knew he had no choice. The clamour for the man's death had grown irresistible, and even though Gaius Valerius Verrens had advised clemency he was not yet in a position to defy the mob. He nodded and his secretary dripped hot wax on a corner of the parchment. Reluctantly, he marked it with his seal and handed it to the man.

'See that it is delivered immediately. Warn the messenger that he will attempt bribery, offer flattery and any other means he can think of to delay the inevitable, but he is to be informed that there is no escape from his duty.' So ends Offonius Tigellinus, and a decade of fear becomes a mere story to scare children to their beds, he thought.

In truth, Tigellinus was a distraction. But then there were so many distractions to divert him from his task that they caused a flutter of panic every time he sat down to consider them. Despite a lifetime following the *cursus honorum*, the ordered progression that steered a young Roman through the foothills of bureaucracy and discipline and prepared him for rule, he found himself ill prepared for the mountain of detail that seemed designed to crush an Emperor. First there had been the problem of the Praetorians, who had carried him to office on a tidal wave of enthusiasm and – there was no denying it – blood. He had made the normal donative of an incoming Emperor, enough to satisfy them, and make them forget the absurd bribe Nymphidius had promised on Galba's behalf. Then there had been the appointment of the new prefects to replace those who had died with Galba. He had promised that they could vote in their own candidates, but by subtle diplomacy and some questionable manoeuvring by Onomastus he had succeeded in having his clients Firmus and Proculus nominated. And yet there had still been some misunderstanding that had brought them rampaging to the Senate threatening to slaughter the entire house after some rumour spread that he was being held there against his will. It had eventually been resolved, but it had taken time he could ill afford and shaken the senators' faith in his ability to control the Guard. The finger of blame pointed unerringly at the Prefect of Rome. If Otho had been stronger he might have acted, but, like Galba, he

297

could not afford to alienate Vespasian in Judaea, so the general's brother Flavius Sabinus would continue in the role he had held under Nero.

The thought of Sabinus made him frown and he called for a document that had arrived the previous day. The prefect was demanding the arrest of Gaius Valerius Verrens on a charge of murder. Some story of a young relative, that useless scrub of a boy Domitianus, attacked, and one of his bodyguards killed. With Valerius out of the city Otho could afford to put the matter aside, but it would have to be dealt with in time. The dark eyes and scarred features swam into his vision. A capable man in any situation that required violence or guile, but with a fierce intelligence that made him doubly useful. Valerius's inflated sense of personal honour made him predictable, but somehow he always managed to overcome this handicap and get the job done. Well, useful or not, there might come a time when Gaius Valerius Verrens would have to be sacrificed on the altar of political gain.

He picked up another report and an involuntary groan escaped his lips. Flood water from the Tiber had inundated thousands of riverside properties, drowning dozens and making many hundreds homeless. Worse, it had demolished granaries and warehouses packed to bursting with grain to see Rome through the winter and supplies for the troops who would inevitably take the field in the spring. Most had been lost, and a bread shortage would bring the mob on to the streets, which he couldn't afford. There was no question of replacing the supplies in the short term, but should he increase subsidies to appease the poor, or use the money to ensure a supply for his army? The thought of the great shadow spilling from the north answered his question. He closed his eyes. He must have more troops.

'One hour until the parade, Caesar.'

'Very well. Summon my military advisers and my brother Lucius.'

When Galba and his cabal had been got rid of that should have been the end of it. No more bloodshed and an orderly return to normality. But he hadn't bargained for the unlikely ambition of Aulus Vitellius and his hold on the German legions. Galba had appointed Vitellius to Germania Inferior because he was harmless and could be relied on to stay that way. Everything Otho knew about the man confirmed his predecessor's evaluation. He had never met a lazier or less likely candidate for revolt. Otho did not want a war, would do anything he could to prevent it. Yet Vitellius's armies were marching on Rome and he must bring together a force capable of defeating them. Valerius was not his only diplomatic weapon, but it was becoming clear from the increasingly belligerent tone emerging from the Vitellius camp that diplomacy wasn't going to work. A few days earlier, his spies had intercepted a pair of assassins who admitted under torture that they had been sent from Colonia Agrippinensis. Alas, he had missed his opportunity to respond in kind. Even now, Valerius might be in a position to wield the knife. Of course, the one-handed nobleman was much too honourable for that, but Otho was human enough to regret not encouraging his murderous-looking Spanish freedman to do the job if the chance arose. Still, what was done could not be undone.

Marcus Salvius Otho recognized that vanity had always been one of his failings, but personal vanity was one thing, political vanity very much another. Political vanity had killed Galba as surely as if it wielded the blade that removed his head. Political vanity had convinced him that every thought that came into his head was correct, and his every decision irrefutable, whatever the evidence to the contrary. Political vanity had led him to ignore the counsel of more prudent, more experienced men, and Otho had resolved he would not make the same mistake.

The three men his aide ushered into the room could not have been more different, yet each was vital to his plan to defeat Vitellius. His elder brother, Lucius Salvius Otho Titianus, grave and stolid, wearing his usual expression of frowning resolve; a man of little imagination, but one who could be entrusted with holding Rome while his Emperor took the fight to the rebels. In the centre, Gaius Suetonius Paulinus, well into his sixties now, still gaunt from his time under house arrest on the orders of Galba, the reward for being consul in the last days of Nero. A hardened survivor who had all but destroyed the province of Britannia in revenge for Boudicca's excesses, been brought low by his over-enthusiasm and then resurrected thanks to the allies who hailed him as the greatest general of his day. It was that generalship Otho needed now, but the question that had occupied the Emperor's thoughts for the past hour remained unresolved. Could Paulinus be trusted? That was why the third man was here. Marius Celsus was one of the few people in Rome Marcus Salvius Otho counted as a friend. It had been Celsus who had steered him through the difficult and depraved years in Nero's court, Celsus who had convinced him that Poppaea must be sacrificed, and, in the end, Celsus who had persuaded the Emperor that Otho could be left alive, albeit in his Lusitanian fleapit. He could trust Celsus and that was why Celsus, who had the added advantage of having commanded a legion, would share control of the army Otho led north.

Yet, and there was that flare of panic again, how many men would they lead?

'Welcome.' He ushered the trio to the map table his aides had prepared. 'The latest positions of the Vitellian forces are as you see them.' He pointed a jewelled forefinger at the upper-left quadrant of the chart. 'Valens is still beyond the western Alps. Caecina has not yet reached Mediolanum. Our spies say Vitellius has yet to join either. The only troops in northern Italia loyal to the usurper are the cavalry of Tiberius Rubrio. We know that Rubrio has forced at least four cities to acknowledge Vitellius, but doesn't have the numbers to garrison them.'

'Then we must act now, before either force has the opportunity to reinforce the cavalry, or, worse, to combine with each other.' Paulinus's voice reminded Otho of a cart wheel skidding on loose gravel and contained a hint of censure he didn't care for.

'We didn't expect them to march so early in the season.' Titianus came to his brother's defence.

'I have already sent for the Balkan legions,' Otho pointed out. 'The advance guard of the Thirteenth Gemina should reach Italia in just over a week, and they will be followed a few days later by the Seventh and the Fourteenth.'

'We can only get stronger.' Celsus smiled. 'While the enemy relies on a network of disgruntled officers to provide reinforcements, the Emperor has the support of the governors of Dalmatia, Pannonia, Moesia, Syria, Judaea, Egypt and Africa. The armies of Vitellius must live off the land, while we can count on the entire resources of the Empire.'

'I am aware of that,' Paulinus growled. He loomed over the map like a hawk hovering on the wind. 'But the incontrovertible fact is that the enemy already has at least four legions, possibly as many as six, in the field, while we have, by my count, precisely none.'

Celsus's face reddened and Titianus opened his mouth to speak, but Otho raised a hand for silence.

'I congratulate the consul on his command of arithmetic, but that will change within the next few hours. The Praetorian Guard is at this very moment preparing to march north. They will be joined by First Adiutrix and every cavalry unit that can be spared from south of the Padus. It is my intention that they converge on . . .' he sought out a point on the map, 'Bedriacum, here, sweep Rubrio's cavalry out of Transpadana, defeat the first rebel column to reach Italian soil, and then turn and confront the other, by which time our Balkan reinforcements will have joined us.'

He smiled, seeking the grizzled general's approval, but Paulinus only frowned and studied the map all the more intently.

'A fine plan,' said Celsus, who had helped Otho form it.

'Not enough troops.'

'General?'

'We do not have enough men to be certain of defeating either of Vitellius's armies.' Paulinus's granite-chip eyes searched the room seeking dissent. 'The Praetorian Guard may be the Emperor's elite, but they are garrison troops and will take time to become campaign-hardened. The men of the First Adiutrix were pulling oars and climbing ropes not four months ago. They may be strong and they may be brave, but they cannot hope to match any of the legions which march against them. I would advise a strategy of manoeuvre, avoiding an all-out confrontation while simultaneously preventing the

Vitellian columns from combining. If I can achieve this until the Balkan legions are under my command you will have your victory. But we still need more fighting men.'

'The urban cohorts?' Titianus suggested nervously.

Paulinus grunted. He would take them, for all the use they were likely to be. 'We need fighters.'

'I have called up every soldier in southern Italia,' Otho pointed out.

'Not soldiers. Fighters.' Paulinus produced a savage smile. 'Gladiators.'

'Gladiators?' Celsus didn't bother to hide his derision.

'Yes, gladiators. Within this city you have some of the best-trained fighting men in the Empire. How many in the *ludi*, one thousand? Two? They are not soldiers, but they are killers and they will fight if you give them something to fight for.'

'And what would that be?' Titianus demanded. 'They are foreigners; slaves, barbarians and criminals. It matters not to them who sits on the throne of Rome, since it is their destiny to die in any case.'

'Then give them an alternative destiny,' the former consul insisted. 'Offer them their lives and their freedom if they fight for the rightful Emperor of Rome.'

'Unthinkable.'

Paulinus ignored Celsus's intervention and turned to stare at Otho. 'If you wish to continue wearing the purple, then I suggest you be prepared to think the un-thinkable.'

Otho studied him for a long moment before he nodded. 'Titianus, make it so. Every gladiator prepared to fight for his Emperor will have his freedom on the day Vitellius is defeated and captured . . . plus a reward equal to a year's pay for a legionary.' He turned to the other two men. 'Then we are agreed? The advance guard will march at dawn and I will follow with the rest of the force within the next two days. But first . . .' Onomastus appeared in the doorway holding the Emperor's cloak of Imperial purple, 'I have a welcome duty to perform.'

Juva's chest swelled as he stood among the massed ranks of the First Adiutrix, an *optio* of the first century, Fifth cohort, second in command to the centurion. It had been an exhausting few weeks since the fateful day Otho had given the legion its name and its eagle, the training hard and the discipline fierce. Day after day they had marched and counter-marched, learned to form line, column and defensive circle, and eventually to move between the three with the deceptive ease of a true legion. Only then had they been issued with their weapons and their armour. It had been the legion's wish that they keep the blue tunic that identified their naval origins. The Emperor had gladly agreed, and because of the special circumstances of their formation the First wasn't expected to pay the usual five *denarii* cost of the equipment. Over the tunic they now wore the *lorica segmentata*, the flexible jointed plate armour which protected the shoulders and chest. Thirty-four separate pieces of iron that Juva, like every other man, had discovered were so difficult to keep polished, oiled and clean of rust that it took up every moment of the little free time they had. Each man had been issued with a new pair of *caligae*, the leather hobnailed sandals that had allowed the legions to march the length and breadth of the Empire. On his dark head, Juva wore the heavy brass helmet that was a legionary's curse on the march and his saviour in battle. It was one of the most modern types, with a reinforced cross-brace on the brow to stop a direct sword blow, a wide neck protector and detachable cheek-pieces. He'd been fortunate to get one with a good fit that needed a minimal amount of padding. From the belt at his waist hung the scabbard that held his *gladius*, the twenty-two-inch, triangular-pointed sword that made the legions so deadly. He had spent countless hours perfecting the lightning-swift stabbing technique and the brutal, twisting withdrawal that created the terrible wounds that made it feared. At rest in front of him he held his *scutum*, the big leather-covered shield that would protect him in battle. Constructed of three layers of oak, close to four feet tall and three wide, it was heavy enough to make even a giant like Juva struggle initially to hold it for any length of time. Yet every man understood it could be the difference between life and death in a fight. None complained when their centurion, a veteran who resented being transferred to 'a useless shower of sailors', insisted on hour after hour of shoving matches between units, or individual contests where the men battered each other into bloody, exhausted submission. No *pilum* for this parade, though the Nubian prided himself on his skill with the heavy, weighted javelin. Four foot of ash, topped with two and a half of iron, tipped with a pyramid-shaped point, and he could throw it further and more accurately than any man in the legion.

Today, on the eve of its first campaign, the First Adiutrix was to be formally recognized. Only his height and colour made Juva stand out from the near five thousand men waiting at attention behind their century and cohort standards. He squared his great shoulders as Marcus Salvius Otho walked to the central reviewing platform accompanied by three men in military uniform and a cloud of senators in purple-striped togas. Tall and confident, Otho looked every inch an Emperor as he took his place in front of them. It had been his decision to honour Rome's newest legion by formally bestowing their eagle standard in a public ceremony. Thousands of spectators had gathered around the great open square of soldiers. It was to those thousands he spoke, with the help of several dozen orators Onomastus had placed strategically to broadcast his message to those beyond the reach of his master's voice.

'Soldiers of Rome.' Juva's fingers tightened on the shield and his spine tingled as he heard the words. 'Soldiers of Rome, tomorrow you march north in a campaign for the very soul of the Empire. Believe me when I tell you the thoughts of all here will march with you, including those of your Emperor, who will soon follow in your footsteps. I did not want war; I have done everything to avoid it. Yet the usurper has contemptuously cast aside every offer of a peaceful solution. I will not say his name here, but you know him. He is celebrated for his greed. It is his greed for a power that is not his to wield that drives him. That same greed will be his downfall.' The added emphasis he gave to the last sentence produced a roar of applause from the crowd, and he allowed it to subside before he continued. 'The soldiers you will face have yet to set foot on the soil of Italia. When they do, you will defeat them. They have been deceived by soft words and false promises and they do not know what they fight for. You are fighting for the rightful Emperor, solemnly appointed by the Senate and the people of Rome. You will go into battle alongside the elite Balkan legions who are already marching to meet you – the Seventh, the Eleventh Claudia, the Thirteenth Gemina and the Fourteenth Gemina Martia Victrix – but even if you did not, victory would still be assured. For when we fight, great Mars and mighty Jupiter will fight at our shoulders. I have sacrificed a white bull in your honour and the signs are auspicious. Orfidius Benignus, a soldier of proven valour, will command you. Step forward, *aquilifer*, take up your sacred charge and make the oath on behalf of your comrades.'

Florus, once a lowly marine, but now attired in the magnificent war gear which marked the legion's standard-bearer, with a full lion's pelt draped across his shoulders and back, marched tall and proud from the ranks. As he approached the platform, Otho took the eagle standard from the centurion who held it and with Orfidius Benignus at his side descended to meet the *aquilifer*.

'I hand this eagle into your keeping; bear it with honour and guard it with your life. For Rome.'

Florus's hands shook slightly as he accepted the wooden pole, but they stilled as his fingers grasped the polished wood. His eyes lifted reverently to the eagle, its golden wings spread wide, the great hooked beak gaping and lightning rods grasped in its talons. With tears clouding his vision, he turned to face his comrades and his deep voice rang out across the square.

'In the name of Jupiter Optimus Maximus I accept this eagle, this sacred symbol of my Emperor's faith, into my keeping and that of Legio I Adiutrix, and I pledge on behalf of my comrades that we will defend it to our last spear and our last breath, or may the god strike us down. For Rome!'

Five thousand throats echoed those final roared words. In the hush that followed, Juva felt a prickle behind his eyes and he gritted his teeth so no man would

see his weakness. He was a Roman legionary and tomorrow he would march to bring retribution on Rome's
enemies.

'For Rome,' he whispered.

XXXIV

'Two men, well mounted and trailing a pack horse as you said they would, lord.'

Claudius Victor nodded absently and the tracker trotted off down the muddy path, his eyes scanning the ground for any deviation in the sign. It was almost eight months since the Batavian's brother had died at the hands of Gaius Valerius Verrens but not a day had passed when he had not thought of the one-handed Roman and vengeance. Now, at last, the fates had brought his enemy almost within Victor's grasp.

The men he sought had left the river road as soon as they were out of sight of Colonia's smoke. In the empty coldness of his heart the Batavian felt the minutest stirring of the blood. Aulus Vitellius Germanicus Augustus had made him aware of the quality of the man he hunted. Even with the fat Emperor's sanction, Valerius Verrens was wary of the patrols he would meet on the road. But in the end it would not matter. Revenge would be his.

He remembered Vitellius's final words. 'It is a pity, he has been a good friend, but for the Empire's sake he must die. Make it quick and make it clean; he deserves that, at least.'

But Vitellius had not searched for a body on a corpse-scattered field in Gaul all those months ago. Claudius Victor turned to the wolfskin-cloaked troopers of his cavalry detachment. 'We will wait until they are beyond Moguntiacum before we take them. The servant can die, but I want the man with only one hand alive or whoever kills him will go to the fire in his stead.'

He felt their fear as he kicked his horse into motion, and the thirty men followed in his wake as he contemplated the many horrors he would inflict on the man who had killed his brother.

'We have Vitellius's pass and a warrant to change the horses at his way stations,' Serpentius pointed out. 'I don't understand why we're creeping about in the bushes again when we could be making another six miles a day.'

Valerius didn't answer immediately. The Spaniard was right. They could have travelled the well-maintained road that followed the Rhenus all the way to Augusta Raurica and into the Alps beyond. Instead, they had taken to the flat, marshy plain to the west, riding through brush and low scrub and avoiding the occasional patches of forest that studded the countryside. It had cost them time, but all he knew was that he could feel an itch on the back of his neck and that itch had never let him down.

'I may consider Vitellius a friend.' Valerius frowned as he tried to put his thoughts into words. 'And perhaps he does likewise, but he's a great man now. He rules half the Empire, and if Otho doesn't get reinforcements soon it may not be long before he rules the rest. I've been around enough great men to know that they do not see the world as other men do.' He glanced over his shoulder, remembering Nero, alone with his ghosts in the great palace he had built so the world would remember him for ever. 'They see threats everywhere. They lash out in self-preservation and call it duty. They order a man's death and call it necessity. If a friend stands in the way of their ambitions, he is a friend no more. Vitellius is a man who has a soothing way with words, but he wears his ambition like a legionary banner. It is his ambition I fear. A dagger in the back is no less deadly if it's accompanied by whispered words of friendship.'

Serpentius murmured acknowledgement. 'Aye.' He grunted. 'It wouldn't be the first time he tried to feed us to the foxes. I was thinking it was strange he didn't just order a fast galley to take us upriver if he was so keen to get his message back to Otho. We could have reached Moguntiacum in two days in comfort instead of three sleeping in the mud.'

Valerius nodded. He'd had the same thought. Unless Vitellius was having them followed, which was more likely than not, he would expect them to head west and follow the Mosella south-west from Confluentes, where it joined the main river. Instead, Valerius had decided to stay with the Rhenus as far south as Cambete. Yet if Vitellius was playing them false there was no sign of it so far. Perhaps he was starting at shadows. He'd noticed that the older a man got, the more he understood of the perils of his existence and the more nervous he became. Still . . . 'I'd rather sleep in the mud for a night or two than in a cold grave for all eternity, and until we're past Vitellius's legions and back in Italia I'll be sleeping with my sword in my hand.'

They camped in a damp, gloomy wood three miles west of Moguntiacum and Serpentius erected a low palisade of brush to shield the glow of the tiny fire Valerius built in the centre of the clearing. When they'd eaten the Spaniard insisted on taking the first watch. Valerius wrapped himself in his blanket and, after a long day in the saddle, instantly slipped into a blessed sleep and dreamed of warm days on his father's estate, acting as a scarecrow among the vines. The tranquil idyll ended abruptly in an explosion of fear. He woke in darkness with a hand covering his mouth and a sandal-shod foot pinning the blade of his sword.

'Wolves,' Serpentius whispered. He removed his foot from the blade. 'But not the four-legged kind. I can smell them. They're all around us, maybe twenty or thirty.'

'Bandits?'

Valerius sensed the Spaniard shake his head and cursed inwardly. Even with two against many, he would have backed them to cause enough casualties to deter a gang of bandits and give themselves a chance to escape. If this was a military unit they'd be well armed and reasonably disciplined; that made a difference. But if it was one of Vitellius's patrols, why hadn't they approached the camp instead of skulking about in the darkness like assassins? He grabbed the Spaniard's arm and drew him close. 'We have to find a way out,' he hissed.

Serpentius stared at him, the whites of his eyes gleaming like fireflies in the soft glow of the dying embers. Without a sound, he dropped to the damp earth and slithered into the darkness. Meanwhile, Valerius backed away from the entrance to the makeshift enclosure to prepare the horses. He worked silently to untie the pack with his left hand and distribute what supplies he could between the two cavalry mounts. No question of taking the lead animal. It would be a quick prayer and a mad neck-or-nothing dash into the darkness with swords

312

flying. The tactic had worked before when Valerius and his patrol had been trapped beyond the Danuvius by a horde of Dacian warriors. If Serpentius could find a weak spot in the enemy perimeter they had a chance; if not . . . well, the gods would decide.

As he worked at the leather straps the slightest movement caught the corner of his eye. A shadow that wasn't quite a shadow. He froze, not daring to breathe. Serpentius? But when his eyes probed deeper he realized the ground beyond the fence was a living carpet. He wrapped the reins of the Spaniard's mount round the wooden fist and vaulted into his saddle, simultaneously drawing his sword and kicking the beast's ribs. Too late. They were on him before the animal reacted, swarming across the fence in a howling rush that matched the wolf cloaks they wore. Hands clawed at his legs and he hacked at a snarling face that fell away in a screaming welter of blood. Another took its place and received the same treatment, but they were all around Valerius and no matter how often the blade connected, a new threat always appeared. With every second he expected to feel the agonizing bite of spear or sword, but it never came. The horse shied and he felt himself being hauled from the saddle and pinned to the damp earth, kicks and punches raining down on him, accompanied by animal grunts and howls. Rough hands pinned his sword arm and prised the blade from his fist. Now, he thought. It will end now. Instead, a guttural command cut short the assault and he was dragged to his feet in a circle of snarling faces that demanded blood vengeance for the four men who lay groaning in pools of darkness.

A tall figure marched out of the shadows, his face hidden by the wolf's mask that covered his head. The

313

soldier bent towards the fire and stirred the glowing ashes until the brand he held caught light. He raised it to illuminate the prisoner's face and the glow caught the expressionless features beneath the hood. Valerius's breath died in his chest when he recognized his captor.

Twenty paces away, hidden in the trees, Serpentius froze as the torch flared and he saw the face from the blood-soaked field by the Rhodanus. He had already killed four of the Germans, but they swarmed in the woods all around and he knew his time was running out. His first instinct was a red-eyed impulse to rush his enemies and free Valerius or die in the attempt. But that would not help his friend. He had to find another way. He slid backwards and disappeared further into the brush as his hunters closed in.

Claudius Victor fixed Valerius with his pale eyes and the Roman flinched at the malignant spark of triumph he saw in their otherwise lifeless depths. The Batavian studied him for more than a minute, as if he was trying to work out what lay beneath the skin of the scarred face. He reached out and his fingers gently caressed the carved walnut fist. Valerius automatically flinched away and felt the skin crawl on a hand that had been buried in the ash of a Celtic hovel for eight years. Fear formed a squirming ball in his guts and he fought it as it rose to fill his chest and throat. He had never needed his wits more, and if he allowed fear to overwhelm his mind all would be lost. Somehow he had to talk his way out of this.

'I carry dispatches from Aulus Vitellius Germanicus Augustus to Marcus Salvius Otho and any man who stands in my way risks the wrath of the one or the other.' He spoke the words with all the authority and arrogance he could muster, but the Batavian barely acknowledged them. His thin lips twitched, not quite a smile, more an acknowledgement that the situation was not without a certain humour. Without warning, the hand that had been touching the wooden fist came up in a backhanded sweep that took Valerius on the right cheek, making him stagger back and filling his mouth with the metallic taste of blood.

'You carry nothing, Roman, and you are nothing. Better for you to think yourself already dead, for you will soon wish you were. I see you remember me. What else do you remember of that day?' The voice was soft and low, almost seductive, but there was an unhinged quality to it, as if the speaker was teetering on the edge of terrible violence or screaming madness. 'Answer me.' The hand came up again, and Valerius reeled from the power of it.

'I remember a fight. Men died when there was no need, as there is no need for this. If my message gets through, war may be avoided. Do you want to be responsible for thousands of deaths?' The question was aimed not at the man who faced him, who he guessed would slaughter thousands at a whim and think no more of it than of sacrificing a chicken, but at the ring of pale faces whose dark eyes gleamed like shards of quartz in the torchlight.

Claudius Victor's eyes narrowed. 'I remember a boy dying, a son and a brother, a young man in the first flower of his manhood, his body torn by the blades of mercenaries and left lifeless on the field by his murderers. I know this, because I buried him with my own hands.'

'An unblooded auxiliary officer who died in a fight he should never have been part of. If you had led the attack instead of cowering among the trees, perhaps he would be here in your place.' Valerius risked the defiance, thinking nothing could make his situation worse. He was wrong.

Victor reached up to hook his fingers into Valerius's cheek, forcing his mouth open. 'Your mouth is like a latrine. Utter another word that is not an answer to my question and I will have you held down and my men will fill it before we gag you.'

He issued an order and Valerius's throat heaved at the thought of what might be to come. But his captors dragged him to a tree where they tore his clothes away before binding him naked to the trunk. Some of the Batavians rushed into the wood and he heard the sound of axes before they reappeared in the clearing, carrying two long stakes and several cuts of green wood. Meanwhile, others dug two pits ten paces apart on either side of the fire, which now burned fiercely, fed by branches from the makeshift palisade. Valerius watched in growing horror as the stakes were placed in the pits and the earth filled in around them and tramped home to create a firm base. The first was about four feet tall and three inches in diameter and the tip had been sharpened to a horrible, jagged point. The second stood twice the height and more than twice the thickness of the other and the Batavians stacked the green wood beside it. His mind rebelled against what it was witnessing and something exploded in his stomach before erupting in a white-hot stream from his throat.

'I see you understand their purpose.' Claudius Victor nodded. 'Good. For the moment, I will leave you to contemplate which end you would prefer. We will begin when I return at first light. Perhaps I will even allow you to make the choice. The impaling stake or the fire.' He pulled a wicked-looking curved knife from his belt and Valerius flinched from the glittering blade. 'But there are certain things you should know first. You have a single hand and that must be precious to you, as my brother was to me, which is why I will personally cut it from you with a blunt axe. You are a proud man, Gaius Valerius Verrens, knight of Rome; that is plain for all to see, and why we will first remove the things that are the source of your pride. Naturally, we will do this with skill, ensuring you live long enough to enjoy their loss.' The import of the words made their targets shrivel, encouraging a roar of laughter from the Batavians, but Claudius Victor only continued in his cold voice, his face so close that Valerius gagged from the rank stench of his breath. 'If you choose the stake, we will first flay the flesh from your body an inch at a time and burn it before your eyes. It is difficult to imagine the pain and the horror of it. Even to think of it must drive a man to the brink of madness.' Valerius closed his eyes and tried not to see the auxiliary decurion who had led the patrol across the Danuvius two years earlier and been captured by the Dacians. He had ended up a whimpering mass of raw, bleeding flesh, squirming on a stake exactly like the one in front of him. 'I have known a flayed man to live for three days on the stake,' Claudius continued. 'Perhaps you would prefer the fire? Yet the fire can be just as entertaining and the agonies last just as long. We will leave you your skin, for which you will at first be grateful, but when that skin begins to shrivel and melt away in the heat, and the flesh beneath it starts to roast, you will perhaps feel you should have chosen the stake. There will be no flame, which would ensure a quick, if painful, end, and no smoke with which to choke yourself. No escape. For this is the slow fire. Fire that begins at the feet and moves up the body an inch at a time, tended by men who know how to make it

317

last. Of course, you will go mad as you feel the flesh fall from your body and your inner parts begin to cook, but you will still be conscious when your heart explodes and finally ends your suffering.' He took Valerius's face in his right hand and looked directly into his eyes. The Roman felt as if he was staring into a furnace. 'If it was in my power, you would die a hundred such deaths.' The Batavian noticed the glint of gold at the Roman's neck and his fingers closed on the boar amulet Valerius's sister had given him. 'You will not require this any further,' he said, and brought his knife up to cut the thin leather strip holding it.

For a moment fear was replaced by fury, but as Valerius raged Victor called for his horse. 'I go now to bring my father, who will wish to enjoy your end, and my sisters and my brother's wife, who may add further refinements to your agony.' He hesitated and his eyes flicked to the wooden hand on Valerius's right arm. 'Perhaps we should start now?' He sawed at the thongs holding the leather stock in place and hauled it clear. As it was taken from him, the Roman wrestled at his bonds, and Claudius Victor came as close as he ever would to a smile. His eyes never leaving Valerius's, he took the walnut fist to the fire and thrust it into the flames, where the leather scorched and charred before igniting and the wood turned black as the fiery golden heart devoured it. Valerius heard the long cry of anguish that was torn from his own throat and felt a sense of violation that went deeper than the loss of his hand.

And this was only the beginning.

XXXV

Valerius fought to hold on to the tiny sliver of hope that still existed deep at the very centre of him, to harbour the mental and physical strength that had seen him through every crisis. In his heart, survival was still possible, however unlikely. But in his mind Claudius Victor had already won. *Better for you to think yourself already dead.* The Batavians kept the fire banked high so he could see the instruments of torture which, by one road or another, would tomorrow bring him an eternity of suffering that could only be ended by merciful death. The guards entertained themselves by spitting in his face or holding a glowing branch against his flesh to remind him of what was to come. Their victim's lack of reaction to his humiliation or the stink of singed hair and burned skin disappointed them, and only made them try all the harder. Valerius endured, drawing deeper within himself to escape the agonizing pain of the ropes cutting into his flesh. Despite his agony and the chill of the night, at one point he somehow managed to sleep, though even here the horrors he would endure at dawn followed him. Yet from within his tormented dreams an unlikely hope tempted him in the whispered voice of a ghost that seemed to come from very far away.

He came instantly alert. In fact, the whisper came from behind the trunk, on the side hidden from the men by the fire. Serpentius. 'I'm cutting the ropes,' the Spaniard informed him, 'so you'll only be held by a single strand. Do you think you'll have the strength to break it when the time comes?'

Valerius felt a renewed surge of energy that almost made him cry out. Instead, he kept his head bowed so his captors wouldn't see his lips move. 'When will that be?'

'Soon. You'll know when it happens.'

'Just free me and go,' the Roman urged. 'There are twenty of them and only one of you. All you're doing is handing them another piece of meat to cook.'

'Maybe, and maybe not,' Serpentius grunted. 'I'm sticking a sword in the ground at the base of the tree. When you free yourself, pick it up and kill anything that gets in your way.'

Valerius waited for further instructions, but there was only silence. His mind whirled. Was it possible they could get out of this alive? He almost laughed, because it didn't matter. All that mattered was that he wouldn't have to endure the horrors these German savages had planned for him. He would escape or die in the attempt, and if he died he'd take as many of these Batavian bastards with him as possible. He was tempted to test his bonds, but he knew that if the rope snapped and fell away prematurely the Batavians would be on him like a pack of the wolves they so admired. He couldn't feel his left hand and he would need it for the sword. He flexed the fingers until the blood flowed again and pains shot up his wrist. *You'll know when it happens.* When *what* happens?

He didn't have long to wait.

A Batavian with a flat moon face and slits for eyes picked up a brand from the fire and marched towards him. Valerius watched him come, the wild, untamed features a vision from Hades in the firelight. When he was halfway to the tree Valerius heard the sharp snap of a branch splitting and the auxiliary appeared to walk into an invisible wall. Without another sound he fell backwards. His slack-jawed comrades stared in stunned disbelief until someone noticed the Scythian throwing axe embedded in their comrade's skull. As one, they began to rise. But they were much too slow.

A second axe took the man closest to the fire in the chest and he pirouetted into the flames with a shriek of agony. In the same instant, a hail of legionary *pila* killed or wounded half the remaining guards and a wave of howling figures launched themselves from the shadows. Most of the Batavians died in those first seconds, cut down by the blades of their attackers. But one warrior decided his last moments would be best used ensuring the prisoner met the painful end his lord had decreed. It might not be the drawn-out torment Claudius Victor had in mind, but the skinning knife in his hand would do the job. Valerius searched the darkness for Serpentius, but the Spaniard was lost in a maelstrom of whirling blades and dying men. He hurled himself from the tree and cried out in astonishment when the ropes snapped so easily that he flopped at his attacker's feet. The Batavian lunged with the curved knife, a scything cut that would have opened Valerius from groin to breastbone if he hadn't rolled out of reach. The Roman scrabbled frantically backwards using the tree as cover, his left hand reaching for the sword he knew was hidden there. A wild burst of elation as his fingers found the hilt, gone in the same instant as a hand wrapped itself in his hair and hauled his head back to expose his throat. With a convulsive heave he threw himself away from the sweeping blade, his vision turning red as a bolt of agony tore through his scalp. At the same time he stabbed blindly with the sword as the cavalryman tried to pin him with his body. With a high-pitched scream the squirming mass above him became a dead weight and Valerius lay back with a warm liquid feeling spreading gently over his stomach and chest. He would have been happy to lie there for ever if someone hadn't hauled the dead Batavian off to reveal a bony, grinning face looming above him.

'You can rest when you're dead, and that might be sooner than you think if we don't get out of here. Is any of that yours?'

Valerius looked down to where the Batavian's life-blood had poured over his torso. 'I don't think so, but my head hurts.'

Serpentius put his hand to the raw pink wound on his friend's scalp and Valerius flinched. 'Nothing that a little sheep fat won't cure.' He pulled the Roman to his feet and looked him over. 'You're a mess, but you'll live. What happened to your hand?'

Valerius glanced at the stump of his right wrist. With all that had occurred since Claudius Victor had thrown the walnut fist in the fire he'd completely forgotten its absence. Now he was assailed by the same agonizing sense of loss he'd experienced at the time. Still he managed a smile. 'It was only a lump of wood. I can always get another, and better to lose it than endure what that Batavian bastard had in mind for me.'

The Spaniard eyed the pair of stakes standing like grave markers in the centre of the clearing and his features darkened. 'If any of them had lived I'd have left their leader something to remember us by.'

Valerius looked to where the fire still blazed and around twenty men were stripping the bodies of the dead and tending to two of their own who would soon be joining them. 'Just who is us?'

'I knew I couldn't do anything alone,' Serpentius explained, 'so I thought I'd look for reinforcements. The big lad, Cornelius Metto, is a centurion from the Twenty-second Primigenia. He's been around, he doesn't think much of Vitellius and he didn't want to end his enlistment as a rebel. The rest are the legionaries from the fort at Moguntiacum who refused to throw down the Emperor's statues. I found out they were being held in a stockade outside the fort. They were for the axe, if they were lucky, so they didn't take a lot of persuading. After that it was simple enough to break them out and they knew the way to the armoury.'

Valerius took a second to consider the frightening reality behind that bald statement before he used the contents of a Batavian water skin to wash the rapidly congealing blood from his body. He picked up his tunic, but it was torn beyond repair.

'I was thinking that one of our dead German friends might have something that would fit you,' Serpentius suggested. 'In fact, I don't think it would do any harm if we all turned into Batavian wolf men for a few days, at least until we're somewhere safer than this.'

When Valerius had found a sweat-stinking, verminous tunic and a mail shirt that more or less fitted he called the legionaries together. There were still at least three hours until dawn and he could see the wariness in their eyes in the firelight. These were men who, in the elation of freedom, had agreed to help their saviour. Who knew how much more they were willing to give? He met their gaze one by one. 'You will for ever have the thanks of Gaius Valerius Verrens and you may call on him for aid if ever you need it. When I return to Rome I will make sure that the Emperor hears of your loyalty and your valour.' At the word Rome a mutter ran through the assembled soldiers and Metto barked a command for quiet. Valerius continued. 'I cannot order you to come with me, and those who do not will not suffer in any way, but there will be rewards and honour for every man who accompanies us. Those who wish to should take a step forward.'

About a third of them complied, which was more than he expected. The rest formed a delegation behind a wiry decurion who said they'd rather take their chances heading for Gaul, if your honour didn't mind. Metto, the bearded centurion, stepped forward threateningly, but Valerius waved him back.

'I don't command these men. They have the right to make their own decisions and I only want willing volunteers.' He told Metto to split the Batavian supplies between the two groups. They were fortunate that most of the remaining legionaries could ride, after a fashion, or were willing to try when the alternative was being hunted down by the comrades of the slaughtered Batavians. He reminded them of what lay ahead. 'They will not give up. Their leader will not allow them to; he is not that kind of man. He said he would not return until dawn, which should give us four hours by the time he works out which direction we've taken. We won't get far in open country, so I intend to go back to the road and make as much distance as we can before daylight without tiring the horses. Remember, without your horse you are a dead man. Gather as much fodder as he can carry, but don't overload him. We'll ride night and day, rest when the horses begin to tire and not before, and stop for water when they need to drink, not us. Now, let us ride.'

Valerius rode at the head of the column with his scalp throbbing and the stump of his wrist hidden under a wolfskin cloak. He and Serpentius discussed what they would do if they met another patrol, or were stopped at a checkpoint.

'We may be dressed like Batavians, but we don't ride like them and we don't speak their language,' the Spaniard pointed out.

Valerius shrugged. 'If it comes to it, we may have to fight our way through.'

'And have every unit this side of the Alps on our tails within the hour? Not to mention giving away our position to a Batavian butcher who won't be satisfied until he feeds you your own entrails?'

Valerius stared at him. 'You have a better idea?'

'Maybe.' Serpentius chewed his lip. 'According to Metto, there's been bad blood between the auxiliaries and the legions on the Rhenus ever since the Batavians were shipped back from Britannia. They're arrogant bastards, the wolf men. They didn't appreciate the fact that the legionaries had been lording it over their people and romancing their women while they were off dying for the Empire.' He darted a sideways glance at Valerius. 'Not that you can blame them for that. Anyway, it's got so bad that they can hardly look at each other without hands twitching for knife hilts. Even the officers barely talk to each other.'

'How does that help us?'

'If we hold our nerve and stick our noses in the air,

all we have to do is ignore any bastard who tries to stop us. If they persist, we snarl and spit in their eye and it'll be exactly what they expect from a surly, suspicious barbarian. Unless we meet a centurion with a head full of hangover I reckon it should get us past most of the units we meet.'

Valerius grinned. It was worth a try. 'All right, but if it comes to it, I'll be the one with my nose in the air. You can do any snarling and spitting that's needed. You have the face for it.'

The Spaniard grunted. 'I'll take that as a compliment.'

Two days of hard riding brought them to the point where the road branched off towards Vesontio, where Divine Caesar had defeated the German king Ariovistus, and more recently Verginius Rufus's legionaries had slaughtered Gaius Julius Vindex's Gaulish rebels. The valley would take them in turn to the Sauconna and the Rhodanus, the rivers that would lead them home. Serpentius's tactic of steadfastly ignoring authority had served them well and the journey passed without incident, if you didn't count the cracked ribs and mild concussion suffered by legionaries who temporarily parted company with their horses.

'They're still with us.'

Valerius didn't need to ask who, or how the Spaniard knew. All he had to do was close his eyes and he was looking at the burning embers in the depths of Claudius Victor's soul. 'He won't give up until one of us is dead.'

'If we sent Metto and his men on upriver to Augusta Raurica while we head west,' the Spaniard suggested, 'it might confuse them, or at worst make him split his forces.'

'I thought you knew me better, Serpentius.' Valerius shook his head. 'Those men helped save my life. I won't ask them to sacrifice themselves for me. That would make me as bad as the man who's hunting us. In any case, he'll have brought a full squadron. Even if he did split his forces we'd still have twenty or thirty on our heels. No, we stay together.'

They rode on, first west, then Valerius planned to turn south, which would take them finally into the wake of Gaius Fabius Valens' marauding army. Enemies to the front and enemies to the rear. Gaius Valerius Verrens had been in tighter situations, but he had never faced an enemy as implacable as Claudius Victor. He knew in his heart that the only way he was ever going to escape the Batavian was to kill him.

At first, the road took them through soft rolling countryside, dotted with farms and homesteads, and between mountain ranges that dominated the landscape to north and south. They saw little military activity, but Valerius knew that would change when they reached Vesontio, which was a major stop on the trade route formed by the Rhodanus, the Sauconna, the Mosella and the Rhenus. Up and down these rivers travelled olive oil, wine and *garum* from Massilia in the south, and grain, furs and timber from Colonia in the north. These were the rivers that had carried Vitellius's western army on its dash south. Vesontio opened up possibilities, but there would be time to think about that.

Early on the third day the ground became more difficult: low hills, rough grassland and swampy, wooded river valleys. They were breasting a rise as the ground fog cleared when Serpentius suddenly stiffened in the saddle and looked back. 'Riders, maybe fifteen or twenty of them, and coming up fast along our trail.'

Valerius followed his gaze and saw nothing in the broken countryside, but the Spaniard was certain.

'Victor has split his forces,' Valerius thought aloud. 'He's sent an advance guard of his best horsemen to either pin us in place or make us turn and fight.'

'Then here is as good as anywhere.' It was Metto. The big centurion's voice sounded weary and his words received muttered support from his men, who were arse-sore and exhausted after days and nights of struggling to stay in the saddle. 'We can ambush the bastards among the trees.'

'There aren't enough of us,' Valerius pointed out. 'Would you fight them on horseback?'

Metto shrugged, but it was clear that a mounted battle with veteran cavalrymen could only have one winner.

'And we can't fight them from the ground, because they'll cut us to pieces.'

'So what do we do?' the centurion demanded.

'There may be a way.' Valerius took Serpentius aside. 'I want you to ride ahead and find a place. Remember the Cepha gap. Somewhere we can't be outflanked.'

The Spaniard's eyes lit up with understanding. 'I know. If such a place exists, I will find it.'

An hour later, Serpentius met them where the road turned sharply from the river valley at the edge of a green meadow. The meadow was almost a mile deep, disappearing into heavy forest at the far end, bounded on one side by a scrubby hillside impassable to a horse, and on the other by the thick trees and bushes that lined the river bank.

Valerius shot a puzzled glance at the Spaniard.

'You'll see,' Serpentius said. 'We ride halfway across the meadow at the trot. When we get there you'll see a branch I've pushed into the turf. That's when you dismount and lead your horse. Go gently and stick close together on the line I've marked.'

The men did as they were ordered, and as he walked his horse through the branches Serpentius had placed Valerius realized the genius of the plan. 'Will it work?'

The Spaniard shrugged. 'It's the best I can do. It depends on how determined they are to get you and how blown their horses are. If it doesn't, we take our chances among the trees.'

When they reached a point about three-quarters of the way across the green sward, Valerius halted the men.

'Now we wait. Metto?' The centurion nodded. 'When they come into view we'll be arguing. You want to go back. I want to go on. Lots of arm waving. The others will mill about looking demoralized and beaten. You hear that, you bastards? They've beaten you. Those sons of dogs have ridden you into the ground and now you're ripe for their spears.'

A pent-up growl of frustration went up from the legionaries, but Valerius silenced it with a snarl. 'Save your anger for the Batavians. If they win, you'll find yourself with a stake up your arse and a flaying knife tickling your foreskin. They believe they're going to win because they outnumber us two to one. But Serpentius thinks we can beat them and Serpentius survived a hundred fights in the arena so he knows what he's talking about.' The men glared at the Spaniard, hating him for bringing them to this place and their potential doom. Each of them was armed with the pair of legionary *pila* they had stolen from the armoury at Moguntiacum. 'When the time comes, you slaughter them.' Valerius's voice rose to a shout. 'You slaughter every last one of the bastards.'

The thunder of hooves heralded the arrival of the enemy. Valerius prayed to Mars and Jupiter for Claudius Victor to be leading the men, but one glance told him the glacier-eyed Batavian had stayed with his main force. Metto was red-faced and roaring obscenities, waving his sword back to the road, and Valerius had a feeling it wasn't entirely an act. His men were doing their best to look defeated.

Valerius recognized the moment the auxiliary leader saw the small group trapped in the middle of a broad field. He knew what his adversary would be thinking: a perfect target, half his strength and ripe for the slaughter. The man swerved off the road and led his troopers at the gallop across the meadow towards the confused fugitives. Of course, he would be suspicious. One part of him would be thinking it was too easy, but he'd have the scent of blood in his nostrils and his commander's warning of the consequences of failure in his ears. It was obvious they'd ridden at a killing pace to get here. The horses were pop-eyed with exhaustion, their coats foam-flecked and silver-bright with sweat, but they still had one last charge in them and against so few their commander would be gambling that one would be enough.

Valerius watched them come, following the innocent hoof pattern. Saw the moment the commander registered the change and lost his certainty. But before the auxiliary's mind could assess the implications of what he was seeing, his mount had covered another four strides. To disaster.

At the battle of the Cepha gap, Gnaeus Domitius Corbulo had used concealed pits and viciously spiked four-toed metal caltrops to confound the elite heavy cavalry of the Parthian host. Here, Serpentius had marked a path for Valerius and his men on the very edge of a bog concealed by heavy grass. By dismounting and leading the horses at a walk, they had ensured that the beasts' hooves had cut into the surface crust of the bog without breaking it. But the Batavian horses covered the ground at the gallop with a fully armed and armoured cavalryman in each saddle. The moment they hit the soft ground their hooves plunged two feet into the clinging black ooze. At best, the horses hurtled to an instant halt in a welter of mud and water, throwing their riders into the mud. Animal screams of terror and pain told Valerius that several had broken legs and would never be ridden again.

'Now!'

Valerius stayed in the saddle while his legionaries dismounted and hefted their heavy javelins with professional ease. Most of the Batavian riders were down, struggling to free themselves from the mud and groping desperately for swords or the long spears they'd lost in the thick sludge. Three had managed to stay in the saddle and were now urging their mounts to the edge of the bog and it was to these that Valerius directed the first of the spearmen. They aimed for the horses, because they were the more certain target, and soon all three were down or standing shaking, knee deep in the mud and with a pair of the deadly *pila* projecting from their rib cages. A well-trained legionary could pin a moving target at forty paces. Now they were confronted with trapped and struggling men at twenty feet. The heavy mail the auxiliaries wore was designed to stop a sword cut, but the triangular points of the weighted javelins carved through the rings like paper to pierce hearts and lungs and guts. Serpentius circled the bog to cut off any retreat. As the remaining Batavians tried to struggle clear, they were chopped down before they touched dry ground. Two tried to surrender, but they were treated to the mercy they would have given their quarry.

When it was done, Serpentius put the injured horses out of their misery and the surface of the swamp was stained red. Valerius ordered his men into the saddle. There was no time to lose. Claudius Victor would be hard on his vanguard's heels and the slaughter of his men would only add to his fury.

XXXVI

They arrived at Vesontio in the first light of dawn with the smoke from thousands of cooking fires rising to merge with the low grey cloud. The city had originally been contained by a narrow-necked bend in the river, made more impregnable by the fortified hill that filled the neck like a stopper in a wineskin. Now the familiar red-tiled roofs and stucco walls spilled over to the east bank and a sturdy wooden bridge linked the two sections.

Serpentius wanted to continue onwards to maintain their slender lead over Claudius Victor, but Valerius knew they were in a race they could never win. 'We have to find another way,' he said as they sat apart from the others in a grove outside the city.

'How? You admitted we could never pass close inspection as Batavians.'

'That's true, but perhaps we don't have to.' The Emperor's sealed warrant had survived the search of his bags by Batavians more interested in gold than parchment and now he drew it from the sleeve of his tunic. 'This order requires every Roman citizen to lend all possible aid to Gaius Valerius Verrens, Hero of Rome, on pain of death. Vitellius probably thinks we're already dead and he can forget about it, but the commandant of this city, or whoever we have to bully into providing us with a boat, doesn't know that.'

'But—'

'We are on a secret mission,' Valerius continued, anticipating the question. 'So secret that it requires a Roman officer to dress in the uniform of a Batavian cavalry trooper. It is vital that we reach General Valens as soon as possible. We'll leave the horses here and use the warrant to replace them somewhere downriver.' He read the look on Serpentius's face. 'You're not convinced?'

'It doesn't matter what I think. By the time we find out whether it's going to work or not, Claudius Victor will have us bottled up like rats in a grain barrel.'

'Then let's make it work.'

Valerius left the legionaries with Metto and took Serpentius to the wharf downstream of the bridge, where he sought out the centurion in charge of shipping. Paladius Nepos was a small, officious martinet of a man, with a permanently angry scowl and a shock of mousy hair. The two rows of clerks under his command cringed away from the rod he carried and he was clearly unhappy at being disturbed by what he perceived as a mere barbarian.

'I will have to consult the *quaestor*, who is away on official business for the next two days,' he sniffed when he saw the seal. 'I do not have the authority to deal with this.' He turned away dismissively, but Valerius dropped the eagle-claw grip of his left hand on his shoulder.

'Then find someone who does. I count three barges out there ready to sail. If I and my men are not on one of them in ten minutes the name Paladius Nepos will be on the Emperor Vitellius's desk within a week. Perhaps you didn't read the Imperial pass carefully enough?' He pointed to the words *on pain of death*, and watched the conflicting emotions run across the other man's face.

Like every Roman citizen, Nepos had been faced with a choice of Nero or Galba. Now it was Vitellius or Otho, and for the moment, by an accident of geography, Aulus Vitellius Germanicus Augustus held his grubby little career and his life in his plump hands. And here was a tall, scar-faced Batavian officer who sounded like a properly educated Roman claiming to be on a vital mission from the Emperor and with the paperwork to prove it. His eyes darted to Serpentius, who stood at the door managing to look disinterested and dangerous at the same time. Beads of sweat appeared at Paladius Nepos's hairline and gravitated together to produce tiny runnels that made their way slowly down each side of his narrow, weasel's nose. The calculations going on behind the bulging eyes and the moment they reached a conclusion were as clear as a badly rigged chariot race. He picked up the pass.

'The *Pride of Sauconna* leaves as soon as she has clearance . . .'

'You mean now?' Serpentius suggested helpfully.

'There should be room aboard for eight men, if some of them sleep on the deck. She's the galley out there on the downstream side. With this height of water behind her, you can be with the . . . the army within two days. The last we heard, General Valens was moving east from Valentia . . .'

'We will only be with the ship as far as Lugdunum. One other thing.' Nepos looked up with startled eyes. 'You will tell no one about this.' Valerius waved the

335

Imperial pass under the other man's nose. 'On pain of death.'

'You don't expect him to keep quiet?' Serpentius said as they headed back to Metto and his legionaries.

'No, but I'm hoping it will make him think about it for an hour or two.'

As it turned out, his estimate was almost fatally optimistic.

The oarsmen of the *Pride of Sauconna*, a double-banked bireme of the Rhodanus fleet, had just got into their rhythm when Valerius heard a commotion behind them on the wharf. A rattle of hooves and a flurry of grey wolfskin told him that Claudius Victor had arrived earlier than anyone could have predicted. By the time they reached the downstream stretch of the bow in the river that encircled Vesontio, a Batavian cavalry patrol was already tracking them beyond the trees that lined the bank. Valerius could hear shouts and he turned to find the young prefect who captained the galley studying him with a question in his eyes.

'Ignore them. They could be rebels,' he said.

'You're the man with the Imperial pass.' The sailor shrugged. 'In any case, I don't take orders from landsmen. I have a schedule to keep and I'm buggered if I'm going to row against this current to get back to Vesontio.'

The Batavians stayed with them for another mile, dropping behind all the time. Valerius watched them disappear into the distance, and when a bend in the river carried the galley out of sight he relaxed for the first time in many days. Barring accidents, they had gained at least one day on their pursuers, perhaps two. He knew Claudius Victor couldn't afford to abandon his horses and follow by boat, because that would mean splitting his forces again and the Batavians had already seen how deadly Valerius and his men could be against superior odds. He would follow the river road at least as far as Lugdunum, and stop there to make enquiries, because that was where Valerius had told Nepos he was going, and Nepos would not stay mute for long in the face of someone like Victor. But Valerius didn't intend to leave the ship at Lugdunum. They would stay with the river until Valentia and then he would make his decision. That night they slept on deck wrapped in their wolfskin cloaks and listened to the rush of water beneath the ship's hull. During the day, the ship's company, always busy in any case, kept a discreet distance from the eight soldiers. There was something about the hard, unblinking eyes and the way their hands never strayed far from their swords that didn't invite pleasantries or questions, and that was the way Valerius wanted it. Marcellus, the captain, was obviously curious about his passengers, but it wasn't until they reached the point where the river they were on met the larger Sauconna that Valerius joined the young man at his place by the stern post.

'How long to Lugdunum?'

'Another day's sailing. The smoke you see is from Cabillonum. Lugdunum is fifty miles downstream, where the Sauconna joins the Rhodanus. The Sauconna is wider and deeper than the Doubus we've just left, but still tricky to navigate in places. Normally, I would berth here and transfer you to another galley, but my orders are to take you as far as you wish to go. The little scorpion seemed happy to be rid of you on any terms.'

Valerius smiled at the nickname, so appropriate for the touchy bureaucrat at Vesontio. 'In that case you will not mind if I ask you to take us as far south as Vienne, or even Valentia?' The sailor's eyes widened a fraction, but he hid his surprise well. 'It depends where we can most easily replace our horses,' Valerius went on. 'And on the best way to catch up with General Valens.'

'In that case, Valentia,' Marcellus said decisively. 'Our transports have been carrying remounts there for weeks.' A shadow fell over the cheerful, pink-cheeked features. 'Even now the general must be preparing to cross into Italia.'

Valerius allowed a sympathetic smile to touch his lips. 'These are troubled times,' he said evenly. 'But a man cannot serve two masters.' It was a statement, but a statement that contained a question and Marcellus eyed him warily.

'My only master is the governor of Gallia Lugdunensis . . . but I have no wish to see Roman fighting Roman.'

Valerius clapped him on the shoulder. 'A good answer, Marcellus. You may even keep your head until this madness is over.'

As he moved away, Valerius's cloak slipped aside and he saw the young man dart a glance at his right arm. The mottled stump identified him as surely as any slave brand and he had been careful to keep it hidden during the voyage. Annoyed with himself, he turned back so his face was close to the younger man's and he kept his voice low and filled with menace.

'Best to forget you ever saw that, boy. There's nothing but grief for you there.'

Valens' main force had used the right bank of the river as their line of march and from time to time the *Pride of Sauconna* would pass piles of charred timbers that had once been a town or a village, often with figures rooting among the ashes for the burned remnants of their lives. All too often there would be a mound of newly dug earth that spoke eloquently of whatever minor tragedy had been enacted there. Once they reached the Rhodanus at Lugdunum that changed. Marcellus explained that the elders of the city had been the first to recognize Vitellius and had welcomed Valens like a conquering hero.

'He entered the city to a triumph worthy of an Emperor,' the sailor said. 'They opened up the storerooms and the treasury and bade him take what he wished. It may be different when we reach Vienne, where people are less enthusiastic about our new Emperor, but possibly not. Two weeks ago bloated corpses were a more common sight on this river than ducks. The Viennese will be aware of the price they would pay if they attempted to delay the army of Vitellius.'

Every mile south brought a small, but welcome, warming of the air and the mood among Valerius's men became almost festive as they realized how close they were to home and relative safety. A few miles downriver from Vienne, with Valentia less than half a day away, he drew Metto aside.

'We are still in hostile territory and the closer we get to the Vitellian army the more hostile it will get. In a few days it will be different, but for the moment the only way we'll all stay alive is to act like surly, incommunicative Batavian barbarians. Make sure your men know that. I don't intend to get killed because some idiot from the fifth rank thinks he's on furlough, and the first one who forgets that will find the point of Serpentius's dagger in his ear.'

'I'll make sure the men understand,' the big centurion growled. 'My arse is as valuable to me as yours is to you, tribune, and you won't need your Spanish assassin to put the fear of death into them. I'll take care of that myself.'

The next morning they woke to find Valentia looming over the river from a hillside on the east bank and
Marcellus brought them into the quay with barely a
bump. Valerius thanked the young sailor and wished he
had some kind of compensation for the crew.

'I will buy them a flagon of wine in the nearest tavern
and they will be happy enough,' Marcellus said soberly.
He looked out over the river. 'A strange journey for
strange times, but at least the chill is seeping from my
bones. Edging your way up and down the Doubus day
after day can be wearing, and the cold wind from the
east gives a man aches that make him old before his
time. I will not shake your hand, but you need not fear
I will broadcast its lack. Though I do not know your
name, I sense an honest man behind that fierce mask
you wear and I wish you well in your mission, whatever
it is.' The last was said with a twinkle that told Valerius
his subterfuge was not as subtle as he thought it had
been. Marcellus grinned at the look of consternation
and saluted farewell.

Valerius, Serpentius and Metto installed the legionaries
in a secluded square behind the market with instructions
to keep their mouths shut and set off to find the cavalry
headquarters. Valerius had no illusions that it would be
easy. This would be no bored functionary like Nepos
who could be bullied into doing what he wanted. They
were in a war zone now, and in a war zone men tended
to be wary and suspicious. As it turned out, though, he
was wrong. The prefect in charge of remounts was a
harassed fat man fit only for garrison duty. His red face
and hoarse breathing hinted at an early seizure and he
was having to deal with twenty similar requests an hour.
With a single glance at Valerius's warrant, he gasped an
order to an equally stressed clerk, and Valerius walked

out with a docket for saddlery and cavalry horses for eight men. He sent Metto off to search out supplies for the journey, while he and Serpentius located the horses.

'Have you noticed that we're as popular around here as a turd in a fruit bowl?' Serpentius asked quietly as they walked across the town forum.

Valerius didn't reply immediately. He too had noticed the angry stares and muttered insults from the off-duty soldiers they passed. At first he'd feared that Claudius Victor had somehow got word to Valentia, but gradually he realized the loathing wasn't aimed at them in particular, but Batavian auxiliaries in general. He studied his companion and laughed as he realized they probably looked more dangerous than the troopers whose disguise they'd taken on. Serpentius's cloak looked as if the wolf it had come from had been dead for a month before he skinned it, and smelled as bad. The plaid *bracae* he wore were ripped at the knees and the arse. His helmet was ill-fitting and rusty and beneath it the menace of the savage eyes and rat-trap mouth was magnified by a week's growth of stubbled beard that covered his upper lip and lower jaw. 'It seems Vitellius's legions and their provincial allies aren't on friendly terms. Remember what Metto said about the auxiliaries at Moguntiacum? Give the Batavians a battle to fight and they're happy, but they're proud and arrogant and they've never been that fond of us. They've come back from Britannia to find legionaries having their way with their women and robbing their villages blind. If they didn't like each other at the start of the march, who's to say what the relationship is like now? A civil war isn't like a war against barbarians. For most of his march, Valens has been in the lands of tribes who support Vitellius, or at least won't oppose him. That means little fighting and less loot. The Batavians won't have liked that. Maybe they've been doing a little raiding on their own. That could help us. The more chaos the better. Claudius Victor is a day or so behind. That should be enough of a breathing space to get through to Otho's lines.'

'Maybe so,' the Spaniard spat. 'But I don't like the feel of this place. The sooner we're out of here, the happier I'll be.'

Valerius agreed, and when they'd gathered up the men and horses they left Valentia by the east gate, towards a land that would soon be filled with the stink of blood and death and war.

XXXVII

The men shivered around the meagre campfire Valerius had allowed in the damp gully that was their refuge. Refuge, not camp. A place to hide from enemies who by now would be sharpening their blades in anticipation of a painful and hideous revenge for the deaths of their comrades.

A dark shape appeared from the shadows and seven hands dropped to their swords in alarm.

'Like a cork in a wineskin.' Serpentius shook the rain from his cloak. 'A camp or a patrol guarding every road and no way past that I could find.'

Valerius cursed under his breath. Things had gone so well for the first three days after they'd left Valentia. They had followed the trail of Valens' army through the mountains from marching camp to marching camp, staying just far enough back to avoid his rearguard. But on the fourth day they found themselves almost colliding with his baggage train and Valerius had been forced to waste precious hours in hiding, waiting for the invasion force to reach open country where there would be ample space to bypass them. But it seemed Valens was in no hurry to reach the plains, because he had halted his army in the mountains west of Augusta Taurinorum, where the hills opened out on to the flatlands of northern Italia.

'Why is he holding back?' Valerius directed the question at Serpentius and Metto, but he knew there were a hundred possible answers. Perhaps some kind of negotiation had begun between Otho and Vitellius and they'd agreed to halt their forces until it was complete. Maybe, somewhere beyond the hills, Otho had put together an army that had bottled Valens up in the passes. Or Caecina could be stuck in the Alps and his rival was wary of taking on Otho's forces alone. He felt the eyes of the others on him and knew the reason didn't matter. What mattered was that they were looking for a decision from their leader because they knew that Claudius Victor and his skinning knife were somewhere close. Very well. 'There is no other option. We have to go back.' He heard a sharp intake of breath and sensed the men's dismay at the prospect of retracing their steps through the narrow, steep-sided valleys where they might meet Victor's Batavians round every corner. 'We'll find a way south and another route home.'

'That could take weeks.' The challenge came from Fuscus, one of the legionaries. It had to be Fuscus, who had moaned and whined all the way from Moguntiacum. Fuscus who couldn't keep his mouth shut. 'Maybe we should split up and try to get through in pairs?'

'In Batavian breeches and cloaks?' The gully rang with a sharp crack as Metto slapped his comrade on the back of the head. 'Without a pass or today's watchword? We wouldn't last beyond the second hour. And then it would be the axe or the fire, maybe even the cross for traitors like us.' The other legionaries growled at the hated word, but Metto was unrepentant. 'Aye, curse you may, but that's what we are as far as those men out there are concerned. Traitors deserving of a traitor's death.'

'Maybe we should turn ourselves in,' Fuscus persisted, rising to his feet. He pointed at Valerius. 'If we handed him over we might even get a reward. They'd pay well for one of Otho's spies . . .' His voice tailed off with a curious hissing sound like an angry snake. Or a man who'd just had a long knife pushed very deliberately between his ribs and into his heart.

Serpentius pulled the blade free and allowed the legionary's body to drop to the earth. 'Only one step from saying it to doing it,' the Spaniard said cheerfully, wiping the blade on Fuscus's cloak. 'Anyone else have any ideas they'd like to share?'

Valerius had been as surprised as any of them by Serpentius's swift response to Fuscus's revolt, but he dared not show it. With barely a glance at the dead man, he met the remaining legionaries' eyes one by one. When he reached Metto, the centurion gave him an almost imperceptible nod that confirmed he still had them. He'd been fortunate that Fuscus was a fool, and a fool who had made himself unpopular at that. If it had been one of the others, the outcome might have been different.

They doused the fire and readied themselves in the darkness. Valerius knew they had to get as far from Valens' army as they could before daylight, but there was another, greater danger to be considered. Claudius Victor was out there somewhere and he would know he had his prey in a trap. They travelled through the hills in single file with every man thanking the gods for the lack of a moon and the pitch black night that hid them from their enemies. Serpentius was mountain born and mountain bred, and he could move in the dark as easily as in the day. With barely a pause, he took them westwards where he had identified a valley that led south and would, in time, hopefully bring them to the plain and Italia. Despite the Spaniard's lead, the men were wary and progress was necessarily slow. Valerius hid his frustration. He knew every moment of delay put his mission at greater risk and might cost thousands of lives. Otho would be aware of his enemy's dispositions by now, but Valerius had learned much that could mean the difference between victory and defeat.

When they reached the valley mouth, Serpentius halted the little column and made his way back to where Valerius waited. 'Something doesn't smell right.'

'Take Metto.' But his words were wasted. Serpentius was already gone.

They waited for what seemed like an eternity, the horses moving restlessly, but cavalry-trained to stay silent. Valerius strained his ears until they hurt and his eyes searched the darkness until every variation of shade seemed to move and threaten. Eventually, he could take no more and lifted his heels to push his horse into motion. 'Only one.' The whisper almost stopped his heart as Serpentius threw a wolfskin cloak across his saddle. The Roman shivered. Mars' arse, he must be getting old. He hadn't had the slightest notion of the former gladiator's return until the weight of the cloak fell on his knees.

They were three more days in the mountains, eking out their rations and watering their horses in the streams that cut every valley. Serpentius had buried the Batavian whose wolfskin cloak now acted as Valerius's saddle cloth, but they knew the fact that the man was missing would be as good as a signpost to Claudius Victor. Valerius could almost feel the Batavian's warm breath on his neck.

Every man felt a surge of relief when they eventually emerged from the claustrophobic embrace of the hills at a tiny settlement beside a small stream the inhabitants laughably claimed was the Padus. The villagers had fled at the first sight of wolfskin cloaks and gleaming iron, but when the strangers made no threatening moves and didn't loot the houses the bravest gradually returned. They called their village Forovibiensis and spoke a guttural Latin that Valerius at first struggled to understand. Still, he managed to trade the dead man's cloak for three loaves of hard country bread and a skin of some earthy drink that might once have been wine. Gossip was as important to these rustic people as trade goods and they listened with dismay as Valerius told them of the great army gathering to their north. One of the elders nodded seriously. Apart from Valerius's men, he said, they had encountered no soldiers, but this information accorded with what their watchers could see from the mountain behind the village. Columns of smoke where no smoke should be seen, thick and dark, towering in the still air over the plain like ominous statues.

'Valens may be too scared to leave the mountains,' Serpentius offered, 'but he's sending out raiding parties to try to goad Otho's forces into attacking him. Fire and iron in the night and a few slaughtered civilians, and soon every town and village in the province is screaming for protection. With a little of lady Fortuna's luck, Otho's army could be within a day's march.'

Valerius wasn't so certain. There was nothing wrong with the Spaniard's logic, but he knew Otho had been relying on the Balkan legions to stop Vitellius and those legions would take time to react. At best, a legion on the march would make twenty miles a day. He tried to remember how many days it had been since they had left Rome, but could only guess. It was possible, but nowhere near certain, that they could be somewhere close to Italia by now.

'What lies that way?' He pointed to the east. The elder shook his head and explained he had never ventured further than the next river. After a moment's thought, he called over a small fat man who peered suspiciously from the doorway of one of the mud and wattle houses.

'Cabour sometimes trades as far as Genua,' he said proudly.

Valerius repeated his question and the trader's brow furrowed. 'When you come to Pollentia, follow the river upstream until you can cross the bridge at Alba Pompeia. There you will find a track that takes you to Aquae Statiellae, where you can join the Julia Augusta. It is a fine road,' he said proudly. 'Two full carts can pass side by side. Turn south and you will eventually reach Vada Sabatia and the great sea. Go north and the next town is Dertona, but I have never been there.' He shrugged as if the place was of little consequence, but the name stirred a memory in Valerius.

'These columns of smoke, could one of them have come from Dertona?'

Serpentius glanced up sharply at the new urgency in his friend's voice, but Cabour only looked mystified. 'Smoke is smoke. You see it in the sky, something is burning. Who knows where?'

Valerius shook his head in frustration. 'Saddle up,' he shouted, and saw the startled looks from his exhausted men.

When they were on the move, Serpentius rode up to him. 'What's so interesting about this Dertona?' The flat plain stretched out ahead of them under an endless

348

blue sky, a patchwork of fields cut with drainage ditches and streams and scattered with workers preparing the land for planting. Despite the relative warmth of the day, Valerius suppressed a shiver as he kept his eyes on the distant horizon.

'Domitia.'

The villa sprawled across a low hill overlooking the town and Domitia Longina Corbulo had a clear view from the balcony over the plain. It was already pitch dark and silk-winged moths the size of gold *aurei* fluttered round the oil lamp, occasionally popping in a hissing splutter of bright flame when they came too close. A similar phenomenon was occurring in front of her eyes. Tiny pinpricks of red and gold dotted the distant blackness, first flaring, then fading quite quickly to a duller glow. With every new conflagration, a claw of cold iron gripped her heart.

What was she to do?

She had come north to evade the attentions of Flavius Domitianus and the growing unrest in Rome, but there was something else too. She had needed to get away to try to come to terms with her feelings for Gaius Valerius Verrens. She was a married woman – true, in name only – yet each time he appeared in her life she remembered the terrible shipwreck and the sun-baked beach in Egypt where it had all begun. The desperate struggle for survival against heat and thirst. The stern, masterful figure who had fought for her life and her honour, and, finally, her love. A man unlike any other she had ever known. She shivered, not entirely due to the chill night air. She was sure Valerius suffered similar feelings, because she had seen it in the soulful eyes that sat so uneasily in a face that was as hard and unyielding as the man who bore it. When news came that Galba was dead and Otho had taken the purple, her first instinct had been to return to him. But her uncle, head of Dertona's *ordo*, the council of a hundred prominent citizens who controlled all civic life in the city, had persuaded her it was too dangerous to travel.

And now it was too late.

Hard on the heels of Otho's elevation had come word that the governor of Germania, Aulus Vitellius, had been hailed Emperor in his turn, and that his legions were marching on Rome. Troops of hard-eyed auxiliary cavalry had appeared at every town along the Padus valley demanding that each *ordo* in turn pledge allegiance to Vitellius. Her uncle, dear, proud old Prixus, had closed the gates on them and a show of force on the walls had been enough to see them off. For now. Prixus argued in council that only the Senate and people of Rome had the right to hail an Emperor, and that Vitellius was a provincial upstart of the worst sort. The townsfolk had heard him out and agreed that a message should be sent to Rome assuring Otho of Dertona's allegiance and asking for troops to be sent to safeguard the city against possible attack.

Since then they had heard nothing.

She flinched as another bright flare briefly pierced the night. A villa, just like this? A farm? Was it closer than the last? So far the German auxiliaries had kept their depredations to the far side of the river, but she knew that could change at any time. A stream of refugees carrying the blackened remnants of their lives had confirmed the cavalrymen were part of a mighty army and that they were becoming bolder by the day. Earlier she had seen a great column of smoke to the north-west that could be no single building. Her uncle had stood beside her with tears in his eyes and said a single word. 'Cuttiae.'

Cuttiae was – had been – a small community less than ten miles away, on the north side of the river. Its people had stayed firm for Otho. Prixus sighed and Domitia tried not to notice as he wiped his eyes. 'I think that tomorrow we must move into the city.'

He was telling her it was only a matter of time before they came.

XXXVIII

'What happens when we reach Dertona?'

Valerius glanced over his shoulder as he pondered his response to a question which had any number of answers. 'Are they still there?'

'Two miles or so back. They're not trying to run us down, so either their horses are as tired as ours, or they have something else in mind.' *They* had been there for two hours, just visible as a dark smudge on the flat, dusty landscape. 'It's the ones we can't see I'm worried about.'

They had ridden through the night, stopping only to water and feed the horses. At dawn there had been grumbles from the worn-out legionaries that they should stop and rest, until Valerius pointed out that Claudius Victor and his vengeful Batavians were probably not far behind and he was unlikely to allow his men that luxury. His instinct had been correct, for not much later Serpentius spotted riders keeping pace with the little column. They would get rest and food at Dertona. If they ever got there. 'You think they've got ahead of us?'

Serpentius shrugged. 'I don't see how, but who knows? You said they did the impossible in Britannia.'

'I didn't witness it, but men who did said the Batavians could swim rivers in full armour and disappear into the ground when your back was turned. The way you do.'

The Spaniard grinned. 'Just be thankful I'm not hunting you.'

Valerius felt a surge of affection for the former gladiator who had become his friend. 'If it wasn't for you we wouldn't have got this far. A lot depends on whether Dertona has declared for Vitellius or stayed loyal. When we reach the city, if Domitia is still there, I'll try to persuade her to come with us. Placentia's not much further ahead, and from there we can take the road south and join Otho.'

'And if she doesn't agree?'

Valerius took a deep breath. 'If she decides to stay, I'll stay with her, and you and the others can go on.'

'You think so?' Serpentius produced the barking cough that passed as laughter with his people.

'It would be wiser,' Valerius said. They both knew it was a likely death sentence to stay.

'I'm a Spaniard, Valerius.' The dark eyes turned dangerous. 'An Asturian. If we were wise, we would never have let the Romans take our country. You can keep your wisdom and your *culture*, I've lived as a filthy barbarian and I'll die a filthy barbarian.'

The Roman smiled. 'Then let's see if we can't put a little more distance between us and our Batavian friends.'

They approached the walls of Dertona just as dawn broke after another night in the saddle. 'Don't expect a warm welcome,' Serpentius warned the men. 'They'll be expecting trouble and we look like the worst kind.'

Valerius rubbed his bearded chin and ran an eye over his six companions; pinch-faced, brooding and full of menace in their stinking furs and rust-pitted armour they looked more like bandits than soldiers. 'I'll go first.'

'Be my guest. And don't worry. If anybody puts an arrow through your throat I'll stick a spear through his.'

'That's very comforting.' Valerius rode slowly towards the gate with his arms raised to shoulder height. He got to within a few paces of the wooden palisade before he was challenged.

'Stop! Who's there?'

Whoever was asking, or someone less inclined to debate, didn't wait for an answer. Valerius saw a blur of movement on the palisade and twisted in the saddle as an expertly thrown spear hurtled towards him. If he hadn't been riding a cavalry-bred mount, trained to obey knee and heel, it would have taken him in the midriff. Instead, the horse danced sideways and the spear passed harmlessly by. 'Friend,' he shouted. 'I'm a friend.'

A voice filled with authority barked an order from the tower beside the gate, and that order must have been obeyed because no more spears came his way. He waited, still with his arms outstretched, feeling like a target for *pilum* practice.

'You don't look like a friend,' the voice said suspiciously. 'You look like one of the barbarian wolf men who threatened to burn us out a few days ago unless we support that fat bastard Vitellius. What about the others? I see some shadows in the murk behind you that don't look like shadows.'

Valerius waved Serpentius and the legionaries forward and heard a reluctant shuffling of hooves from behind. He didn't blame them. He didn't feel particularly brave himself, parading within range of unknown numbers of frightened and suspicious spearmen.

'You look even less like friends now.'

'If we weren't friends there'd be hundreds of us, not just seven, and we wouldn't be standing here. We'd have already swarmed over your pathetic little walls and I'd have cut your throat before your sentry there had even woken up.'

'Pathetic, is it?'

'You know you won't last five minutes when they come for you. You should pack up now and get everyone to Placentia while you can. At least you'll have a chance there.'

The man laughed nervously. 'You're just trying to get us into the open, so we'll be easier to slaughter.'

'No,' Valerius said with exaggerated patience. 'I'm trying to get a message to Prixus Lucianus Longinus, the man who represents your interests in the Senate.'

A grey-bearded elder wearing a centurion's helmet appeared behind the palisade. He reminded Valerius of Falco, the militia commander who had helped defend Colonia from Boudicca. 'What message?' the man demanded, but now his voice sounded more curious than suspicious.

'That is between myself and the senator.'

There was a long pause before the man made up his mind. 'Then you can carry it to him yourself.' The words were spoken with exaggerated dignity. 'He's too stubborn to come and live with us ordinary mortals, even if it gets him killed. Take the road round the walls and up to that fancy villa on the hill there. You can't miss it.'

Valerius hesitated before turning away. 'My advice is good.'

The other man nodded gravely. 'Perhaps.'

They rode wearily up the hill in single column and

the growing light showed them approaching a well-maintained villa of substantial proportions along a track running between cultivated rows of vines. There was no wall, only a low hedge that formed a barrier between those who owned the land and those who only worked it. Valerius pushed his horse forward through the carved wooden gateway into a courtyard formed by the three sides of the white stucco building. As they reached it, a large bell began tolling in the city below, triggering a flurry of activity within the house. Four fluted pillars flanked the doorway and the shadows between them filled with figures that gradually became recognizably human. In the van was a tall, balding figure holding an old-fashioned sword of a pattern that might have been carried by Divine Caesar himself. Behind him stood a short, almost square peasant wearing a savage scowl and wielding a woodman's axe. They were backed by what looked like the household ladies and their servants, each armed with whatever had come to hand at short notice. Less enthusiastic were the slaves, who sidled round the angle of the building carrying staves and mattocks.

'Raaaargh!' Serpentius's lion's roar broke the silence and the slaves disappeared like morning mist under a bright sun. The Spaniard grinned. Valerius darted an annoyed glance at his friend and turned to the man in the formal toga with the sword.

'Prixus Lucianus Longinus?'

The aristocrat peered at his visitor through rheumy eyes. 'Yes, and I am prepared to die for what is mine.' As he said the words he raised the sword, but Valerius backed his horse away and pulled back the wolf's head hood that had left his face in shadow. He dismounted and advanced on the old man. The sword shook in wrinkled hands and the axeman's eyes flared dangerously.

In the shadows of the portico Domitia held the knife that would, if necessary, end her life with honour, but something about the commanding figure in the wolf-skin cloak awoke a memory. When the hood went back her heart seemed to stop. What was it? Unkempt dark hair. A stubbled face, the expression savage, as if the man who wore it had spent an eternity in the company of death. Battle-scarred and grim, it was marked by hunger and privation so every bone seemed ready to cut through the skin. Yet there was something about him that made her pause. The eyes. She recognized the eyes.

'Valerius?'

He heard the question and turned to the slim figure who stood to the right of the little tableau, cloaked in what looked like a shroud. The exhaustion of the past few days had threatened to overwhelm him, but the very sight of her made the blood pound in his veins and he felt a new energy course through him. He wondered that he had not seen her immediately, because she shone out from the drabness around her like the brightest star in the night sky. More careworn, perhaps, than the last time he had seen her, but still with a hypnotic beauty unmatched by any woman he had met.

'My lady.' The gentle smile he attempted appeared as a fierce wolf's grin. 'I hope you are well.'

The cushioned benches, soft drapes and perfumed oil lamps could have come from another world, but it was being in a room with a ceiling that was most disconcerting after more than three weeks sleeping under the stars.

'My place is with my uncle.'

It was the third time Domitia had spoken the words and each time with increased emphasis. For the third time, Valerius repeated his argument.

357

'To the west, General Gaius Fabius Valens is camped not more than fifty miles away with an army of twenty-five thousand men. To the north, General Aulus Caecina Alienus, with another twenty-five thousand. Soon, probably in less than a week, they will combine somewhere very close to Dertona and prepare to march on Rome—'

'Unless the Emperor stops them, surely.'

Valerius bowed to acknowledge Prixus Longinus's intervention. 'That is true, senator, but you must ask why we have seen no sign of his cavalry. Why Dertona, which has been so loyal, has had no message of reassurance or encouragement. I give you a soldier's answer. His forces in Italia are not sufficient to defeat either of Vitellius's armies without reinforcement from the legions of the Balkans and the Danuvius frontier. They are close, I am certain of that, but not close enough yet to intervene in time to save Dertona. You must seek refuge in Placentia, which has stout walls and is prepared for defence. Already Valens' auxiliaries have crossed the river. They will come for you soon and you will have the choice of surrender or annihilation.'

Prixus flinched and walked to the balcony where the twisting, tree-lined course of the Padus was just visible as a dark line on the horizon.

Domitia raised herself to her full height. 'Nevertheless, I must stay with my family.'

'Then we all die.'

In the long pause that followed her eyes pleaded with him for understanding and he remembered again her father's mantra. *A Corbulo does not have the luxury of choice . . . only duty.*

'No.'

They turned automatically to the figure at the window. Prixus Longinus's eyes were bright as he addressed Domitia, but his voice remained steady.

'You must go with your friend.' He raised a hand as Domitia opened her mouth to protest. 'In the absence of your husband, I stand here as your guardian, and as such your safety is in my hands. The household will prepare to leave for Placentia within the hour and I will arrange the evacuation of Dertona, but you will accompany Gaius Valerius Verrens.' He turned to Valerius. 'I place Domitia Longina Corbulo's life and her honour in your hands. May you protect both to your last breath.'

Valerius felt Domitia's eyes on him and his mouth went dry. 'I pledge it.'

'What are your intentions?'

'I will ride to Placentia as soon as the lady Domitia has made her preparations, with word that you are on your way and seeking refuge. If the road is clear we will continue south to meet the Emperor.'

Prixus nodded solemnly and Domitia rushed to her uncle and took his hands in hers. The old man met her gaze with the ghost of a smile. 'It is for the best, my dear.'

Another woman might have hesitated, but with the decision made Domitia left the room calling for her personal slave, and by the time Valerius had gathered his men she was at the villa's entrance dressed in a long cloak. Behind her came a house slave carrying two leather bags and Valerius realized that, despite her protests, she must have prepared for this day. She saw his look.

'I am my father's daughter,' she said. 'A soldier's daughter.'

Valerius fought the urge to smile. It had been the watchword that sustained her through the long ordeal of thirst and heat in Egypt. She proved the truth of it moments later when her uncle offered her the use of his four-wheeled cart.

'You will need it for the journey to Placentia,' she told him. She turned to Valerius. 'My father ensured I was taught to ride, though it was not thought seemly by some. I am having my horse saddled. A woman's saddle,' she added, 'but you will not be delayed.'

As they prepared to leave Domitia embraced her tearful slave girl, assuring her that she would send for her. A sleek, lean-limbed roan was brought to the mounting block and she settled on the side saddle with all the grace of a Roman maiden taking her place at the dinner table. Valerius led the roan to the centre of the column and placed it beside Serpentius. Domitia greeted the Spaniard with a warm smile that made him blush. There was little formality between the two. Serpentius had also been stranded with them after the shipwreck and people who have spent a week together surviving on tepid water and roasting like fish on a griddle in the Egyptian heat can have few secrets.

Valerius grinned at the Spaniard's discomfiture. 'As you know, he is less dangerous than he looks, at least as far as his friends are concerned. You will be safe with him.'

'It is a relief to be travelling with such a capable guardian. I hope I see you well, Serpentius?'

Serpentius produced a scowl that was meant to be a reassuring smile. 'At your service, my lady, as always.'

They rode, not down the slope towards the town, but due east through the hills until they came to flatter ground. There they turned north and eventually joined the Via Aurelia, where it hugged the south bank of the Padus. Valerius had debated long and hard whether to risk using the open road, but with Claudius Victor undoubtedly closer than ever speed was more important now than guile. Placentia drew him like a moth to a flame. They would be safer there, although he knew it might only be exchanging one trap for another. But if the road south was clear . . . if Otho's army had marched north . . . if the Balkan legions were close by . . . so many ifs.

'Will there be war?'

He had been so preoccupied he hadn't heard Domitia rein in beside him and her voice came as a surprise. Metto, who had ridden at his side, dropped back to allow them privacy.

'Yes. It cannot be stopped now, though neither Otho nor Vitellius wants it.'

'Then why must it be? Surely if both of them will it so it can be prevented. There has already been too much destruction and death.'

Valerius knew she was remembering the little farmstead they had passed, one of many ravaged by Valens' auxiliary cavalry; bodies barely recognizable as human tossed carelessly on the funeral pyre of their former home.

He tried to explain. 'It can only be resolved if one or other gives up his title to the purple. Vitellius is being dragged like a charioteer behind a runaway team by the ambition of his officers and the enthusiasm of his soldiers. They have been promised rewards and plunder and advancement. They have tasted blood. There is no turning back. Vitellius could not rein them in now even if he wanted to. If he tried . . . ? Poison in his wine or a dagger in the night and Valens or Caecina would step into his place.'

By now it was past midday. He twisted in the saddle to

check the positions of the troop, and instead found himself looking into her eyes. She seemed incredibly young. The narrow face strained and serious, with half-moons of weariness just visible beneath the dark eyes, and the lovely chestnut tresses covered by the hood of her linen *stola*. Melancholy gave her a different kind of beauty, the way a ripe cornfield is still beautiful when the sun goes behind a cloud, or a breeze ripples the surface of a glassy pond. His breath caught in his throat, but somehow he managed to stumble on. 'Otho, for all you hear otherwise, is a man of honour. He has Galba's blood on his hands, but he can rationalize it. He tells himself that Galba betrayed the people of Rome, though the reality is that the only reason he acted was because Galba betrayed Otho. Now he has been confirmed Emperor of Rome, in Rome, by the Senate and people of Rome; he is Emperor by right and by rank.' He shrugged. 'To walk away at the first challenge to his authority would be cowardice and Otho is no coward. I believe the thought of having Romans die on his behalf appals him and that Otho the man might well go into exile to save lives. But it is not Otho the man who sits in the Domus Aurea but Otho Imperator, and his honour and his responsibility to the office of Emperor will not allow it. So he too is trapped, as Nero was, in his gilded cage.'

'So now they will fight.' Domitia frowned as she recognized the truth in his words. 'How will it happen?'

Valerius had been asking himself that question for days and always coming up with the same answer. 'Vitellius has taken a risk by splitting his army. If Otho had been able to bring enough of his legions together to meet either individually the war would be over. Valens and Caecina must combine or be destroyed in sequence. The fact that Otho has not attacked tells me he does not yet have his full strength. That means his Balkan legions, from Moesia and Pannonia, are still on the march. Yet he must do something.' His war-sharpened eyes roved across the tree-lined hills to their right, which had forced the road close to the river. In an enemy commander's place, Valerius would have launched his cavalry from those hills and smashed the little column. With no place to run, the outcome would have been certain. He watched a little longer, but could see nothing. 'I believe he will bring what troops he has to the Padus, where he can harass Valens or Caecina as he chooses, possibly stop them from joining forces, and block their march south. When his Balkan reinforcements arrive from Aquileia, along this very road, he will be in a position to combine with them somewhere close, possibly a little further east. Once he has done that, he will meet the enemy on a field of his own choosing with a stronger force. Then it will not matter if Valens and Caecina have united. He will destroy them.'

'You sound very certain.'

'I am.' He smiled.

'And we are riding to meet them?'

Valerius nodded. 'I will join Otho, if he will have me.'

'And Domitia Longina Corbulo?' She said it lightly, but the question took on more weight in his mind than the mere words suggested.

'Domitia Longina Corbulo will return to Rome to take up her life as a Roman lady.' He tried to match her mood, but could not hide the raw edge of emotion in his voice.

'But what if that is not what she wishes?' Her whisper was so low he couldn't be certain he'd heard her correctly. She sensed his hesitation and now it was her turn to smile. 'You are right not to reply. For it is a question only Domitia Longina Corbulo can answer.'

With a graceful nod she dropped back to join Serpentius. Valerius shook his head at the contradictions and confusion she caused in him. Soon he had a battle to fight and a war to win. Tomorrow or the next day he could be dead. So why did his mind refuse to focus on anything but a pair of wide walnut eyes and the way the pupils were flecked with gold and contained shadows and unfathomable secrets?

Serpentius heard the bark of bitter laughter and darted a glance at Domitia. She kept her face expressionless and her eyes on the road, but he noticed her lips twitch.

Half a mile behind, the horseman who had stood silently beneath the tree canopy on the wooded hills Valerius had studied waited until he was certain the column of riders was out of sight before kicking his mount towards the road.

XXXIX

Through the crimson veil of his rage, Claudius Victor
had to remind himself it was not the messenger's fault,
though his hand itched to ram a sword through the
man's guts. He couldn't believe they had escaped him
again. When the Batavians had reached the walled town
he had sent patrols ahead on the Placentia road, but
they saw no sign of the one-armed spy and the strangers
who had slaughtered his men in the woods. They had
gone to ground. There could be no other conclusion.
Victor didn't have enough men to besiege the place, but
he posted guards on every side so that even a mouse
couldn't escape without his knowledge. When it was
done, he sent to General Valens for reinforcements, who
would arrive within a day. He had decided to demand
the commander of the place hand over the fugitives as
payment for not destroying his town, but to destroy it in
any case. The men were becoming bored and it would
give them the opportunity for plunder he had promised
them and which had been so scarce thus far.

And now this. Ten miles, the scout said. They would
be almost at Placentia by the time the Batavians caught

up with them. To ensure that they did, every man with him was leading a spare horse – it meant he could afford to ride at twice the Romans' pace, but also that he had been forced to leave half his men behind. He fought the urge to push on even faster. Patience. If they killed the horses he would never lay hands on the crippled bastard who had murdered Glico. He had promised his brother's shade the cripple would die the very worst of deaths, and now he vowed to himself that as Valerius Verrens wriggled on his spike, the others would be roasting in the slow fire. And what about the woman? Well, there was more than one kind of impalement.

He cursed himself for the indulgence that had made him delay Valerius Verrens' execution. It had led to the loss of more than twenty men and a long, frustrating ride south. Yet he had never lost faith that his Batavian hounds would run down the Roman fox. They had come within minutes of their quarry at Vesontio, and again in the passes, only to be frustrated at Dertona. This time he would finish it.

Valerius had insisted they ride through the night, stopping only to water and feed the horses. By daylight he reckoned they could be no more than a few miles from their goal, and his belief was confirmed a few minutes later when Metto pointed to a smudge on the horizon that must be Placentia. Valerius turned back to join Serpentius. Domitia rode head down, asleep in the saddle. Exhaustion made her face the colour of whey. Should he wake her? He reached out, but she must have sensed his presence because her eyes opened and she blinked in surprise to see him so close.

'Tribune?' Her voice was wary.

'Lady.' He bowed in the saddle. 'I thought you would

like to know we are almost there.' He pointed to the grey haze. 'When we reach Placentia you will be able to bathe and rest while I try to discover what I can of the local situation. With Fortuna's favour, we will have time to allow the horses to recover before we move on. When we do, it will be with a large enough escort to deter any enemy cavalry we come across.'

She sighed with relief and the tired eyes slowly closed again. 'I do not think I ever want to sit on another horse.'

'If Otho is close perhaps we will be able to hire a wagon. But I may have to ask you to endure another day in the saddle.'

Domitia smiled and his heart seemed to skip. 'I am in your hands, tribune, and I will endure what I must. But I will be glad to see the inside of a bath house.'

'Another hour and I promise you will have as much water as you please.' But he had forgotten that they were the playthings of the gods.

He had ordered the man at the tail of the column to hang back so they had warning of any threat from the rear, but it was Serpentius who sensed their presence. He shouted to Valerius to stop and sat for a moment with his ears cocked like a fox listening for a rustle in the grass.

'Riders, coming up fast.'

Valerius scanned the far horizon. At first he could see nothing, but then a grey mass appeared at the very periphery of his vision.

'Do we fight them?' Metto's voice was close to panic.

Valerius frantically searched the surroundings for some sort of defensive position, but the ground was flat as a gaming board. The river? He looked to his left. The tree-lined bank was about a mile from the road. As a last resort . . . ? The nervous horse danced beneath him and he saw Domitia looking to him for some kind of reassurance. No, he couldn't risk it. He tried to judge the distance between himself and the riders, himself and the city. Could they make Placentia before they were overtaken?

'We run!' As he shouted the order, he grabbed her reins and kicked his horse into motion, leading her towards the hazy smudge on the horizon. The others followed suit and soon even the worst-mounted legionary had passed him as he kept pace with Domitia and Serpentius, who would not leave her side. It was clear that riding side saddle she couldn't keep pace with the other riders. She realized it as soon as Valerius did.

'You must leave me,' she cried.

He found himself grinning. 'Not as long as I have breath in my body.'

Serpentius glanced over his shoulder. 'They're gaining and they're very good.'

Domitia's mind raced. 'Look away,' she said. Valerius thought he'd misheard. 'I said look away.'

He did as she ordered and heard the sound of tearing cloth above the thunder of hooves. A cry of triumph and the roan surged ahead. When he looked again, he saw she was riding astride, with the torn material of her skirt flapping in the slipstream and barely covering her long legs. Truly she was her father's daughter.

Now it was Domitia's turn to overtake the least proficient horsemen among the legionaries and they found themselves in the middle of the charging pack. Placentia was plainly visible now as a dark hump on the horizon. How far? Three miles? Four? Could their mounts keep up this pace? Valerius dared a glance back. Mars' beard, how could they have caught up so fast? He could see individual riders now, and Serpentius was right. He had served with cavalry long enough to know veterans when he saw them.

'Their horses are fresher than ours,' the Spaniard rasped.

A gap had opened up between the main group and three of the legionaries, riding wide-eyed with fear and lashing at their mounts. Valerius looked again for somewhere to make a stand, but he could see nowhere that would give them even the ghost of a chance. Their pursuers outnumbered them by at least thirty. They rode hunched over their horses' necks and he imagined the grim resolve on the barbarian faces. By now it was clear, if there had ever been doubt, that they were Claudius Victor's Batavians. The relentless pursuit and disregard of their horses' condition were proof enough that they were being driven on by a madman. Valerius's three stragglers dropped back further and he winced at the thought of what would happen when the Batavians reached them. If they gained the outskirts of the town and could find a building or a yard, they might have a chance, but Placentia was still a good mile distant. He knew there was nothing anyone could do for them. Instead, he crouched low in the saddle and tried to coax another fraction of speed out of his mount.

Closer. Closer. He recognized the bulk of Placentia's amphitheatre and beyond it the city walls with their stone towers. Something was different and he realized that where the arena had been crowded by other buildings, it now stood alone. The defenders must have torn down every house outside the walls to give themselves a clear field of fire. The knowledge brought a new thrill of panic. What if the city was already under siege?

The thunder of hooves rang louder. He didn't risk a

look back, but he knew it meant that the Batavians must be close to spear range. A prolonged shriek that died away on the breeze confirmed his suspicion, quickly followed by a second, and then a third. Domitia heard it too. He saw a flash of fear in her eyes, but she held her nerve and rode her horse like a cavalry trooper. Valerius moved his mount in behind the roan to shield her from the hunters, but he knew that if they got close enough to do her harm they were finished in any case. Gradually they drew ahead of Metto and the surviving legionary, and as they did so, the centurion drew his *spatha* and shouted an order. Valerius watched the two men haul up and turn to meet the charging Batavians. Serpentius would have gone with them, but Valerius snarled at him to stay with Domitia. Looking over his shoulder, he saw the centurion flick a spear point aside and run his attacker through with his sword. Metto's cry of triumph split the air, only to turn into a shriek as the following Batavian spitted him with his lance, hurling him backwards from the saddle. The other legionary was already dead. Remembering the fallen soldiers were followers of Mithras, Valerius sent up a prayer to the bull-slayer to take them into his keeping.

With a flare of hope, he found himself in the shattered foundations of what had once been streets, with Serpentius and Domitia just ahead. He looked up to see astonished faces lining the city walls. A collective howl of frustration and rage erupted from behind him and a spear, hurled at full range, clipped his shoulder to tumble harmlessly away. The gate – where was the gate? He flinched as a flurry of arrows rattled around them like a sudden summer shower. Of course, the defenders couldn't know they were friends. 'Otho!' he roared. 'Otho Augustus!' Serpentius and Domitia took up the cry, and whether at Otho's name or the shrill female voice, the arrows stopped coming. Domitia's mount stumbled and might have gone down if Serpentius hadn't grabbed its bridle and held its head up. Their horses were almost done, red-eyed, breath snorting through flared nostrils, flanks slick with sweat. Finally they passed under the shadow of the amphitheatre, and before them appeared a pair of twin towers flanking the great wooden gate of Placentia. They clattered to a halt in front of it and Valerius called up to the defenders studying him suspiciously from the walls.

'Otho,' he gasped. 'I demand entry in the name of the Emperor Marcus Salvius Otho Augustus.'

'You'll stay where you are or I'll fill you so full of holes we'll be able to use you as a window,' a voice answered from above.

Valerius's reply was cut off by the sound of their pursuers drawing up just outside arrow range. He dismounted and slowly drew his sword, turning to face the Batavians as Serpentius helped Domitia from the saddle and manoeuvred the horses to shield her.

The Spaniard came to his side and they waited silently as Claudius Victor slid from the saddle, followed by half of his men. Victor advanced towards the little group in front of the gate with his sword sheathed, undaunted by the spears and arrows that threatened him from the wall. The other Batavian troopers were warier, but their spears of iron-tipped ash never wavered from Valerius and Serpentius. Valerius sensed a slight figure at his side. 'Are you trying to get yourself killed?' he said through clenched teeth. Domitia carried a small dagger he recognized as one he'd given her on the Egyptian beach when the mutinous crew of the *Golden Cygnet* were lining up to kill them.

'This is my fight as much as yours, tribune.' There was no time for further conversation.

'That's far enough.' The warning was aimed at Claudius Victor, but the auxiliary commander ignored the shout from the walls until it was reinforced by the arrow that ricocheted from the hard-packed earth at his feet. Behind him, his troopers shambled to an uncertain halt. 'The next one will be in your gullet.'

The Batavian surveyed the gate towers with cold grey eyes. 'These men are thieves and murderers, the woman too. Renegades who have the blood of innocents on their hands. I claim them in the name of the Emperor.'

'Which Emperor would that be?'

Victor shrugged, as if it was of no consequence. 'We have no quarrel with the people of Placentia. All we ask is justice for these scum.'

'He's lying.' Valerius pitched his voice just loud enough to reach the wall. 'I carry dispatches for Marcus Salvius Otho Augustus, the only true Emperor and proclaimed so by the Senate and people of Rome. This man serves the usurper Vitellius.'

'You came from the west,' the voice from the wall challenged. 'The only troops between here and Augusta Taurinorum are with Vitellius. Why would you be carrying dispatches from them? Maybe you're a spy and this is all a trick to get you inside.'

Valerius kept his eyes on Claudius Victor and the Batavian watched him as a snake watches a mouse. 'I passed through here less than two months ago. You have an inn on the far side of the town, called the Fat Sturgeon. I made a promise, which has yet to be fulfilled, to buy a drink for your gatekeepers, who gave me a warmer welcome than I am getting now.'

The words brought a chortle of laughter from somewhere on the wall. He could feel Victor's hatred reaching out to him in the long pause that followed, the silence only broken by the soft murmur of a debate being conducted in whispers. Eventually, the Batavian's patience ran out. 'Enough of this time-wasting.'

'Take them, then.' It was a new voice, heavy with the ring of command. Valerius felt as if he'd been kicked in the stomach. He saw something flare in Claudius Victor's eyes. Domitia moved a little closer to his side, her face grim with determination, and he vowed she would not be taken alive.

Victor waved his spearmen forward, but the voice cracked like a whip. 'No. Not them. Just you. You and one other.'

The Batavian froze as the impact of the words struck. Ten paces away, Valerius heard them too and felt something swelling up inside him: a snarling beast with an appetite for only one thing. Blood. For a month this man had dogged his footsteps and his dreams with his promises of pain and death. One step forward and he would finish it one way or another.

'What are you waiting for?' he spat. 'Perhaps you aren't so brave without your wolf pack?'

Claudius Victor's face twisted with revulsion, but he remained where he was. He had formed an image of the man he hunted and that image was of a victim to be humiliated and destroyed. The man he faced across the dusty ground was a new Valerius Verrens, and the savage certainty on the scarred face made the odds less than favourable. Cripple or not, the sword the Roman held in his left hand was killing sharp and rock steady and the Batavian felt an unfamiliar thrill of fear as he imagined the blade slicing at his throat. He glanced at Serpentius and the Spaniard met the look with a barking laugh that sent a shudder through the cavalrymen facing him. Relaxed and loose, he stood with a sword in his right hand and one of the deadly little Scythian throwing axes in his left. The message in his eyes was that Claudius Victor wouldn't get within a sword swing of Valerius before he felt the bite of the axe. Victor looked up at the walls, judging the threat from the arrows and spears, still tempted to launch his men in an attack that would sweep away the three upstarts whose continued existence was an insult to his brother's shade. Even as he made his decision, the gate opened and fifty armoured men trotted out to form a line in front of Valerius, Serpentius and Domitia.

'You had your chance,' the voice from the wall shouted. 'Now leave or I will see you and your men dead.'

For a moment, Valerius thought that Claudius Victor would attack the legionary shield line single-handed. His whole body shook as if he was having some kind of seizure, his eyes bulged and his jaw was clenched so tight that spittle drooled from between his lips. When one of his men tried to pull him towards the horses, he back-handed him across the face so that the auxiliary fell away with blood streaming from smashed lips. Eventually, Victor recovered his reason. When he spoke his voice was thick with loathing and the words were aimed directly at Valerius.

'Do not think you can hide from me for ever, Roman. This little place will soon be squashed flat and when it is I will come for you. The death I promised earlier will seem merciful compared to the torment you will meet then. I will geld you and blind you, cut the tongue from your head and remove your fingers and toes with a blunt axe. My men will use you as a woman and my women as a slave. Every moment of every day you will pray for the release of the impaling spike or the slow fire.'

He marched back to the horses and tugged at something attached to the saddle of the latest arrival. A round object flew through the air and rolled through a gap in the line of defenders to Valerius's feet. With a last look of pure hatred Claudius Victor leapt into the saddle and rode away at the head of his men. It was only when he was out of sight that Valerius looked down and found himself looking into the startled eyes of Cornelius Metto.

XL

'In these unhappy times it is sometimes difficult to tell one's friends from one's enemies.' The grey-haired general pursed his lips and studied the man in front of him with a mixture of puzzlement and distaste. Tall and well set, but with a month's growth of beard and dark hair that hung low over hard, unyielding eyes, Gaius Valerius Verrens looked more brigand than soldier in his ill-fitting tunic and mail. 'You say you have dispatches for the Emperor?'

'Information, rather than formal dispatches. I have come from the north.'

Titus Vitricius Spurinna's lips pursed and Valerius allowed himself a smile at the patrician's reaction. The north meant enemy territory and Vitellius, and the manner of their coming had been mysterious enough to confirm what that hinted at. No one liked a spy, at least not until they needed the intelligence he'd risked his neck for. They were talking in the *principia* at the centre of Placentia's fort. Valerius had sent Serpentius to find them fresh horses, while Domitia had been welcomed by the wife of the town's leading magistrate and would even now be enjoying the bath she'd craved.

'You were fortunate the guard commander vouched for you.' Spurinna gave a sniff, followed by what might almost have been a resigned sigh. 'And as it happens, I have heard the name Gaius Valerius Verrens. News of your exploits in Britannia spread even as far as the German frontier, and, of course, your missing hand confirms your identity more certainly than any papers.' Valerius bowed his head in acknowledgement of the compliment, but he found himself disliking this pompous little man with his narrow, heavy-browed eyes. Still, Spurinna's dispositions and the way he had dealt with Claudius Victor and his Batavians marked him as a soldier. As did his next words. 'An officer who has experience of a siege may be an asset in the days ahead.'

'My information . . .'

Spurinna waved the protest aside and called to his aide to fetch wine. 'I fear you have left it too late. Caecina's cavalry have been probing south of the river for two days. I am only surprised you did not meet them. The road is cut. I do not intend that to continue, but, for the moment, I have other priorities.' He stood up and took a long scroll from a wooden rack attached to the wall. A servant poured the wine and handed Valerius a cup while Spurinna unrolled the map on the table and pinned it flat.

'You know about Valens, of course. He proceeds cautiously.' He looked up and met Valerius's eye. 'Strange given his reputation, but fortunate for us. One of our patrols picked up a deserter yesterday, and he talked of a possible mutiny, but . . . Any detail of his troops and their numbers would be helpful, but that can wait for now. For the moment, my main concern is Caecina Alienus. His main body, which we estimate at something approaching twenty-five thousand men, including the elements of at least three legions, reached Cremona yesterday and is encamped outside the town between the Via Postumia and the Brixia road. You see?' He placed his finger on the map where Cremona and Placentia nestled just twenty miles apart, the one north of the river, the other south. 'Together the two cities make up the lock that holds the entire north, but whoever wishes to open it must have both keys. If Caecina wants to march south, he must first take Placentia, or he knows I will sally out to cut his supply lines and use my forces to harass his flanks and rear. Likewise, the Emperor must take Cremona if he is to hold the north until his Balkan legions arrive and give him overwhelming strength.'

Valerius didn't hide his surprise. 'The Emperor is here?'

The general frowned. 'He is marching north. His advance guard, of which I am nominally part, is stationed astride the Via Postumia to the east of Cremona, here, at Bedriacum, threatening Caecina's flank. We do not yet have the strength to attack, but that will change when the Emperor comes with his main force, or the Thirteenth Gemina arrives.'

'And until then you must hold Placentia.'

The old soldier nodded slowly, his eyes fixed on the map. 'When I said an officer of your experience would be helpful, I was in earnest. In fact, you may be invaluable, Gaius Valerius Verrens, Hero of Rome. With Fortuna's aid, I do not doubt I can make Caecina Alienus wish he had never heard the name Placentia. But the truth is that my greatest obstacles do not lie without the city walls, but within. Including the original garrison of five hundred auxiliaries, I have a force of just under four thousand men to hold this city against

Caecina's twenty-five thousand.' He walked to a display of cohort standards and ran a hand over a brass laurel wreath, one which Valerius recognized. 'Otho sent me three cohorts of the Praetorian Guard. Veteran troops admittedly, but years of garrison work have made them soft. Still, I would stake my life on their holding a wall to the last man. In his wisdom, he has also provided me with a vexillation of a thousand men from a newly formed legion, First Adiutrix. You have heard their story?'

'Marines and sailors.' Juva's determined face swam into Valerius's mind. 'They proved their loyalty when they refused to be deterred by Galba's cruelty. Raw troops, but keen to prove their worth.'

'A fair assessment,' Spurinna agreed. 'Yet their greatest asset is also their greatest failing. They have an over-high estimation of their military potential. Once they have learned the discipline of the shield line, perhaps they might be as good as they think they are. Yet civil war stirs the blood in ways that no other contest will. They, and the Praetorians, are so eager to get their hands on the throats of Vitellius's rebels that they are almost beyond discipline. Two nights ago the troops' blood was so hot I was forced to lead an armed reconnaissance. Hopeless, of course. Behind a wall they will be as formidable as any, but out in the open Caecina's veterans would destroy them in moments.' Valerius nodded in understanding, if not acknowledgement. 'Fortunately, our heroes did not find chasing shadows through swampland as much to their liking as they thought. I was able to persuade them home before dawn and they now work to strengthen the walls with renewed vigour, so perhaps the lesson is learned.' The old general smiled. *The things I have to put up with.*

Valerius stood up and saluted. 'How may I be of assistance to you?'

'As you see, we have razed the houses outside the ditch,' Spurinna pointed out as they made a circuit of the walls that evening. 'So we have clear fields of fire for our artillery.' He laid a hand on one of the many *scorpio* catapults that had been placed at intervals along the walls and in the towers. The *scorpio* fired a five-foot arrow that could gut a man or a horse at four hundred paces, and its effect on close-packed ranks had earned it the title Shield-splitter. The defenders had a similar number of *onagri*, which could launch a stone the size of a man's head the same distance. Two enormous *ballista* catapults were strategically positioned in the town to support the outer defences. They would hurl their cauldron-sized missiles while the attackers assembled out of range of the smaller artillery pieces. Valerius's respect for Spurinna grew when he saw the full extent of his preparations. Spearmen and archers lined walls sturdily built of dressed stone and thirty-five feet high where they dropped into the ditch. Placentia stood on a slightly raised platform of land in the curve of the Padus and was a city experienced in war. It had its origins as a frontier *colonia*, populated by legionary veterans, with potential enemies on every side, and had endured siege and struggle for a hundred years before Caesar's peace. On the walkway behind the parapet bundles of javelins and arrows lay heaped in readiness every few yards and thousands more were piled high at the base of the wall ready to replace them. Long poles with V-shaped tops for pushing away scaling ladders stood easily to hand. At the places the general judged most vulnerable to assault or undermining, piles of massive stones had been placed on rough wooden boards, ready to be released at the pull of a lever on to the attackers. These were flanked by braziers to heat oil that would cause horror and agony when poured on a packed scaling ladder.

'You will see that I have concentrated the bulk of our defensive capability on the south and west walls,' Spurinna said. Valerius studied the two lengths of wall. The first looked out towards the amphitheatre, was between eight hundred and nine hundred paces long, and included six individual towers and the pair guarding the gate. Any attacker would have to negotiate the foundations of the houses Spurinna had ordered demolished before they could reach the wall. To defend this stretch, Valerius had one thousand legionaries of the First Adiutrix, plus two hundred Gaulish auxiliaries, whose job was to protect the towers and load and fire the artillery machines, a force he reckoned just about adequate. For replacement and reinforcement he could count on a cohort of Praetorian Guards, who would lie concealed until they were needed. The west wall ran barely half the length of the south and required fewer defenders, although it would depend on the same Praetorians for reinforcement. Spurinna waited until Valerius had absorbed the position before he explained his other concerns. 'The open ground by the river is too narrow for Caecina to assemble an assault of sufficient force, and that to the east is swampland. I have gambled that it is boggy enough to deter an attacker in full armour.' The general shrugged. 'If I am wrong, it is relatively simple to reinforce along our internal lines.'

Valerius noticed that despite his casual dismissal of the possibility of attack from the lightly defended sectors, Spurinna had made sure that, like those most likely to be assaulted, the ditches had been filled with hedgehogs of spears fixed to logs and piles of bitumen-soaked brush that could be fired in an instant. One thing puzzled him. He pointed to the great arena that dominated the ground to the south. Constructed of wood and stone, it lay well outside spear or arrow range, but it could have other uses. 'You have gone to great trouble to clear the houses, yet you have left the amphitheatre, which would appear to offer a fine position for an attacker, who might safely position his artillery within the protection of its walls.'

Spurinna's eyes twinkled. 'You have outed me there, young man. I could tell you that I do not believe Caecina will have carried siege weapons across the Alps, and that would be true. Nevertheless, though I doubt he has the capacity to construct siege towers, he will undoubtedly be able to whip up a few catapults. No, the true reason is that the Placentians are more attached to their amphitheatre than they are their homes.' He produced a disbelieving laugh at the foolishness of civilians. 'It is, apparently, a symbol of the town's wealth and power. That feeling is so strong that I fear if I took the proper military course and destroyed it I would lose their cooperation, which might be fatal in the event of a long siege. I have decided to take the easier approach and leave it where it is.' The smile broadened. 'Who knows what can happen in the course of a battle?' His voice turned serious. 'Now you understand why I want you to oversee the defence of the south wall for me, while I maintain overall command. If I am right, this will be the place of greatest danger and I need someone I can trust to hold it whatever Caecina throws at us.'

'You talk as if Valens' army does not exist. Is it wise to discount him?'

'Not wise, perhaps, but realistic.' The words were accompanied by a savage grin. 'If Valens and Caecina can combine before the Emperor reaches the Padus, they will have enough strength to crush us like a grape in a walnut press.'

They carried on round the walls until they came to the gateway. Below them, a squad of legionaries dressed in the distinctive blue tunics of the First Adiutrix worked to strengthen the gates with massive baulks of wood, stockpiling others that would be braced against the rear of the doors if the Vitellians attacked them with a ram. Valerius recognized a familiar figure supervising the men.

'Hail, Juva of the *Waverider*,' he called. 'It seems we are ever destined to meet in interesting circumstances.'

The Nubian looked up with a broad smile that turned serious when he recognized the general. He slammed his fist against his chest in a salute that would have graced a twenty-year veteran. The dark eyes looked Valerius up and down.

'Of the *Waverider* no more. *Optio* of the first century Fifth cohort.' Pride suffused Juva's voice. He looked Valerius up and down, taking in the filthy clothing and the beard, and the new shadows under the eyes. 'It appears that larks' tongues are no longer part of your diet, lord, if you have eaten at all this past week. But do not concern yourself. If you have fallen on hard times there is always a place for you in the First Adiutrix.'

Valerius raised the stump of his right arm. 'Even for a man with but one hand?'

The big man considered for a few seconds. 'Perhaps on half pay, then.'

When the laughter had died, Juva addressed the general. 'When will they come, sir? The First would rather be fighting than playing at being carpenters.'

'Then you are already a true legionary,' Spurinna

laughed. 'For, in my experience, the sign of a true legionary is that he would rather do anything than work. Soon.' His face turned solemn. 'They will not keep you waiting for long.'

The big man saluted again and, with a nod to Valerius, returned to his section.

'Well, you have seen my preparations,' Spurinna said. 'Does your experience at Colonia allow you to add anything that might be of help?'

Valerius looked out over the town and the ants' nest activity of the soldiers working on the walls and shook his head. 'At Colonia the lack of walls forced us to take the battle to the enemy. We took what advantage we could of the terrain and made the enemy pay for every inch of ground in blood. When it was clear the battle was lost, we fought our way to the temple and held out for another two days. The defenders of the Temple of Claudius had no hope of victory or survival. The defenders of Placentia have both. My only reservation is the arena. I would burn it now. The military disadvantages outweigh any loss of morale to the citizens.'

'I do not disagree with your assessment, but—' Spurinna broke off as his eyes were drawn to something on the rampart ahead.

Valerius followed his gaze to where Serpentius hovered protectively beside a slight figure in a cloak who stared out towards the southern horizon.

'General, may I introduce the lady Domitia Longina Corbulo.'

Domitia turned to meet them, nodding graciously as she recognized the legate's scarlet sash. Spurinna's eyes twinkled and the old soldier carried off a low bow with the poise of a much younger man. 'I had enormous respect for your late father, lady; if ever there was a soldier's soldier it was he. My nephew Gaius served as his surgeon during his Armenian campaigns and said his men would follow him to the very gates of Hades. A great loss to the Empire.'

'Thank you, general. I understand that we are not to be permitted to travel south?'

'It is not a question of permission, more that I cannot assure your safety. You will have had your fill of Batavian auxiliaries for today.'

'When will they come?' She repeated Juva's question.

Spurinna looked distracted, as if his mind was elsewhere. 'When they come, they will come from there.' He pointed out along the snaking line of the river. 'From the east, not the south. Ah.' A tiny pin prick of brightness rose slowly on the far horizon before arcing back to earth. The flaming arrow was quickly followed by a second. With the signal from his scouts, the general's whole bearing changed, as if an enormous burden had been removed from his shoulders. He smiled. 'As to when? I do believe they are already on the march and we can expect them in the morning.'

XLI

'They look well.' Spurinna laughed appreciatively as he looked out from the parapet at the great army massing before the city.

Standing beside him among his aides, Valerius had to agree with the general. They did look fine, marching like a crimson tide across the broad farmland beyond the line of razed buildings, in their tight-ranked centuries and their cohorts, armour twinkling in the early morning sun and the brightly coloured shields identifying their legions. The only thing he didn't share was the older man's enthusiasm for the sight.

'Twenty-first Rapax, sir.' A sharp-eyed young tribune noted the twin boars on the scarlet and yellow background. His voice echoed his general's zeal. 'A full legion, more or less, and every man a veteran. They've been keeping the Helvetii honest up at Vindonissa for the last five years.'

A horn blew its familiar hoarse call and the legionaries came to an instant halt, not a man out of line and their standard-bearers placed exactly in front of each individual unit. Spurinna turned to Valerius. 'They can drill, but can they fight?'

'We'll find out soon enough.' They watched as a second unit and then a third came into sight and took their places to the right and left of the Twenty-first.

'Twenty-second Primigenia and Fourth Macedonica.' The aide noted the names down on a wax tablet. 'They're a long way from Moguntiacum. Plus about five cohorts of auxiliaries and another three of cavalry.'

A never-ending line of wagons and carts, mules and livestock crawled in after the legions, but Valerius's eyes were drawn to a tall figure at the centre of a cloud of immaculately dressed officers which halted in front of the assembled troops.

'If he's a fool,' Spurinna commented, 'he'll keep them sweating in their ranks while he comes and makes his obligatory offer of terms. If he's not, he'll have them make camp while we discuss the pointless niceties. Ah, good. Always better to fight a man who knows what he's doing.' As the soldiers dispersed, an individual officer rode out from the group of horsemen. When he was close enough they saw he carried a green branch. 'Valerius? Young Mettelus? Anyone feel like surrendering? Well then, let's not keep them waiting.' They unbuckled their swords and strode out to meet the emissary.

'My legate wishes to discuss the possibility of a peaceful solution,' the young man said when they were within hearing distance.

'Well, get him here, you fool,' the general snapped. 'We haven't got all day.'

The aide raised his branch and waved it above his head. Immediately, four riders broke away from the group and rode towards Placentia. As they approached, Spurinna let out a choking grunt. 'Mars' arse, the man's dressed like a Celtic farmer and . . . is that a bloody woman with him?'

Caecina's emissary shot the general a startled glance. 'I believe it's his wife, sir,' Mettelus offered. 'They say she travels everywhere with him.'

Spurinna studied the slight figure in the centre with undisguised admiration. 'Yes, well, you would keep her close, I'll say that. But it's not proper. Not proper at all.'

He turned his attention to the curious figure in the Celtic breeches and tunic. A less confident man would have stayed in the saddle and looked down on his enemies. Instead, Aulus Caecina Alienus vaulted effortlessly to the ground and threw his mount's reins to an aide. A broad smile creased his handsome, fine-boned face as if this were a surprise encounter with old friends, but Valerius noticed that the smile didn't quite reach the over-bright eyes. His hair was dark as a raven's wing and worn long in the fashion of his barbarian auxiliaries. A fine torc of twisted gold strands graced his neck, and others encircled his wrists. The only thing that distinguished him as a Roman soldier was the sculpted breastplate he wore and the scarlet sash at his waist that identified him as a legionary legate. A barnyard cockerel, strutting and proud, Valerius thought, but, it seemed, not a cockerel looking for a fight.

'Aulus Caecina Alienus.' He bowed. 'Legate of the Fourth Macedonica and commander of the armies of the North. My Emperor regrets this unfortunate misunderstanding. He desires only peace and prosperity throughout this land.' The voice was soft and persuasive; charming, but, despite all the owner's efforts, lacking in sincerity. 'He believes you have been misled by your superiors and he would welcome you into his protection. All you must do is march your men from the gates within the hour. You have my promise that they will not be molested and they may retain their weapons, their standards and their honour.' He shrugged as though the rest was not his concern. 'After that, they may join us or go home, as they please.'

Spurinna nodded thoughtfully, as if he were considering the offer. 'And the people of Placentia?'

Caecina waved a careless hand towards the city walls, but Valerius knew he would be taking in every helmet, spear and artillery position. 'They are my Emperor's subjects,' Vitellius's general said smoothly. 'They will be unharmed as long as they are prepared to take the oath to him.'

'And if not?'

Caecina shrugged. They both knew what would happen if the city fell after a prolonged siege.

The old general drew himself up to his full height and his voice took on a new power, reaching out to the soldiers working on the closest encampment. 'Marcus Salvius Otho Augustus was proclaimed Emperor in Rome by the Senate and people of Rome. He is the only true Emperor: Imperator, Princeps and Pontifex Maximus.' Spurinna reeled off the titles one by one. 'He regrets that the officers and soldiers of his northern armies have been deceived and believes the governor of Germania Inferior has acted rashly. Still, he is prepared to take him as a friend if he will only kneel and take the oath of loyalty. Even now, Aulus Vitellius is considering an offer of gifts and further preferment that would raise him among the highest in the land. In addition, the soldiers of the Rhenus legions will receive a payment equal to half a year's wages a man in recognition of their previous petitions if they return to their posts today.'

Valerius saw Caecina dart a nervous glance towards his lines. This was not how Emperors dealt with their rivals, or the troops who followed them. The suggestion

389

that Vitellius might be tempted by Otho's bribes had unsettled him. Spurinna noticed his unease and took his chance to exploit the opening. 'They know your friend and ally Valens has deserted you. What is the excuse? Sickness? Lack of supplies? We hear mutiny being spoken of. You cannot win alone. Take your soldiers home and you too could be elevated among the highest in the land. You know the true Emperor is marching north. If you do not reduce Placentia in days, you will be caught between the hammer of the Emperor's legions and the anvil of my walls. He will be on your neck like a ravening wolf. And Placentia will . . . not . . . be . . . reduced.' The old general's nostrils flared as he remembered past triumphs and he glared defiance at his enemy. 'Men with strong hearts and strong arms will stand behind those walls and oppose you until the Mare Nostrum freezes over. Placentia will be the graveyard of your army and your hopes, Aulus Caecina Alienus.'

While the verbal sparring continued, Valerius found himself the undisguised focus of dark, slanting eyes from behind Caecina's left shoulder. He returned her stare, trying desperately not to smile. Spurinna was right. A true beauty. A long aristocratic nose, with high cheekbones and pouting cherry-red lips. The look she gave him was languid, considering and . . . he almost choked . . . heavy with promise. It shouldn't be possible, but it was true. He could almost hear her purring. But look again and there was something else in those eyes, the kind of gold-flecked shadows you saw in a hungry leopard's. He decided that he didn't envy Aulus Caecina Alienus his nights after all. He dragged his eyes away, but not before he saw a knowing smile touch her lips.

'. . . and we promise you a warm welcome.'

Caecina sighed. 'I am a generous man. I will give you

two hours to accept my Emperor's offer. After that, there will be no more talk and no more mercy.' He leapt athletically into the saddle and dragged his horse's head round. 'Two hours,' he repeated. 'Two hours and then it begins. Surrender and you will live. If my legions have to take those walls, everyone inside them will die.'

As they marched back towards the gate, Spurinna's face split in a savage grin.

'Two hours, my . . . I know his kind. Aulus Caecina Alienus could sell a wooden leg to a four-legged dog, but at heart he's a backstabber. He'll have them on us as soon as he can get spears in their hands.'

By the time he reached the makeshift camp, Caecina was having doubts about the wisdom of his generosity. Spurinna's talk of ravening wolves had made him nervous, because he knew the old man was right. He had to finish this quickly, not least because that dog's turd Valens might arrive soon to steal the glory. He exchanged a glance with his wife and she nodded.

'We will attack immediately,' he said. 'Have the leading cohorts ready with their scaling ladders in thirty minutes.'

His military tribune frowned. 'But, general, we haven't sited the artillery yet and the heavy *ballistae* won't be here until nightfall.'

But the legate wouldn't be moved. 'They think they have two hours. We will take them by surprise. One swift charge will take the walls, and I will be drinking from Spurinna's cup before nightfall.'

Domitia was waiting for Valerius on the battlements where she had watched the negotiations. 'Was she pretty?'

The question left him groping for an answer that

wouldn't offend and a short-lived thrill of panicked guilt. How could she have known? 'Does it matter?' The walnut eyes pinned him in their frank stare and he stumbled on. 'As it happens, she was very beautiful.'

She nodded as if it was only right and reached down to touch his left hand, running soft fingers over skin calloused to the texture of leather by daily sword practice. 'If I were to have my life again, I would choose to be a warrior queen riding into battle side by side with my king.' The fingers fluttered away, but he dared not look at her and his throat felt as if it was filled with pebbles.

'You should go,' he said, as gently. 'It will not be safe here for much longer.' But when he turned she was already gone.

Valerius tightened the straps of the bronze helmet Serpentius had brought him from Placentia's armoury and tested the point of his sword. He knew it was keen enough, because he'd sharpened it himself, but it was a warrior's ritual and rituals were important to a soldier. When Domitia had left him on the battlements he'd felt a curious mixture of loss and elation. He wanted her to be safe, but he missed the warmth of her touch and the strength she gave him. He knew she was in danger, but her presence in Placentia made something inside him soar; a terrible feeling of anger and power and violence, and a sense of invincibility he had never felt before. What better reason to fight and die than to protect the one you . . . yes, he could admit it to himself now . . . the one you loved. Today, he would fight at the right hand of the gods. Today he was Mars the Avenger come to earth, and any man who crossed this wall would live only long enough to regret it. His face set in a grim half-smile he could barely control and he knew – *knew* – that though he had tested the gods' patience with his unspoken boasts he would live to enjoy this day. Let them come. He felt Serpentius's eyes on him and he saw that the Spaniard sensed the change in him.

'A pity we didn't have time for me to carve you a new hand,' the gladiator said. 'A man without a shield on a day like today is only asking to get killed.'

'Then you'll have to be my shield.' It was said half in jest, but Serpentius nodded gravely and for Valerius that was as good as a solemn vow. They would fight as a pair, the arena way, the Spaniard never leaving his right side. A former slave and a part-man, but together they would be worth ten of the enemy.

Who had broken their truce.

At the sound of the massed trumpets, Spurinna came to join them on the parapet for the last time before he would retire to coordinate the defence from his headquarters in the city. Caecina's forces marched out from their compounds, the clatter of armour and the tramp of feet clear in the still air even at this distance. Valerius had witnessed the sight of his enemies massing in overwhelming numbers before, at Colonia, where he had faced Boudicca, and again at the Cepha gap where Corbulo had fought the Parthian King of Kings to a standstill. But this was different. In some ways, the barbarians had been more frightening to watch; a great swirling mass of hatred, a cacophony of colour and noise designed to instil terror. Yet this was the first time he had faced Roman soldiers in battle. The thought stayed with him and for a moment he felt a curious mix of confusion and sadness that was alien and potentially fatal on a battlefield. These men were Roman citizens, soldiers of the Empire. They should not be his enemies.

He savagely thrust the feeling aside, conjuring up Domitia's face in his head and reminding himself what would happen to her if he failed. *If my legions have to take those walls, everyone inside them will die.* Well, these walls would stand. Must stand. If the blood of every man out there had to be spilled to ensure it. The massed ranks came on at their familiar, unhurried pace. Here was none of the bluster and posturing of barbarians, only deadly intent. Caecina was using the two part-legions, six thousand veteran troops, as his battering ram. Primigenia's symbol, a golden Wheel of Fortuna, was clearly visible on the shields to the right front, beside Fourth Macedonica's white bull to the left, with a horde of anonymous auxiliaries on their flanks. Valerius had a moment of unease as Twenty-first Rapax marched off towards the right flank. Was it possible Caecina would use his crack legion to attack the west wall? No. Five cohorts of auxiliary infantry jogged past them and it seemed the Vitellian commander had decided to keep them in reserve in the shadow of the amphitheatre walls.

'I thought so,' the general grunted. 'The south wall and the gate. He may use those auxiliaries for an attack on the west side, but most likely it will be a feint. We'll keep a cohort of Praetorians in the angle of the two walls, ready to support whichever is under the most pressure. I was wrong.' His voice was almost affronted. 'He *is* a fool. Unless he has a trick up his sleeve, this throwing his men at stone walls is an affront to military science. He should have allowed an hour or two to flay us with his *onagri* and *scorpiones*. At the very least, it would have kept our heads down. You are happy with your dispositions?'

Valerius nodded. He had checked them a dozen

times. Men and weapons where they were needed, the legionaries crouched behind the walls for the moment for protection. No point in taking unnecessary casualties. Reserves in position where they could easily reach the places they were needed. Water to hand for extinguishing fires and slaking thirst. Cauldrons of hot oil bubbling on the braziers and glowing irons ready to be slapped on a wound to stop the blood flow. This wall would be defended by the men of the First Adiutrix and he felt an unlikely confidence in the face of the great odds as he noted Juva's reliable presence a little way to his left. The general saw his look and placed a hand on the younger man's arm. 'This is where it will be won or lost, Valerius. Win it for me.'

As the general walked away, Valerius dismissed the surge of foolish pride he had felt at the words. He was aware of the Vitellian auxiliaries deploying in front of the west wall just out of range of the *onagri* and *scorpiones*, but he forced himself to concentrate on what was happening to his front. Feint or not, he had to rely on the commander of the western defences to do his job. For the moment, he ignored the great mass of soldiers and studied what was going on around them. The first thing he noticed was the men struggling with what looked from this distance like wooden carts, but he knew were the legion's mobile light artillery. Oddly, the sight pleased him. It would take time to deploy the machines and, for the moment at least, the defenders wouldn't be plagued by the giant arrows and rocks. He faced upwards of ten cohorts, which meant they could deploy a dozen *onagri* and ten times as many *scorpiones*. He frowned. No, many more than that. Caecina wouldn't leave the Rapax's artillery lying idle while Primigenia and Macedonica were doing the dying.

The 'Shield-splitters' and their 'Wild Ass' counterparts, so named for the enormous kick they gave when they were triggered, were nothing like as lethal against a fortified city as they were against a packed mass of men. Still, it was daunting for any man to raise his head when he knew it could be taken off by a ten-pound boulder. Satisfied they were in no danger for the moment, he searched among the baggage carts for the sight he feared, but there was still no sign of the big siege *ballistae* that the Vitellians were undoubtedly constructing.

Well, he would show them what they were missing.

'Ranging shot,' he called down to the messenger stationed at the base of the wall. 'Five hundred paces beyond the gate on a direct line.'

The big machines were notoriously inaccurate and he had no great hope of causing any damage, but it would give the enemy something to think about. The problem with the *ballistae* was the exact opposite of that with their smaller cousins. It was all very well firing them at a mile-long wall when you had every chance of hitting the city behind it, but hurling rocks blind and inside the machine's most effective range was like throwing pebbles over your shoulder into a fishpond and hoping to catch your supper. The theory was confirmed when a few moments later a resounding thud seemed to shake the wall and he instinctively ducked as something split the air above him with a powerful whooshing surge. He searched for the missile and thought he saw a black dot curving far above the assembled legions below him and arcing into the baggage carts packed around the newly built camp. The impact was invisible, but he could imagine the damage and consternation the huge rock would have caused if it hit anything and he consoled himself with the thought that, if nothing else, he would make it difficult for Caecina's legionaries to sleep that night. If Placentia survived that long.

For they were coming.

A wall of bright iron, proud banners and triple-layered shields of ash and oak. Valerius's mind assessed the threat without conscious effort. Ten cohorts made up the attack. A front rank of four, each containing six centuries of eighty men, five hundred to a cohort, more or less, so a total of around two thousand men. Behind the front rank came two further ranks of three cohorts, an additional three thousand battle-hardened legionaries. The centuries marched in open order, with a six-foot gap between every man, a formation designed to minimize casualties from Placentia's death machines. They were close enough now for him to see the hundreds of scaling ladders carried by the men in the front ranks. Part of him hoped the ladders would be too short, which had happened in attacks before, but he guessed Caecina's engineers would have done their calculations properly. The legionaries would have practised this manoeuvre often, but never against walls of this scale and never without the diversionary support of the artillery. Valerius knew from experience that once they were in the shadow of the walls and safe from the defenders' *ballista* bolts and missiles the centuries would close their gaps to a single space and adapt to a denser formation of eight ranks of ten. It made them a more compact target, but it allowed the century to form *testudo*, the near impenetrable carapace of shields that would protect those within from spears and arrows. From the shelter of the *testudo* they would raise the siege ladders and begin the long perilous climb to meet their enemies. It was all about numbers. Caecina's soldiers would not attack along the entire wall. They would choose the most vulnerable points around the gate and between the towers to concentrate their efforts. Three or four ladders converging on the same limited space. If they could get enough men to the top of the ladder to overwhelm the defenders Placentia would fall and the slaughter of innocents would begin.

But Valerius had other ideas.

By now, Caecina's leading cohorts were entering the killing ground Spurinna's engineers had marked, four hundred paces out among the dirt mounds that were all that was left of Placentia's suburbs. The defenders saw it and howled insults and defiance at their attackers.

'Enough,' Valerius roared and the centurions re-inforced the order with their gnarled vine sticks. The one-handed Roman stared at his enemy, counting their steps and allowing as many as he dared to enter the marked space. He raised his left hand. 'Now,' he said, allowing the hand to drop.

Ropes that had been tensed to breaking point thrummed with released energy and the distinctive chopping sound of the *onagri* and *scorpiones* echoed all along the wall. 'That'll teach the bastards,' he heard Serpentius mutter.

In the centre of the leading cohort a centurion, recognizable by the scarlet horsehair crest on his helmet, his armour glinting with the *phalerae* of a dozen campaigns, was whipped backwards by an invisible hand, smashing into the ranks behind and causing momentary chaos. Valerius didn't see what had caused the casualties, but armour counted for nothing against five-foot bolts and heavy boulders. The centurion had either been gutted or smashed to bloody pulp and the men of the Macedonica had lost a leader and a comrade. All along the line, shields were shattered and gaps

398

appeared in the ranks as the heavy missiles smashed home. Men were left bleeding and broken as their tent mates marched reluctantly over their bodies.

'Close up! Close the ranks!' Valerius heard the first shouts of the centurions, decurions and *optiones* as they struggled to maintain the cohesion of the formations. A discernible growl went up from the legionaries as they came on, leaving a scattering of still figures in their wake like jetsam discarded by a ship. He felt an involuntary flare of triumph as he watched his enemy fall, but he understood that he could not let passion control him. His artillery salvos would hurt them, but would not stop them. The machines were slow to load and their commanders might get five shots away before the angles of fire meant more would be useless. A few dozen casualties, possibly a hundred. Just a pinprick, but Valerius was satisfied.

Something whirred past his helmet.

'Keep your head down, idiot, unless you want a hole in it.'

Valerius ignored Serpentius's admonition and concentrated on the battle unfolding before him. From the gaps between the attacking formations, and on their flanks, swarms of auxiliary archers and slingers ran forward to close on the walls. When they were within range, he ordered the bowmen scattered among the defenders to engage them. But the archers were a sideshow; the *gustatio* before the meat. It would soon be time for the main course.

XLII

'It won't be long now.' Valerius drew his *gladius* free from its scabbard for the first time.

Serpentius heard the doubt in his voice. 'Would you rather be somewhere else?'

'It doesn't feel right to be killing Romans.'

The Spaniard's only reply was to spit in the direction of the attackers and Valerius knew he was thinking of his burning village and the long years fighting for his very survival in the arena. Serpentius called Gaius Valerius Verrens friend, but he had as much reason to hate Romans as any man alive and today he would get his chance to cleanse that stain on his honour with blood.

'Ready.' Valerius had seen the attacking formations first tighten and then break up into individual components as each century homed in on its target area of the walls. When they reached a line of white pegs hammered into the earth, he shouted the command. 'Fire.'

From the cleared area where they had waited within the walls, an entire wing of green-cloaked auxiliary archers from Syria loosed their bows, sending a shower of arrows soaring into the air in a great hissing swarm.

Before the first volley had reached the top of its arc, a second followed, and then a third. Fifteen hundred arrows in the space of twenty seconds. The sky above the attackers turned black. Valerius had seen barbarian assaults decimated by the arrow storm, but he watched with a feeling close to pride as the legionaries' *scuta* came up in a single movement and the arrows rattled harmlessly against the big shields. A few more casualties as the shafts found gaps and weak spots. It would slow them – the archers would fire until they were out of arrows – but it could never stop them.

This was war. Move and counter-move. Caesar's Tower on a larger stage, with human pieces.

A gigantic crack seemed to sunder the air and Valerius flinched as something stung his cheek. He put his hand up and it came away bloody. When he looked to his left three men were down, writhing among the shattered remains of their *onager*, which had been struck by a missile identical to the boulders they had been firing at the enemy. One tried to stand, his face a mess of blood, but before anyone could go to his aid he staggered blindly off the edge of the parapet and fell thirty feet to smash on the cobbles below. The others, a tangled mess of entrails and shattered bone, went still.

'Clear this mess away,' Serpentius ordered, and a section of replacements carried the dead men off before taking their place. The Spaniard reached up and tugged something from Valerius's face. He held up an oak splinter the length of his finger. 'A few inches higher and it would have had your eye out.'

Valerius met his gaze. 'That's why I have two.'

By now an increasing number of missiles were striking the walls and causing casualties among the defenders, but Valerius knew that this would soon cease, as their attackers became fearful of hitting their own men. For the two legionary formations had reached the wall and pools of brightly coloured shields formed as the individual centuries went into *testudo* to protect the ladder crews.

The first ladder rose by the gate above which Valerius stood, quickly followed by another and then another. With the battle joy rising inside him, he stood up to his full height. He knew he looked nothing like a Roman officer with his beard, his wild hair and his badly patched Batavian chain mail. But he was a warrior. A warrior invested with the confidence of the gods. A warrior to follow. To victory.

'First Adiutrix,' he roared. 'Ready!'

Officers repeated the cry all along the wall and a host of wide-eyed glaring faces anticipated the next order, twitching with the eagerness of starved hunting dogs. A few of the marine legionaries, driven half-mad by the waiting, would have risen, but checked at Valerius's snarl. 'Wait, you sons of sea spawn. You'll have your chance. Wait!'

They waited until the ladders appeared on the wall. They waited until the wooden uprights began to vibrate beneath the feet of the men climbing them. And still he made them wait. Arrows lashed the air above the parapet and turned it into a place of death. 'Wait!'

A first red and yellow shield appeared, raised high to protect the owner's head from arrows and spears that had never appeared. The legionary was puzzled by the lack of opposition. He had expected to be dead by now. Valerius's ears reverberated with the roars of the attackers, the shrieks of the dying, the deadly *zupp* of passing arrows and the clatter of iron spears breaking impotently against the walls.

'Now!' He roared the order above the cacophony.

Juva rose to tower over the twin boar emblem of the leading legionary's *scutum*, a double-headed woodman's axe held like a toy in his great paws. 'Give a sailor an axe and watch the blood and teeth fly,' an old friend had once told Valerius. Now he watched as the big Nubian brought the curved head down and in three terrible blows chopped the shield to splinters, leaving the incredulous owner holding little more than the boss and a few scraps of wood. But the men of the Fifteenth did not lack courage. With a scream of defiance, the man attempted to take the final step that would put him on the parapet. It was too easy. Valerius leaned out and stabbed down, forcing his *gladius* into the gaping mouth until blood vomited past the blade and the point scraped on backbone. The dying legionary went rigid and his fingers lost their grip on the ladder so that he fell backwards, taking the man below with him to his death. In the same instant, a second big sailor hurled a boulder that crushed a third attacker's chest and splintered the rungs so that the whole construction fell apart, sending the remaining men into the ditch to be impaled on the iron-tipped hedgehogs, where their tent mates used them as human stepping stones. A similar combination of pitiless assaults saw off a second ladder. Meanwhile, powerful hands, long educated to push and haul on ships, expertly hooked the V-shaped ends of two specially prepared poles against the top rungs of the outermost of the four ladders. Desperate fingers scrabbled to free them, but the marine legionaries heaved until the ladders slowly swayed upright. With a terrible inevitability, they pitched slowly backward with the combined wail of a dozen doomed men heralding their entry to the Otherworld. A marine capered on the parapet, screaming insults at the seething mass of men below until an arrow took him in the eye and the caper turned into an elegant pirouette that sent him over the edge.

Valerius turned and a shudder of unease ran through him as he found himself staring into Juva's smouldering eyes. Before he could react, the Nubian had run past him along the wall to where the occupants of a new ladder were just completing their climb. The topmost legionary swung his leg over the parapet and with a casual swing of his axe Juva severed it at the knee. While the shocked owner was staring incredulously at the mutilation, the axe reversed and looped up to take him below the chin, splitting his screaming face in two and sending his brass helmet spinning. The second man on the ladder advanced, head down, unaware of the fate of his comrade. When he finally raised his helmet to be confronted with Juva's savage face and the plunging axe, he threw himself backwards, taking two men down with him. Juva waited at the top of the ladder, roaring defiance and daring anyone to meet him. The next man hesitated until a *pilum* thrown from the wall took him in the side and he fell away. Still, another took his place and scrambled doggedly upwards to where a spray of scarlet marked his end. Arrows peppered the parapet where they stood and Valerius hauled the Nubian away as a dozen new ladders targeted the gate. 'You are more use to me alive than dead,' he snarled. Juva glared at him for a moment and the axe twitched in his hands before he obeyed.

At their side, Serpentius grinned. 'And I always thought sailors were soft.'

All that long day they held the walls, and all the long day the attackers fought and died. Fell back to regroup, attacked and died again. They were so brave that Valerius became sick of killing them. The life expectancy of any man who reached the parapet could be measured in seconds, but still they came and still the left-handed sword rose and fell, its blade clotted thick with the blood of countless victims. He killed, because if he did not kill Domitia Longina Corbulo would die. He killed to survive and he killed because Serpentius fought at his side and the Spaniard's relentless savagery never waned.

Urged on by Aulus Caecina Alienus, the near-exhausted legions attacked a third time, reinforced by four fresh cohorts from their comrades of Twenty-first Rapax. The assault was coordinated with an all-out bid by the Vitellian auxiliaries to take the west wall. For the first time they reached the parapet in enough numbers to make Titus Vitricius Spurinna throw in his reserves. Serpentius, Valerius and Juva found themselves fighting alongside black-tunicked Praetorians in a desperate street brawl where helmets and teeth replaced swords and spears and Juva somehow laid hands on a long-handled Celtic blade that sang as it carved great swaths through the screaming enemy ranks. At some point it must have ended, because the only living Vitellians in Placentia lay groaning and bleeding their lives away on the stone slabs. Valerius found himself with his back against the parapet, his whole body shaking as if he had a fever and his tongue cloven to the roof of his mouth by thirst. He watched Serpentius and Juva move among the enemy wounded giving the mercy stroke and noticed a dullness in the sky that heralded night and made him wonder where the day had gone. He wanted only to sleep, but Spurinna had given him command and a commander must record who still lived and who had died, ensure his men were fed and watered, and replenish the stocks of weapons. First he had to help heave the enemy dead over the walls to take their place among the great heaps of corpses clogging the ditch. Corpses who had once been the cream of the Rhenus legions. Who had once been Roman citizens. With the last body gone, the futility of civil war almost swept him away and he leaned against the cold stone and would have wept if Serpentius hadn't cuffed his shoulder and thrust a water skin at him. Thankful that only the Spaniard had witnessed his weakness, he drank deeply and the moment was gone.

'We'll have to do it all again tomorrow.' He wiped his cracked lips.

Serpentius's blood-streaked features were a picture from Hades. 'Let them come.'

'First I have a job for you.'

Serpentius turned to stare at him. 'Are you trying to get me killed again?'

What seemed like an eternity later, Serpentius lay in the cellar of what had once been a house by the amphitheatre whose giant shadow he could feel looming above him. The groan and creak of iron-shod wheels rent the air as he went over Valerius's instructions in his head.

The one-handed Roman had predicted that Caecina would ask for a truce to recover his wounded and they'd watched as a whey-faced emissary confirmed the request. In the growing gloom it had been simple enough for the Spaniard to slip out among the cloaked and hooded men who quartered the battlefield with torches, seeking out the living from amongst the countless, anonymous dead. Eventually they concentrated their efforts where they were needed most, on the charnel house ditch below the walls, and he was able to squirm his way across the battlefield to the hiding place.

The groaning wheels meant he would have to wait a little longer, but he had been fed and watered and the battle fatigue that affected other men was alien to Serpentius of Avala, so he was content enough. He lay back in the darkness and closed his eyes.

All was quiet when he opened them again. He checked the bag at his waist to ensure he hadn't dropped anything, and slithered noiselessly towards the massive bulk of the amphitheatre. The door was where Valerius had said it would be, on the north-west side, away from the legionary camps, and he found the handle after only a minimum of groping. Inside, he followed the steps downwards and through a maze of corridors that were etched on his brain from the plan Spurinna had provided. His nose told him this was where they penned the animals that were to die in the arena, and he passed a room that smelled of liniment and fear and stirred a familiar anger inside him. Eventually, he knew he was beneath the arena because he could hear thumps and murmurs from the earth-covered wooden floor above, where Aulus Caecina Alienus had sited his recently constructed great siege weapons. Without hesitation, Serpentius felt about in the darkness until he found the door he was looking for. Behind it lay piles and piles of bitumen-soaked brush and bales of straw, stockpiled here by Placentia's defenders for just this purpose. Just one place, Valerius had said. You need to light it only in one place. The reason was apparent in the smell of newly applied paint that filled his nostrils. Paint that covered every inch of the wooden structures around him and the seats in the amphitheatre above. Spurinna had said it was some infernal compound of sulphur and bitumen that could be relied on to combust. It seemed almost witchcraft and his fingers twitched in the sign against evil, but he was pledged to carry out his mission. Cautiously, he held the iron rod he carried over the nearest bundle of gleaming brush and struck the flint against it until a single glowing spark twirled through the gloom.

XLIII

Domitia Longina Corbulo looked out from the walls of Placentia with the flames of the city's blazing amphitheatre dancing in her eyes.

'You are not safe here.'

She had sensed his presence, so Valerius's voice came as no surprise, but his words made her lips purse. Who was safe amid all this butchery? She had spent the day helping care for the wounded, tying bandages and trying to staunch wounds that would not be staunched. She had seen things that no human being had a right to see and held men as they died. When she had tried to wash the blood from her hands there always seemed to be traces left. Perhaps it would never leave her. Domitia turned to meet his gaze, hastily concealing her unease at the change a few hours had wrought. His eyes held the shadows of fresh sorrow, and exhaustion and strain had deepened the lines around them. The wound on his left cheek would leave a new scar on a face that might have been fashioned for war. 'Were you safe today, Valerius?'

Today? Surely the moon said it had been yesterday, and the stink of blood and torn bowels answered her better than he ever could. 'I am a soldier,' he said simply.

The crackle of sparks drew them back to the arena. A moment passed as they watched the flames leap higher before she spoke again. 'Will we be together?'

The change of direction momentarily confused him. Did she mean tonight, or tomorrow, or for the rest of their lives? 'I think that is for the gods to decide.'

The angry hiss of her breath told him it was the wrong answer. 'I have watched you, Valerius. I have seen you preserve life and I have seen you kill. You stood on these walls today like a god of old, yet you would allow them to dictate to you, to us?'

He wanted to argue, to be the man he had been when the sword was in his hand, but before he could reply Spurinna appeared with a shadowy figure at his elbow. Valerius took a step away from Domitia.

'Lady.' The general bowed. Domitia nodded gravely and directed a smile at the dark spectre, who turned out to be Serpentius. She walked by Valerius on the way to the stairs. He watched her go and wished more than anything in this world that he could follow.

'By the gods, if you had but been a Roman you would have had the Gold Crown today.' Spurinna's eyes held a glint of triumph as he commended the Spaniard. 'It was a good plan, but it took a special man to turn it into reality. You have done the Emperor a great service and you may be assured he will hear of it.'

Serpentius spat into the darkness. He knew all too well that the gratitude of Emperors could be unreliable and short-lived. In the torchlight the gleam of his grim smile was a stark contrast to his soot-stained face, and he no longer had any eyebrows. He glared at Spurinna. 'You said it would burn well,' the general frowned, uncertain whether he was hearing a compliment or an accusation, 'but you didn't say *how* well. I was lucky to get out with only a singed arse . . .' The gaunt Spaniard was interrupted by a great, grumbling roar from the amphitheatre. A flurry of sparks and flame shot hundreds of feet in the air as the floor of the burning arena collapsed beneath the weight of the giant siege catapults. 'But at least they won't be throwing rocks at us tomorrow.'

'No.' Valerius's voice was deadly serious. 'But they'll be throwing everything else.'

'Then we'd better be ready for them.'

The attack that began at daylight took on a new dimension. Valerius had been right. Caecina did throw everything he had at the south wall. While his auxiliaries hammered at the rampart in a repeat of the previous day's tactics and with as much success, the men of the three legions, protected by portable wooden huts and screens they'd worked through the night to produce and hardened by years of digging forts and roads, worked to undermine the walls. Valerius tried to use fire arrows to destroy the thatched huts, but he discovered his counter-measure had been anticipated. The reeds the legionaries had used to roof the structures had been dampened and the burning shafts simply smouldered and died. Anyone who attempted to improvise an angle to loose an arrow or throw a spear at the occupants became the target of the dozens of archers placed to protect the diggers and enthusiasm for the tactic soon waned. The only victories were achieved where the piles of big stones happened to be stockpiled above the point where the legionaries were digging. A single small boulder would make little impact, but an avalanche of them smashed the shelters to splinters and crushed those inside. Juva witnessed one successful strike and later he came to Valerius during a lull in the fighting. 'I have an idea, tribune.'

Valerius listened to what the Nubian had to say and grinned. 'Take as many men as you need.'

Spurinna appeared on the wall an hour later. He was clean-shaven and as immaculate as usual in his legate's polished armour and scarlet cloak, but the grey pallor on his cheeks was proof he had not slept for days and the snap in his voice reinforced the fact. 'I've had a complaint from Antiochus, one of the city's *aediles*, that some legionaries are demolishing his house.'

Valerius showed him the shelters and explained what Juva had in mind.

'Well.' The general's lined face relaxed. 'I'm sure the gentleman has other houses, and we all have to make sacrifices.'

The 'house' was a rich villa constructed of large blocks of cut sandstone that would take two normal men to lift. But the former oarsmen of the marine legion were no ordinary men. Broad as a pick handle at the shoulder, with necks like bulls, they had upper arms that, over the years, had developed to the thickness of a man's thigh. Now a line of these giants struggled up the stairs to the parapet with their haul. Juva showed how it should be done. Bending low to avoid the arrows that were a constant threat to the defenders, he dragged his block to a point just above one of the wood and thatch huts. When he was in place, he waited patiently until the others reached their positions.

Every eye was on the big Nubian as he crouched over the massive stone, huge muscles taking the strain until the tendons stood out like tree roots and his neck looked as if it might explode. Just when it seemed he must admit defeat he straightened in a single smooth movement and heaved the block over the parapet. A heartbeat later the roof of the shelter exploded, followed by a long

412

moment of silence before the screaming started. One of the diggers had taken the full force of the block and his blood and brains now coated the other occupants, who scuttled through a shower of arrows into the safety of the *testudo* where their comrades waited their turn to dig. A second man's arm had been sheared off at the shoulder. Valerius watched as the exercise was repeated simultaneously all along the wall to similar satisfying effect.

A great cheer went up from the defenders, but the roar faded as the legionary ranks opened to allow a new set of shelters to be trotted forward into place, along with a fresh set of diggers.

'It seems they're not ready to give up,' Valerius commented.

Juva's eyes were red-rimmed with exhaustion and his face was grey with dried sweat and mortar dust, but he managed a smile. 'Neither are we.' He waved a huge arm to take in the roofs of Placentia. 'When this house is finished there are plenty more to choose from.'

Valerius always knew there would be a crisis and it came as the sun reached its height and the pressure on the walls threatened to overwhelm the exhausted defenders. Thousands of dead auxiliaries filled the ditch, lying on the already bloated carcasses of those who had been killed on the first day, but still they came. The shelters and diggers had been renewed several times. Juva had lost a dozen of his strongest in the cat-and-mouse game with the archers, and the survivors were close to collapse.

Serpentius noticed it first. 'What in the name of the gods is that?' he demanded through a throat choked with dust and thirst. *That* was a shelter four times the length of those the legionaries had used for their mining expeditions, and it appeared more sturdily constructed. Valerius followed his gaze and felt a thrill of genuine fear as he watched it carve a route through the legionary ranks.

'To the gate!' He ran in the direction of the flanking towers.

When they reached the walkway above the gate the curious structure was close enough for the foremost occupants to be visible. Its size was explained by the fact that, as well as the men who carried it, the interior had to be wide enough to accommodate two lines of legionaries and the massive tree trunk they struggled to carry between them. The clue was in the huge stone carved in the shape of a horned ram that tipped the trunk.

'Juva? Brace the gates and concentrate the strongest of your men here with as many of the big blocks as they can find.'

By the time he heard the sound of the braces being knocked into position the battering ram was already being manoeuvred towards the gate through a storm of spears and arrows. But the roof of the shelter wasn't thatched, rather plated with some kind of metal sheets, and the weapons simply bounced off. Sweat ran down Valerius's back, but it had nothing to do with the warmth of a spring day.

The builders had set the gate back from the line of the wall, so that from above the overhang obscured the front of the shelter. A big legionary staggered up with a stone block, but before he could hurl it an enormous splintering crash froze everyone in place. 'Jupiter save us,' someone whispered. It wasn't until he saw Serpentius staring at him that Valerius realized it had been he himself. Now it was the Vitellian forces who cheered, and they attacked the walls with renewed vigour as the battering ram's rhythmic, ear-splitting crash echoed across the field.

'I'll show those bastards.' With a roar, the legionary heaved the block up to the parapet and dropped it on to the shelter below with a mighty clatter. For a moment the battering stopped, but when Valerius risked a glance to inspect the damage he saw that although the metal roof had been badly dented, the occupants were untouched.

'Try again,' he snarled, but in his heart he knew the result would be the same.

'How long?' Serpentius asked.

Valerius shrugged. The gate was made of a double layer of seasoned oak and barred with three thick beams. It was strong, but unless the ram could be destroyed the result was inevitable. 'An hour, maybe less.'

The Spaniard nodded solemnly. 'In that case, we'll slaughter the bastards when they come through the gate.'

Valerius smiled at his friend's assurance, but they both knew that if the ram broke through, this would be their last fight.

When he inspected the gate, it was holding up reasonably well, with only a few white splinters showing the damage done so far. Yet every blow had an effect and men flinched with each strike of the ram and the wooden beams shivered at the strain placed on them. Valerius had ordered two centuries of Spurinna's Praetorians to the gateway, ready for the breakthrough when it came. For the moment, they sat with their backs to the wall darting nervous glances at every thundering crash. The defenders on the walls above were still full of fight and Caecina would be lamenting the loss of his siege *ballistae*, but none of that would matter when the ram breached the gate.

Even as he watched, the pressure on the wooden beams grew, and when he looked closely Valerius saw the first cracks beginning to form in the central bar, which was taking the worst of the pounding. How much longer could it last?

He was still brooding on the question when he heard the sound of snarled orders and tramping feet. Puzzled, he turned to find Juva bearing down on him at the front of a stout pole being carried by six of the marine legionaries, every man cursing the great load they bore and their faces uniform masks of pain and effort. The pole was bent almost to breaking point by the weight of an enormous millstone from one of Placentia's bakeries; four feet of black granite as broad as a glutton's waist, transfixed by the pole through a hole at its centre.

Valerius realized in an instant what the big Nubian had in mind. 'Clear the stairs,' he shouted.

Grunting with effort and legs straining, Juva and his men hefted the massive stone one agonizing step at a time up the steep stairway to the parapet. Valerius wondered that the millstone didn't slide back and crush the rearmost carriers until he noticed that someone had jammed cloth into the gap between stone and pole to hold it in place. Eventually the carrying party reached the wall above the gateway and thankfully lowered their burden to the flagstones before collapsing groaning beside it. Valerius looked over the parapet down to where the metal-plated shelter covered the ram. Would it be enough? They were about to find out.

'You are not finished yet,' Juva snarled at his comrades. 'One more effort.' He picked up one end of the pole and took the strain. Reluctantly, and easing their aching muscles, his tent mates returned to their places so that three men gripped the pole on either side of the great stone. 'On the count of three. One, two . . .'

With one convulsive heave they lifted the pole to shoulder height and somehow managed to get the mill-stone on top of the parapet, where it teetered for a moment before a last effort sent it plunging down on the ram shelter. The massive block instantly caved in six or eight feet of roof, buckling the metal and shattering planks. Animal shrieks of pain and terror testified to the effect on those within. Only the bulk of the ram itself had stopped the roof being crushed to ground level. Inside would be a welter of smashed bodies and shattered limbs. Even those not in the immediate area where the millstone had fallen would not have escaped as the trunk was torn from their hands or the wooden frame battered to the ground. Eventually, a few figures started to crawl out, or were supported from the wreckage, to be scythed down by a merciless hail of arrows and spears, before two centuries of Caecina's legionaries formed *testudo* to rescue the survivors. In the hours that followed, a few half-hearted attempts were made to salvage the smashed shelter and its ram, but eventually the young legate's men gave up the unequal battle. In fact, the destruction of the ram had a curiously debilitating effect on the whole attack. The assault against the city walls lost its impetus and by nightfall the Vitellians were back in their camps, leaving only a few archers to harass the defenders with fire arrows.

That evening Spurinna joined Valerius on the parapet and stared into the darkness. 'Your men did well today. You should get some sleep.'

'They're up to something.'

Spurinna nodded. It was impossible to see anything,

but like Valerius he could sense some great effort out there in the darkness. 'They'll have some new trick to torment us with in the morning. Even more important that you get some rest.'

But when the sun rose the camps were empty and the only movement on the battlefield was the flapping of wings as the crows fought over the bloating corpses of the dead.

XLIV

'What will happen now?' Domitia asked. The 'to us' was unspoken, but there just the same.

'It depends what the Emperor decides.' Valerius rode beside the covered wagon Spurinna had provided for his guest as they travelled from Placentia on the Via Aemilia to meet Otho's advancing forces. It was the same road he and Serpentius had followed north on their journey six weeks earlier. Blue skies and spring sunshine had replaced the glowering clouds, but Valerius only had eyes for Domitia, who wore a blue cloak of fine cotton which set off her dark hair in a way that made the gulf between them seem all the wider. 'He'll furnish you with an escort back to Rome, while I . . .' He shrugged. 'He may give me a command, or he may not, but I'm a soldier and if there is a battle I will fight.'

'So it is finished.' It wasn't a question and the pain was clear in her eyes.

'Only if you want it be so.' The words fell like stones into a void and each one proclaimed him a coward. His heart cried out to him to make her his; to send her back to stay with Olivia at the villa until he returned. But the Domitia Longina Corbulo who had stood with him on the parapet overlooking the battlefield, the Domitia who had not hidden her love for him, had been replaced by another woman. He had witnessed before how the bonds created by the shared hardship and racing blood of battle could be sapped by the realities and responsibilities of peace. If he wanted her, he must win her, but this Domitia was again her father's daughter and that made his task more difficult. Duty was a Corbulo's watchword and he doubted she would shame his memory by leaving her husband. There was another, equally complicating, factor. In what seemed like another lifetime Valerius had sworn an oath to protect her life *and her honour*. That oath now stuck in his throat, but it had been made to a man who had died for honour and duty and it was an oath he couldn't break, even for Domitia.

With a last look of frustrated hurt she stared ahead and they continued the journey in silence.

Two days earlier, while the dead were still being cleared from Placentia's ditch, Spurinna had summoned Valerius while he questioned the commander of a patrol that had just returned from harassing the retreating Vitellians.

'Caecina is licking his wounds back at Cremona.' The general didn't hide his exultation. 'He will be vulnerable until Valens can reach him. I have had word that the Emperor is on the way to Brixellum and I would ask you to ride there and tell him that I advise an early attack while the traitor's men are still demoralized by their failure here.' From somewhere close by came the sound of female laughter and Valerius could smell the scent of cooking meat from the kitchens. Spurinna hesitated as if he were mulling a decision, then nodded as he made it. 'The lady Domitia will accompany you – I am sure he will see that she is safely taken south. I will give you a squadron of cavalry as escort. Oh, and he will need every man he can get, so I will send him five centuries of the First Adiutrix as soon as I've cleaned up this mess.'

Brixellum was a hard day's ride from Placentia, but Vitellian cavalry patrols still plagued the road and it was late afternoon on the second day by the time they arrived at the settlement thirty miles south-east of Cremona. The town had been heavily fortified and six cohorts of the Praetorian Guard were encamped on the outskirts, but when Valerius asked for the Emperor he was told Otho had already ridden north to link up with his main force. The officer who gave him the news said there were rumours of a great victory near Cremona the previous day and Valerius wondered aloud if the war was already won.

The man's mood changed. 'No, there will be fighting yet. They say the armies of Vitellius have combined, and the false Emperor is on his way with reinforcements drawn from the legions of Britannia.'

'I should send you south with Serpentius.' Valerius despised himself for the emotionless formality in his voice. Domitia responded with a shake of the head and a smile marked with weary resignation.

'My sentence is delayed for another day. Besides, I have never met the Emperor . . .' She hesitated and he sensed she wanted to say more, but she turned and walked back to the coach.

They crossed to the east bank and followed the road to the town of Bedriacum where the Emperor's main force had made their headquarters. The first thing Valerius noticed as they approached the great military encampment outside the walls was the golden lion of the Thirteenth Gemina on the shields of the gate guards. The sight raised his spirits because it meant Otho's reinforcements had begun to arrive from the East. The second was a curiously unmilitary sprawl of tents with an odd-looking assortment of men lazing around campfires among them. Many wore makeshift bandages and bore signs of recent wounds. It was as he was studying them that one of the reclining figures rose to his feet and hailed him.

'Still alive, Valerius? And unless I miss my guess, that ugly bastard behind you is a Spanish horse thief of my acquaintance.'

Valerius gaped in disbelief at the man who had spoken. He was grey-haired and stocky and he carried a brass cock's comb helmet that had seen hard use. The helmet marked him as a gladiator, even if the deep scar that split his right cheek and his missing left ear weren't familiar enough. 'Marcus?' He shook his head at the sight of his old friend, who should be back in Rome, running the *ludus* where he trained the Empire's most sought-after gladiators. Serpentius leapt from his horse to wrestle with the *lanista* who had coached him for the arena and whose tricks had kept him alive long enough for Valerius to rescue him from certain death.

'You're a long way from the training ground. I thought you never ventured more than a mile from the Argiletum and the Green Horse. Have they retired you?'

The lined face took on a solemn look. 'Not much need for a beaten-up old *lanista* at the best of times, but when every *ludus* in Rome is closed down and every gladiator signed up to fight for the Emperor, you know the game's up. I couldn't let my lads march away on their own, so here I am. A year's pay for every man who fights and his freedom if he survives.'

'You already have your freedom, and I doubt you

need the money.' Valerius didn't hide his puzzlement.

Marcus shrugged. 'Aye, but these men are fighters – man for man, they are a match for any legionary – but what they are not is leaders.' His face split in a self-conscious grin. 'They elected me commander of the second century and here I am.'

'It looks as if you've already been in a fight,' Serpentius observed.

'Not a fight.' Marcus's face clouded. 'A massacre. Two nights ago our commander volunteered to destroy a bridge the enemy had built near Cremona. They had already tried with fireships, but the wind drove them ashore. We were to capture an island upstream of the bridge and launch an attack from there. We were betrayed.' He glanced up and Valerius thought he read a message in the pale eyes. 'Yes, you'll find there is much talk of betrayal and cowardice in this camp. When we reached the island it was already crawling with Tungrian auxiliaries. Hundreds were killed in their boats. Some of us managed to reach land and fought, but when our brave leader turned and ran the rest of us followed as fast as we could row. When we started out from Rome there were two thousand of us. Now there are just one thousand. The rest are dead, or have deserted.'

Valerius studied the sullen, suspicious faces of the men watching the conversation. They were of a mix familiar to him from the days he had trained at Marcus's school and ranged from hulking giants who looked as if they could crush a skull with their fingers to men so small they could almost be called midgets. Their exotic paraphernalia was the same equipment they wore in the arena – strange helmets and armour from barbarian tribes and the troops of long-forgotten empires – and they carried the same weapons: curved swords, boar spears and even tridents. They had two things in common: they were some of the fittest men he had ever seen and every man had been marked by defeat. 'Will they fight again?'

Marcus hesitated for only a moment. 'If they are well led.'

Otho had taken over the *praetorium* in a tented pavilion at the heart of the First Adiutrix camp. As he approached, Valerius didn't know what to expect. After all, he was the man the Emperor had been prepared to have killed and who had failed in his mission. The welcome turned out to be warmer than he had a right to expect. Otho immediately broke off his discussion and led the one-handed tribune aside. The other man had changed since Valerius last saw him, the handsome features more drawn and careworn, and to Valerius's surprise he was wearing a simple legionary's tunic and armour. 'I fear I did not expect to see you again, but I am glad you are here. We are in need of every seasoned soldier who can carry a sword. You have come from where?'

'I carry news from General Spurinna.'

'You fought at Placentia?' Otho didn't hide his surprise. 'The last word we had was that the city was still under siege and might be taken any day.'

Valerius explained how Caecina's forces had been defeated and Otho closed his eyes. 'Victory,' he whispered. 'A victory that balances all else. Yes, a victory against great odds and an omen for what is to come.'

Valerius was bemused. 'In Brixellum they spoke of another great victory at a place called Ad Castorum.'

A shadow fell over the Emperor's face and he directed a pained glance to where Suetonius Paulinus stood having a heated debate with three other officers. 'A victory of sorts, but not one to be celebrated. An opportunity lost. If my generals but had confidence in their troops, Caecina might have been destroyed; instead he was allowed to withdraw. You know he has been joined by Valens.'

Valerius opened his mouth to reply, but the Emperor noticed the slim figure hovering by the doorway and for a moment the old predatory Otho reappeared. 'You have not introduced me to your companion.'

'May I present the lady Domitia Longina Corbulo.'

The Emperor's eyes widened at the name. 'You are most welcome, lady, but I fear your father would have been more welcome still. A great man and a fine soldier.' Domitia acknowledged the compliment with a slight nod.

'The lady Domitia wishes to return to Rome and hoped you would be able to spare an escort.'

'Of course.' Otho smiled. 'And she will also have my carriage. I find it much more agreeable to march with my soldiers than to ride past them like some preening golden peacock.' He lowered his voice so that what he said would be inaudible to the other men in the pavilion. 'It will also give me an opportunity to rid myself of an irritant. He came north insisting he would fight alongside his cousin, who commands my Praetorians, and I could not send him away for fear of insulting his father.' He called to an aide. 'Send me young Domitianus.'

It took Valerius a moment to recognize the tall young man who appeared in the doorway. Titus Flavius Domitianus was dressed in a tribune's armour instead of the tunic he'd worn in the garden outside Domitia's house, but the look of loathing that contorted the pale features left Valerius in no doubt that he hadn't been forgotten – or forgiven. The look lasted less than a second before it transformed into a puzzled, moonstruck half-smile as Domitianus sensed the identity of the feminine presence half hidden by the two men. Domitia's mouth fell open and she darted a glance of dismay at Valerius. Fortunately, she recovered before the Emperor noticed.

'But Caesar, I must not deny you the services of such a brave warrior,' she said earnestly. 'Surely you have a slave woman who could accompany me?'

Domitianus was caught between preening at the compliment and alarm that his opportunity to spend an extended period with the woman whose beauty made the blood pound in his ears was threatened. Otho sensed some undercurrent and his face creased in a puzzled smile. He vaguely remembered the letter from Flavius Sabinus and the hint of some conflict between Valerius and this boy. For a moment he was tempted to accede to Domitia's suggestion, but the chance to rid himself of the Flavian irritant was too good to miss.

'No, I insist. This young nobleman will protect you and entertain you on your journey, although I agree that you must have a woman to attend you. We will find a slave of suitable age and ability to accompany you in the carriage. You will leave after dawn.'

The final words allowed no further argument. Otho gestured at Valerius to accompany him and with a last look of fury Domitia reluctantly followed the tall young man from the tent, taking all Valerius's hopes with her.

'You already know Suetonius Paulinus, of course.' All thought of Domitia was swept from Valerius's mind as Otho introduced the three men who stood around the table at the far end of the room. 'Marius Celsus, who also advises me on military matters, and Orfidius Benignus, commanding First Adiutrix. I want you to act as Benignus's second in command. You have heard of our gladiators?' Celsus gave a derisive snort and shot a sneering glance at Paulinus, who ignored him. Valerius nodded.

Otho continued, echoing the words of Marcus the *lanista*. 'Brave men and hardy fighters: a potentially telling weapon, but one that must be wielded by a skilled hand. We lost many of them in a misguided attempt to split Caecina from Valens, but they can still be of use. You will form them into a single cohort and integrate them with First Adiutrix. It will help compensate for the loss of the cohort to Placentia.' Valerius mentioned that Spurinna was sending five centuries of the marine legionaries back to join their legion. 'Better still. Let us hope they will be in time.' Valerius noticed the look of surprise Paulinus shot the Emperor, but Otho continued unperturbed. 'Benignus, you are happy with this?'

Benignus was the scion of a rich patrician family and their wealth had helped furnish the tent with ornate wall hangings and statuary by famous sculptors, including a very recent bust of Marcus Salvius Otho Augustus. It was an unusual display of affluence in a military camp, but he had a reputation as a fair man and a good soldier. He was clearly anything but happy, but he looked to Valerius. 'As long as they will fight.'

Valerius met his gaze. 'They will fight.'

'You said you hope they will be here in time, Imperator?'

Otho looked down at the table before he answered Paulinus. Its top was covered in sand and formed a detailed map of the terrain between Bedriacum and Cremona. His gaze ranged over the bumps and hollows, taking in every detail. Finally, he made his decision. 'I am convinced we must bring the enemy to battle.' The two men stared at each other and Valerius had the feeling this was an argument that had begun before Paulinus entered the tent.

'And *I* must advise against it.' The tone was polite, but the voice of Boudicca's conqueror held a core of iron. 'We have an excellent defensive position here. I believe we are still outnumbered by the enemy, but our strength increases with every passing day. We have supplies in plenty, while the enemy goes hungry. If we have patience, the enemy will be forced to attack us on this ground; the ground of our choosing.' He stabbed a finger at the table. 'If we attack him, *he* will have the advantage of choosing where we meet. In another two days Fourteenth Gemina will be here. In another week we will have two more legions and victory is certain.'

Valerius watched Otho's reaction and was reminded of another conference in another tent, when Corbulo had outlined the detailed plan for the battle of the Cepha gap. His army had been outnumbered almost three to one and his commanders had opposed his plan, but Corbulo had never allowed his council of war to turn into a debate. The Emperor drew himself up to his full height and Valerius knew before he spoke that he would dismiss Suetonius Paulinus's perfectly logical military reasons for not meeting the enemy.

Otho nodded slowly, still staring at the contours on the table. 'I respect the venerable general's regard for caution. He was cautious at Ad Castorum and no doubt we still have our army as a result of it.' Paulinus visibly flinched at the words and Valerius remembered Marcus's comments about betrayal and cowardice. Was Otho accusing the great general of running away? 'But I do not have the time for caution,' the Emperor went on. 'The longer I wait, the weaker becomes my position in Rome. If I do not act, it appears I am inviting Vitellius to take my throne. Valens and Caecina have combined, but I believe we are more than strong enough to defeat them. Have patience, you say, and they will attack us? But what if they divide their army again?' He met Paulinus's unflinching glare. 'What if Caecina pins us here and Valens moves to attack Rome? Must I stand idly by while they ravage my people?' The Emperor's voice shook with suppressed emotion. 'No, the time is now. One decisive battle, and the usurpers will run like beaten dogs. Their soldiers are dupes who fight not for Rome but for plunder and for Rome's enemy. When they see the true might of Rome, their hearts will fail them.'

Valerius studied the sand table. The raised causeway of the Via Postumia ran arrow-straight from Bedriacum to Cremona, with the Padus river five miles to the south-west. On the river flank of the road the ground was relatively clear, but to the north-east small notes on the map identified fields clogged with bushes and vines, and beyond them terrain that was mostly bog and scrub. He decided it was a good road for marching down, but ground more suited to ambush than battle.

Otho was still speaking. 'My brother Titianus will join us later today or tomorrow to take overall command.' Paulinus met the news of his demotion with a deeper scowl, but he made no protest and the Emperor continued: 'In two days we will march down this road and force them to meet us or flee. Now, to the dispositions.'

Boudicca's conqueror continued to argue for delay, but his voice was that of a man who knew he was already defeated. Benignus, an aristocrat whose bloodline went back to Romulus, tapped his manicured fingers on the table as he studied the road. Valerius had the feeling he agreed with Paulinus, but having been only recently appointed was unwilling to speak out. Celsus, who Valerius was certain had been about to vote against the plan, threw his wholehearted support behind Otho now the decision was made. Belatedly, Vedius Aquila, legate of the Thirteenth legion, made an appearance, apologizing for his absence, but bringing news that the advance guard of the Fourteenth Gemina were only a few miles to the east.

Otho was elated. 'You see, Suetonius,' he said fiercely. 'You will have your Britannia heroes with you after all.' Even Paulinus's thin lips twitched in a smile. The Fourteenth had been the core of his army in the final battle to defeat Boudicca and he had a huge affection for the legion. 'The order of march will be this,' the Emperor continued. He addressed Aquila first. 'Thirteenth and elements of the Fourteenth in the van will form the right of the line when battle is joined. Orfidius? Your Adiutrix will follow and hold the left, and your gladiator villains with them, Valerius. The ground is more open there, so you will also have the bulk of the cavalry. The Praetorian Guard will follow and take the fight to the enemy in the centre.' He smiled. 'We have seen that they don't have the legs of a veteran legion, but they are eager enough. Are there any questions?'

Hearing the plan for the first time, Aquila studied the sand table with the deep frown of a worried man. 'We will be advancing on a narrow front. I take it that our action, if we meet an enemy force of similar strength, will be to assume defensive positions and draw them on to us?'

'No.' The Thirteenth's legate flinched at the force in Otho's voice. 'If we meet the enemy we will take the initiative and attack. This will be a decisive battle. The traitors must be given no opportunity to run away.'

Valerius exchanged a glance with Paulinus. The general's face was grim, but he kept his thoughts to himself.

Aquila had another question. 'Will the Thirteenth have the honour of your presence on the right?'

Otho's face froze and the atmosphere in the room changed as if a cloud had just covered the sun. It was Celsus who answered. 'Tradition dictates that the Emperor has no place on the field of battle.'

'But . . .'

'No Emperor since Augustus has fought on the front line,' the adviser continued. 'It has already been decided. The life of Marcus Salvius Otho Augustus is too valuable to be risked on the battlefield. He will take up a position in Brixellum with our strategic reserve and await your call, or the outcome, of which he is not in doubt.' More than one pair of eyes widened at the words 'strategic reserve'. If they met the enemy in any strength, the fighting power of every auxiliary and legionary in Otho's army would be needed. Brixellum was twenty miles and more from the potential site of the battle. It would take Otho's 'strategic reserve' a day's hard marching even to reach it. Celsus sounded as if he were trying to convince himself. 'Vitellius the usurper is not with his army, so . . .'

Otho laid a hand on his arm and his eyes sought out each man in the room in turn. 'Please do not question my courage . . .' Valerius joined the chorus of denial. 'I am more than willing to lay down my life for this cause. But I am an old-fashioned man who believes it is the job of his generals to fight battles. And now, if there is nothing else, I must rest.'

The five officers saluted and as the Emperor talked quietly with Celsus the others left the tent to brief their junior commanders. Aquila and Benignus whispered together and Suetonius Paulinus hung back deliberately to walk beside Valerius through the long lines of eight-man legionary tents towards the gates. They were not friends. Paulinus might have created him Hero of Rome, but Valerius had good reason to believe the consul would have been happy to see him dead two years earlier when Nero's torturers were 'cleaning up' after the Piso conspiracy. Now, however, it seemed he was seen as a potential ally.

'Have you ever heard such rubbish?' Paulinus squinted into the afternoon sun. 'Titianus in overall command? The man has never fought a skirmish, never mind a battle. Our Emperor is an old-fashioned man who leaves his generals to fight battles? Yet the first thing he does is tie one hand behind their backs.' He stopped suddenly and the grey eyes pierced Valerius like a pair of javelins. 'Mark my words, young man, we will be in the fight of our lives.' The gravelly voice softened and his gaze dropped to the stump of Valerius's right arm. 'I am glad you will be with Adiutrix. They are a young legion, none younger, and they need to be directed by experienced hands. Benignus is a good man, but I have no doubt he will appreciate a steadying influence.' He turned to retrace his steps to his own tent, then hesitated. 'I do not doubt his valour, but he is wrong, you know. I was with the Eighth during the invasion of Britannia and I saw Divine Claudius charge a barbarian line on a ceremonial elephant. He was worth two legions to us that day.'

In the morning, Valerius broke his fast with Serpentius among the gladiators who were his new command, and waited until the Emperor's convoy began to line up for the journey back to Brixellum. The carriage carrying

432

Domitia had a place in the centre of the column, as part of the Emperor's baggage train and close to the civil servants who travelled everywhere with him. He'd hoped at least to see her and try to convey some message, but the vehicle's heavy curtain remained closed.

'I would have thought you would have better things to do with your time.' The familiar sneering voice came from behind and he turned to find Titus Flavius Domitianus looking down at him from the saddle of a fine black stallion. Just for a second it seemed a good idea to tip him off into the churned-up dirt, but Valerius resisted the impulse and the younger man continued. 'You may find it difficult to believe, but I hope you survive the battle. My servant died and my uncle Sabinus is preparing murder charges against you. It will be my pleasure to see you in the *carcer* as you await your fate. As for the lady,' he sniffed condescendingly, 'she is my responsibility now.'

There was something about the way he said *responsibility* that conveyed much more. Valerius smiled and moved closer to the fidgeting horse. Domitianus froze when he felt the point tickling his thigh.

'I hope you understand your obligations, little man. Because if any harm comes to the lady, I will cut off your balls and feed them to you one at a time. Nod if you understand.' Domitianus's head twitched. 'Good, we understand each other. Now go away. I'm sure you have something better to do.'

Domitianus reluctantly complied with his dismissal, but with a murderous look that told Valerius he had made an enemy for life. And a dangerous enemy at that. With a last glance at the coach, he walked away towards the gladiator lines. To a new command, a new battle, and, if the gods willed it, a new victory.

He was a heartbeat too late to see the curtain flick back and catch the desperate eyes and the lips that moved in a silent message.

'Come for me.'

XLV

Marcus Salvius Otho Augustus delayed his departure long enough to make a rousing speech which extolled honour, duty and courage and his right to rule as directed by the Senate and people of Rome. It was a fine speech, with Otho at his charming, persuasive best, and its message was that they could not lose. The legions cheered him to the heavens.

But later, as they watched the Emperor ride away with an escort of six cohorts of elite Praetorian Guards, Valerius felt the mood change. There were no cries or protests, but he could see the looks of puzzlement and disappointment in the faces of Juva and the First Adiutrix, and Marcus and his gladiators. For the first time he realized the true magnitude of Otho's misjudgement.

'They think he's deserting them,' Serpentius voiced the unspoken thought.

Celsus had claimed no Emperor since Augustus had fought beside his legions. But those legions had not been fighting a civil war, they had been fighting for the expansion of the Empire against barbarians. In the coming days, Otho's legions would meet fellow Roman citizens in battle, and would be fighting not for the Empire, but for a man. Now that man was riding to safety, leaving them to serve under leaders in whom they had little or no trust, and, worse, he was taking with him three thousand men who should have been fighting at their side.

Valerius was reminded of that moment during a conference of senior officers two days later beside the Via Postumia. They had covered barely twelve miles on the first day, delayed by confusion in the baggage train. Today they had marched until the sixth hour across the flat, featureless landscape on a raised causeway barely wide enough to take eight men, bounded by ditches that would hamper the legions' ability to deploy into battle order. Paulinus wanted to leave the road and make camp for the night, arguing there was no point in going any further before nightfall. 'We can set up a defensive position here and be on the outskirts of Cremona tomorrow with a full twelve hours of daylight ahead. There is ample water and the ground is soft enough to dig.'

'We should continue.' Licinius Proculus, the Praetorian prefect, had accompanied Otho's brother Titianus from Rome and shared his authority. 'We can march another four or five miles before we have to make camp. Perhaps age wearies you, consul?' The words were accompanied by a smile but his voice was heavy with sarcasm. 'I'm sure we can find you a carriage.'

Paulinus had commanded great armies and fought more battles than he could count. The insult made no more than a scuff on his armour. 'You are right, Proculus, I am getting old, but I am perfectly capable of riding another five miles. And age means I need not defer to a man whose closest acquaintance with the blood and guts of battle has been breaking plebeian heads in the Forum during a bread riot.' The barb was accompanied by a vicious, shark-toothed smile. 'If we meet the enemy on the march, he will have travelled four miles and be as fresh as the moment he broke fast. We will have marched thirty in two days and even you must have noted the shambles behind us.' He gestured back along the road, where auxiliaries mixed haphazardly with legionaries, and pack mules and baggage carts had forced great gaps between cohorts and centuries. 'Only a fool would put himself in a position where his foes could bring him to battle with two hours to darkness. You have fought a night action, perhaps, Proculus, in your bed at the Castra Praetoria?'

Benignus, who had ridden at Valerius's side all day, nodded quietly in agreement. Aquila, the Thirteenth's commander, had bristled at the suggestion of lack of organization in the column, but he gave his support to Paulinus. 'And we should send our scouts further ahead. If we meet Vitellius's forces on the march they will smash the column before we can deploy. You have seen the ground to the north: a nightmare of bushes, vines and ditches. We must have time to clear a line of fire or they will be on us before we know it.'

'Or we among them,' Titianus suggested tartly, 'if we show more offensive spirit than has been hitherto displayed. My brother's orders were to press the enemy.'

'Your brother is not here,' Paulinus snapped.

They were still arguing when an exhausted Imperial messenger rode up, instantly identifiable by the yellow cape that warned no man to delay him. He looked from one officer to the other, seeking a leader and evidently not finding one. There was an odd moment of comedy while Paulinus and Celsus jostled for position with

Proculus and Titianus before Titianus accepted the dispatch. He broke the seal and opened the cylindrical leather pouch. Proculus stood at his shoulder frowning as he read the contents.

'My brother chides us for our lack of progress.' His tight smile said the wording was more forthright. 'He demands to know why we have not brought the enemy to battle.'

Paulinus sniffed. 'Very well, we will continue, but I ask that my protest be noted in case of disaster. And Aquila is right: those idle cavalrymen must probe another five miles further ahead.'

There was no disaster, just another few weary miles and a camp site with little water on stony ground that defeated even the strongest mattocks. The following day began like any other with its dawn chorus of coughs and farts, the soft murmur of thousands of men lost in the low mist.

Valerius was preparing for another long day in the saddle when Marcus, the *lanista* who was now a centurion, approached apologetically.

'We lost another twenty in the night,' he said, confirming what Valerius had feared. A few men had deserted before the march began, and more on the first night. 'They're not soldiers,' Marcus explained. 'They expected a quick campaign, a little bit of glory and the chance to spend their winnings as free men. What they've had is day after day of ankle-breaking marches, bad food and lives thrown away by a man who wasn't fit to command a tannery's piss pots.'

'They signed up for this.' Valerius tried unsuccessfully to work up the anger the desertions merited. These men weren't soldiers, they were slaves trained to fight. 'And the prize wasn't just money, it was their freedom. If they're caught they will either die on a cross or go back to the arena, where they'll die anyway.'

Marcus nodded, but the look in his eyes told Valerius he should be asking why men marked for death should be prepared to take their chances on the run rather than fighting under the command of men like Titianus, Proculus and Celsus.

'Tell them Orfidius Benignus is a fine man and a fine soldier. The First Adiutrix will be in good hands when it meets the enemy.' He hesitated. 'And tell them Gaius Valerius Verrens, Hero of Rome, will be proud to stand beside them with a sword in his hand tomorrow.' Marcus grinned and strode off to carry the message, but Valerius's thoughts were already elsewhere. A sword, but no shield. For the first time in days he felt the loss of the wooden hand and he tried to shrug off the feeling that it might be some kind of omen. He had survived the siege of Placentia. He would survive the battle, if there was a battle. He looked out over the encampment to the north, where the pale line of the Alps showed where he and Serpentius had risked their lives all those weeks earlier. What had it all been for? The thought came to him like a whisper on the air. There was one way to make the trials of recent months worthwhile. When it was over he would go to Domitia and offer her his protection. The decision gave him comfort, but he drew his *gladius* and set off to find an armourer in any case.

On the march an hour later, he noticed that the men were warier and less eager than on previous days. The marine legionaries of the Adiutrix kept up the pace, fired by pride and a determination to be as good as the men of the Thirteenth and Fourteenth who marched in front of them, but gradually the gladiators began to lag behind. Valerius rode forward and found Benignus at the head of the legion.

'I'd like to borrow your eagle and a few of your men,' Valerius said, and explained what he had in mind.

Benignus had noticed the gap between the leading cohorts and the gladiators. 'Of course, as long as you bring them back.'

Valerius laughed. 'If I don't I will find you another.'

Dismounting, he handed the reins of his horse to Serpentius. He called to Florus, the *aquilifer*, marching at the head of the legion's headquarters staff in his lion headdress and polished breastplate with the gleaming symbol of office he had vowed to fight and die for. Together, they dropped back through the column until Valerius saw the man he was looking for.

'Juva, I need you and your best singers. I seem to remember the crew of the *Waverider* had good voices.'

The big Nubian grinned and chose four men to join them. They strode back to where the gladiators loitered, and Valerius told him what they intended. Juva snorted dismissively. 'If they do not want to fight, send them home. The Adiutrix does not need them, the crew of the *Waverider* does not need them and Juva does not need them.'

Valerius leaned close and said softly: 'You may have been in bar brawls, my friend, and you have withstood siege behind strong walls, but you have never been in battle. Believe me, when the time comes you will welcome any man who stands beside you as the enemy comes, and dies, and dies again, and keeps coming, and be pleased to call him brother.'

Juva's nostrils flared, but the dark eyes softened and he nodded solemnly. Soon they were among the gladiators, with their odd weapons and ludicrous, antiquated

440

armour: *secutores*, with their short swords; *provocatores* with their long, thin blades; a giant *murmillo* in full war gear and a fish tail helmet; a dark-skinned Scythian with a pair of throwing axes at his belt of the type Serpentius, who had once been one of these men, favoured; fighters dressed as griffin-crested Thracians, and Celts with bare chests and checked trews; even a few men without armour carrying the three-pronged spear of the *retiarius*. They had only two things in common: Valerius had insisted that every man should be issued with a *scutum*, the big curve-edged shield every legionary carried that was as much an offensive weapon as a defensive one, and their reluctance to be part of the army of Otho.

He had arranged for Marcus's century to lead the cohort and he fell in step beside the *lanista*, greeting him as a friend and talking to him as an equal in a voice loud enough for twenty or thirty men around him to hear. 'They tell me the gladiator cohort isn't prepared to fight?'

'No!' a veteran of the arena shouted. 'We're just fussy about who we fight and what we fight for.'

'You're fighting for your Emperor.'

'Then why isn't he here to fight with us?' This voice came from further back in the ranks.

'Because he has better things to do.' A laugh rippled through the column. 'And because he's not as stupid as we are.' The laughter gained intensity. Valerius continued. 'You took an oath. You're fighting for your lives . . .'

'And money.'

'. . . and money. But before you live, you have to be prepared to die.'

'I don't want to die for some rich bastard who's sitting back in Brixellum drinking wine and screwing somebody else's woman.'

'Neither do I.' This time Valerius joined in the laughter and he felt himself warming to these men.

He gestured to Florus to raise the eagle and the former marine flourished the standard high, turning the gilt pole so that every man could see the spread wings, gaping beak and fierce, glinting eyes. '*This* is what you're fighting for. This piece of brass covered in gold. But it's not just brass and gold. It's an eagle. It is *your* eagle and it contains the spirit of *your* legion.' The laughter died away and the murmurs of dissent faded. Every man's eye was on the eagle and the only sound was the metallic crunch of hundreds of marching sandals. Valerius allowed his voice to grow in strength, remembering a speech Suetonius Paulinus had made more than eight years earlier on a slope that soon after was slick with blood. 'You're not just a mob now. You're not just a rabble of ex-slaves trained to kill each other. You are the Tenth cohort of the Legio I Adiutrix. You don't fight for a man. You don't even fight for an Emperor. You fight and die for this, and you fight and die for each other. Forget everything that's gone before. You are part of a legion now, and some time tomorrow or the day after you will meet other legions. Good legions. Veteran legions. Who will do their best to kill you.' A murmur ran through the listening men and he thought he'd gone too far, but, from somewhere, he found a moment of inspiration. 'And while they're doing their best to kill you, you'll be killing them, because you're better than them. Those legions will have an eagle and if you take away a legion's eagle, you take away its soul. You take away its courage. If you take its eagle, it means you've won.' He sensed them rising to him, the heat of battle joy swelling inside them. 'So tomorrow or the next day you will bring me an eagle, and together we will present it to

Emperor Marcus Salvius Otho Augustus, and I promise you that Marcus Salvius Otho Augustus will not just give you your freedom, and your money, he will give you land, so much land that you will live like kings for the rest of your lives.' The message was passed along the lines of marching men and they roared their approval. He had another message, the message he had intended to send, but now that message stuck in his throat as he heard the chant. '*Valerius! Valerius! Valerius!*' He found Marcus grinning at him and a smile split Juva's dark face. 'Sing, you bastards,' he somehow found his voice, 'and pick your feet up, because tomorrow we will fight and tomorrow we will win and tomorrow the Emperor will have his eagle.'

Juva's deep, resonant tones roared out the first verse of the pornographic marching song that had driven the legions of Rome from the snow-capped mountains of west Britannia to the deserts of Africa from the super-heated sands of Syria to the cool blue seas off Lusitania. The March of Marius.

> *There was a mule, he was no fool,*
> *He had a girl in every fort,*
> *Another one in every port.*
> *In Allifae she was not shy . . .*

They didn't know the words, and in truth it was not Homer, but they joined in with a will and Valerius felt them surging behind him, their legs automatically taking the rhythm of the song. Up ahead he knew the men of the First Adiutrix would have heard it too and would push on harder still. He grinned, because this was what he lived for. Hardship, yes. But comradeship, too. These men would stand together and die together, and that

443

was all he needed. And, perhaps, they just might bring the Emperor his eagle.

Away in the mist another man listened to the song with a semblance of a smile on his pale features. He did not smile because of the song, but because of the name that had preceded it. Something primeval gripped the very centre of Claudius Victor's being. If the gods of battle were kind, his brother would have his revenge. He wrapped the wolfskin cloak tighter around him and led his patrol back towards Cremona.

XLVI

The rhythm of the march dulled a man's senses, but Valerius was so attuned to the distinctive sounds that formed an army's heartbeat that he came instantly alert as a troop of Pannonian cavalry galloped up to rein in opposite the army's commanders. His racing mind took in the agitation of the Pannonian commander and the moment of confusion and consternation as Titianus, Paulinus, Proculus and Celsus digested the information they had been given.

'We should be ready to move,' he warned Benignus. The legionary commander shot him a nervous glance and called up his *cornicen*, the signaller who would relay his commands to the ten cohorts of the First Adiutrix. The cohort commanders all had their orders, but Valerius wondered how they would react. Paulinus had said the First was a young legion and he was right. For all the drill they had performed in the last three months, they couldn't hope to deploy as quickly as a veteran formation. A clarion call rang out from the command group and was taken up by the legionary trumpeters. His blood quickened, because like every man in the miles-long column he knew it meant the enemy was in sight. Valerius had witnessed the smooth transformation of a legion from column of march into battle formation a hundred times, but it never ceased to awe him. Thousands of men moving as if they were controlled by a single hand in precise, perfectly choreographed movements. With a sinking heart he saw this was going to be different.

'Mars' arse,' Serpentius muttered. 'I hope the bastards aren't in a hurry for a fight.'

The Via Postumia, with its hardened, well-drained surface, had provided the legions with good marching, but it was a narrow causeway constricted by deep ditches on either side of the raised surface. It meant the two full legions, their baggage and heavy weapons, and the Praetorian cohorts who would make up the centre of the Othonian line, were strung out over at least five miles of road. Thirteenth Gemina, leading the column, was a veteran legion, with a long history. A Thirteenth had crossed the Rubicon with Divine Caesar and helped raise him to the purple. Now the Thirteenth, and its reinforcing cohorts from the Fourteenth, had to disperse into attack formation over the ditch and into the fields on the north side of the causeway. As the road ahead cleared, theoretically, the First Adiutrix would move forward and deploy to the left and align with the Thirteenth's formations, allowing the Praetorians to advance to fill the centre and create an unbroken line. But the fields on the north side of the road were choked with trees and bushes strung with vines, and deep ditches had been cut to drain the swampy land. The four cohorts who would make up the front rank hacked their way through the vines to take up their positions and the legion's engineers sweated and cursed to cut some kind of space that would allow the *onagri* and *scorpiones* to provide support against the enemy. Behind them the six cohorts who would form the second and third ranks struggled to hold position in the maze of vegetation. A further three cohorts attempted to get off the road into a supporting position, but only added to the chaos and confusion. Officers roared orders and standard-bearers screamed out the name of their units, trying desperately to unify their commands. Meanwhile the road ahead of Valerius was jammed with men trying to join their centuries and cohorts, a bustling mass of bobbing iron helmets and frantically waving unit standards. Beacons of red indicated where the scarlet-plumed centurions battled to regain order, but it still looked more like a bread riot than a military operation. He could see that it might be an hour and more before Aquila, the Thirteenth's legate, could bring any sort of cohesion to his ranks.

'We have to move now,' Valerius urged. 'The enemy must be close and if they have any sense they'll stay out of that jungle, take us on the flank and slaughter us.'

Benignus looked towards Paulinus's standard, desperately seeking some kind of signal, but the four commanders of Otho's army were too busy arguing to notice.

'Now,' Valerius's voice was a vicious snarl that brought startled looks from the junior tribunes surrounding the legionary commander. Benignus's chin came up at the suggestion of insubordination, but when he saw the certainty in his deputy commander's eyes he realized what he must do.

'Sound deploy,' he ordered the *cornicen*.

Valerius thanked the gods that Otho had opted to deploy First Adiutrix on the left of the line. It was the natural position for a less experienced formation, and whether through accident or design the legion would fight its battle on open ground with a clear view of the enemy. The men spilled over the side of the roadway and through the ditch, automatically moving into centuries and cohorts and marching towards the positions marked by the engineers who had galloped ahead. Valerius abandoned his horse to a groom and ran to join his gladiators, with Serpentius always at his right side. Marcus and the rest of the centurions tried valiantly to emulate the other cohort formations, but compared to the marine legionaries they were little more than a shambling mass. Benignus had accepted Valerius's advice that the gladiator cohort should occupy the centre position in the second rank. That way, they would have a regular cohort on either flank and others to their rear to steady them if things began to go badly.

Serpentius gave a hoot as he watched his former comrades attempt to copy the legionaries, but Valerius was impressed by the unflinching way they made for their position and by the determination on the gaunt faces. 'They may not march very well, but they seem steady enough,' he ventured.

The Spaniard frowned and it took him a moment to find the words he sought. 'They are gladiators,' he said simply. 'Death is no stranger to them. They face it, or live with its presence, every day. A lonely death at that, in front of and for the pleasure of thousands of strangers.' His face went hard and Valerius knew he was remembering every time he had entered the ring. Pride swelled in the Roman's chest that he could call this man a friend. Serpentius stared out over the ranks of glittering helmets as he continued. 'It seems to me that for them – for us who have fought – the opportunity to die with other men in support of a cause . . .' he shook his head at this unlikely sentimentality, 'no matter the worthiness of the cause, is a privilege. They have always had the right to die with a sword in their hand, but here they will have the chance to die with a sword in their hand and a friend by their side.'

The formation First Adiutrix took up was the same the Thirteenth was attempting to achieve with so much effort and cursing on the far side of the road. A front rank of four cohorts, followed by two staggered ranks of three cohorts each, a total of just over five thousand men, give or take the sick and the stragglers. Little groups of engineers struggled in the gaps between, siting the legion's artillery and cursing the damp ground that would affect their aim after a few shots. Whatever crops had been in these fields were long since trampled flat, but Valerius, raised on an estate, gave the name winter barley to the crushed green shoots. Another troop of Pannonians trotted past on the left and Benignus had one of his junior tribunes hail them, hoping for some intelligence on the enemy's movements. A bearded decurion carrying a bloodied spear heard the shout and rode up to salute the legate and Valerius strode across to hear what was said.

Benignus nodded gravely to the cavalryman. 'You have been in some action already, I see?'

The Pannonian grinned. 'Their cavalry thought a couple of squadrons would be easy meat, but we taught them differently. They would have been running yet if their infantry hadn't turned them back.'

'So you've seen the main force?' the tribune blurted.

Valerius saw the decurion's face turn grave. '*You'll* be seeing them soon enough.' He pointed the bloody spear west. 'They are advancing slowly, because their left flank is obstructed by the vines and ditches on the

449

far side of the roadway, but they're coming. At least three full legions as far as I could tell, and swarms of auxiliary infantry and cavalry . . .'

'What about their right flank?' Benignus grunted in annoyance, and the junior tribune who'd posed the question in a voice frayed with nerves blushed under his glare.

'Judging by the fat boars on their shields, you'll soon have the honour of fighting the Twenty-first Rapax. Their ranks are a little thinner after Placentia, but from what my lads tell me it looks as if they've been brought up to strength by a cohort or two of the Twenty-second. Caecina's put most of his cavalry on the flat ground to his right, but you won't have to worry about them because we'll keep them busy for you.' A glint in his eye said he was looking forward to the contest. 'As for the rest,' he shrugged, 'First Italica is in the centre and advancing up the line of the road. Who's among the trees is anybody's guess, but we know Fifth Alaudae and First Germanica were with Valens when he reached Augusta Taurinorum.'

Valerius listened with growing dismay to the account of the enemy's dispositions. They would be facing four legions and elements of a fifth with two legions, the exhausted advance guard of another, and a few Praetorian cohorts. And one of those legions had never fought a battle. He could still hear the roars of the centurions on the far side of the road attempting to bring order to the confusion among the vines. Paulinus had been right. Given time, the engineers could have turned this terrain into a killing ground, but by marching into the enemy's arms the legions of Otho had committed themselves to a fight on the worst possible ground. The only consolation was that the nature of the landscape would hamper Vitellians and Othonians alike. On the roadway, the Praetorians would be outnumbered, but the narrow front would tend to negate the First Italica's advantage. He realized with increasing clarity that the battle would be won or lost on the plain where First Adiutrix stood.

A messenger arrived from the command group ordering the legion to advance, keeping station with the Praetorians on the raised roadway to their right.

'Why should we advance if they're already coming to us?' Benignus complained. 'If we fight here, at least the Thirteenth will have a little time to clear some space to see the enemy.'

'Titianus is frightened Valens and Caecina might decide to run away,' Valerius ventured. 'His brother ordered him to bring them to battle and he's doing what he's told.'

'If he had any sense he'd be more scared of the enemy than he is of his brother,' the legate snapped. 'Very well, order the advance and make sure the lead centurions know to keep station with the standards of the Thirteenth. We will form line when the enemy is at six hundred paces.'

Valerius saluted and ran off with the other tribunes to pass on the orders and join his gladiators. When the trumpet sounded its command they shuffled forward, keeping station on the cohorts ahead and to their flanks, the centurions using their vine sticks to straighten the ranks. It was painfully slow because they could only move as fast as the men of the Thirteenth forcing their way through the trees and the vines, cursing as they fell into hidden ditches. A murmur ran through the leading cohorts and the centurions barked their commands for silence. Valerius strained his eyes and he saw the reason for the noise. On the far horizon, perhaps two miles distant, polished metal glinted in the bright spring sun and he imagined he could see a dark shadow spreading across the fields. An image came to him of blood spilling across a marble floor and he swallowed hard and thrust it from his mind. But he couldn't prevent his heart from beating faster or stop the flame that lit deep in his belly and flared to fill his chest. Part of it was fear, because no man could march into battle without feeling fear. Its smell filled the air like the earthy scent from some noxious flower. What mattered was how a soldier used that fear. Every man had courage, but experience had taught Valerius that courage was not infinite and no man could predict when the supply would run out. He had seen scarred veterans who moments earlier had been boasting how many enemy would die on their swords collapse quivering with fright before a battle. The *phalerae* and awards for valour that weighed them down meant nothing then. All around him men hitched their armour into more comfortable positions, or checked their grip on sword and shield. They had cursed the big, cumbersome shields on the march, but they didn't curse them now, because in a few minutes those three layers of ash or oak could be the difference between life and death.

As he strode over the dark earth he shouted instructions. 'I don't want to hear a sound when you see the enemy. A Roman legionary does not waste his breath with threats and taunts. He does his talking with his sword.' He allowed a hint of savagery to infuse his voice. 'But when you charge I want to hear you scream like the beasts of Hades, because a good scream keeps a man's courage up and turns his enemy's blood to vinegar. Wait for my order before you throw your *pilum*, I know you're not spearmen, so I'll leave it until we're close, but not so close that you don't have time to draw your sword, or whatever exotic killing implement you arena scum prefer. Stay together and keep your discipline. That shield will protect you as long as you stay in line, but get isolated and you'll be holding off one man and too busy to notice his mate until he starts carving your kidneys.'

He looked over his shoulder to where Juva marched beside his standard-bearer in front of the right-hand cohort of the third rank. The Nubian's *pilum* looked small in his big fist and his face was a mask of menacing concentration. He felt Valerius's eyes on him and turned and met the Roman's waved salute with a broad grin. Beyond him, the tight-packed cohorts of the Praetorian Guard held to the line of the road, and far off on the right flank the standards of the Thirteenth rocked and stuttered as their bearers forced their way through the vegetation.

A centurion's bark cut through the silence. 'Stay in line, you bastards, you'll get there soon enough.' Valerius noticed that now the enemy was closer the gladiators strained against the enforced leisurely pace like dogs on a leash. And not just the gladiators. The marine legion marched with the pent-up energy of men determined to prove themselves worthy of the eagle they followed. By now, in the space between the leading cohorts, he could see the individual formations that made up the enemy legion and identify the colours that marked them as the Twenty-first Rapax. A shiver ran through him at the sight. They looked impressive. No, they looked invincible.

Yet this was one of the legions Spurinna had sent from Placentia with their tail between their legs. The question was how it would react to that defeat. Valerius was again burdened by a sense of unease at facing Roman soldiers on Roman soil. Spurinna had told him Twenty-first Rapax had been raised and recruited in the Padus valley. Some of the men he faced behind the big shields would have been born here, perhaps even ploughed these very fields. He shrugged off a melancholy he could ill afford and felt an icy calm settle on him. Well, they would die here and their own earth would provide them with a permanent resting place. Perhaps he would die with them. After all, he was a soldier, and that's what soldiers did. No matter how good you were, there was always the chance that someone was faster or better. As he had told Juva, a battle was very different from a siege and he had never fought Roman soldiers in battle before. He remembered a recurring dream that had haunted him in the years following his return from Britannia. He would be fighting for his life when his legs suddenly felt as if they were encased in mud and his sword weighed ten times more than normal. He'd feel Boudicca's warriors chopping him to pieces and wake screaming. These legionaries he would fight today were the veterans of the Rhenus legions. They carried the same arms and equipment as the First Adiutrix, but they were battle-tested and had years more training. Perhaps among them was a man who was faster, or better, or had Fortuna on his side.

Well, Valerius Verrens had Serpentius on his side. He looked to his right and took comfort from the former gladiator's presence. The Spaniard had found a set of auxiliary armour from somewhere, but he preferred not to fight in a helmet because he said it restricted his vision. The hatchet face read his thoughts and twisted into a smile. 'Would you rather die in your bed?'

Valerius grinned back, but whatever he had been going to say was lost in the clamour of horns.

'Form line!'

XLVII

The leading ranks moved swiftly from four cohorts, including the elite First with its double strength contingent of eight hundred legionaries, into two solid shield walls manned by eleven hundred men apiece. Legionary training dictated that each man required three feet of space to fight in, roughly the width of a standard *scutum*. Against Boudicca's champions or German tribesmen the combination of a stout shield, a *gladius* with a strong arm behind it and Roman discipline would all but guarantee victory. But the men of First Adiutrix were fighting Romans – Romans with the same stout shield and short, deadly sword, who were just as disciplined. When they met, it would be a question of who had the strength of will, the strength of arm, and who cracked first.

With less elegance, Valerius helped shepherd the gladiators into their place in a third shield line, formed by the three centre cohorts of the original formation. When men fell or were wounded, or when their sword arms tired, the third line would provide replacements for the first and second under the directions of their centurions. As he had agreed with Benignus, he kept four centuries back as a mobile reserve to reinforce any weak spots in the Othonian ranks, or capitalize on any weakness in the enemy's. The three remaining rear cohorts would perform the same function, but on a larger scale, and their very presence would be a constant threat to the opposition because of the danger they posed of a flanking movement.

On the far side of the field the men of Twenty-first Rapax went through similar motions, but in a series of much smoother movements. 'Soon now,' Serpentius muttered.

As he said the words, a clarion call rang out over the battlefield and told Valerius the Twenty-first's legate had completed his dispositions and sounded the advance. The hair on his neck felt as if it was standing on end. A shiver ran through him, the last vestiges of a fear that would soon fuel the fury building inside. To his front, the extended ranks of the First Adiutrix seemed to shimmer as men checked their station and tightened the grip on their *pila*. 'Now, Benignus,' he whispered. 'Now.' The braying notes of the *cornicen* were echoed all along the line by brisk orders from the centurions.

The battle had begun.

Six hundred paces separated the two legions. Three hundred paces before the collision. Some men counted their steps as they marched; anything to keep their minds off what was to come. Others stared at their enemies, but saw only the faces of their bastard children or their sweethearts. A few ejected the day's breakfast and claimed it was not fear but excitement. Many muttered prayers and wished there had been time for a sacrifice that would have given some indication of the day's outcome. A surprising number relished the thought of the coming battle. The men of the First were proud of their legion. Proud of the fact their Emperor had called on them for help. It didn't matter that another had treated them worse than dogs, or that it was a third who had given them their eagle to follow. What mattered was that they had an eagle. They were the Legio I Adiutrix and they would make the name of the First Adiutrix ring through the ages. It began today. Hadn't Juva and the five centuries who'd returned victorious from Placentia taught these rebel scum a lesson? They had trained and marched and counter-marched, spent countless hours hammering at posts and each other with the heavy practice swords, dug roads and built bridges. They were the First and they were the best. Now they would do what they were trained to do. Fight.

They marched in silence, with the measured, implacable tread that had made the legions feared from one side of the world to the other. They marched for Rome.

And towards them marched five thousand men equally certain of victory.

At four hundred paces, the *scorpiones* and *onagri* began the killing, the five-foot arrows of the 'Shield-splitters' living up to their feared nickname and the big boulders crashing through shields to smash bones and crush skulls. 'Close up! Fill the gaps!' The cries of the centurions rang out along the line, as they would until the day was won or lost. Men moved forward from the second line of shields to the first, and from the third to the second. Valerius stepped over a twitching body with half a head and a single staring eye. To his right, where Benignus had taken up position, an ambitious young tribune on the legate's staff cried out in agony as a *scorpio* bolt tore a gaping hole through his mount's chest and carried on to pierce his thigh, pinning him in place as the beast fell and crushed his ambitions for ever. And still the missiles came.

'Close up. Fill the gaps.'

Less than three hundred paces now, and the enemy was an unbroken line of brightly painted shields, the twin boar legend of the Twenty-first Rapax proclaiming their identity to the world. If the veteran centurions of the First hadn't been so occupied, they could have scanned the enemy ranks for faces they knew beneath the distinctive transverse crested helmets of their counterparts. Men they had fought with in bar brawls and screwed alongside in brothels during twenty years of postings. But they concentrated on holding their men in check. They could feel the eagerness of the marine legionaries and hear the distinctive throaty snarls of dogs desperate to be unleashed. But not yet.

'Steady. Hold the line.'

Valerius dropped back to Marcus, who marched beside his century's *signifer* with the mobile reserve. 'Remember, when the first three lines charge, these men's instinct will to charge with them. But we must hold them fifty paces back and wait.'

'They won't like watching other men doing the fighting,' the *lanista* warned him.

'I don't care what they like. They're legionaries and they'll obey orders. The first man who gets ahead of me will find my sword up his arse.'

'Aye.' The old gladiator grinned. 'That should do it. I'll let them know.'

A hundred and fifty paces. 'First three ranks at the trot.' Three and a half thousand men moved instantly from the walk to the steady-paced jog that could carry them for miles. Across the divide, the sight of the unit banners and standards wavering as their bearers increased pace confirmed that the Rapax's legate had issued the same orders.

'Hold your spacing, you bastards,' Marcus growled.

Seventy-five paces. 'Ready.' Three and a half thousand fists closed on the shafts of the heavy, weighted javelins they carried.

Sixty paces. 'Throw.' Three and a half thousand arms pulled back and launched their *pila* towards the enemy. The moment the javelins flew, the legionaries drew swords with a metallic hiss that sent a shiver through every man.

Forty paces was the ideal killing range of the *pilum*, the heavy spear that consisted of a length of ash tipped by a shaft of iron the length of a man's arm and a pyramidal point designed to pierce shield and armour. But the *primus pilus*, the senior centurion and tactical commander of the first wave, had judged his distance perfectly. By the time the javelins fell in three great hissing arcs, the front ranks of the opposing lines had just entered the killing ground. The heavy spears punched into shield, or armour, or flesh. If point met shield at the optimum angle, the spear would rip through layers of ash as if they were silk. With good fortune the owner would survive with a dent in his armour, but for the rest of the battle his shield would be hampered by the heavy javelin. Plate armour might stop a direct hit by a *pilum* if the impact was not perfect, but its wearer's charge would be stalled and the shock was capable of cracking ribs and breaking bone. Any man foolish enough to look up as the spears fell would end up with a shaft of iron through his skull.

The converging attacks faltered like boxers staggered by a simultaneous opening punch, but the legionaries on each side recovered swiftly to launch the final rush with a spine-chilling howl that echoed their fear and their rage and their pride. With a splintering crash that rippled like distant thunder, the two shield lines met. Swords hammered at oak shields and individual pairs of warriors tested their strength, heaving, twisting and pushing. Screams and curses and pleas to a dozen different gods filled the air.

Watching with his reserves fifty paces to the rear, Valerius tried to still his own thundering heart as he spoke quietly to his men. He knew that the initial casualties in these encounters would be relatively low. Armoured men, fighting from behind the big curved shields, do not present many targets. The only thing an enemy would see was the gleaming sword point that probed to find his weakness, a bobbing helmet and perhaps a glimpse of a pair of eyes that mirrored his; eyes that contained a potent mix of savagery and terror. Those were his targets: the eyes, the throat and possibly a carelessly presented armpit where a point might find its way to the heart.

But casualties there were, because suddenly men were crawling back through the ranks with blood hanging in skeins from gaping mouths, or reeling clear with scarlet spurts from a severed jugular clouding the air. A young legionary staggered from the line with one hand clapped over his eye and blood running through his fingers. A veteran centurion, transferred in from Moesia to give the First a backbone of experience, checked the sobbing man and inspected the wound, a diagonal cut that had split the eyeball like an over-ripe grape.

'An honourable wound, son, taken in the front.' Should he send the boy back to the wounded? He sniffed the air, as if he could scent the course of the battle, and made his decision. 'Still, a man can fight with one eye.

461

You can stand and you've kept hold of your sword. Get back there and let the *medicus* patch you up, and when you've had a bit of a rest join the reserves.'

The boy shambled off and the veteran nodded to Valerius. 'A good lad, keeping hold of his sword with a wound like that. They're all good lads, tribune; they'll do.'

'Close up. Fill the gaps.'

Similar small dramas were being played out all along the line, but the line held and in places it even forced the men of the elite Twenty-first Rapax back a few paces. The marine legionaries fought with a terrible ferocity fostered by the memory of their humiliation by Galba and hatred of an enemy whose aim was to oust the man who had given them their precious eagle. But it was the big former oarsmen from the Classis galleys who were making the difference. Their opponents couldn't match their enormous strength and it was where the oar-hardened sailors were concentrated that the Rapax line bulged.

Like the gladiator he'd once been, Serpentius sensed weakness and smelled an opportunity. 'With your permission, tribune.' Without waiting for Valerius's answer he ran forward, dodging spears and skipping over dead bodies, to the centre of the third rank where a reserve century of gladiators awaited their opportunity. An animated conversation followed with the centurion of the unit and Valerius used the interval to check the progress of the five cohorts of Praetorian Guard on the roadway. His heart stuttered as he realized they were being forced to fight for their very existence against the might of the veteran First Italica. Whatever was happening in the trees beyond was hidden. He had an ominous feeling, but Serpentius returned before he could give it further thought.

Valerius glared at him. 'What was that about?'

'You'll see.' Valerius looked towards the century the Spaniard had chosen. It stood opposite one of the weak points he had identified in the Twenty-first's line. Adiutrix's former sailors had created a bulge in the enemy front rank, but couldn't break the wall of shields. Serpentius tried to explain, but the air around the two men seemed to shake with the growing cacophony of sound as tens of thousands of men attempted to slaughter each other. Valerius had to put his ear to the Spaniard's mouth to hear him. 'Your problem is that you think of them as soldiers,' Serpentius shouted. 'They're not soldiers, they're killers, and they can do things that no soldier would even attempt. But being in the arena isn't just about killing, it's about entertaining.' He shook his head at the memory. 'Old Marcus taught me that. Please the crowd and the rewards will come. One day it might even be your freedom. But the crowd always wanted something more, something they'd never witnessed before. We would practise things that might never be seen in the arena, but made us faster and harder and turned us into athletes and acrobats. Watch.'

A dozen men in the gladiator century dropped to the ground and slithered their way like snakes through the legs of the fighting lines. At the same time, more men withdrew in threes from the unit and moved behind the third line, two of them holding a shield between them and one, the lightest and most agile of the three, backing further away.

'What . . . ?'

'Wait.'

Even as Serpentius said the word, the sound of battle altered. The screams of the dying and the maimed remained undiminished, but the normal cursing and insults changed to cries of consternation and confusion. In that instant, Valerius understood what had happened and what would happen next.

'Marcus, tell the men to prepare,' he called urgently. 'Serpentius, since you're so fond of giving orders, tell Juva to bring his cohort forward.'

He ran across to Benignus and told him what was planned. The legate frowned. 'You're sure? It will weaken our reserves and it doesn't seem very honourable.'

'The only place for honour on a battlefield is when it's over and you honour the dead.' Valerius's voice emerged harsher than he intended and the other man flinched. Valerius glanced back to the battle line. They didn't have time for an argument. They must act now or the chance would be gone. 'We have one chance to break them.' The young legate recoiled from the savagery that accompanied the words, but Valerius was relentless. 'You've seen what's happening on the road.' He pointed to their right, where the Praetorians were fighting and dying. 'If we are to win, we have to win here.'

Benignus's face flared red with fury. He had taken enough insubordination from this crippled upstart foisted on him by the Emperor. He opened his mouth to order Valerius back to his men, but the one-armed tribune laid a hand on his arm and the look on the scarred face silenced him.

'One chance, Benignus. One opportunity for glory. But it *must* be now.'

The legate's jaw clenched and unclenched and he felt the eyes of his aides on him. One chance. His eyes softened. 'Very well.' His voice was thick with emotion. 'But give me a victory, Gaius Valerius Verrens, or die in the attempt.'

By the time Valerius reached his men, Juva's cohort

had lined up to their right. He called the Nubian and his senior centurion across and told them the plan. The centurion looked sceptical, but Juva's eyes lit up with visions of glory. With a final check of their flank, Valerius gave the order. 'Gladiators, forward, at the trot. Marcus, they know what to do?'

The *lanista* grinned. 'What their tent mates are already doing.'

It was not the legionary's way, but they weren't legionaries, they were gladiators: trained killers. And it was effective.

Serpentius had sensed weakness in the enemy line the way he could sense weakness in an opponent's defence. He knew the gladiators. Knew their qualities. And he knew that they were wasted in the reserves. He had ordered some of the century to crawl between the legs of their comrades and below the line of shields opposing them. A fully armoured legionary was difficult to kill. He fought from behind the protection of the curved *scutum*. Beyond the shield, his head was protected by an iron helmet and his body by the polished plates of the *lorica segmentata*. But get under the shield and a man with a short sword and no mercy could do terrible damage. Now those short, needle-pointed blades ripped up into unprotected groin and belly and the screams took on a new, horrifying dimension that sowed consternation and the seeds of panic among the tent mates of the screamers. At the same time, the remaining gladiators launched a second unorthodox assault. Acrobats, Serpentius had called them, and now they proved it. While two men held a shield face down between them, a third gladiator sprinted forward to leap on to the wooden platform and with perfect timing was propelled across the lines of fighting men and into the second and third lines of

Vitellian troops to cause chaos and carnage. Their triumphs were short-lived – theirs was a virtual suicide mission – but their very existence caused dismay in the enemy ranks. These first efforts encompassed a section of line only a few dozen paces wide, but now Valerius threw more men into the attack and used all four centuries of gladiator reserves to broaden the point of contact. He waited behind the line, trying to gauge the effect of the new tactics. Gradually, the enemy's first line disintegrated into a hundred individual fights. The shield wall was crumbling. Now was the time to break it. He ran back to where Juva's Fifth cohort waited, eager to be part of the battle.

'Form wedge.'

In a series of smooth movements, the cohort's six centuries transformed from a square to an arrowhead formation, with Juva's first century – eight men wide and ten deep – as the tip, two centuries at their backs, and finally three centuries to add critical mass in the rear. Valerius had seen Boudicca's horde of warriors crushed to dust between Paulinus's flying wedges. Now he would use the boar's head to tear the heart out of the Twenty-first Rapax. He and Serpentius attached them-selves to the middle rank of Juva's first century.

'Charge!'

Marcus and his gladiators had been warned of their coming and those who could made way. Those who couldn't were smashed aside or trampled mercilessly underfoot. The first two lines of defenders had no warning and no chance as the equivalent of an armoured rhinoceros battered them down. The third line snapped like a piece of silk thread under the combined weight of four hundred and eighty men in tight formation. Without warning Valerius found himself in the open ground between the three Vitellian attacking lines and their reserve cohorts.

'On,' he screamed. 'On!'

He wasn't worried about what was happening behind him because he knew that the moment the line broke Benignus had agreed to throw his final two cohorts of reserves into the gap to guarantee victory. They would pour through the hole the Fifth cohort had punched and roll up the lines from the centre. Caught between two irresistible forces, the legionaries of Twenty-first Rapax would have the choice of retreating or dying where they stood. There would be no surrendering today.

Valerius's task now was to keep the Vitellian reserves occupied until the attackers had done their job and could come to his aid. But there was another more powerful reason for the raw emotion in his cry.

'On! On to victory! Kill the bastards!'

Because in the front rank of the centre enemy cohort, less than sixty paces away, he had seen a glint of gold. His mind transformed it into a spread of wings, a beak opened wide in a shrill cry of defiance and cruel eyes that glinted in the sunlight. An eagle. The eagle of the Twenty-first Rapax.

'On! The eagle! Take the eagle!'

They were charging now, all cohesion lost, with Juva at their head. The Nubian's long legs covered the ground faster than any other man and he ran with teeth bared in a face filled with elemental savagery, emitting a raw keening sound as he went. Valerius screamed until he thought his throat would tear and beside him Serpentius growled like an attack dog.

'On!' The centurions took up the cry. 'The eagle!'

It was the symbol of the legion's power, presented personally by the Emperor, but it was more than that.

A legion which lost its eagle lost its soul, and even its identity. Legions which had lost their eagles could be not just disgraced, but disbanded. And somewhere in the raging inferno of his mind, Valerius desperately wanted to inflict that humiliation on these men who had dared to support a false Emperor. It didn't matter that Vitellius was his friend. He should not have taken arms against his own country and condemned its people to the horrors of civil war. The eagle of the Twenty-first Rapax was Vitellius's eagle and in that moment Valerius wanted more than anything else to take it from him.

'Kill!'

The boar's head had caught the Twenty-first's commander by surprise and it took time for him to react, but the centurion in command of the centre reserve cohort understood that his formation was the focus of this attack. For the moment, his only option was to hold out until his neighbouring cohorts could reinforce him. He ordered his men to form square, with the legion's eagle and the cohort standards in the centre. A special guard of his best men had orders to keep the *aquila* safe or die in the attempt. It was a sensible strategy and he was happy that it would work. The wedge might have broken three fragile lines, but it was only a single cohort and it could not break a stoutly defended square. He decided not to use his javelins, because when it came to it a javelin would outreach a sword and the threat would keep the attackers from closing. All he had to do was survive for a short time and these brave fools would die.

But the centurion did not take into account the fury and the strength of the attackers, nor the fact that they still had their own *pila*.

Valerius waited until they were close. 'Throw!' The spears sailed out and the defenders automatically raised their shields to protect themselves from the hail of missiles. By the time they recovered the Fifth was on them.

Juva smashed his way into the first rank, taking two defenders with him and turning the air red with sweeps of his short sword. Men ignored the spears that jabbed at them from behind the *scuta* and tore at the curved shields with their bare hands, reeling back only when they received some mortal blow or had their clutching fingers removed by a blade. The first few ranks battered their way into the square and the Vitellians fought with a terrible ferocity to seal the gap. Valerius and Serpentius, at the centre of the first century, added their weight to the attack and hacked at the survivors who rose, stunned, among the carnage. A hand clutched at Valerius's leg and he sliced down with his *gladius* to cut a snarling face in two. Serpentius dispatched victims with the dismissive ease of a man who had spent half his life in the arena. But gradually, as the Fifth penetrated deeper into the Vitellian square, the men ahead in the formation were cut down and subsumed in the carpet of maimed and dead or sucked into individual combats, and the friends found themselves near to the point of the wedge. Valerius felt the Spaniard move closer to his right side.

'Remember, I am your shield.'

Valerius blinked. He'd entirely forgotten his plan that they would fight together. Without warning, something flashed across Valerius's vision and Serpentius's blade swept up to divert the spear point that had been about to take out his throat. Before he could react, they were surrounded by scarlet and yellow shields and fighting for their lives. The sword in Valerius's left hand hammered at a painted boar and Serpentius spun a web of bright iron to keep the attackers beyond striking distance. A hulking figure launched itself from Valerius's left. He knew he was too slow to save himself, but it was Juva, driven beyond madness, his helmet gone and his face a mass of red from a cut that had sliced open his forehead. His bulging eyes were fixed on something in the distance and Valerius followed them to where the Twenty-first's sacred eagle danced above a swirling mass of men. With a terrible roar the big Nubian tore apart the shields barring his way. A legionary lunged at him with his spear, but as the Roman raised his arm Valerius rammed his sword into the gap above his armour and the man froze as he felt the cold iron enter his body. With a twist of the wrist Valerius hauled the blade free in time to parry a scything cut from a soldier in a centurion's helmet. The *gladius* deflected the blow, but his attacker kept coming and his weight smashed Valerius to the earth. The centurion's sword was gone, but he still had the advantage. All Valerius could do was hack at his armoured ribs in a futile attempt to dislodge him. Strong hands gripped his helmet and the chin strap bit into his throat. He tried desperately to wriggle free, but the centurion was so close his nostrils filled with the stink of the other man's breath and spittle dripped on his face. Lightning exploded in his head as his opponent battered it repeatedly into the ground until his skull rang like the inside of a bell. He knew he was done, but as his mind began to fade the hands loosened and the centurion went limp, his snarls turning into a scream as the point of Serpentius's *gladius* severed his spine. Valerius lay pinned by the dead weight and for the first time became aware of the screams of the wounded and dying, the howls of men turned animal and the cloying stink of fresh-spilled blood and torn bowels. Serpentius kicked the corpse off his chest and hauled him to his feet.

'The eagle,' Valerius gasped. 'Follow Juva.'

Ten paces ahead, the Nubian was a roaring presence who surged through the carnage like one of the galleys he once rowed and, as if in a dream, Valerius followed in his wake. The men who faced Juva's awesome savagery were paralysed for a heartbeat and the marine legionaries accompanying their *optio* used that precious interval to ensure those heartbeats were their last. Juva had taken a dozen minor wounds, but he felt nothing but elation. All he knew was that the eagle was there, just beyond his grasp in the midst of the honour guard, who screamed their defiance at their attackers. They were big men, weighed down with *phalerae*, each at least a ten-year veteran, and they feared no enemy. At their centre stood the a*quilifer*, in a leopardskin cloak with the beast's mask framing his face as he brandished the eagle high and howled for the Twenty-first to honour their oath to Jupiter. Valerius wondered why they hadn't retreated to the rear of the cohort, but a glimpse of a First Adiutrix shield beyond the group answered his question. The guard had created a ring of spears around the standard-bearer and dared anyone to enter it. A dozen corpses testified to that ring's resilience, but they had not reckoned on Juva. The Nubian launched himself at the nearest spear, one big hand brushing it aside while the other bent a second just behind the point. Still he would have died but for the little Scythian throwing axe that appeared magically in Serpentius's hand and spun to take a third spearman in the face. Valerius and the Spaniard followed him into the gap and the slaughter began. When it ended Valerius stood panting with blood to his elbows and the familiar dull, metallic taste of it on his lips. The guards had died hard, but none harder than the *aquilifer*, who had beaten back every attack until Juva lifted him bodily from the pile of corpses that protected him and crushed him in his great arms so that Valerius heard ribs snapping and the legionary's body flopped forward as his spine cracked.

Juva stood on the charnel heap he had helped create and lifted the eagle to the skies. His challenge echoed across the battlefield and Valerius experienced a moment of Elysian stillness on that field where two thousand men had already died. The Fifth cohort echoed their champion's roar of triumph. All except one.

'Shit. Time we were out of here.'

Valerius turned at the sound of Serpentius's shocked whisper. Was the Spaniard mad? He shook his head, wincing at the pain. 'We need to hold here until the reserves are finished with the front lines. The battle is won, Serpentius. It is only a matter of time.'

But the battle wasn't won, and it was only a matter of time before the Fifth cohort was annihilated, because Benignus had betrayed them. The two reserve cohorts hadn't moved from their position and the gap the Fifth cohort had opened was quickly closing.

If they didn't retreat they would be slaughtered.

XLVIII

Valerius would remember the remainder of the battle the way a man remembers a night march in a lightning storm; as a series of disjointed, flashlit images that had no connection with his own reality, in a world where time meant nothing.

Stumbling on someone else's legs through a fog of confusion and death with Serpentius at one elbow and Juva, still clutching the Twenty-first Rapax's eagle, at the other. Hacking another human being into bloody ruin until the Spaniard screamed meaningless words into his face and dragged him to safety through the swiftly closing gap moments before an avalanche of fresh Vitellian troops fell on what was left of the Fifth. Juva on one knee presenting a disbelieving Benignus with the eagle that would bring the legate and his legion eternal fame and glory, and in the same instant winning immediate promotion to centurion and the Gold Crown of Valour that would make him a Hero of Rome. A terrible empty feeling as Benignus, with tears on his cheeks, explained that an order had come from Paulinus forbidding him to use his reserves. Standing with Serpentius in the shield line as wave after wave of attacks broke themselves against it until men were so exhausted they could barely lift their swords and the attackers were impeded by heaped piles of their own dead. The oddly detached sense of disbelief as old Marcus threw his surviving gladiators into a break in the line before being swept away to oblivion amid a tide race of flashing swords. The legate lying on the crushed grass with the last of his lifeblood leaking in dying spurts from the sword wound in his neck – 'Save them, Valerius. Do not let the name Benignus be for ever linked with the loss of an eagle and the loss of a legion' – and the noble head falling to one side. A desperate rearguard action as the First Adiutrix attempted to extricate itself from a battle already lost and the roars of triumph at the left of the line as Valens threw in his Batavian cavalry.

And a sudden moment of terrible clarity.

Claudius Victor had prayed to the old gods that his one-armed quarry was not already dead, and his prayers had been answered. Fifth Alaudae and First Italica had already won their battles among the trees and on the road when two full cavalry wings smashed into the left flank of the First Adiutrix. In a single moment, the Othonian line collapsed like a mud dam in a thunderstorm. This was what horse soldiers had been born for as three thousand surviving foot soldiers fled in terror, their backs inviting the spear points that punched their way through armour into living flesh with the weight of horse and man behind them. Helmets and skulls crushed as the heavy *spatha* swords hammered down and faces cleaved in two by a perfectly timed back-cut. Chaos and confusion everywhere, apart from the centre where one man had managed to hold two centuries in square and was attempting to screen the legion's eagle as the *aquilifer* carried it to safety.

A man with a missing right hand.

'Form on me,' Victor screamed, and the auxiliary wing's decurions took up the cry. Within moments he had four troops of cavalry at his back. Four troops. Less than a hundred and fifty men. Not enough, but the defeated legionaries were already close to breaking point so he would make it enough. 'Sound the charge.' The signaller at his right shoulder echoed the command on the *lituus*, the curved trumpet he carried. His eyes never leaving the man who had killed his brother, Claudius Victor lashed his tired mount into motion and urged his Batavians forward.

As the battle ebbed and surged around the little square of shields, Valerius watched the compact mass of cavalry surge across the battlefield, running down friend and foe alike. All around him was blood and pain and death as men, or small groups of men, fought their individual battles for survival. With the help of Serpentius and Juva he had somehow gathered the remnants of two centuries around the eagles and the walking wounded. Those too hurt to move received the mercy of a quick end from their comrades. Better that than be left on the battlefield to die by inches, or be tortured for sport by some looter or camp follower. With danger on every side, they backed slowly away through the fighting across the gore-stained earth, stepping on the corpses of friend and enemy, slipping and slithering through the obscene detritus of the human form. Valerius didn't know where they were going, only that he had promised Benignus he would save his eagle and he would die trying to fulfil that oath. As they edged their way east, more fleeing legionaries sought the disciplined sanctuary of the square, staggering up on spent legs and trying to claw their way into the interior. 'You'll get in when you deserve it, you bastards,' Valerius roared at them, ordering them to form a new outer rank. Yet if the men of the First Adiutrix were exhausted, the enemy was equally so, and that was what kept the eagles safe. They were content to butcher the small knots of legionaries who stood and fought, or take a hack at a fleeing man. But they shied away from Valerius's square to find easier prey. Still, Valerius knew Fortuna couldn't protect them for ever. If they were to stay alive, they had to fight their way to safety, wherever safety was. In the distance he heard the strident call of a trumpet and he felt a surge of hope. Somewhere, someone was trying to rally the shattered remnants of the army of Otho. Yet that hope was immediately tempered with doubt, because the horsemen he had seen had only one object in mind and that was the eagle of the First Adiutrix. He blinked to clear vision that was still blurred from his earlier knock on the head and a shudder ran through him as he recognized his enemy. The cavalrymen bearing down on the square wore wolfskin cloaks and at their head rode a tall figure whose features were engraved in ice on his heart.

'Spears.' The fear in his voice shamed him, even though he knew it was shared by every man in the formation. 'Prepare to receive cavalry.'

The square stuttered to a clumsy halt and the front rank of each of the four sides crouched behind the big curved *scuta*, while those behind locked their shields in place to protect the heads of the front line and form a solid wall almost seven feet high. But it was a fragile wall, close to breaking just at the sight of the charging horses. Men who had suffered more than any man

476

should endure wept and cursed and prayed and Valerius knew he would have lost them but for the massive presence of Juva, snarling at his former shipmates with the eagle of Twenty-first Rapax still held in his great fist. A pitiful few *pila* poked through between the big shields, held by men who'd had the foresight to scavenge enemy javelins from the battlefield. Being static left the formation more vulnerable to an infantry attack, but the square would have been impossible to defend on the move against cavalry. No ordinary commander would throw his horsemen at a well-formed square, for to do so was to endure certain defeat and heavy casualties. But Valerius understood that the man he faced was no ordinary commander, but one driven mad by a visceral need for vengeance. A man prepared to sacrifice everything in his lust for the blood of his brother's killer. Even as the thought formed, he saw Claudius Victor drop back from the front rank of the charge, and the first squadron converge into four ranks of eight in front of him. The thunder of hooves seemed to shake the earth and reverberated in the very air around him. A horse will not charge home against formed-up infantry; that was the philosophy that had dictated tactics from Marius down to Otho and Vitellius. Yet the men who rode these horses were goaded by Claudius Victor's screams of encouragement, promises of advancement and threats of painful death. They were so close Valerius could see the individual features beneath the iron helms. Savage, bearded faces, lips drawn back and mouths gaping as they screamed to cow the enemy and disguise their own fear. Faces that had no intention of avoiding the inevitable collision.

Behind the shield wall, Valerius ran along the line of spearmen calling out his orders. In a normal fight, the *pila* would form an impenetrable palisade of glittering spear points, but there were not enough of them and these horses were not stopping.

'On my command.' He swayed as he fought the exhaustion that fogged his brain and tried desperately to gauge the distance between the horses and the square. Too early and the javelins would be wasted. Too late and even if they did strike home the dead and wounded horses would smash the square into so much human wreckage. 'The front rank only. Only aim for the front rank.'

Fifty paces.

He licked his lips and tasted blood. Somewhere in the front rank of the square a man was whimpering.

'You know your orders.'

'For fuck's sake, let us throw.'

Forty paces.

One heartbeat.

Two heartbeats.

'*Now!*'

The upper layer of shields dropped for a split second and a ragged volley of javelins sailed towards the charging cavalry. Valerius had positioned himself to witness the effect of the throw. *Pray Jupiter he'd got it right.* Eight horses all in line, some already shying away from the impact and the others catching their fear. The grey on the left of the Batavian line took a *pilum* in the neck and swerved sharply, pitching its rider howling from the saddle. Three others, on the right, went down like sacrificial bulls under a pole-axe and the rider of the new right flank horse sprouted four feet of ash from his screaming mouth and was catapulted backwards to be trampled by the second line. Of the remaining horses two were mortally wounded, but their riders continued to urge them on. A third fought in vain to turn away, trapped between its dying stable mates.

Valerius was moving even before the riderless mount swerved across the front of the line and collided with the charge. He screamed at Juva to get the eagles to safety, but his words were drowned in a splintering crash and the shrieks of crushed men as a mountain of horseflesh scythed into the wall of shields. The second line of cavalry, followed by the third, swerved to avoid the mayhem, knowing there were easier victims to come, but Claudius Victor leapt through the carnage with a squadron at his heels and charged into the centre of the already disintegrating square.

'He's mine!' The screamed order was directed at a Batavian trooper who had lined up the square's one-handed commander with his long spear. The cavalryman swerved away. In the same moment, Valerius heard the shout and turned to find his nemesis bearing down on him. Victor crouched low in the saddle with a smile on his pale features and the leaf-shaped iron blade aimed at his enemy's lower belly. For once Valerius couldn't depend on Serpentius to be his strong right hand; the Spaniard was elsewhere, fighting his own deadly battle. He had nowhere to run; his only defence was his sword and his speed. He feinted left, but the spear point went with him. Victor held the shaft close to his steed's flank, to give his enemy no chance of getting inside the point. Another second and the spear would tear through the iron mail and gut him. The Batavian expected Valerius to break and run in that final heartbeat. Instead the one-armed Roman danced to his right, bringing the sword up in a scything, unwieldy slash that bit into the cavalry horse's throat. A cloud of scarlet and the animal screamed as it felt the bite of iron and Valerius threw himself to the side as it surged past, already going down on its knees. In the corner of his eye he registered Victor tumbling from the saddle and the snap as the long spear broke, but there was no time to be pleased with himself. For now the exhausted legionaries of Twenty-first Rapax had found new strength and were tearing at the shattered formation like a pack of wolves on a dying deer calf. Suddenly, Victor was no longer Valerius's greatest threat as he tripped on a body, lost his grip on the *gladius* and found himself sprawling among the feet of a knot of men hacking at two gladiators who had tried to surrender. Unarmed and wriggling backwards through someone's entrails, Valerius flinched away as one of the legionaries stepped into position with his sword poised for the killing blow.

'Mine!' The guttural Germanic roar was punctuated by a butcher's block slap that registered the moment Victor's long cavalry *spatha* took the man's head off at his shoulders. As the torso collapsed, Valerius's worst nightmare loomed over him. 'The remaining hand, I think. We will start with the hand.'

Victor raised the sword high as Valerius lay helpless. The Roman looked into his killer's eyes and saw a madness there that told him the hand was only the least of it. He groped frantically for his lost *gladius*. Instead, his fingers connected with something obscenely soft, with the slimy texture of a fresh-caught eel. He threw the still-warm guts of the anonymous gladiator into Victor's face and the Batavian reeled back, but recovered when he realized what had struck him. A savage smile wreathed his face as he made the decision to end the games. All around them was chaos and slaughter, the screams of the dying and the victory cries of their killers. From nowhere, a bay horse, out of control with its Pannonian rider dead in the saddle, galloped blind-eyed with panic towards them and Valerius rolled away from the flashing hooves. He heard Victor curse even as he found his escape blocked by the bulk of the auxiliary commander's dead mount. A kaleidoscope of images: blue sky, blood-soaked earth, a dead man's staring eyes, a glint of bright metal. The sword flashed down and he twisted desperately to one side, some voice screaming a message at him that his mind struggled to decipher. The sharp slap of metal slicing into muscle, but surprisingly he felt no pain and he realized Victor's blow must have struck the dead horse. Without conscious thought, his hand wrapped around the shaft of the broken spear embedded in the ground to his left. His arm whipped round and he felt the moment the point tore through cloth into the sucking embrace of flesh, the crunch of iron scraping on bone and then the breakthrough into the softness beyond. An agonized shriek that combined pain, torment and frustration filled his ears and he looked up as Claudius Victor's shuddering body collapsed on top of him.

The random, panicked thrust of the spearhead had taken Victor deep in the groin, slicing through the big artery there and into his lower stomach. The Batavian's body shuddered uncontrollably with each wave of shock and agony. He knew he was dying, but the animal instinct to destroy his foe was overwhelming. Powerful warrior's hands fought their way to Valerius's throat and the Batavian's eyes bulged as he used the last of his strength to throttle the man who had killed his brother. Trapped beneath the armour-clad body, Valerius struggled to free his good hand and somehow prise the iron grip of the fingers from his throat. His vision blurred and he heard the sound of a rook cawing and knew it was the sound of his dying. Claudius Victor's face was in his, and he felt the other man's spittle on his cheek and remembered the foul breath of his enemy from their previous terrifying meeting in the woods of Germania. His mind screamed at him. He . . . would . . . not . . . die. His fingers closed on the object at his belt and somehow he forced his left hand upwards between their two bodies. Victor was oblivious of what was happening, his mind lost in the divine, unearthly madness of victory and death. He barely felt the point of the knife that forced its way through the skin beneath his chin. Only in the lightning-flash moment when it entered his brain did he accept defeat.

Blood surged from the gaping jaws over Valerius's face and he almost vomited at the foulness of it in his mouth. A moment of relief, darkness and finally despair threatened to overwhelm him, but he took the time to cut the leather strip holding the golden boar amulet that had hung at Claudius Victor's neck and push it into his tunic. What seemed like much later rough hands dragged him clear of the body and he heard a familiar voice in his ear.

'Can't lie about here as if you're already in the Senate, lord,' Serpentius chided.

Someone put a sword in his hand as Juva placed a giant arm round his waist and between them the Nubian and the Spaniard half carried him through the fighting and the heaped bodies of the dead and the dying. Somehow they found themselves among a group of gladiators still battling for their lives.

'The First's eagle?' Valerius demanded.

Serpentius shrugged and the Roman knew it was gone. A pain pierced him that was more terrible than anything he'd suffered this day as he remembered his promise to Benignus. But he was their leader. He could not surrender to despair. 'We fight on. Otho's reserve will be here soon. While we live, there's still a chance.'

'I don't think so.' Serpentius's voice was bleak. The first time Valerius had heard it bereft of hope. Because Aulus Caecina Alienus had thrown in his reserves to finish it.

A massed wave of charging infantry and cavalry swept across the plain towards them. 'If I'm to die, I will die like a man.' Still clutching the eagle of the Twenty-first, Juva of the *Waverider*, centurion of the first century, Fifth cohort of Legio I Adiutrix, gave a final nod to his two friends and was gone before Valerius could stop him. His last memory of the Nubian was of Juva standing like a colossus at the heart of the full cohort sent to squash the insolent slaves who had tarnished the honour of a legion, before he was consumed by a whirling maelstrom of bright iron.

As he waited with Serpentius at his side, his strong right hand for one final time, Valerius felt the same mix of pride, loss and anger he had experienced in the final moments of the siege of the Temple of Claudius. There was no glory in defeat, but what did that matter when a man had known warriors like these and had a friend such as this. He planted his feet more firmly in the rich, dark soil and held the *gladius* at the ready as a squadron of cavalry charged the two defiant figures who stood firm among the dead and the wounded. Valerius managed to sidestep the first spear, but moved too late to avoid the bulk of the galloping horse. He felt something break in his left shoulder and the moment the sword dropped from his nerveless fingers.

Then, only darkness.

XLIX

Gaius Valerius Verrens recognized the soot-stained walls of the burned-out villa on the hill and each detail of the defence and fall of the Temple of Claudius returned, as if it was carved on his brain by the point of a dagger. Falco and his militia dying where they stood so that the others could escape. Lunaris, like a hero of old, holding back Boudicca's horde on the steps of the temple. And Messor, poor Messor, slipping into the dark tunnel that would have been better being his tomb. With a start, he realized he wasn't alone. The cloaked figure who worked in the gloom by the shuttered window seemed familiar and his heart soared as he realized her identity.

'Maeve?'

She turned and he reached out to her and it was only then he realized that his arms ended in ragged stumps. Both hands had been chopped off above the wrist. As the first shuddering scream escaped his tortured throat he looked up into a face from the gates of the Otherworld; not his Maeve, not the beautiful Trinovante who had loved and betrayed him, but Claudius Victor, and a Claudius Victor straight from the grave, eyes turned to puddles of white pus, a gaping crater for a nose and a yawning mouth filled with worms and nameless crawling things. Hands like skeletal claws reached for something at his neck. He screamed again. And again.

Rough hands shook his shoulders. 'Valerius.'

No, they wouldn't take him.

'Valerius, open your eyes.'

Reluctantly, he obeyed a voice that had an authority that could not be ignored. Staring at him was another face from Hades; burning eyes glared out from features tanned to the colour of a house tile, the nose narrow with an edge like a woodsman's well-used axe and below it a razor-lipped rat-trap mouth. Beyond this nightmare the world was the uniform pale blue of a song thrush's egg.

'Serpentius?'

The word emerged as a hoarse croak and the Spaniard put a cup to his lips. Valerius gulped down what he discovered was well-watered tavern wine. He choked and Serpentius removed the cup.

'Don't talk now. I've put your shoulder back in place, the fever's gone and you're getting stronger every day. Rest, and we'll speak later.'

But there was one thing Valerius had to know, and he dared not look himself. 'My hand?' Serpentius smiled gently and raised the left arm, so Valerius could see his hand was intact. The Roman allowed his head to fall back and closed his eyes. 'My worst nightmare,' he whispered.

'No,' he heard the former gladiator say, 'your worst nightmare is yet to come.'

'Where are we?' Valerius surveyed the rough stockade that enclosed the parade ground of beaten earth that was their prison, along with over a hundred other ragged, bearded men.

'Somewhere outside Cremona. When Otho died . . .' The Spaniard hesitated as he saw the question in Valerius's eyes. Otho had been nowhere near the battle; there was no reason why he shouldn't have escaped and joined the Eastern legions who had been marching to join him. Serpentius shrugged. 'They say that the officers who were with him at Brixellum urged him to fight on. Said that when the Seventh and the Fourteenth arrived they'd outnumber Vitellius's men. But Otho hadn't just lost the battle, he'd lost his heart. He said he'd killed enough men and went into his tent . . . well, you can guess the rest.'

Valerius felt a pang of compassion for the man who had been, if not his friend, then at least a colourful and entertaining companion. A man who, against all odds, would have made a fine Emperor, given time. The gods had presented Marcus Salvius Otho with everything he had ever desired, and just as quickly taken it away.

'Who are these *they*, so free with their information? Who's to say it's true?'

'The guards.' Serpentius waved a hand towards the men watching from the perimeter. 'They're not bad sorts. Now that the war is over they feel a bit sorry for us. We fought well, but we lost. They're just glad it's not them sitting here, so they make sure we're well fed and let us do pretty much what we please, as long as we don't cause any trouble.'

Valerius stared suspiciously. This wasn't the Spaniard he remembered. Perhaps Otho wasn't the only one who'd lost heart. For the first time he noticed that Serpentius was working on a block of wood with a small fruit knife.

'Not bad sorts? Fools, surely, to give a man like you

486

a blade. I've seen the day you'd have slit half a dozen throats and been halfway to Rome by now, and taken the others with you.'

The Spaniard chewed his lip. 'Maybe so, but it's different now. For one thing, as far as they're concerned every man here is a gladiator, and he'll be treated as an escaped slave if he runs. You know what that means?'

'The cross.'

'That would be the best of it.'

'And the other reason?'

Serpentius shrugged. 'They knew I had reasons for staying.'

Valerius snorted and shook his head. 'Fool. That still doesn't explain why we're here.' Something occurred to him. 'Gladiators?'

'It's the only reason we're still alive. We were with what was left of the gladiators when you got your second knock. They were about to butcher the lot of us when Caecina rode up and called off his dogs. Turns out he had a better use for us.'

'What kind of use?' Valerius didn't hide his suspicion.

The Spaniard stared at him, the dark eyes deadly serious. 'We do what gladiators do best. We fight. To the death.' Valerius's brain fought against the reality of the final three words. Execution he had expected, exile or imprisonment at best. But not that. Never that. Serpentius explained that Caecina, ever eager to stay one step ahead of his rival Valens, had ordered a great games for the Emperor and the climax would be a hundred and fifty captured gladiators fighting to the death. 'What do you expect? As far as Vitellius is concerned we're slaves who rose up against him. No better than Spartacus and his lads.'

They had a month.

'In a month we'll get you fit enough to fight.' He saw the stricken look in Valerius's eyes. 'Don't worry. I'll think of something.'

L

May, AD 69

'Ready?'

Valerius nodded, but he had a lump in his throat the size of a goose egg and his feet seemed to be encased in lead. They sat in the stifling heat of the arming room below the arena outside Cremona and all around them were the sounds of men praying, or sobbing. Somewhere close was the thick, bitter scent of fresh vomit.

Serpentius kept his voice low. 'We'll fight together and if the gods will it, we'll be the last men standing.'

'What happens then?'

The Spaniard shrugged. 'Maybe we'll have been so good they'll let us both live.'

Valerius nodded slowly, knowing it was unlikely, no matter how well they fought. 'And if not?'

He saw a glint in the dark eyes. 'I'll make it quick and clean.'

Valerius swallowed as he imagined the coldness of bright iron piercing his heart, but he managed a smile. 'What if it's the other way round?'

Serpentius stared at him. They both knew that was

not going to happen. 'Do not concern yourself. If you die, you will die with a sword in your hand and a friend by your side.' He reached down to retrieve a bag from between his feet. 'Here, take this.'

Valerius opened the bag and the contents took his breath away. Inside was a rough replica of the wooden hand he had watched burn all those months ago on the Rhenus. It had a laced cowhide stock and without a word he pulled it over his right forearm and deftly tied the laces with the fingers of his left hand. He turned it slowly as if he might be imagining its existence.

'I told them you'd fight better with a shield,' Serpentius said gruffly. 'It should fit this.' He produced a round shield, in the Thracian style, but Valerius only had eyes for the crude oak fist his friend had carved. For a moment, the world seemed to spin around him. No words could ever express what he felt and all he could think of was to reach across with his good hand and touch the Spaniard's arm.

If he was going to die, he would die a whole man. A whole man with a sword in his hand and a friend by his side.

It was enough.

'Prepare yourselves.'

Valerius's left hand rose to touch the golden boar amulet at his neck.

Aulus Vitellius Germanicus Augustus frowned as the guards brought them out in batches of ten. Caecina hadn't even thought to create a better spectacle by arming them properly. They looked like a bunch of bearded peasant farmers with spears and swords. At first they stood around, frightened and bewildered, but the *lanistae* ran between them pushing them into match-ups and pointing out the hundreds of archers who ringed the packed dirt and had orders to kill any man who refused to fight. Soon the arena rang to the roars of the spectators, the clash of swords and the screams of the dying.

He pinned the young man sitting next to him, the architect of this farce, with a smile, muttered some unintelligible words of praise and turned away. By the gods he was bored.

After the victory at Bedriacum he had been feted from Moguntiacum to Mediolanum and Lugdunum to Rome. He had eaten and drunk until he had been surprised to discover that even *his* gargantuan appetites had limits. Not four days earlier, Valens had held his own little spectacle, and in truth it was infinitely more cultured than anything this upstart youth had provided thus far.

His mind returned to the day when he had finally visited the battlefield between Cremona and Bedriacum, forty days after the fighting had ended. A charnel house. A slaughterer's yard two miles long and a mile and a half wide. Tens of thousands of putrefying corpses piled as high as temple walls and hanging from the trees. Legs, arms and severed heads littering each yard of blood-soaked earth, every inch blanketed by the flies that swarmed insatiable to the feast. His court had gagged at the stink of rotting flesh, the yards of blackened, festering intestines torn from gas-filled bodies by the feral dogs which still roamed that awful field of death, and the black clouds of crows who fought for the softest parts – the best of it, the eyes, the lips, had long gone, but there were still opportunities for the determined – but to Aulus Vitellius Germanicus Augustus the stink of a rotting corpse was the sweet smell of victory.

A cry of appreciation from the crowd brought him

back to the 'entertainment'. A pair of gladiators had been clever enough to fight together for a time, but the taller of the men, a well-muscled bruiser, had taken the opportunity to stab his comrade in the back the instant that particular contest had been won. It appeared the victim had some special skill his murderer had feared. Perhaps the spectacle was not going to be as dull as he'd believed.

A second pair had also decided to fight as a team and he admired their skills until his attention was drawn to two equally matched men armed with terrible, curved knives. The blades darted and threatened, sang in great scything arcs that would have removed a head if they'd been successful, until the sublime moment when, with a scream that rent the air, they simultaneously ripped each other's guts out and fell, spilling viscera on to ground already pooled with blood and gore. The numbers were down to twenty or thirty now, with the rest dead . . . or, like one of the gutted men who was entertainingly trying to crawl somewhere with his insides trailing behind him, certainly dying.

His gaze drifted back to the double team. By the gods, they weren't bad. A tall spare bullwhip of a fighter with a long sword that seemed to have a life of its own, and a stockier man – no, not stocky, just not as tall as the other – who fought with a short sword and shield. So quick and coordinated that at times it seemed they fought as one man, entertaining the crowd with spectacular executions and imaginative ends, quite literally carving their way through their opponents. Vitellius thought he recognized something in the taller man. He had seen him fight before, he was certain.

Amusing. What would happen when . . . ?

Valerius seemed to see the world through a red veil

and a mist of scarlet droplets coated every inch of his skin and clothing. How many men had he killed? It didn't matter. All that mattered was to kill the next one, and the next. Make it look good, but make it quick. They deserved that at least. He was glad Serpentius had insisted they stay away from the other prisoners and that he had never learned their names, otherwise . . . well, otherwise didn't mean anything now. He fought on, always conscious of Serpentius's immense presence at his side, not immense in mass, but in speed and style and efficiency. With a thrill of fear he realized the red mist had cleared and only one man faced them. The big man who had fought beside his friend, right until the moment he'd stabbed him in the back.

'Come on, Lucius, let's get it over,' Serpentius coaxed. Valerius saw a moment of recognition in the other man's face, and then he ran. The crowd shrieked their disgust and within five paces a dozen arrows from the archers on the walls had pierced his body.

Valerius stood, head down and panting, until he realized the attention of the entire crowd was focused on him. A wall of sound pounded him from every quarter. He turned to find the Spaniard four paces away, with his sword at the ready.

'Remember,' Serpentius said quietly. 'Fight hard and die well.'

He fought hard, because Serpentius made him fight for his life. He only lived because Serpentius made it so. This was a different Serpentius from the man he had faced on the training ground so many times. An implacable, stone-cold killer who could have finished it at any time of his choosing. Valerius looked good because Serpentius made him look good. A dozen times he was able to avoid a killer stroke by the merest whisker, because of the Spaniard's whispered instructions. A dozen times he stepped back, amazed to be alive, with the cheers of the crowd ringing in his ears. But it couldn't last. There had to be an end.

Gradually, he realized that Serpentius was man-oeuvring him to the precise spot he had chosen for the kill. As he fought for his life, he wondered how many other men had experienced this despairing hopelessness. This feeling of being a fish in a tank chosen as someone's horribly eviscerated supper.

'Now!'

The long sword came down in an arc that chopped the shield from his right hand. He heard a shout from somewhere in the distance, but already the Spaniard's wrist had twisted to deliver the counter-stroke and Valerius's short sword was an age too slow to parry it. Lightning seemed to flash in his brain and he experienced a terrible pain. As he fell, he felt an odd relief that it was over.

Aulus Vitellius had seen the shield drop to reveal the wooden hand. For the first time he realized the identities of the two men and instinctively he heaved himself to his feet shouting: 'No!'

Too late. The sword flashed a second time and the stockier man's head exploded in a cloud of bright scarlet. He went down like a stone, but such was the bloodlust of his opponent that he hacked at the fallen body with his sword and reached down to tear the viscera from the corpse, raising it high to the ecstatic roars of the crowd.

When the cheering subsided, the fighter trudged wearily through the carnage to where Vitellius sat beside Aulus Caecina Alienus in the Imperial box.

'You fought well,' the Emperor congratulated him –

was there a hint of regret in his voice? – 'as did your . . . friend.'

The gladiator, his skin streaked with the blood of his last victim, fell to his knees in supplication. 'I would ask a favour of the Emperor.' The harsh voice was respectful, but not pleading. Aulus Vitellius doubted this was a man who would ever plead.

Beside him, Caecina growled and started to rise, but Vitellius placed a hand on his shoulder. 'Ask it.'

'I beg the right to bury my comrade with the honour he deserves.'

It was too much. 'You have your life, traitor,' Caecina snapped. 'Be satisfied with that or it will be taken from you. Do not try your Emperor's patience.'

But Vitellius only sighed. His eyes roamed the arena, testing the mood of the crowd. Finally, he nodded.

'I grant you that right, gladiator.' He reached up to his neck and there was a collective gasp as he unclipped the golden brooch holding his cloak. Aulus Vitellius Germanicus Imperator raised his voice so his words echoed around the walls. 'He was a nobleman, I think, and a Hero of Rome. Let him be buried in the purple.' He threw the heavy cloak to Serpentius. The Spaniard gave a curt nod and stalked back to where Valerius lay. Taking the utmost care, he wrapped his friend in Imperial purple and, with a last baleful look around the arena, picked up the body and carried it to the doors with the cheers of the crowd ringing unwanted in his ears.

Epilogue

Valerius opened his eyes, but the darkness was as total as the grave. So, not Elysium, then, but the inside of a tomb.

'How does it feel to be dead?'

He started at the unexpected voice in his right ear. 'Better than the alternative, but my head hurts. Did you have to hit me so hard?'

'Another scar to add to your collection.' Serpentius rose and went to the door, drawing back a ragged curtain to allow a shaft of moonlight into the hut. 'I made it look real, that's all that matters. Everything went as we planned. I turned the blade at the last moment, but they needed to see blood. It helped that we were fighting on top of two who'd gutted each other – one man's guts looks exactly the same as another's.'

Valerius lay back and closed his eyes. His throbbing head cleared for a moment and he felt as if a spear had pierced his chest. She was lost to him for ever. 'So it's exile then,' he said wearily. 'A new life. I have always wanted to see the mountains of your home and you have always wanted a servant.'

It was an old jest and should have brought a smile, but when he finally spoke Serpentius's voice was grave.

'Word reached the village yesterday that the legions of Syria and Egypt have hailed General Titus Flavius Vespasian as Emperor and the Balkan units who would have fought for Otho have joined them. They say they're already marching on Italia to bring Vitellius to battle.'

So, more war, more bloodshed and more death, but, oddly, Valerius felt a wellspring of hope. There was still a chance. He would do what he did best, fight, and defeat his old friend. He would regain his honour and win back Domitia. He turned to the Spaniard.

'So it begins again.'

Historical Note

Gaius Valerius Verrens lived in interesting times, and none more interesting than the tumultuous period of civil war erroneously dubbed The Year of the Four Emperors. The year was actually eighteen months and it would be unfair not to count Nero, whose policies and fatally flawed decision making were the genesis for all that followed, among its key players, taking the Emperor count to five. It was a remarkably untidy and sprawling civil war, which had a devastating impact on every subject of the empire from Lusitania in the west to Alexandria in the east, and from Britannia to Africa. With a little more composure and confidence, Nero might have survived to do more damage. His successor, Galba, was the worst possible candidate; arrogant, elderly, stubborn – admittedly not in themselves a barrier to high office – a skinflint who refused to pay the Praetorian Guard their due, and so aloof he could not see what was happening under his nose. He was also a poor judge of character who, of several possible alternatives, chose an heir in his own image, alienating all others. Marcus Salvius Otho came to the throne with Galba's blood on his hands and a reputation as the man who sold his own wife to Nero for Imperial favour. Our main sources, Plutarch, Tacitus and Suetonius, portray him in a poor light for different reasons. Yet despite all the carnage and political upheaval of his succession, and the horrors that followed, some decisions he took in office point to a thoughtful, if impetuous, leader who might have grown to become a fine Emperor. Otho's misfortune was to inherit power without strength, and to be presented with a military crisis before he could create political stability. The man who faced him, Aulus Vitellius, is another who suffers from the record; a spendthrift glutton who cared for nothing but his own belly. Again there are certain facts that cloud this judgement, which is why I've chosen to portray Vitellius as a man carried along by flattery and events, unfortunate in his choice of collaborators. If the civil war was untidy, the first major confrontation between the two sides – at Bedriacum – was diabolically so. It was so badly botched on both sides that it's a wonder anyone emerged a winner, and afterwards Otho's supporters cried 'Betrayal', possibly with some justification. In the aftermath, a devastated Otho chose to commit suicide, and his death probably paints him in a much more flattering light than his life, because it prevented further bloodshed. If he had waited a week, or even a few days, he would have been joined by an overwhelming force of veterans from the Danube frontier. His impetuosity was literally the death of him.

Whereas the final battle in *Avenger of Rome* was entirely a work of fiction, the major events of *Sword of Rome* are as accurate as I can make them. The scratch marine legion, First Adiutrix, recovered from the massacre at the Milvian Bridge to acquit themselves heroically at Bedriacum. Otho was so starved of soldiers that he recruited Rome's gladiators to his cause, though his generals wasted many of their lives in futile engagements, and they ended up fighting each other for Vitellius's entertainment. Aulus Vitellius did borrow Julius Caesar's sword from the temple of Mars Ultor to make himself look more of a general.

The result of First Bedriacum leaves Vitellius on the throne of Rome and soon to be confirmed as Emperor by the Senate. His old friend Gaius Valerius Verrens is an outcast, stripped of his rights and his property. The only way to have them returned is to join the growing insurrection of the new contender for the purple, Titus Flavius Vespasianus, the elder, and become an Enemy of Rome.

Glossary

Ala milliaria – A reinforced auxiliary cavalry wing, normally between 700 and 1,000 strong. In Britain and the west the units would be a mix of cavalry and infantry, in the east a mix of spearmen and archers.

Ala quingenaria – Auxiliary cavalry wing normally composed of 500 auxiliary horsemen.

Aquilifer – The standard bearer who carried the eagle of the legion.

As – A small copper coin worth approximately one fifth of a **sestertius**.

Aureus (pl. Aurei) – Valuable gold coin worth twenty-five **denarii**.

Auxiliary – Non-citizen soldiers recruited from the provinces as light infantry or for specialist tasks, e.g. cavalry, slingers, archers.

Ballista (pl. Ballistae) – Artillery for throwing heavy missiles of varying size and type. The smaller machines were called scorpions or onagers.

Batavians – Members of a powerful Germanic tribe which lived in the area of the Rhine delta, now part of the Netherlands. Traditionally provided auxiliary units for the Roman Empire in return for relief from tribute and taxes.

Beneficiarius – A legion's record keeper or scribe.

Boars Head (alt. Wedge) – A compact arrow-head formation used by Roman infantry and cavalry to break up enemy formations.

Caligae – Sturdily constructed, reinforced leather sandals worn by Roman soldiers. Normally with iron-studded sole.

Centurion – commander of a century (see next entry). A long serving veteran who would have had various responsibilities within the legion.

Century – Smallest tactical unit of the legion, numbering eighty men.

Classis Germanica – Fleet of galleys which patrolled and carried military traffic on the River Rhine frontier.

Cohort – Tactical fighting unit of the legion. Normally contained six centuries, apart from the elite First cohort, which had five double-strength centuries (800 men).

Consul – One of two annually elected chief magistrates of Rome, normally appointed by the people and ratified by the Senate.

Contubernium – Unit of eight soldiers who shared a tent or barracks.

Cornicen (pl. Cornicines) – Legionary signal trumpeter who used an instrument called a *cornu*.

Decimation – A brutal and seldom used Roman military punishment where one man in every ten of a unit found guilty of cowardice or mutiny was chosen for execution by his comrades.

Decurion – A junior officer in a century, or a troop commander in a cavalry unit.

Denarius (pl. Denarii) – A silver coin.

Domus – The house of a wealthy Roman, e.g. Nero's Domus Aurea (Golden House).

Duplicarius – Literally 'double pay man'. A senior legionary with a trade, or an NCO.

Equestrian – Roman knightly class.

Fortuna – The goddess of luck and good fortune.

Frumentarii – Messengers who carried out secret duties for the Emperor, possibly including spying and assassination.

Gladius (pl. Gladii) – The short sword of the legionary. A lethal killing weapon at close quarters.

Governor – Citizen of senatorial rank given charge of a province. Would normally have a military background (see **Proconsul**).

Haruspex – Soothsayer, sometimes a priest.

Hispania Tarraconensis – Roman province covering a large part of what is now Spain.

Jupiter – Most powerful of the Roman gods, often referred to as **Optimus Maximus** (greatest and best).

Legate – The general in charge of a legion. A man of senatorial rank.

Legion – Unit of approximately 5,000 men, all of whom would be Roman citizens.

Lictor – Bodyguard of a Roman magistrate. There were strict limits on the numbers of lictors associated with different ranks.

Lituus – Curved trumpet used to transmit cavalry commands.

Lusitania – The Roman province which covered a territory now southern Portugal and part of western Spain.

Magister navis – A ship's captain.

Manumission – The act of freeing a slave.

Mars – The Roman god of war.

Mithras – An Eastern religion popular among Roman soldiers.

Nomentan – A superior variety of Roman wine, mentioned by Martial in his Epigrams.

Optian/optiones (pl) – second in command of a century, officer ranked immediately below a centurion.

Phalera (pl. Phalerae) – Awards won in battle worn on a legionary's chest harness.

Pilum (pl. Pila) – Heavy spear carried by a Roman legionary.

Praetorian Guard – Powerful military force stationed in Rome. Accompanied the Emperor on campaign, but could be of dubious loyalty and were responsible for the overthrow of several Roman rulers.

Prefect – Auxiliary cavalry commander.

Primus Pilus – 'First File'. The senior centurion of a legion.

Principia – Legionary headquarters building.

Proconsul – Governor of a Roman province, such as Spain or Syria, and of consular rank.

Procurator – Civilian administrator subordinate to a governor.

Proscaenium – The area where plays were staged in a Roman theatre.

Quaestor – Civilian administrator in charge of finance.

Scorpio – Bolt-firing Roman light artillery piece.

Scutum (pl. Scuta) – The big, richly decorated curved shield carried by a legionary.

Senator – Patrician member of the Senate, the key political institution which administered the Roman Empire. Had to meet strict financial and property rules and be at least thirty years of age.

Sestertius (pl. Sestertii) – Roman brass coin worth a quarter of a **denarius**.

Signifer – Standard bearer who carried the emblem of a cohort or century.

Spatha – a long, heavy sword carried by auxiliary cavalry troopers.

Testudo – Literally 'tortoise'. A unit of soldiers with shields interlocked for protection.

Tribune – One of six senior officers acting as aides to a Legate. Often, but not always, on short commissions of six months upwards.

Tribunus laticlavius – Literally 'broad stripe tribune'. The most senior of a legion's military tribunes.

Urban cohorts – Force founded by Augustus to combat the power of the Praetorian Guard. Used for policing large mobs and riot-control duties.

Vascones – Roman auxiliaries from a tribe inhabiting northern Spain. Gave their name to the Basque region.

Victimarius – Servant who delivers and attends to the victim of a sacrifice.

Victory – Roman goddess equivalent to the Greek Nike.

Vigiles – Force responsible for the day-to-day policing of Rome's streets and fire prevention and fighting.

Acknowledgements

I'm grateful to my editor Simon Taylor and his team at Transworld for helping me make *Sword of Rome* the book it is, and to my agent Stan, of Jenny Brown Associates in Edinburgh, for all his advice and encouragement. As always my wife Alison and my children, Kara, Nikki and Gregor, have been the rocks on which this book has been built. Apart from the primary sources, Plutarch, Tacitus, Suetonius and Dio, Gwyn Morgan's *69 AD, The Year of the Four Emperors* was constantly at my side, and any gaps in my ever-advancing knowledge of life in the legions were filled by Stephen Dando-Collins's *Legions of Rome*. Special thanks to my friend Moira Pringle in Milan for her help in guiding me through the swampland and forests of northern Italy in the 1st century AD.

CALIGULA
Douglas Jackson

Can a slave decide the fate of an Emperor?

Rufus, a young slave, grows up far from the corruption of the imperial court. He is a trainer of animals for the gladiatorial arena. But when Caligula wants a keeper for the emperor's elephant, Rufus is bought from his master and taken to the palace.

Life at court is dictated by Caligula's ever shifting moods. He is as generous as he is cruel – a megalomaniac who declares himself a living god and simultaneously lives in constant fear of the plots against his life. His paranoia is not misplaced however: intrigue permeates his court, and Rufus will find himself unwittingly placed at the centre of a conspiracy to assassinate the Emperor.

'Jackson brings a visceral realism to Rome in the days of the mad Caligula'
Daily Mail

'Light and dark in equal measure, colourful, thoughtful and bracing'
Manda Scott, bestselling author of the *Boudicca* series

'A gripping Roman thriller'
Scotland on Sunday

CLAUDIUS
Douglas Jackson

Rome 43AD. Emperor Claudius has unleashed his legions against the rebellious island of Britannia.

In Southern England, Caratacus, war chief of the Britons, watches from a hilltop as the scarlet cloaks of the Roman legions spread across his land like blood. He must unite the tribes for a desperate last stand.

Among the legions marches Rufus, keeper of the Emperor's elephant. Claudius has a special role for him, and his elephant, in the coming war.

Claudius is a masterful retelling of one of the greatest stories from Roman history, the conquest of Britain. It is an epic story of ambition, courage, conspiracy, battle and bloodshed.

'What stands out are Jackson's superb battle scenes . . . I was gripped from start to finish'
Ben Kane, author of *The Forgotten Legion*

'If I were Conn Iggulden or Simon Scarrow, I'd be rather worried by the new Scottish kid on the block'
The Scotsman

HERO OF ROME
Douglas Jackson

The warrior queen Boudicca is ready to
lead the tribes to war.

The Roman grip on Britain is weakening. Emperor
Nero has turned his face away from this far-flung
outpost. Roman cruelty and exploitation has angered
their British subjects. Now the Druids are on the rise,
stoking the fires of this anger and spreading the spark
of rebellion among the British tribes.

Standing against the rising tide of Boudicca's rebellion
is Roman tribune, Gaius Valerius Verrens, Commander
of the veteran legionaries of Colonia. One act of
violence ignites the smouldering British hatred
into the roaring furnace of war.

Colonia will be the first city to feel the flames of
Boudicca's revenge, and Valerius must gather his
veterans for a desperate defence.

'A splendid piece of story-telling and a vivid
recreation of a long-dead world . . . The final battle
against Boudicca's forces is as vivid and
bloody as anyone might wish'
Allan Massie

'One of the best historical novelists writing today'
Daily Express

AVENGER OF ROME
Douglas Jackson

THE EMPEROR'S GRIP ON POWER
IS WEAKENING . . .

In every shadow Nero sees an enemy and, like a
cornered animal, he lashes out at every perceived
threat. His paranoia settles on Rome's greatest
general, Gnaeus Domitius Corbulo, who
leads the imperial legions in the East.

So popular is Corbulo with his men that he effectively
presides over an empire within the Empire. Could he
be preparing to march and seize the purple?

Gaius Valerius Verrens, Hero of Rome, is ordered to
Antioch with the power of life and death over Corbulo,
a soldier he worships. However, the general's eyes are
not on Rome, but on a new threat. The Parthian King
of Kings, Vologases, is leading his massive
army to wage war against Rome.

In the barren lands beyond the Tigris, Valerius stands
at Corbulo's side as they confront the Parthian hordes.
And he must decide whether to complete his
mission – or risk his Emperor's wrath . . .

'Superb battle scenes . . . I was gripped
from start to finish'
Ben Kane

'A splendid piece of story-telling and a vivid
recreation of a long-dead world'
Allan Massie

DEFENDER OF ROME
Douglas Jackson

A DIVIDED EMPIRE CANNOT STAND

The biggest threat to the Empire comes not from the armies of Boudicca or the hordes of Germania but from within the walls of Rome itself. A new religious sect, the followers of Christus, are spreading sedition, denying the divinity of the Emperor. And Nero is not a man to be denied.

Calling on his 'Hero of Rome', Gaius Valerius Verrems, to become a 'Defender of Rome', Nero orders him to seek out the rebel sect and capture its leader. If he fails not only will his own life be forfeit, but so too the lives of twenty thousand Judeans living in Rome.

His quest will take his from the backstreets of Rome to the slopes of Vesuvius and Valerius will quickly discover that success may cost him as much as failure.

'One of the best historical novelists writing today'
Daily Express